PENGUIN BOOKS

TALES OF TWO AMERICAS

John Freeman is founder of the literary biannual *Freeman's*. He has written two books of nonfiction, *How to Read a Novelist* and *The Tyranny of E-mail*, and *Maps*, a collection of poems. *Tales of Two Cities: The Best and Worst of Times in Today's New York*, an anthology about inequality in New York, was published by Penguin in 2015. The former editor of *Granta*, his work has appeared in *The New Yorker*, *The Paris Review*, *The New York Times*, and has been translated into more than twenty languages. He lives in New York City, where he is writer in residence at New York University and teaches at The New School.

A portion of the proceeds from sales of this book will be donated to homeless charities in the United States.

TALES OF
TWO AMERICAS

Stories
of Inequality
in a Divided Nation

EDITED BY

John Freeman

PENGUIN BOOKS

PENGUIN BOOKS

An imprint of Penguin Random House LLC
375 Hudson Street
New York, New York 10014
penguin.com

Published in Penguin Books 2017

Published by arrangement with OR Books LLC, New York.

Pages 327–330 constitute an extension of this copyright page.

LIBRARY OF CONGRESS CATALOGING-IN-PUBLICATION DATA
Names: Freeman, John, 1974– editor.
Title: Tales of two Americas : stories of inequality
in a divided nation / edited by John Freeman.
Description: New York : Penguin Books, 2017.
Identifiers: LCCN 2017011506 | ISBN 9780143131038 (paperback)
Subjects: LCSH: Social problems—United States—Fiction. |
Social justice—United States—Fiction. | Social conflict—
United States—Fiction. | United States—Ethnic relations—Fiction. |
United States—Race relations—Fiction. | Short stories, American.
Classification: LCC PS648.S58 T35 2017 | DDC 813/.0108355—dc23
LC record available at https://lccn.loc.gov/2017011506

Printed in the United States of America

11th Printing

Set in Adobe Caslon Pro

DESIGNED BY KATY RIEGEL

This book is for my brother Andy,

who has lived in many countries

CONTENTS

INTRODUCTION

John Freeman

LAST WINTER I flew home to Sacramento for a short visit. On a mild December night I slipped on a coat and set out walking from the capitol to a bookstore not far away.

Very quickly, as in most American cities, I was approached and asked for money. Each man—and they were all men—spoke a reason. *Spare some change for the holidays? A dollar for a veteran? Do you have any money for food?* Taken in isolation, their requests had a stark, brutal simplicity. They were each a call to basic kindness. *Will you see me, will you help?* Of course even the most strapped of us has a quarter for a hungry person. So I gave, I always do. I know it is quite possible the reasons were ploys to get money for other things, but I cannot stand the other possibility—which is that the need was actual, and dire.

I walked on after speaking to the last man, and approached my destination in a state of dismay and déjà vu. I had been traveling a lot that fall and winter and everywhere I went I saw an unkind America. It was a constant refrain in Chicago, in Seattle, in Portland, in Miami: *got some change, can you help, got some money for a veteran?* Most people walk right by. Somewhat understandably. The only way in which to reside or work in much of America for many is to ignore these requests, in essence to deny our mutual humanity in order to live our lives. My dismay had another source, however. I had actually traveled to Sacramento that December to have an event at Time Tested Books to discuss this very issue of homelessness and inequality in New York. I had just published an anthology called *Tales of Two Cities: The Best of Times and Worst of Times in Today's New York*, and I decided to walk because some of the most important essays in that book came from walkers, from people who saw New York at a human pace and so saw the stories it was not telling itself.

I thought about it and realized that most of my memories of Sacramento were seen at the speed of a car. I couldn't remember a single walk I had taken with my grandfather, who moved to the city in 1933, and helped build the church we attended; or my father, who was born six years later and grew up downtown; or my brothers, who moved with me to the suburbs of Sacramento from Pennsylvania in 1984. We drove, parked, and walked a short distance to our destination. Now, thirty years later, I was on foot and seeing a very different city, wondering if I had been passing by it all along, or if something important had changed. As I approached Twenty-First Street I began to despair that I had come to Sacramento to speak about New York. That's when another man dressed in jeans and a work shirt stepped into my path, looking like he might be needing directions. He did: "Do you know where the Meals on Wheels truck is, man?" he asked.

■ ■

America is broken. You don't need a fistful of statistics to know this. You just need eyes and ears and stories. Walk around any American city and evidence of the shattered compact with citizens will present itself. There you will see broken roads, overloaded schools, police forces on edge, clusters and sometimes whole tent cities of homeless people camped in eyeshot of shopping districts that are beginning to resemble ramparts of wealth rather than stores for all. Thick glass windows and security guards stand between aspirational goods and the people outside in Portland, Oregon; in San Francisco; in Seattle; Los Angeles; New York; and Miami. The soaring cost of living in these cities— which have become meccas for luxury and creative economy work, but depend on service labor to run their dream machines—has a lot to do with this state of affairs. Adjusting for rent and costs, the middle-class residents of these cities now have the lowest real earnings of any metropolitan area. And across the nation at large, America's[1] top 10 percent earns nine times as much as the bottom 90 percent.[2]

This is not just an urban problem. In smaller cities and towns and in rural America the gulf between the haves and have-nots stretches just as wide, even if its symptoms are not so visible. California might be home to more than one hundred billionaires—whose collected assets dwarf the GDP of most nations in the world—but nearly a quarter of the state is poor. The jobs that were once done by hand are increasingly done by machine. Appalachia, upstate New York, Michigan—inequality stretches to almost unthinkable gulfs there too. No matter how much one hears of recovery and new jobs, what those jobs are and what they promise tend to get left out. These jobs are often short-shift work, work without benefits, work so temporary it has created a new term: the *precariat*. This unease became the pivot point of the 2016 presidential election.

■ ■

Financial inequality is not just a symptom of bad public policy, though, or something that has emerged only in tandem with the forces of the recent election. It was formed by decades of injustice and structural inequality in America produced by the nation's growth on the back of stolen labor, the failure of Reconstruction, the entrenchment of racial bias in the culture, restrictions on immigration and the way immigration law is enforced, the long aftermath of the war on drugs, sexism, gender imbalances, and the complicity of financial services in preying upon populations afflicted by these inequalities with predatory loaning. We also haven't

---

1 *Forbes*, http://www.forbes.com/sites/joelkotkin/2014/03/20/where-inequality-is-worst -in-the-united-states/#6a2ca2eb56ce
2 http://inequality.org/inequality-data-statistics/

introduced meaningful progressive taxation in decades. Whatever benefits the once-robust welfare state ensured have been all but demolished by this deeply enmeshed system of inequality, putting far more at risk than just upward mobility. It has put people's bodies at risk. Writing in the wake of a lethal police shooting in Charlotte earlier last year, the pastor William Barber II noted: "When Charlotte's poor black neighborhoods were afflicted with disproportionate law enforcement during the war on drugs, condemning a whole generation to bad credit and a lack of job opportunities, our elected representatives didn't call it violence. When immigration officers raid homes and snatch undocumented children from bus stops, they don't call it violence. But all of these policies and practices do violence to the lives of thousands of Charlotte residents."

■ ■

The way systems of oppression have entrenched themselves in the United States calls out for a new framework for writing about inequality. We need to look beyond statistics and numbers and wage rates. We need to create a framework that accounts for what it feels like to live in this America, a framework that can give space to the stories that reveal how many forces outside of wages lead to income inequality, which is a symptom of a network of inequalities. The work of writing has been done for decades by writers who do not have a choice but to pay attention to these forces. This anthology is an attempt to bring together the best of these writers and recast the story of America in their words.

■ ■

Piece by piece you will watch as these writers demolish the myth of Horatio Alger and replace it with the reality of what it feels like to try to keep a foothold in America today. In a poignant essay, Manuel Muñoz pays tribute to his dying father, who came north from Central America to pick lettuce and cotton—jobs that are all but vanishing as work that can sustain a family. The U.S. poet laureate Juan Felipe Herrera contributes a short poem that salutes the unnamed and undocumented workers who still try. Very often what is left behind isn't in the past at all. In her short story "Dosas," Edwidge Danticat conjures a home health aide whose ex-boyfriend returns with a request for money because his new wife has been kidnapped back home in Haiti.

The problems of America are indeed not just based in the United States, but they follow populations here and take root in this landscape. The poet Lawrence Joseph writes of the tectonic tension global forces brought to bear on Detroit, the city demolished by fleeing manufacturing industries that have shipped jobs overseas. Timothy Egan remembers the days when you could find such work to sustain you in Seattle—that is no longer the case. The novelist Richard Russo muses on what a blow it is to a person's dignity when their work is taken away, how that destroys a part of their soul. So what do you do? Sarah Smarsh's brother— like many thousands of Americans—sells his blood plasma to the growing global industry of plasma sales in Kansas. In RS Deeren's short story, two men in Michigan mow lawns of recently repossessed homes: they do not lack for work. Jess Ruliffson describes veterans returning to the lower Plains from Iraq to precarious employment.

This does not of course stop new families from coming to the United States, there is just a much steeper ladder for coming out of poverty—and also a crisis of identity of what America is, and who counts as citizens. In her short story, Ru Freeman brings to life housekeepers and nannies who live in the orbit of families but get very little of the benefits. In her essay, Patricia Engel describes how an influx of labor in these industries from Cuba, the Caribbean, Mexico, and elsewhere call Miami home now, as whites in the same city redefine their notion of home in terms of racial purity and exclusion. Rebecca Solnit's devastating account of a shooting in San Francisco describes how the incident came as a direct result of the encroaching gentrification of the victim's neighborhood. The people who called the police on the day of the victim's death would have known him had they lived in the area for years, as so many residents around them did.

Too often the police are in an adversarial relationship with people they are meant to protect. In her powerful poem, "American Arithmetic," Natalie Diaz meditates on the fact that while Native Americans make up less than one percent of the population, they are killed at an alarming rate. "When we are dying," she writes, "Who should we call?" In Kiese Laymon's potent essay, he recalls a friend who was arrested in his college town for allegedly doing what so many of its students do—selling drugs. Only, in his friend's case, since he wasn't a student, the law was far swifter and more severe. The deterioration of this relationship between police and Americans of color has created a sense that there are two Americas, one black, one blue, and the dream that America tells itself is possible feels not like a dream but like a lie—something the poet Danez Smith circles in his beautiful poem. It's been this way for a long time, Kevin Young's poem on Howlin' Wolf reminds, something that demands a song of protest.

How are white Americans to situate themselves before this blunt fact? How do they acknowledge it while also respecting that it is far easier for them to protest than their brothers and sisters who pay far more dearly for their voices? In Joyce Carol Oates's story "Leander," an older white woman visits an African American church that hosts a Black Lives Matters–type protest and finds herself feeling like an intruder; all of her instincts lead to self-consciousness. In her essay, Eula Biss changes the concept from white guilt to white debt, a far more useful idea in the face of the economic benefits of being white. Brad Watson learned these lessons early growing up in Mississippi, when his mother hired a woman of color to be their housekeeper for a daily wage that was less than he made in a few hours mowing lawns.

Education has so long been held aloft as the way that America can correct the systemic imbalances of its history and culture. Several pieces here explore the loopholes in that equation. Kirstin Valdez Quade remembers working as a counselor at an elite prep school's summer program, where a Hispanic student from a lower-income background flunked out due to the lack of support the program gave her—even as that program coveted the girl's diversity. Quade makes a powerful argument for why schools that run such programs made to enhance diversity in their student body need to do more for their enrollees upon their arrival. No such programs existed when Dagoberto Gilb was growing up in Los Angles and Texas—he had to make the possibility for himself, and in his memoir describes the agonies and leave-takings such a discovery entailed. In Nami Mun's short story, two parents who have sacrificed everything for their child to have opportunities they never did pay the ultimate price when their debt comes crashing down on them.

One of the powerful sensations that arises from these pieces concerns the ethics of our times. How can some of us live when we know others are not experiencing the same comfort? In Héctor Tobar's memoir, he recalls reporting on a gang shooting casualty, a young boy his son's age, in a neighborhood adjacent to his own in Los Angeles. Meanwhile, over in Idaho, Anthony Doerr returns home to his house tired from a day with his children and discovers a man parked in his driveway, possibly asleep in his car. Who is this man, he wonders, and what has led him to a remote cul-de-sac near Boise? Is he simply tired or out of steam in an existential sense? Where the stress falls and where it does not can feel—in a culture that has so eagerly ripped out certain social nets—almost cruelly random. In Joy Williams's story, a man prepares to dismantle the estate of a wealthy politician in Maine, his house and liquor stocks suddenly, without the late man's presence, highlighting the absurdity of accumulation for its own sake.

There is a lurking feeling of estrangement in America. Of people from their lives, of Americans from one another, of all of us from places as they race to change. In his poem "Visible City," Rickey Laurentiis wishes he could make all the cities within his city of New Orleans more visible. Larry Watson bemoans the loss of the Bismarck, North Dakota, that he called home once, where the well-to-do and the middle classes lived on the same block, and the cathedrals of accumulation one sees now circling the city were unthinkable. Chris Offutt bemoans such changes, too, but he isn't about to become a spokesman for the working classes by selling his heritage back to well-to-do buyers in the form of essays on "trash food," as one editor asks him to write.

What is required to make it in America often requires leaving home—and grappling with a new place. In her barbed and lovely essay on Chicago, Sandra Cisneros remembers how the city that raised her also trained her to leave it in order to survive, to become herself. A far greater threat to personhood lurks in wait for the women in Roxane Gay's short story. Raised by an abusive out-of-work drunk, married to husbands who don't pull their weight, they sense their time to escape is running out. Claire Vaye Watkins remembers the many houses and trailers she grew up in across the West, and how she and her sister kept eyes on each other as their mother spiraled close to giving up.

I hope there is a bandwidth of care that still exists in America. One where people don't give a hand just because it suits them, but because it is the right thing to do—it is how we all get by. Annie Dillard recommends this to writers on days when they wonder what they are for. Whitney Terrell practiced this generosity with a next-door neighbor and realized what a complicated network of expectations he was entering. In her essay, Ann Patchett recalls a priest in Nashville who lived by this credo, and all the good work he did. And in Portland, Oregon, today, Karen Russell describes a city with a homeless problem so large, an epidemic of generosity among all its citizens might be the only way out.

It might sound trite—the notion that the solution to our problems in America lies *between us, not above us,* and not in the governments that have let us down. Perhaps, but all one has to do is get stuck overnight at an airport, as Julia Alvarez did on her way home to Vermont one night, to realize that the thin boundaries between people can easily be broken down by one shared experience. Alvarez watches as people of all colors and backgrounds help one another find places to sleep, blankets to wrap themselves in, food to eat. In America today we have come to view inequality as a problem that afflicts only the needy. What a mistake. For it is in sharing that we can alleviate a situation that pains us all.

■ ■

I do have one memory of Sacramento that came to mind not long after I left behind the man looking for the Meals on Wheels truck. Christmas 1986. In those years my father worked as director of a family service nonprofit that created drug and alcohol recovery programs, Meals on Wheels trucks for seniors, counseling for families who could not afford it otherwise. That year he decided it was a good idea to take us around south Sacramento giving out toys and turkeys to families who could not afford them. And so we piled into our station wagon with a trunk full of food and presents.

I was used to knocking on doors back then—I had a paper route, and every month I had to ride a few miles around my suburban neighborhood chasing down the $8.50 it cost for home delivery of the *Sacramento Bee*. Most people paid, no one ever invited me in, and a few people dodged me. That latter group made me wonder, *Who doesn't pay an eleven-year-old who has been riding to your doorstep at five-thirty every morning?* And there were different sorts of houses, like the ones we visited that Christmas. The screen doors open even in winter. The dogs did not look particularly friendly. But the people were. That holiday as we drove from house to house we were invited in, welcomed, hugged, and even when people felt uncomfortable—one teenager our age ran off crying—we shared a few words. My father stood in living rooms and asked where people were from.

My parents never told me what this trip was supposed to mean. It was clear. Arriving back at our home felt surreal—there was no cosmological reason why my brothers and I were allowed to grow up there rather than in one of the homes we just left. Improbability demands stories. Each one of us in America could have grown up someone else had the universe's mysterious finger touched a different key. Later in life, when both of my brothers were briefly homeless at separate times, I discovered how even with comfortable upbringings the ladder of society can slip from right beneath you. Back then I didn't have the stories I needed to know this was possible—I just had this one trip. I was lucky.

TALES OF TWO AMERICAS

DEATH BY GENTRIFICATION: THE KILLING OF ALEX NIETO AND THE SAVAGING OF SAN FRANCISCO

Rebecca Solnit

On what would have been his thirtieth birthday, Alejandro Nieto's parents left a packed courtroom in San Francisco shortly before pictures from their son's autopsy were shown to a jury. The photographs showed what happens when fourteen bullets rip through a person's head and body. Refugio and Elvira Nieto spent much of the rest of the day sitting on a bench in the windowless hall of the federal building where their civil lawsuit for their son's wrongful death was being heard.

Alex Nieto was twenty-eight years old when he was killed in the neighborhood where he had spent his whole life. He died in a barrage of bullets fired at him by four San Francisco policemen. There are a few things about his death that everyone agrees on: he was in a hilltop park eating a burrito and tortilla chips, wearing the Taser he owned for his job as a licensed security guard at a nightclub, when someone called 911 on him a little after seven p.m. on the evening of March 21, 2014. The police officers who arrived a few minutes later claim that Nieto defiantly pointed the Taser at them, and that they mistook its red laser light for the laser sights of a gun, and shot him in self-defense. However, the stories of the four officers contradict one another's and some of the evidence.

On the road that curves around the green hilltop of Bernal Heights Park is an unofficial memorial to Nieto. People walking dogs or running or taking a stroll stop to read the banner, which is pinned by stones to the slope of the hill and surrounded by fresh and artificial flowers. Alex's father, Refugio, still visits the memorial at least once a day, walking up from his small apartment on the south side of Bernal Hill. Alex Nieto had been visiting the hilltop since he was a child: that evening his parents, joined by friends and supporters, went up there in the dark to bring a birthday cake to the memorial.

Refugio and Elvira Nieto are dignified, modest people, straight-backed but careworn, who speak eloquently in Spanish and hardly at all in English. They had known each other as poor children in a little town in the state of Guanajuato in central Mexico and emigrated separately to the Bay Area in the 1970s. There, they met again and married in 1984. They have lived in the same building on the south slope of Bernal Hill ever since. She worked for decades as a housekeeper in San Francisco's downtown hotels and is now retired. He had worked on the side, but mostly stayed at home as the principal caregiver of Alex and his younger brother, Hector.

In the courtroom, Hector, handsome, somber, with glossy black hair pulled back neatly, sat with his parents most days, not far from the three white and one Asian policemen who killed his brother. That there was a trial at all was a triumph. The city had withheld from family and supporters the full autopsy report and the names of the officers who shot Nieto, and it was months before the key witness overcame his fear of the police to come forward.

Nieto died because a series of white men saw him as a menacing intruder in the place he had spent his whole life. Some of them thought he was possibly a gang member because he was wearing a red jacket. Many Latino boys and men in San Francisco avoid wearing red and blue because they are the colors of two gangs, the Norteños and Sureños—but the colors of San Francisco's football team, the 49ers, are red and gold. Wearing a 49ers jacket in San Francisco is as ordinary as wearing a Saints jersey in New Orleans. That evening, Nieto, who had thick black eyebrows and a closely cropped goatee, was wearing a new-looking 49ers jacket, a black 49ers cap, a white T-shirt, black trousers, and carried the Taser in a holster on his belt, under his jacket. (A Taser shoots out wires that deliver an electrical shock, briefly paralyzing its target; it is shaped roughly like a gun, but more bulbous; Nieto's had bright yellow markings over much of its surface and a fifteen-foot range.)

Nieto had first been licensed by the state as a security guard in 2007 and had worked in that field since. He had never been arrested and had no police record, an achievement in a neighborhood where Latino kids can get picked up just for hanging out in public. He was a Buddhist: a Latino son of immigrants who practiced Buddhism is the kind of hybrid San Francisco used to be good at. As a teen he had worked as a youth counselor for almost five years at the Bernal Heights Neighborhood Center; he was gregarious and community spirited, a participant in political campaigns, street fairs, and community events.

He had graduated from community college with a focus on criminal justice, and hoped to help young people as a probation officer. He had an internship with the city's juvenile probation department not long before his death, according to former city probation officer Carlos Gonzalez, who became a friend. Gonzalez said Nieto knew how criminal justice worked in the city. No one has ever provided a convincing motive for why he would point a gun-shaped object at the police when he understood that it would probably be a fatal act.

Like a rape victim, the dead young man underwent character assassination as irrelevant but unflattering things were dredged up about his past and publicized. Immediately after his death, the police and coroner's office dug into his medical records and found that he'd had a mental health crisis years before. They blew that up into a story that he was mentally ill and made that an explanation for what happened. It ran like this: Why did they shoot Nieto? Because he pointed his Taser at them and they thought it was a gun. Why did he point his Taser at them? Because he was mentally ill. Why should we believe he was mentally ill? Because he pointed his Taser at them. It's a circular logic that leads some-where only if your trust in the San Francisco Police Department is great.

Nieto carried a Taser for his guard job at the El Toro Night Club, whose owner, Jorge del Rio, speaks of him as a calm and peaceful person he liked, trusted, admired, and still cares about: "He was very calm, a very calm guy. So I was very surprised to hear that they claim that he pulled a Taser on the police. Never have seen him react aggressively to anyone. He was the guy who would want to help others. I just can't believe they're saying this about him." He told me how peaceful Nieto was, how brilliant at defusing potentially volatile situations, drawing drunk men out of the rowdy dance club with a Spanish-speaking clientele to tell them on the street "tonight's not your night" and send them home feeling liked and respected.

From the beginning the police were hoping that Alex Nieto's mental health records would somehow exonerate them. The justi-fication that he was mentally ill got around, and it got some trac-tion in local publications committed to justifying the police. But it was ruled inadmissible evidence by the judge in the civil suit brought by his parents, Refugio and Elvira Nieto. The medical records said that three years earlier Alex Nieto had some sort of breakdown and was treated for it. Various terms were thrown around—psychosis, paranoid schizophrenia—but the entire file was from 2011 and there seemed to be no major precedents or subsequent episodes of note. The theory that mental illness is rel-evant presumes not only that he was mentally ill on March 21, 2014, but that mental illness caused him to point a Taser at the police. If you don't believe he pointed a Taser at the police, then mental illness doesn't supply any clues to what happened. Did he? The only outside witness to the shooting says he did not.

Here's the backstory as I heard it from a family friend: Devas-tated by a breakup, Alex got very dramatic about it one day, burned some love letters, and was otherwise over the top in the tiny apartment the four Nietos shared. His exasperated family called a city hotline for help in de-escalating, but instead got escalation: Nieto was seized and institutionalized against his will. The official record described burning the letters as burning a book or trying to burn down the house—something might have gotten lost in translation from Spanish. That was in early 2011; there was another incident later that year. In 2012, 2013, and until his death in 2014 there appear to have been no problems. There is no reason to believe that, even if what transpired in 2011 should be classified as mental illness, he suddenly relapsed on the evening of his death, after years of being exceptionally calm in the chaos of his nightclub job. And shortly before his encounter with the police, he exercised restraint in a confrontation with an aggressor.

■ ■

On the evening of March 21, 2014, Evan Snow, a thirtysomething "user experience design professional," according to his LinkedIn profile, who had moved to the neighborhood about six months earlier (and who has since departed for a more suburban location), took his young Siberian husky for a walk on Bernal Hill. As Snow was leaving the park, Nieto was coming up one of the little dirt trails that leads to the park's ring road, eating chips. In a deposition prior to the trial, Snow said that with his knowledge of the attire of gang members, he "put Nieto in that category of people that I would not mess around with."

His dog put Nieto in the category of people carrying food, and went after him. Snow never seemed to recognize that his out-of-control dog was the aggressor: "So Luna was, I think, looking to move around the benches or behind me to run up happily to get a chip from Mr. Nieto. Mr. Nieto became further— what's the right word?—distressed, moving very quickly and rapidly left to right, trying to keep his chips away from Luna. He ran down to these benches and jumped up on the benches, my dog following. She was at that point vocalizing, barking, or kind of howling." The dog had Nieto cornered on the bench while its inattentive owner was forty feet away—in his deposition for the case, under oath, his exact words were that he was distracted by a female "jogger's butt." Snow said, "I can imagine that somebody would—could assume the dog was being aggressive at that point." The dog did not come when he called, but kept barking.

Nieto, Snow says, then pulled back his jacket and took his Taser out, briefly pointing at the distant dog owner before he pointed it at the dog baying at his feet. The two men yelled at each other, and Snow apparently used a racial slur, but would not later give the precise word. As he left the park, he texted a friend about the incident. His text, according to his testimony, said, "in another state, like Florida, I would have been justified in shooting Mr. Nieto that night"—a reference to that state's infamous "stand your ground" law, which removes the obligation to retreat before using force in self-defense. In other words, he apparently wished he could have done what George Zimmerman did to Trayvon Martin: execute him without consequences.

Soon after, a couple out walking their dogs passed by Nieto. Tim Isgitt, a recent arrival in the area, is the communications director of a nonprofit organization founded by tech billionaires. He now lives in suburban Marin County, as does his husband, Justin Fritz, a self-described "e-mail marketing manager" who had lived in San Francisco about a year. In a picture one of them posted on social media, they are chestnut-haired, clean-cut white men posing with their dogs, a springer spaniel and an old bulldog. They were walking those dogs when they passed Nieto at a distance.

Fritz did not notice anything unusual but Isgitt saw Nieto moving "nervously" and putting his hand on the Taser in its holster. Snow was gone, so Isgitt had no idea that Nieto had just had an ugly altercation and had reason to be disturbed. Isgitt began telling people he encountered to avoid the area. (One witness who did see Nieto shortly after Isgitt and Fritz, longtime Bernal Heights resident Robin Bullard, who was walking his own dog in the park, testified that there was nothing alarming about him. "He was just sitting there," Bullard said.)

At the trial, Fritz testified that he had not seen anything alarming about Nieto. He said that he called 911 because Isgitt urged him to. At about 7:11 p.m. he began talking to the 911 dispatcher, telling her that there was a man with a black handgun. What race, asked the dispatcher, "Black, Hispanic?" "Hispanic," replied Fritz. Later, the dispatcher asked him if the man in question was doing "anything violent," and Fritz answered, "Just pacing, it looks like he might be eating chips or sunflowers, but he's resting a hand kind of on the gun." Alex Nieto had about five more minutes to live.

■ ■

San Francisco, like all cities, has been a place where when newcomers arrive in a trickle, they integrate and contribute to the ongoing transformation of a place that is not static in demographics and industries. When they arrive in a flood, as they have during economic booms since the nineteenth-century gold rush, including the dotcom surge of the late 1990s and the current tech tsunami, they scour out what was there before. By 2012 the incursion of tech workers had gone from steady stream to deluge, and more and more people and institutions—bookstores, churches, social services, nonprofits of all kinds, gay and lesbian bars, small businesses with deep roots in the neighborhoods—began to be evicted. So did seniors, including many in their nineties, schoolteachers, working-class families, the disabled, and pretty much anyone who was a tenant whose home could be milked for more money.

San Francisco had been a place where some people came out of idealism or stayed to realize an ideal: to work for social justice or teach the disabled, to write poetry or practice alternative medicine—to be part of something larger than themselves that was not a corporation, to live for something more than money. That was becoming less and less possible as rent and sale prices for homes spiraled upward. What the old-timers were afraid of losing, many of the newcomers seemed unable to recognize. The tech culture seemed in small and large ways to be a culture of disconnection and withdrawal.

And it was very white, male, and young, which is why I started to call my hometown "Fratistan." As of 2014, Google's Silicon

Valley employees, for example, were 2 percent black, 3 percent Latino, and 70 percent male. The Google bus—the private luxury shuttles—made it convenient for these employees who worked in the South Bay to live in San Francisco, as did shuttles for Facebook, Apple, Yahoo!, and other big corporations. Airbnb, headquartered in San Francisco, became the engine that devoured long-term housing stock in rural and urban places around the world, turning it into space for transients. Uber, also based here, set about undermining taxi companies that paid a living wage. Another tech company housed here, Twitter, became the most efficient way to deliver rape and death threats to outspoken feminists. San Francisco, once a utopia in the eyes of many, became the nerve center of a new dystopia.

Tech companies created multimillionaires and billionaires whose influence warped local politics, pushing for policies that served the new industry and their employees at the expense of the rest of the population. None of the money sloshing around the city trickled down to preserve the center for homeless youth that closed in 2013, or the oldest black-owned, black-focused bookstore in the country, which closed in 2014, or San Francisco's last lesbian bar, which folded in 2015, or the Latino drag and trans bar that closed the year before. As the Nieto trial unfolded, the uniquely San Franciscan African Orthodox Church of St. John Coltrane faced eviction from the home it found after an earlier eviction during the late-1990s dotcom boom. Resentments rose. And cultures clashed.

■ ■

At 7:12 p.m. on the evening of March 21, 2014, the police dispatcher who had spoken to Fritz put out a call. Some police officers began establishing a periphery, a standard way to de-escalate a potentially dangerous situation. One police car shot through the periphery to create a confrontation. In it were Lieutenant Jason Sawyer and Officer Richard Schiff, a rookie who had been on the job for less than three months. They headed for Bernal Heights Park when they got the call, tried first to enter it in their patrol car from the south side, the side where Alex's parents lived, then turned around and drove in from the north side, going around the barrier that keeps vehicles out and heading up the road that is often full of runners, walkers, and dogs at that time of day. They moved rapidly, but without lights or sirens; they were not heading into an emergency. But they were rushing past their fellow officers and the periphery without coordinating a plan.

At 7:17:40 p.m., Alejandro Nieto came walking downhill around a bend in the road, according to the 911 operator's conversation with Fritz. At 7:18:08 p.m., another policeman in the park, but not at the scene, broadcast: "Got a guy in a red shirt coming toward you." Schiff testified in court, "Red could be related to a gang involvement. Red is a Norteño color." Schiff testified that from about ninety feet away he shouted, "Show me your hands," and that Nieto had replied, "No, show me your hands," then drew his Taser, assuming a fighting stance, holding the weapon in both hands pointed at the police. The officers claim that the Taser projected a red light, which they assumed was the laser sight of a handgun, and feared for their lives. At 7:18:43 p.m., Schiff and Sawyer began barraging Nieto with .40-caliber bullets.

At 7:18:55 p.m., Schiff shouted, "Red," a police code word for out of ammunition. He had emptied a whole clip at Nieto. He reloaded, and began shooting again, firing twenty-three bullets in all. Sawyer was also blazing away. He fired twenty bullets. Their aim appears to have been sloppy, because Fritz, who had taken refuge in a grove of eucalyptus trees below the road, can be heard shouting, "Help! Help!" on his call to the 911 operator, as bullets fired by the police were "hitting the trees above me, breaking things and just coming at me." Sawyer said: "Once I realized there was no reaction, none at all, after being shot, I picked up my sights and aimed for the head." Nieto was hit just above the lip by a bullet that shattered his right upper jaw and teeth. Another ripped through both bones of his lower right leg. Though the officers testify that he remained facing them, that latter bullet went in the side of his leg, as though he had turned away. That while so agonizingly injured he remained focused on pretending to menace the police with a useless device that drew fire to him is hard to believe.

Two more officers, Roger Morse and Nate Chew, drove up to the first patrol car, got out, and drew their guns. There were no plan, no communications, no strategy to contain the person they were pursuing or capture him alive if he proved to be a menace, to avoid a potentially dangerous confrontation in a popular park where bystanders could be hit. Morse testified in court: "When I first arrived I saw what appeared to be muzzle flash. I aimed at him and began shooting." Tasers produce nothing that resembles muzzle flash. Chew, in contrast to his partner officer's account, testified that Nieto was already on the ground when they arrived. He fired five shots at the man on the ground. He told the court he stopped when he "saw the suspect's head fall down to the pavement."

Several more bullets hit Nieto while he was on the ground—at least fourteen struck him, according to the city autopsy report. Only one out of four of the bullets the officers fired reached their target—they fired fifty-nine in all. They were shooting to kill, and to overkill. One went into his left temple and tore through his head toward his neck. Several hit him in the back, chest, and shoulders. One more went into the small of his back, severing his spinal cord.

The officers approached Nieto at 7:19:20 p.m., less than two minutes after it had all begun. Morse was the first to get there; he says that Nieto's eyes were open and that he was gasping and gurgling. He says that he kicked the Taser out of the dying man's hands. Schiff says he "handcuffed him, rolled him over, and said, 'Sarge, he's got a pulse.'" By the time the ambulance arrived, Alejandro Nieto was dead.

Nieto's funeral, on April 1, 2014, packed the little church in Bernal Heights that his mother had taken him to as a child. I went with my friend Adriana Camarena, a civic-minded lawyer from Mexico City who lives in the Mission District, the neighborhood on Bernal's north flank that has been a capital of Latino culture since the 1960s. She had met Alex briefly; I never had. We sat near a trio of African American women who had lost their own sons in police killings and routinely attend the funerals of other such victims. In the months that followed, Adriana became close to Refugio and Elvira Nieto. Their son had been their ambassador to the

English-speaking world, and gradually Adriana was drawn into their grief and their need. She stepped in as an interpreter, advocate, counsel, and friend. Benjamin Bac Sierra, a novelist and former marine who teaches writing at San Francisco's community college, was a devoted friend of and mentor to Alex. He has become the other leader of a small coalition named Justice for Alex Nieto.

In that springtime of Nieto's death, I had begun to believe that what was tearing my city apart was not only a conflict pitting long-term tenants against affluent newcomers and the landlords, estate agents, house flippers, and developers seeking to open up room for them by shoving everyone else out. It was a conflict between two different visions of the city.

What I felt strongly at the funeral was the vital force of real community: people who experienced where they lived as a fabric woven from memory, ritual and habit, affection and love. This was a measure of place that had nothing to do with money and ownership and everything to do with connection. Adriana and I turned around in our pew and met Oscar Salinas, a big man born and raised in the Mission. He told us that when someone in the community is hurt, the Mission comes together. "We take care of each other." To him, the Mission meant the people who shared Latino identity and a commitment to a set of values, and to one another, all held together by place. It was a beautiful vision that many shared.

The sense of community people were trying to hang on to was about the things that money cannot buy. It was about home as a whole neighborhood and the neighbors in it, not just the real estate you held title to or paid rent on. It was not only the treasure of Latinos; white, black, Asian, and Native American residents of San Francisco had long-term relationships with people, institutions, traditions, particular locations. *Disruption* has been a favorite word of the new tech economy, but old-timers saw homes, communities, traditions, and relationships being disrupted. Many of the people being evicted and priced out were the people who held us all together: teachers, nurses, counselors, social workers, carpenters and mechanics, volunteers and activists. When, for example, someone who worked with gang kids got driven out, those kids were abandoned. How many threads could you pull out before the social fabric disintegrated?

Two months before the funeral, the real estate website Redfin looked at the statistics and concluded that 83 percent of California's homes, and 100 percent of San Francisco's, were unaffordable on a teacher's salary. What happens to a place when the most vital workers cannot afford to live in it? Displacement has contributed to deaths, particularly of the elderly—and many in their eighties and nineties have been targeted with eviction from their homes of many decades. In the two years since Nieto's death, there have been multiple stories of seniors who died during or immediately after their eviction. A survey reported that 71 percent of the homeless in San Francisco used to be housed there. Losing their homes makes them vulnerable to a host of conditions, some of them deadly. Gentrification can be fatal.

It also brings white newcomers to neighborhoods with nonwhite populations, sometimes with appalling consequences. Local newspaper the *East Bay Express* recently reported that in Oakland, recently arrived white people sometimes regard "people of color who are walking, driving, hanging out, or living in the neighborhood" as "criminal suspects." Some use the website Nextdoor.com to post comments "labeling Black people as suspects simply for walking down the street, driving a car, or knocking on a door." The same thing happens in the Mission, where people post things on Nextdoor such as "I called the police a few times when is more then three kids standing like soldiers in the corner," chat with one another about homeless people as dangers who need to be removed, and justify police killings others see as criminal. What's clear in the case of Nieto's death is that a series of white men perceived him as more dangerous than he was and that he died from it.

On March 1, 2016, the day the trial began, hundreds of students at San Francisco public schools walked out of class to protest Nieto's killing. A big demonstration was held in front of the federal courthouse, with drummers, Aztec dancers in feathered regalia, people holding signs, and a TV station interviewing Nieto's friend Benjamin Bac Sierra. Nieto's face on posters, banners,

T-shirts, and murals had become a familiar sight in the Mission; a few videos about the case had been made; demonstrations and memorials had been held. For some, Nieto stood for victims of police brutality and for a Latino community that felt imperiled by gentrification, by the wave of evictions and the people who regarded them as menaces and intruders in their own neighborhood. Many people who cared about the Nietos came to the trial each day, and the courtroom was usually nearly full.

Trials are theater, and this one had its dramas. Adante Pointer, a black lawyer with the Oakland firm of John Burris, which handles a lot of local police-killing lawsuits, represented Refugio and Elvira Nieto, the plaintiffs. Their star witness, Antonio Theodore, had come forward months after the killing. Theodore is an immigrant from Trinidad, a musician in the band Afrolicious, and a resident of the Bernal area. An elegant man with neat shoulder-length dreads who came to court in a suit, he said he had been on a trail above the road, walking a dog, and that he had seen the whole series of events unfold. He testified that Nieto's hands were in his pockets—that he had not pointed his Taser at the officers, there was no red laser light; the officers had just shouted "stop" and then opened fire.

When Pointer asked him why he had not come forward earlier, he replied: "Just think: it would be hard to tell an officer that I just saw fellow officers shooting up somebody. I didn't trust the police." Theodore testified cogently under questioning from Pointer. But the next morning, when city attorney Margaret Baumgartner, an imposing white woman with a resentful air, questioned him, he fell apart. He contradicted his earlier testimony about where he had been and where the shooting took place, then declared that he was an alcoholic with memory problems. He seemed to be trying to make himself safe by making himself useless. Pointer questioned him again, and he said: "I don't care to be here right now. I feel threatened." When witnesses are mistrustful or fearful of police, justice is hard to come by, and Theodore seemed terrified of them.

The details of what had happened were hotly debated and

often contradictory, especially with regard to the Taser. The police had testified as though Nieto had been a superhuman or inhuman opponent, facing them off even as they fired into his body again and again, then dropping to a "tactical sniper posture" on the ground, still holding the Taser with its red laser pointing at them. The city lawyers brought in a Taser expert whose official testimony seemed to favor them, but when he was asked by Pointer to look at the crime-scene photos, he said the Taser was off and that it was not something easily or accidentally turned on or off. Was Nieto busy toggling the small on-off switch while also busy having his body hammered by the bullets that killed him on the spot? The light is on only when the Taser is on. Officer Morse had testified that when he arrived to kick it out of Nieto's hands there were no red light or wires coming from it. The Taser wires are, however, visible in the police photographs documenting the scene.

The Taser expert told the court that Nieto's Taser's internal record said the trigger had been pulled three times. The Taser's internal clock said these trigger pulls had happened on March 22, after Nieto was dead. The expert witness also said it was set to Greenwich mean time and recalculated the time to place these trigger pulls at 7:14 p.m. the night he died. The police didn't have contact with him until 7:17 p.m. The Taser expert then created a new theory of "clock drift," under which Nieto's Taser fired at exactly the right time to corroborate the police version that the Taser was on and used at the time they shot him. Even if the trigger was pulled, it is not evidence that he was pointing the Taser at them. When a Taser is fired, confetti-like marker tags are ejected; none were found at the scene of the crime. Taser has, incidentally, just negotiated a $2 million contract with the police department.

One piece of evidence produced was a fragment of bone found in the pocket of Nieto's jacket. Some thought this proved that his hands had been in his pockets, as Theodore said. Dr. Amy Hart, the city coroner, said in the trial on Friday, March 4, that there were no photographs of his red 49ers jacket, which must have been full of bullet holes. The following Monday, an expert witness for the city mentioned the photographs of the jacket that the city had supplied him. The jurors were shown photographs of Nieto's hat, which had a bullet hole in it that corresponded to the hole in his temple, and of his broken sunglasses lying next to a puddle of blood. The coroner testified to abrasions on Nieto's face consistent with Nieto wearing glasses. Before this evidence was shown, Officer Richard Schiff had testified under oath that he made eye contact with Nieto and saw his forehead pucker up in a frown. If the dead man had been wearing a hat and dark glasses, then Schiff could not have seen these things. Finally, how could four police officers fire fifty-nine bullets at someone without noticing that he was not firing back? And what are we to make of their reports of "muzzle flash" from an object incapable of producing muzzle flashes?

When Elvira Nieto testified about her devastation at the death of her son, Pointer asked her about her husband's feelings as well. "Objection," shouted Baumgartner, as though what a wife said about her husband's grief should be disqualified as hearsay. The judge overruled her. At another point, Justin Fritz apologized to the Nietos for the outcome of his 911 call and seemed distressed. Refugio Nieto allowed Fritz to hug him; his wife did not. "Refugio later said that at that moment he was reminded of Alex's words," Adriana told me, "that even with the people that we have conflict with, we need to take the higher ground and show the best of ourselves."

Adriana sat with the Nietos every day of the trial, translating for them when the court-appointed translator was off duty. Bac Sierra, in an impeccable suit and tie, was right behind them every day, in the first of three rows of benches usually full of friends and supporters. Nieto's uncle often attended, as did Ely Flores, another young Latino who was Nieto's best friend and a fellow Buddhist. Flores later told me that he and Alex had been friends who tried to support each other in living up to their vows and ideals. He said that they wanted to be "pure lotuses" in their communities, a reference to the key Buddhist phrase about being "a pure lotus in muddy water," something spiritual that arises from the messiness of everyday life.

Flores had been studying to be a police officer at City College, seeing this as the way he could be of service to his community, but when Nieto was killed, he told me he realized he could never wear a badge or carry a gun. He abandoned the career he'd worked toward for years and started over, training in a culinary academy as a chef. He suggested that Nieto didn't see the police as adversaries and thought that he might instead not have understood that they were coming for him when he walked around the bend in the road that evening, not acted according to the rules for men who are considered suspects and menaces in everyday life.

It was a civil trial, so the standard was not "beyond a reasonable doubt," just the "preponderance of evidence." No one was facing prison, but if the city and officers were found liable, there could be a large financial settlement and it could affect the careers of the policemen. The trial was covered by many journalists from local TV stations and newspapers. On Thursday, March 10, 2016, after an afternoon and morning of deliberations, the eight jurors—five white, one Asian woman, and two Asian men, none black, none Latino—unanimously ruled in favor of the police on all counts. Flores wept in the hallway. The American Civil Liberties Union of Northern California published a response to the verdict headlined WOULD ALEX NIETO STILL BE ALIVE IF HE WERE WHITE? Police are now investigating claims that Officer Morse posted a sneering attack on Nieto on a friend's Facebook page that night.

■ ■

San Francisco is now a cruel place and a divided one. A month before the trial, the city's mayor, Ed Lee, decided to sweep the homeless off the streets for the Super Bowl, even though the game was played forty miles away, at the new 49ers stadium in Silicon Valley. Online rants about the city's homeless population have become symptomatic of the city's culture clash. The open letter to the mayor published in mid-February by Justin Keller, founder of a not very successful start-up, was typical in tone: "I know people are frustrated about gentrification happening in the city, but the reality is, we live in a free market society. The wealthy working people have earned their right to live in the city. They went out, got an education, work hard, and earned it. I shouldn't have to worry about being accosted. I shouldn't have to see the pain, struggle, and despair of homeless people to and from my way to work every day." And like Evan Snow, who wanted to blow away Alejandro Nieto after their encounter, Keller got his wish in a way. Pushed out of other areas, hundreds of homeless people began to set up tents under the freeway overpass around Division Street on the edge of the Mission, a gritty industrial area with few residences. The mayor destroyed this rainy-season refuge too: city workers threw tents and belongings into dump trucks and hounded the newly property-less onward. One of the purges came before dawn the morning the Nieto trial began.

When the trial ended with a verdict in favor of the police, 150 or so people gathered inside at the Mission Cultural Center and outside on rainy Mission Street. People were composed, resolute, disappointed, but far from shocked. It was clear that most of them had never counted on validation from the legal system that what happened to Alex Nieto was wrong. Their sense of principle and history was not going to be swayed by this verdict, even if they were saddened or angered by it. Bac Sierra, out of his courtroom suits and in a T-shirt and cap, spoke passionately, as did Oscar Salinas, who had just posted on Facebook the words "Alex you will never be forgotten, your parents will always be taken care of by us, the community. As I've always said, the unspoken word of La Mision is when someone is hurting, needs help, or passes we come together as a family and take care of them."

The Nietos spoke, with Adriana translating for those who did not understand Spanish. And Adriana spoke on her own behalf: "One of the most important changes in my path being involved in the Alex Nieto case has been to learn more about restorative practices, because as someone trained in legal systems, I know that the pain and fear that we are not safe from police in our communities will not go away until there is personal accountability by those who harm us."

Adriana, her historian husband, and their friends—including an AIDS activist and a queer choreographer—who live nearby in a ramshackle old building, had faced their own eviction battle last year, and won it. But the community that came together that night was still vulnerable to the economic forces tearing the city apart. Many of these people may have to move on soon; some already have.

The death of Alex Nieto is a story of one young man torn apart by bullets, and of a community coming together to remember him. They pursued more than justice, as the case became a cause, as the expressions became an artistic outpouring in videos, posters, and memorials, and as friendships and alliances were forged and strengthened. On April 7, less than a month after the trial, the police shot longtime San Franciscan Luis Gongora to death, claiming he was rushing them with a knife. Eyewitnesses from the little homeless community he was part of and from surrounding buildings and a security video suggested otherwise. People became angrier about the police they saw as part of a city government wiping out the black and Latino communities.

After the verdict and the killing of Gongora, five people went on a hunger strike in front of the Mission police station, fasting for eighteen days in their Hunger for Justice campaign to force the police chief to resign. Conventional wisdom dismissed their perspective and their effort, but on the afternoon of the day that police killed an unarmed mother—Jessica Nelson Williams—in her twenties, the police chief was forced to resign. At the demonstration that night at the industrial site where Williams died of a single bullet, two women held a banner that said WE ARE THE LAST 3%. The black population had plummeted since its peak in the mid-teens thirty years earlier. Down the block tucked under a freeway overpass, gentrifying homes were visible, styled in what you could call fortress modernism.

That night in March, in the gathering for the anniversary of Nieto's killing, Adriana Camarena told the crowd: "Our victory, as the Nietos said yesterday, is that we are still together." That too is a fragile and insecure condition.

i'm sick of pretending to give a shit about what whypeepo think

on the best days, i don't remember their skin
the kingdom & doom of it, their coy relationship to sunlight

band-aids are the color of the ones who make the wound
& whats a band-aid to a bullet to the rent is sky high & we
    gotta move?

i have no desire to desire what they apparently have
i want quiet & peace & enough weed to last through Saturday

so now that we're done talking about them, do you think
its appropriate to call that nigga Obama a nigga in public?

i have accepted that they who is always they will always be
looking so what's the use in holding back my black cackle

& juke? what's the purpose in being black if you have to spend
it trying to prove all the ways your not? i'm done with race

hahahaha could you imagine if it was what easy? to just say
i'm done & all the scars turn into ravens

the trees forget their blood memory & the city
lose all it's teeth? when people say they're post race

i think they're saying their done with black people
done with immigrants, officially believing America

began when the white people demanded their freedom
from the other white people i'm post America in that case

i'm so far in the future i'm on the beaches of Illinois
southern coast of a has been empire

telling my grandkids about the dust that use to rule us

—Danez Smith

NOTES OF
A NATIVE DAUGHTER

Sandra Cisneros

How to explain, Chicago, why you and me split?

Nelson Algren dubbed you a woman with a broken nose, albeit a lovely one, but you are guilty of breaking more than noses. Gwendolyn Brooks painted you as "grayed in, and gray," and this is how I remember your bruised skies of October, November, December, January, February, March, April till May. Lorraine Hansberry fumigated your cockroaches. Richard Wright stalked your rats. Studs Terkel quoted a Chicagoan who said, "I always feel a chest-swelling when I drive along the lake. . . . Yet I know four blocks over is desperation."

So much desperation in our neighborhood. We thought we deserved what we got because we were willing to live in such flimsy buildings. *What did you expect? Rent's cheap.* Just like my mother and father thought they'd been punished when the baby died from the flood of bronchial pneumonia. Blamed themselves. Not the cold apartments, not the city, never the landlords, nor the building inspectors.

On the northwest corner of Western and Le Moyne, a Puerto Rican classmate drowned in a sea of fire; an open casket and the ugly wig terrible as a lie. On Twenty-First Street and Wolcott, a prizewinning poet and her daughters leaped from third-story flames and survived. But did not escape the aftermath of nightmares. Fire department blamed ladders too short for the buildings, not enough trucks, not enough equipment. Never enough of anything for a neighborhood not worth saving.

Our neighborhoods were the ones earmarked for urban renewal, we were told, and told to move. They didn't tell us someone else's renewal, not our own.

But I have you to thank, Chicago, for my education. Slim luck enough to have been born when museums had free admission on Sundays so working folks were welcome. My teachers were Hokusai and Brancusi at the Art Institute; my schoolroom, the basement of the Field Museum in the Egyptian tombs; color I learned at the Shedd Aquarium; Yesterday's Main Street was my lesson at the Museum of Science and Industry; the Chicago History Museum taught me about fire.

In the neighborhoods we knew, booze was easier to find than books. On every block, liquor stores or taverns to mute the pain of dreams deferred. Few and far and rare, libraries to ignite aspirations. Before we learned to read and ever after, Mother took us to the library weekly.

My immigrant father's overdose of Mexico City pride gave us the self-esteem to survive you, Chicago. We *were* the border. Between black and white at war with one another and at war with us. We knew from visits to our father's home, there was more than one story in "history." Knew to distinguish what was said in textbooks from what we knew ourselves from traveling south.

I discovered *The Autobiography of Malcolm X* and thereafter refused to serve the Master. I changed my name from *sand-druh sis-narrows* to *sohn-druh seez-neh-ros*, though I had to repeat and repeat it. And when my listener gave me back my name beautifully whole, it was a gift of respect and self-respect.

Those days were sick-and-tired times of I-can't-wait. The Democratic convention of '68 camped in our backyard, Humboldt Park; the first time I'd seen white people come visit. Those days were the days dimmed with Dr. King's death. The city consumed by fire that gave no light. Our relatives, the last of the Mexicans on their black block, fled their Lawndale home. Walked, abandoning family photos, all their personal things, though aunty, with her indigenous Guanajuato skin, was the hue of her neighbors, if not darker.

Each night, sun hunkered in the West and gilded our rowdy village. I needed sunsets like I needed books. I needed an eternity of serene. Had to wait till Sunday to get my dose of lake. The blue coastline too expensive daily. I made do with what was affordable, within reach. When you least expected it, you might come upon an astonishing cloud, wild morning glories climbing an electric pole, the first green pips of spring breaking through the crust of winter. Something beautiful was necessary, needed to keep one nourished for the inevitable grief.

One long, hot summer, Mayor Jane Byrne sent Tito Puente to Humboldt Park to drum on his garbage cans for us instead of sending the Department of Sanitation to empty our cans, trash collection halved from twice a week to once, even though population and trash had doubled. And with that, doubling the population of urban creatures. Mother and I avoided our garden after sunset. Our curfew—fear.

What could a city girl like me do but major in human behavior? I knew since I was a teenager, a passenger grunting on the Armitage bus could take delight of himself in open day and force others to watch for added pleasure. For good measure, I sat thereafter next to the driver.

The crash of a windshield with a baseball bat meant the disappearance of a purse. Gold about the neck attracted the only runners our neighborhood knew. When driving, I knew to lock all doors. Once, at a stoplight, Father was escorted by knife a few blocks, deposited curbside, and kindly divested of his van. At least he made it to his bed that night, unlike cousin's husband found asleep at the wheel, a bullet and a this-can't-be-happening-to-me look lodged to the head.

To feed nine meant weekly visits to the local supermarket that stank of black fruit and sour beer. Nothing to transport the groceries home but me and Mother, a collapsible shopping cart, and our collapsible bones. Sweets meant another trek beyond the park and the Kedzie armory, to day-old vending machine doughnuts sold at half price to sugar the deal.

Every place we ever lived never had enough bedrooms for seven kids. Nights, we camped where we could. Three or four together, head to feet. On La-Z-Boys, rollaways, couch cushions. In rooms not meant for beds.

When I came home at night from work, I knew enough to avoid sidewalks and parked cars and sprinted the center runway of our street from bus stop to the safety of my door.

I answered Ginsberg's "Howl" with my own poetry for those who lived like me, afraid for themselves and of one another. "North Avenue." "Roosevelt Road." "South Sangamon." A house on a street named Mango.

I was all of twenty-two when on a car trip through Carolina's Blue Ridge, I saw a country house with a swing dangling from a thick branch and a careless bike abandoned on the fenceless lawn. And thought, Kids grow up like this? I never knew.

Chicago's Magnificent Mile made others feel magnificent but only made me ashamed of my shoes. To us, Michigan Avenue shops meant: *Do not enter if you have to ask, "How much?"*

Our downtown was South State Street. Smokey Joe's for *Super Fly* wear. Ronny's Steak House's $2.95 T-bones. George Diamond's, home of the original iceberg wedge salad. Three Sisters Dress Shop: *Yes, we have layaway.* Sears for boxes of popcorn. Van Buren Street temptation row—peep and burlesque shows where Harold's library now stands.

And Goldblatt's. A carnival. Department store bells dinging nervously. Escalators filled to capacity in both directions. Chaos in enticing bins. A sea of pastel nylon undies. Mountains of mismatched socks. An explosion of double-D brassieres. Miniature Lincoln Log cabins spouting incense from chimneys. Queen-size pantyhose. Windmill cookies. Butter toffee peanuts. Candy in glass bins. All within reach. *Gimme a quarter pound of orange slices, please.*

I was afraid for myself and of others. Tired of being on high alert, watching for the tiger in the grass from the corner of the eye. The walls at night that came alive with amber shimmering at the flick of a light. The scuttling and squeaking behind plaster.

Father said, pointing around our home, "Why would you want to leave? You have everything here."

How could I tell him this was not the everything I'd asked for? What did I want? No one had ever thought to ask me.

I longed for a space all my own to think. Quiet enough to hear my pen move across paper. Affordable but safe. Serene and clean. Peonies on the kitchen table. No mice, or rats, or crispy bugs allowed, ever. A lock on the door. A door, please.

"A city should be a place to live."

The truth was, I was trying not to die.

Mother said, *Go to school. Study hard. And wear a bra.*

Father said, *Go to college. And while you're at it, bring back a husband.*

Chicago said, *We need girls like you . . . to teach high school.*

I said to me, *If you stick around, you're everybody's but your own.*

I ran off at twenty-eight with that wild boy—my pen.

I'm sixty-one. My mother and father gone.

Chicago, how do I explain? For home to be a home, you have to feel that you belong.

DOSAS

Edwidge Danticat

ELSIE WAS WITH her live-in renal failure patient when her ex-husband called to inform her that his girlfriend, Olivia, had been kidnapped in Port-au-Prince. Elsie had just fed Gaspard, the renal patient, when her cell phone rang. Gaspard was lying in bed, his head carefully propped on two foam pillows, his bloated and pitted, and sometimes itchy, face angled toward the gray-tinted bedroom skylight, which allowed him a slanted view of a giant coconut palm that had been leaning over the lakeside house in Gaspard's single-family development for years.

Elsie removed the empty plate from Gaspard's nightstand and wiped a lingering string of spinach from his chin. Waving both hands as though conducting an orchestra, Gaspard signaled to her not to leave the room, while motioning for her to carry on with her phone conversation. Quickly turning her attention from Gaspard to the phone, Elsie pressed it close to her lips and asked, *"Ki lè?"*

"This morning." Sounding hoarse and exhausted, Blaise, the ex-husband, jumbled his words. His singsong tone, which Elsie often attributed to his actually being a singer, was gone. It was replaced by a nearly inaudible whisper. "She was leaving her mother's house," he continued. "Two men grabbed her, pushed her into a car, and drove off."

Elsie could imagine Blaise sitting, or standing, with the phone trapped between his neck and shoulders, while he used his hands to pick at his fingernails. It was one of his many obsessions, clean fingernails. Dirty fingers drive him crazy, she'd reasoned, because Blaise had been raised by a market woman and a mechanic and had barely missed having dirty fingers all his life.

"You didn't go with her?" Elsie asked.

"You're right," he answered, loudly drawing an endless breath through what Elsie knew were grinding teeth. "I should have been with her."

Elsie's patient's eyes wandered down from the ceiling, where the blooming palm had sprinkled the skylight glass with a handful of tiny brown seeds. He'd been pretending not to hear, but was now looking directly at Elsie. Restlessly shifting his weight from one side of the bed to the next, he paused to catch his breath. He wanted her off the phone.

Gaspard had turned seventy that day and before his lunch had requested a bottle of champagne from his daughter, champagne which he shouldn't be having, but for which he'd pleaded so much that the daughter had given in on the condition that he would take only a few sips after the toast. The daughter, Mona, who was a decade younger than Elsie's thirty-five years, was visiting from New York and had gone out to procure what was surely the most expensive bottle of champagne she could find. And suddenly she was back.

"Elsie, I need you to hang up," the daughter said in Creole as she laid out three crystal champagne flutes on a folding table by the bed.

"Call me back," Elsie told Blaise.

After she hung up, Elsie moved closer to the sick man's spindly daughter and watched as she gently slid a champagne flute between her father's fingers.

"*À la vie.*" She chose to toast him in French. "To life," she then added. Though there might not be much life left.

■ ■

That afternoon, Blaise called back to tell Elsie that Olivia's mother had heard from her kidnappers. The mother had asked to speak to Olivia but her captors refused to put her on the phone.

"They want fifty thousand." Blaise spoke in such a rapid nasal voice that Elsie had to ask him to repeat the figure.

"American dollars?" she asked, just to be sure.

She imagined him nodding by slowly moving his egg-shaped head up and down as he answered, *"Wi."*

"Of course her mother doesn't have it," Blaise said. "These are not rich people. Everyone says we should negotiate. Can maybe get it down to ten. I could try to borrow that."

For just a second, Elsie imagined him meaning ten dollars, which would have made things easier. Ten dollars and her old friend and rival would be free. Her ex-husband would stop calling and interrupting her at work. He, of course, meant ten thousand American dollars.

"Jesus, Marie, Joseph," Elsie mumbled a brief prayer under her breath. "I'm sorry," she told Blaise.

"This is hell." He sounded almost too calm now. She wasn't surprised because he was always subdued by worry. Weeks after he was kicked out of the popular konpa band he'd founded and had been the lead singer of, he did nothing but stay home and stare into space whenever she tried to talk to him. Then too he had been exceedingly calm.

■ ■

Elsie's former friend Olivia was seductive. Everyone who ever met her acknowledged it. Chestnut colored, with a massive head of hair that she always wore in a gelled bun, Olivia was beautiful. But what Elsie had first noticed about her when they'd first met was her ambition. Olivia was Elsie's age, but was a lot more outgoing and charming. She liked to touch people on either the arm, back, or shoulder while talking to them, whether they were patients, doctors, nurses, or other nurses' aides. No one seemed to mind, though, her touch becoming something not just anticipated or welcomed but yearned for. Olivia was one of the most popular certified nurses' aides at the agency that assigned them work. Because of her good looks and near-perfect mastery of textbook

English, she often got assigned the easiest patients in the most upscale neighborhoods.

Elsie and Olivia had met at a two-week refresher course for home attendants and upon completion of the course had gravitated toward each other. Whenever possible, they'd asked their agency to assign them the same group homes, where they mostly cared for bedridden elderly patients. At night when their wards were well medicated and asleep, they'd stay up and gossip in hushed tones, judging and condemning their patients' children and grandchildren, whose images were framed near bottles of medicine on bedside tables, but whose voices they rarely heard on the phone and whose faces they hardly ever saw in person.

■ ■

The next morning Elsie brought Gaspard his toothbrush and toothpaste and helped him change out of his pajamas into the now too-small slacks and shirt he insisted on wearing in bed during the day. Just as he had every morning for the last week or so, he reached over and ran his coarse fingertips across Elsie's high cheekbones and whispered, "Elsie, my flower, I think I'm at the end."

Compared to some mornings, when Gaspard would stop to rest even while gargling, he seemed rather stable. His entire body was swelling up, though, blending his features in a way that made him look less and less singular all the time. Soon, Elsie feared, his face might become like an ever darkening balloon that someone had just drawn a few translucent dots on. Much to Elsie's and his daughter's dismay, Gaspard was still refusing dialysis, which was the only thing that might help.

"Where's Nana?" he asked, using his nickname for his daughter.

The daughter was still sleeping in her old bedroom, whose walls were draped from floor to ceiling with sheer white fabric that the daughter purposely opened the windows to let flow in the early morning April breeze. Elsie knew little about the daughter except that she was living in New York, where she worked for a famous beauty company, designing labels for soaps, skin creams, and lotions that filled every shelf of every cabinet of every bathroom in the house. She was unmarried and had no children and had been a beauty queen at some point, judging from the pictures around the house in which she was wearing sequined gowns and bikinis with sashes across her body. In one of those pictures, she was Miss Haiti-America, whatever that was.

Elsie had also gathered from pieces of overhead conversations that some years ago, Gaspard's wife, his daughter's mother, had divorced him and moved back to Haiti. ("My wife took two good kidneys with her," she'd once heard Gaspard tell a friend on the phone.) The daughter was willing to donate one of her kidneys to him, but Gaspard refused to even consider it.

Sometimes Gaspard would also share a few things with Elsie, to explain, she suspected, why his daughter couldn't leave the city she'd been living in since college and move back to Miami to take care of him. He would often add, when his daughter showed up on Friday nights and left on Sunday afternoons, that his daughter was living the life he and her mother had always dreamed of for their only child, a free life where she earned enough money to never want for anything from anyone.

"I don't want you to think she's deserting me, like a lot of people forget their old people here," he said.

"But she's here often enough, Mesye Gaspard," Elsie had said. "That's what counts."

Aside from his daughter, he hated having visitors. He minced no words in telling the people who called him, especially the clients and other accountants he'd worked with at his tax-preparation/multiservice business, that he wanted none of them to see him the way he was.

The daughter walked to Gaspard's room as soon as she woke up. In order to avoid tiring him, they didn't speak much, but for the better part of the morning, she read to him from an old Haitian novel with a prescient title, *L'Espace d'un cillement (In the Flicker of an Eyelid)*.

■ ■

Blaise called once more that afternoon as Elsie was preparing a palm hearts and avocado salad that Gaspard had especially requested. It was something his wife used to prepare for him, he said, something he now wanted to share with his daughter, who this time would be spending an entire week with him.

"I think they hurt her, Elsie," Blaise said. His speech was garbled and slow, as though he'd just woken up from a deep sleep.

"Why do you think that?" Elsie asked. Her thumb accidentally slipped across the blade of the knife she was using to slice the palm hearts. She squeezed the edge of the wound with her teeth, the sweet taste of her own blood filling her mouth.

"I don't know," he said, "I can feel it. You know she won't give in easily. She'll fight."

The night Olivia and Blaise met, Elsie had taken her to see Blaise's band, Kajou, play at Dede's Night Club in Little Haiti. The place was owned by Luca Dede, a man in his late forties but who had a teenager's face, a Haitian of partial Ghanaian origin whose maternal line was, like Elsie's family, from the southern town of Les Cayes. Luca Dede's music promoter father had discovered Blaise in Port-au-Prince and had gotten him a visa to tour the United States. Blaise overstayed his visa, kept playing, and never went back to Haiti. Elsie was so used to going to Dede's, Blaise's most consistent gig, that she didn't even bother dressing up that night. She chose instead to wear a buttoned-up white shirt and a pair of casual dark slacks as though she were going to an office. Hungry for a night out, Olivia wore a too-tight, sequined cocktail dress that she'd bought in a thrift shop.

"It was the most soiree thing they had," Olivia said when Elsie met her at the entrance. "They didn't have one, but I wanted a red dress. I wanted fire. I wanted blood."

"You need a man," Elsie said.

"Correct," Olivia said, tilting her body forward on five-inch heels to plant a kiss on Elsie's cheek. Though they'd known each other for a while, it was the first time Olivia had greeted her with a kiss, rather than one of her usual intimate-feeling touches. They were out to have fun, away from their ordinary cage of sickness and death. Perhaps Olivia was simply celebrating that.

Being with Olivia that night gained Elsie a few glances from several men, including Luca Dede. Minding the bar as usual, Dede sent winks and drinks their way until it was clear that Olivia only a passing interest in him. While Elsie didn't dance that night, Olivia danced with every man who trotted over to their table and held out a hand to her. Several rum punches later, Olivia even got up between sets, and on a dare from Dede, sang, in a surprisingly pitch-perfect voice, the Haitian national anthem. Olivia got a standing ovation. The crowd whistled and hooted and Elsie couldn't help noticing that, his voice magnified by the microphone Olivia had just returned to him, her husband cheered loudest of all.

"I'll put her in the band," he hollered.

"Make her president," Dede echoed from the bar.

Three years before, Elsie and Blaise had met more quietly, but also at Dede's. She too had walked into Dede's with a friend, an old school friend from Haiti, the head of the agency who'd helped her get her visa to the United States, mentored her through her qualifying exams, hired her, and put her up until she was able to live on her own. Her friend had since moved to Atlanta to start another business there, but introducing her to Blaise was one of the many ways she'd tried to make sure Elsie wasn't alone.

That night Elsie had heard Blaise sing with Kajou for the first time. She was not impressed. Blaise and his band sounded like every other konpa band out there, repeating the same bubbly beats and endlessly urging everyone to raise their hands up in the air. He would later tell her that it was her look of disinterest, and even disdain, that had drawn him to her.

"You seemed like the only woman in the room I couldn't seduce," he said, while sliding into the empty chair next to her and ordering them rum sours after the show. He could never pass up a challenge.

■ ■

"I got a couple of loans," Blaise announced when he called yet once again a few hours later. His voice cracked and he stuttered and Elsie wondered if he'd been crying.

"I have forty-five hundred now," he added. "Do you think they'll accept that?"

"Are you going to send the money just like that?" Elsie asked.

"I think I'll bring it," he said, sounding as though he hadn't quite made up his mind. "I think I'll get on the plane once I have all the money and bring it myself."

"What if they take you too?" Elsie's level of concern shocked even her. Selfishly, she wondered who would be called if he were kidnapped. Like her, he didn't have any family in Miami. The closest thing he had were Dede and the bandmates, who'd parted company with him over money problems he'd refused to discuss with her. Maybe that's why he'd left her for Olivia. Olivia would have insisted on knowing exactly what had happened with the band and why. Olivia might have tried to fix it, so he could keep playing at all cost. Olivia probably believed, just as he did, that he needed all his time for his music, that working as a parking attendant during the day was spiritually razing him.

"How do you know this isn't some kind of plot to trick you out of your money?" Elsie asked.

"Something's wrong," he said. "She'd never go this long without calling me."

"You would know," Elsie said.

It was something she'd said to him before, when she'd desperately tried to hide her jealousy with mock suspicion.

Soon after Olivia met Blaise, Olivia would also reach up to kiss his cheeks the way she had Elsie's. At first Elsie had ignored this, however every once in a while she would bring it to their attention in a jokey way by saying something like, "Watch out, sister, that's my man." From her experience working with the weak and the sick, she'd learned that the disease you ignore is the one that kills you, so she tried her best to have everything out in the open.

Whenever Blaise asked her to invite Olivia to his gigs, she always obliged because she also enjoyed Olivia's company outside of work. And when the band broke up and he was no longer singing at Dede's or anywhere else, the three of them would go out together to shop for groceries or see a movie, and even attend Sunday morning Mass at Notre Dame Catholic Church. They were soon like a trio of siblings, of whom Olivia was the *dosa*, the last, untwinned, or surplus, child.

"I'm sorry I haven't called before all this." Blaise spoke now as though they were simply engaged in the dawdling pillow talk Elsie had once so enjoyed during their six-year marriage. "I didn't think you wanted to hear from me."

"That's how it goes with the quick divorce, *non*?" she said.

She was waiting for him to say something else about Olivia. He was slow at parceling out news. It had taken him months to inform her that he was leaving her for Olivia. Perhaps it would have been easier to accept had he simply blurted something out that first night he'd seen Olivia at Dede's. Then she wouldn't have spent so much time reviewing every moment the three of them had spent together, wondering whether they'd winked behind her back during Mass or smirked as she lay between them in the grass after their Saturday afternoon outings to watch him play soccer in the Little Haiti soccer park.

"Anything new?" she asked suddenly, wanting to shorten their talk.

"They called me directly." She could hear him swallow hard. Her ears had grown accustomed to that kind of effortful gulp from working with Gaspard and others. *"Vòlè yo."* The thieves.

"What did they sound like?" She wanted to know everything he knew so she could form a lucid image in her own mind, a shadow play identical to his.

"I think they were boys, men. I wasn't recording," he said, sounding annoyed.

"Did you ask to speak to her?"

"They wouldn't let me," he said.

"Why not?"

"Do you think I'm in their heads and know what they're thinking?"

"Did you insist?"

"Don't you think I would?"

"I'm sure you did—"

"They're in control, you know."

"I know."

"Doesn't sound like you do."

"I do," she conceded, "but did you tell them you wouldn't send money unless you speak to her? Maybe they don't have her anymore. You said it yourself. She would fight. Maybe she escaped."

"Don't you think I'd ask to speak to my own woman?" he shouted.

The way he spat this out irritated her. Woman? His own woman? He had never been the kind of man who called any woman his. At least not out loud. Maybe his phantom music career had secretly made him think that all women were his. He'd never yelled at her either. They had rarely fought, both of them keeping their quiet resentments, irritations, and boredom close to the chest. She now hated him for shouting. She hated them both.

"I'm sorry," he said, calming down. "They didn't speak to me for very long. They just told me to start planning her funeral if I don't send at least ten thousand by tomorrow afternoon."

Just then she heard Gaspard's daughter call out from the other room. "Elsie, can you come here, please?" The daughter's voice was laden with the permanent weariness of those who love the seriously ill.

"Please call me later," she told Blaise and hung up.

■ ■

When Elsie got to Gaspard's room, the daughter was sitting there with the same book on her lap. She'd once again been reading to her father when Elsie had slipped away with the intention of stacking the dishwasher with the lunch plates, but ended up answering Blaise's call instead.

"Elsie," the daughter said, as her father pushed his head farther back into the pillows. His fists were clenched in stoic agony, his eyes closed. His face was sweaty and he seemed to have been coughing. The daughter raised the oxygen mask over his nose and turned on the compressor, which had just been delivered that morning, and whose sound made it harder for Elsie to hear.

"Elsie, I'm sorry," the daughter said to her in Creole. "I'm not here all the time. I don't know how you function normally, but I'm really concerned about how much time you spend on the phone."

Elsie didn't want to explain why she was talking on the phone but quickly decided she had to. Not only because she thought the daughter was right, that Gaspard deserved more of her attention, but also because she had no one else to turn to for advice. Her friend in Atlanta had tried to stay out of her separation and divorce, and, perhaps seduced by Olivia, had stopped returning her calls. And so she told Gaspard and his daughter why she had been taking these calls and why the calls were so frequent, except she modified a few crucial details. Because she was still embarrassed by the actual facts, she told them Olivia was her sister and Blaise her brother-in-law.

"I'm very sorry, Elsie." The daughter immediately softened. Gaspard opened his eyes and held out his hand toward Elsie. Elsie grabbed his fingers the way she did sometimes to help him rise to his feet.

"Do you want to go home?" Gaspard asked in an increasingly raspy voice. "We can get the agency to send someone else."

"I'm not in her head, Papa," the daughter said, sounding much younger when she spoke in Creole than she did in English, "but I think working is best. Paying off these types of ransoms can ruin a person financially."

"It's better not to wait." Gaspard said, still trying to catch his breath. "The less time your sister spends with these *malfetè*, the better off she'll be."

Gaspard turned his face toward his daughter for final approval and the daughter yielded and nodded in agreement.

"If you want to save your sister," Gaspard said with an even more winded voice now, "you may have to give in."

■ ■

"I have five thousand in the bank," Elsie told Blaise when he called again that afternoon. She actually had sixty-seven hundred, but she couldn't part with all her savings at once, in case another type of emergency came up in either Haiti or Miami. Somehow she felt he already knew about the five thousand, though. It was roughly the same amount she'd had saved when they'd been together. She'd hoped to double her savings but had been unable to after moving to a one-bedroom efficiency in North Miami, plus sending a monthly allowance to her parents, and paying school fees for her younger sister in Les Cayes. This is what Blaise had been trying to tell her all along. He desperately needed that money to save Olivia's life.

■ ■

Sometimes Elsie was sure she could make out the approximate time Olivia and Blaise began seeing each other without her. Olivia started pairing up with someone else for the group home jobs and turned Elsie down when she asked her to join the usual outings with Elsie and Blaise.

The night Blaise left their apartment for good, Olivia sat outside Elsie's first-floor window, in the front passenger seat of Blaise's red four-door pickup, which he often used to carry speakers and instruments to his gigs. The pickup was parked under a streetlamp, and for most of the time that Elsie was staring through a crack in her drawn bedroom shades, Olivia's disk-shaped face was flooded in a harsh bright light. At some point Olivia got out of the car then disappeared behind it and Elsie suspected that she'd crouched down in the shadows to pee before getting back in the front passenger seat, what Elsie had always called the "wife seat" during a few of their previous outings when Olivia would sit in the back. Only when the pickup, packed with Blaise's belongings, was pulling away did Olivia finally look over at the apartment window, where Elsie quickly sank into the darkness. Sitting on the floor of her nearly empty apartment, Elsie realized she had to move. She couldn't stay there anymore.

■ ■

The next evening Gaspard fell out of bed while reaching over to his bedside table for the book his daughter had been reading to him. Elsie heard the thump from her bedroom, and by the time she dashed down the hall, his daughter was already there, her bottom spiked up in the air, her face pressed against her father's. With one arm under her father's bulbous legs and the other wrapped around his back, she dragged him off the floor and raised him onto the edge of the bed.

Elsie paused in the doorway to watch the daughter lower her father into bed as though he were an oversized child. Raising a comforter over his chest, she gently kissed her father's forehead. They were both panting as their faces came apart, the daughter from the effort of carrying the father and the father from having been carried.

Suddenly their panting turned into loud chuckles.

"There are many falls before the big one," he said.

"Thank God you got that good carpet," she said.

Then, her face growing somber again, the daughter said, "How can I leave you, Papa?"

"You can," he said, "and you will. You have your life and I have what's left of mine. I want you to always do what you want. I don't want you to have any regrets."

"You need dialysis," she pleaded. "Why don't you accept it?"

The daughter reached over and grabbed a glass of water from the side table. She held the back of her father's head as he took a few sips. Elsie rushed over and took the glass from her as she lowered her father's head back onto the pillow. The daughter nearly pierced her lips with her teeth while trying to keep tears from slipping down her face.

"I know you're having your family problem, Elsie," the daughter said, straining not to raise her voice, "but why did it take you so long to get here after my father fell out of his bed? I think Papa's right. I'm going to call the agency to ask for someone else."

Elsie wanted to plead to stay. She liked Gaspard and didn't want him to have to break in someone new. Besides, after wiring that money to Blaise for Olivia's ransom—he had specially asked that she wire it rather than bring it to him—she now desperately needed the work. However, if they wanted her to leave, she would. She only hoped her dismissal wouldn't cost her other jobs.

"I'll wrap things up," she told them, "until you get someone else."

■ ■

One night after Elsie and Olivia heard Blaise play at an outdoor festival at Bayfront Park in downtown Miami, they were walking toward the part of the parking lot that was reserved for the performers when Olivia announced that she was going to find a man to move back with her to Haiti.

"Do you have to love him or can it be just anyone?" Elsie had asked.

Mildly drunk from a whole afternoon of beer sipping, Olivia had mumbled, "Anyone."

"How can you live without love?" Blaise had said, waxing lyrical in a way Elsie had never heard before, except when he was onstage and chatting up the women who came to hear his band with his idea of public come-ons. ("You're looking like a piña colada, baby. Can I have a sip?") Corny, harmless stuff that Elsie was accustomed to.

"I can live without love," Olivia had said, "but I can't leave without money and I can't live without my country. I'm tired of being in this country. This country makes us mean."

Elsie guessed at that moment that Olivia was still thinking about one of their patients' sons from the day before, a middle-aged white man, a loan officer at a bank. In their presence, as they were changing shifts, the man, obviously drunk, had turned over his senile father and slapped the old man's wrinkly bottom with his palm several times.

"See how you like it now," he'd said.

Calling the agency that had hired them, then the Department of Social Services, over a mistreated patient yet again, Olivia had barely been able to find the words.

The night of the concert, to distract Olivia from her thoughts of abused patients, and to distract each other from thoughts of losing Olivia, the three of them had returned to Blaise and Elsie's apartment and had wiped off an entire bottle of five-star Rhum Barbancourt. Sometime in the early-morning hours, without anyone's request or guidance, they had fallen into bed together, exchanging jumbled words, lingering kisses, and caresses, whose sources they weren't interested in keeping track of. That night, they were no longer sure what to call themselves. What were they exactly? A triad. A ménage à trois. No. *Dosas.* They were *dosas.* All three of them untwinned, lonely, alone together.

When they woke up Olivia was gone.

■ ■

Blaise called again early the next morning. Elsie was still in bed but was preparing to leave Gaspard for good. Gaspard and his daughter were still asleep and, aside from the hum of Gaspard's oxygen compressor, the house was quiet.

"I shouldn't have let her go," Blaise whispered before Elsie could say hello.

When Blaise was with the band, he would sometimes go days without sleep in order to rehearse around the clock. By the time his gig would come around, he'd be so hyper that his voice would sound mechanical, as though all emotion had been purged out of it. He sounded that way now as Elsie tried to keep up.

"We weren't getting along anymore," he said. "We were going to break up. That's why she just picked up and left."

A light came on down the hall, in the room where Gaspard's daughter was sleeping. Elsie heard a door creak open then the shuffling of feet. A shadow approached. The daughter slid Elsie's door open an even larger crack and peeked in, rubbing a clenched fist against her eyes to fully rouse herself.

"Is everything all right?" she asked Elsie.

Elsie nodded.

"I wish I'd begged her not to go," Blaise was saying.

The daughter pulled Elsie's door shut behind her and continued toward her father's room down the hall.

"What happened?" Elsie asked. "You sent the money, didn't you? They released her?"

The phone line crackled and Elsie heard several bumps. Was Blaise stomping his feet? Banging his head against a wall? Pounding the phone into his forehead?

"Where is she?" Elsie tried to moderate her voice.

"We had a fight," he said. "Otherwise she wouldn't have gone. We had a spat and she left."

The daughter opened Elsie's door and once again pushed her head in.

"Elsie, my father would like to see you when you're done," she said, before pulling the door behind her once more.

"I'm sorry, I have to go," Elsie said. "My boss needs me. But first tell me she's okay."

She didn't want to hear whatever else was coming, but she couldn't hang up.

"We paid the ransom," he said, now rushing to get his words out before she could hang up. "But they didn't release her. She's dead."

Elsie walked back to the bed she'd called hers for the last few months and sat down. This was the longest she'd ever been at any single job. For a while she had allowed herself to forget that this bed with its foamy mattress, which was supposed to use numbers to remember the shape of your body, was not really hers. Taking a deep breath, she moved the phone away from her face and let it rest on her lap.

"Are you there?" Blaise was shouting now. "Can you hear me?"

"Where was she found?" Elsie raised the phone back to her ear.

"She was dumped in front of her mother's house," Blaise shrieked like a wounded animal. "In the middle of the night."

Elsie ran her fingers across her cheeks where, the night they'd fallen in bed together, Blaise had kissed her for the last time. That night, it was hard for Elsie to differentiate Olivia's hands from Blaise's on her naked body. But in her drunken haze, it felt perfectly normal, like they'd all needed one another too much to restrain themselves. Now the tears were catching her off guard, coming much quicker than she'd expected. She lowered her head and buried her eyes in the crook of her elbow.

"You won't believe it," Blaise said, frantically gargling the words as they came through.

"What?" Elsie said, wishing, not for the first time since he and Olivia had not stopped talking to her, that the three of them were once again drunk and in bed together.

"Her mother says that before she left the house, Olivia wrote her name at the bottom of her feet."

Elsie could imagine Olivia, her conked, plastered hair wild as it had been that night with the three of them, and wild again as she pulled her feet toward her face and, with a marker that she'd probably brought all the way from Miami just for that purpose, scribbled her name on the soles of her feet. Knowing Olivia, she'd probably seen this as the only precaution against the loss of identity that might possibly follow her being beheaded.

"They didn't, did they?" Elsie asked.

"No," Blaise said. "Her mother says her face, *her entire body*, was intact."

He put some emphasis on "her entire body," Elsie realized, because he wanted to signal to her that Olivia had also not been raped. Elsie let out a sigh of relief for both, a sigh so loud that Blaise followed with one of his own. "Her mother's going to bury her in her family's mausoleum, in their village out north," he added.

"Are you going?" she asked.

"Of course," he said. "Would you?"

She didn't let him finish. Of course she wouldn't go. Even if she wanted to, she couldn't afford the plane ticket. She had already booked a flight to go to Les Cayes in a few months to visit her family during their town's annual celebration for its patron saint, Saint Sauveur, and she'd need to bring her family not just money but all the extra things they'd asked for, a small fridge and oven for her parents and a laptop computer for her sister.

Just then his line beeped twice, startling her.

"It's Haiti," he said. "I have to go."

He hung up just as abruptly as he had reentered her life.

"Elsie, are you all right?" Gaspard was standing in the doorway. Short of breath, he spread out his arms and grabbed both sides of the door frame. His daughter was standing behind him with a portable oxygen tank.

Elsie wasn't sure how long they'd both been standing there, but whatever sounds she'd been unconsciously making, whatever moans, growls, whimpers, and squeals had escaped out of her mouth, had brought them there. She moved toward them, tightening her robe belt around her waist. Grunting, Gaspard looked past her, his eyes wandering around the room, taking in the platform bed and companion dresser.

"Elsie, my daughter seems to think she heard you crying." Gaspard's blood-drained lips were trembling as though he were cold, yet he still appeared more concerned about her than about himself when he asked, "Is your sister all right?"

Gaspard's body swayed toward his daughter. The daughter reached for him, anchoring him with one hand while balancing the portable oxygen tank with the other. With a fearful glance at Gaspard's shadow swaying unsteadily on the ground, Elsie rushed forward and grabbed him before saying, "Please reconsider your decision to release me, Mesye Gaspard. I won't be getting these phone calls anymore."

■ ■

She was right. He never called her again.

A week later, after Gaspard had ceded to his daughter's pleas and agreed not just to dialysis but to have his name placed on a transplant list, Elsie had a weekend off while Gaspard was hospitalized, and with nothing else to do, she stopped by Dede's on Saturday night, hoping Blaise might be there after returning from Haiti.

It was still early so the place was nearly empty, except for some area college kids whom Dede allowed to buy drinks without ID. Dede was behind the bar. Elsie walked over and sat across from him as a waitress shouted a few orders at him.

"How you holding up?" Dede asked after the waitress walked away with the drinks.

"Working hard," she said, "to get by."

"Still with the old people?" he asked.

"They're not always old now," she said. "Sometimes they're young people who've been in car accidents or have cancer."

Eventually they got to Blaise.

After she and Blaise had met at Dede's, she kept coming back to the bar with him whenever she was free and he was playing there. He then asked if he could move into her apartment so they could save money and see more of each other, since she was working so much. She found out that his tourist visa had expired long ago, and even though she'd just gotten her green card and wouldn't be eligible for citizenship for another five years, they went to city hall and got married with the hope that one day she might be able to help him with his immigration status. After the three-minute city hall ceremony, at which Dede and the friend who had introduced her to Blaise were witnesses, Dede hosted a small wedding lunch for them at the bar. Elsie's parents, who, just like Blaise's, were also still living in Haiti, had been unable to attend.

"I always thought you should have married me." Dede now reached across the bar and playfully stroked Elsie's shoulder. He had never been married and, according to Blaise, he never intended to.

"You didn't ask then and you're not asking now," she said.

"Maybe I'm asking for something else." He moved his fingers under her white oversized collarless blouse, across her clavicle down to the top button, and let his hand linger there for a few seconds. In his steadfast and unyielding gaze seemed to be some possibility of relief, or a few hours of sweaty comfort masked as excitement, like the kind she'd initially been seeking with Blaise. As pathetic as it seemed now, she loved Blaise most when he was onstage. She was seduced by something she didn't even think he was good at. His devotion to his mediocre gifts had melted her heart. Watching other women pine over his singing excited her too. She was jealous of their ability to fantasize about him, imagining that life with him would be one never-ending songfest. But every once in a while it went beyond that, during ordinary moments like when she watched him cook a salty omelet filled with smoked herring, which he would bring to her at the breakfast nook where they ate all their meals. This is when they would talk about one day having a baby.

She'd promised him that they would have a child after they'd saved enough money to move into a white single-family house she'd seen for sale in North Miami. She had driven by the house dozens of times, imagining the two of them and their future children living there. She knew the address so well that she could recite it to herself, even in her sleep, like a prayer. A For Sale sign had been dangling in front of the house for so long that she believed the house was destined for them, that no one else would be able to buy it before they could. She learned from looking it up on one of the computers at the public library that the house was 1,847 square feet with three large bedrooms and two full baths. It also had a stand-alone efficiency with a separate entrance in the back. They could rent out the efficiency, she told him, to help pay for their mortgage.

"Have you heard from him?" Dede now asked her, as she slowly removed his hand from inside her blouse.

"Not in a while," she said.

"I hear he's in Haiti for good now," Dede said, winking after her rejection had sunken in. He reached over and grabbed a few glasses from under the bar and started wiping the insides with a small white towel. And maybe this was his revenge, or maybe he had been waiting to tell her, but between putting one glass down and picking up another, he said, "He's living in Haiti with his old band's money and a lot of cash from some kidnapping scam he and your friend Olivia came up with together. I promise you I have people on this. If they ever see them, they're going to pay."

If this were happening to someone else, she would wonder why that person didn't grab Dede's neck and demand more details, why that person didn't pound her breasts with her fist, tear off her clothes, and thrash around on the floor. But she did none of those things. It was as if suddenly some shred of doubt, which had been plaguing her, some small suspicion she'd harbored for days, were finally being confirmed.

"So she's alive?" she asked.

"Oh, he told you *she* was dead?" Dede said, putting down the glass he was holding.

"She's not dead?" she asked again, just to be sure.

"They took turns, I suppose," he said. "She called to tell me he was kidnapped, then she told me he was dead, until I heard different."

She grasped for a few more words but could find none. How could she have let herself be fooled, robbed, so easily? How could she have been so naïve, so stupid? Maybe it had something to do with Gaspard being so sick that week, with the possibility of his dying and his daughter being there to see it happen. She had been distracted.

Blaise and Olivia must have trained or practiced for weeks, to take more and more away from her, to strip her of both her money and her dignity. They also must have been convincing to the point that no one could even doubt them. They had fooled Dede too.

"I guess we're both Boukis," she finally said. "Imbeciles."

"Suckers, idiots," he added, wiping the insides of the glasses harder. "I'd understand if they were starving and couldn't make money any other way, but they decided to become criminals so they can go back to Haiti and live the good life."

"It's not right," she said, though nothing felt right anymore.

They were interrupted by some drink orders from another waitress. Dede worked silently filling the orders, then, when he was done, he said, "I promise you. They're not going to enjoy all the money they stole from me."

"You're going to have them killed?" she asked.

"Maybe not killed." He seemed surprised at how casually she uttered the words.

"Would you hurt them?" She heard the pleading tone in her voice, as though she were begging for their execution.

"You *should* want them dead," he reassured her. "At least he didn't marry me."

"She might have married you," Elsie said.

"Clearly I wasn't her type. Wasn't enough for her. Your husband was."

She was asking herself now why he had married her. There were other women with a lot more money than she had, women who could have gotten him his papers faster. Maybe he was hoping she would commit a crime, steal one of her richer patients' life savings for him. She was glad Gaspard's daughter was there that week, otherwise Blaise might have possibly talked her into stealing from him, or even killing him. Who knows?

"What would you do if you went to Haiti and found them?" she asked, while considering the possibility herself.

"I'd give them a chance to pay me back first." He grabbed a bottle of rum from the mirrored table behind him and pushed one of the glasses he'd been cleaning toward her. She demurred at first, waving it away, but then she realized that she wanted to keep talking to him. She also wanted to keep talking about Olivia and Blaise, and he was the only person she could talk to about them now.

"What would you do to her first?" he asked her.

"I'd shave her head," she said, without even giving it much thought. "I'd shave off that head of hair she gelled so much."

"That's all?" he asked, laughing.

After taking a gulp of the rum, she said, "That's not all. After shaving her head and cutting off all his fingers, I'd pound both their heads with a very big rock until their brains were liquid, like this drink now in my hand."

"*Wouy!* That's too much," he said, pouring himself a glass. "I never want you mad at me."

"What would you do?" she asked him.

"The stuff they do to the terrorists. The stuff with water I saw in a movie the other night. I'd wrap their heads with a sugar sack and pour water in their noses and make them think they're drowning. And I wouldn't do that to just them. I'd get all the other thieves who steal from people like us—"

"The Boukis. The naïve people."

"Again, I'd understand if he was broke or she was starving," he said.

"The more money they have, the greedier they are," she said, feeling herself drifting away from Blaise and Olivia and slipping into some larger discussion about thieving and justice that she didn't have the energy to pursue.

"Your revenge would be better than mine," she said, circling back to Olivia and Blaise. "Those two would suffer a lot more with you."

It was also not the first time he had been burned. Once, a seemingly-pregnant woman walked into the bar in the middle of the afternoon. She pretended to suddenly go into labor, and while he was looking for his cell phone to call an ambulance, she pulled out a gun and forced him to empty the cash register. He was bringing up that robbery now, saying he preferred that, being confronted face-to-face, to being robbed behind his back.

"This situation is not ending the same way," he said, his voice growing louder and the pace at which he was speaking becoming faster. "I'm not turning this one over to the police to just drop. And what police? The Haitian police?"

She was thinking about going to a police station near her house and filing a report, in case Blaise and Olivia ever decided to move back to Miami. But how embarrassing would that be? She imagined the police calling her stupid or even lovestruck. They might even laugh behind her back. She had willingly given that money to Blaise anyway. She didn't think it would do her much good either.

"That's why I'm having them caught myself," Dede was saying. "For you, for me, and for everyone else they did this to. Even if it's the last thing I do before I die. Believe me, you're going to start dreaming about killing them more and more from now on."

She hoped not. She would rather think ahead, though she wasn't sure anymore what lay ahead. She was glad Gaspard was still alive, that he had not died in her care. She wanted to keep moving, keep working. Alive or dead, neither Blaise nor Olivia was going to be part of her life anymore.

The details. They'd been so good at the details. Whose idea had it been, for example, to tell her that Olivia had written her name, like a tattoo, at the bottom of her feet? They might have also told her that Olivia had drawn a cross there too, as a symbol that she wanted a Christian burial. That last call, she realized, was to make sure she wasn't coming to the supposed funeral.

Dede poured her another glass of rum. Then another. And even as the news of Olivia being alive slowly began to sink in, she was surprised that a kind of grief she hadn't lingered on was now actually lifting, that a distant ache in her heart was slowly turning to relief. She wanted to fight that relief. She did not want to welcome, embrace, the slight reprieve she'd felt she'd been given in learning that someone she believed to be dead was now alive, as though Olivia had been resurrected after a week under the ground.

She now felt tears flowing down her face, tears she couldn't stop. She didn't want them to be tears of joy, but a few of them were. The country seemed a bit less scary now. Her parents and sister, whom she'd gone back to speaking to more regularly, seemed like they might be in less danger, say, from being kidnapped. Yet the tears kept flowing. Tears of anger too. Of being robbed of money that took years to save, of seeing her dream of owning the white house in North Miami disappear along with the children that, thankfully, they'd never have. She felt even more alone now than before she'd met either Blaise or Olivia, lonelier than when she'd just arrived in this country having only one friend.

Dede kept his eyes on her, but they were now filled with more concern than lust. Her tears were becoming moans then grunts, then, before she could fight her screams, a new revenge fantasy emerged. She was now wishing that her voice alone could destroy Dede's place, that it could smash the glass bottles and turn them into shards. Her screech, her bawl, which was coming from so deep inside that she felt as though it were raising her off the ground, would help her float above Dede's head, above the permanent drunks in the booths, and the college students, and the empty stage that Blaise had so often sung on, all of it shattering so fast and blending into the air so quickly that she could easily inhale it and bury it inside her body.

"I'll take you home," she heard Dede say, and the next thing she knew she was curled up in a ball in the backseat of his car, the same old black Mercedes he'd had for years, and which she thought was no longer working until he was heading down what, between opening and closing her eyes, she recognized as North Miami Avenue. He had somehow managed to obtain her address from her, or maybe, she thought, smiling, he had known it all along.

"You're living in North Miami now?" she heard him say.

She was talking to him in her head, but no words came out of her mouth, which felt like it was full of vomit. Yes, she was living in North Miami, in the house of her dreams, but not in the way she'd intended. Soon after Blaise moved out, she'd driven by the house, and, unlike every other night she'd stopped by, there were lights on. Replacing the For Sale sign was now a rental sign for the one-room efficiency in the back. She saw this as a kind of miracle, a sign that she was truly meant to live there.

The new owners were young doctors from Jamaica and they told her they were happy to have her. Having her own separate entrance made it easy for her to make herself scarce. They often left her notes inviting her to dinner at the main house, but she was always working and was barely around. She sensed that they were being friendly because they felt sorry for her since she seemed to have no one. She was resisting becoming friends with them. She no longer wanted to make friends.

When they reached the house, she handed Dede the keys and he somehow managed to open the door and hold her upright at the same time. She felt him cradle her as she stumbled to the bathroom and emptied out her stomach in the toilet. When he carried her to the twin bed across from the door, she felt as though she were flying, not the good kind of flight, but the kind where you're tumbling through the air and terrified of crashing.

On the bed, she felt herself slipping in and out, between half consciousness and a deep darkness in which Olivia and Blaise were waiting, like they had been waiting the night they'd all slept together. That night she had performed acts and said things she could no longer remember in detail. Maybe in the throes of passion she had even given them permission to be together. Maybe that's why they'd both abandoned her.

She kept opening her eyes to fight this image of the three of them, but particularly of her telling them to go off and be together, to go live out their love, because it was obviously what the two of them wanted. She was now the *dosa*, the surplus one.

She felt a damp washcloth land gently on her forehead. Dede had made her a compress and was whispering comforting words in the air above her head. She could not make out most of the words, but after a long pause she heard him say, "You're home now."

She nodded in agreement.

"Yes, I'm home," she managed to say.

"Do you want me to stay?" he asked.

Having him stay would calm her down, even if he just sat on the floor across the room and watched her sleep. But then she would still wake up in the morning feeling alone with her own losses and pain.

"You can go," she said, feeling a bit more confident now in her ability to speak.

"You sure?" he asked, while stroking her cheeks with his index finger. His finger, wet and slow, felt as though it were carving a warm stream into her skin, a stream that was soaking up her whole body.

"I'm sure," she said.

"I wish I'd met you first," he said, widening the circle he was now drawing with his finger on her face. "I wish I'd seen you first. I wish I'd known you first. I wish I'd loved you first."

"You sound like one of his stupid songs." She stuttered through the words, not sure whether he would find them funny or insulting.

"Those songs were stupid." He chuckled, raising his hands over his mouth as if to suppress a deeper laugh. "The man was ruining a treasured kind of music and he didn't even realize it. Or he didn't care."

"Why did you tolerate him?" she asked.

"Why did you?" he countered.

"He had his charms," she said, and he did. One of them was how he became very conversational before sex. Talking was his foreplay. He would ask her to recount her day to him. He would want to hear all about her patients, her thoughts, her dreams, as if to help him expand, or reinvent, the person he was about to make love to.

"I tolerated him because he was my friend," he said. "Because he was like a brother to me."

"You're sounding like one of his songs again," she said.

"Maybe not all his songs were stupid," he said. "Only people you care about can hurt you like he did."

"Only people you love," she said.

She didn't realize that she had this many words left in her, and for Dede of all people. He was the one dragging these words out of her. He was making her speak. He was making her want to speak.

"That will never happen to me again," she said.

"Maybe it won't be him, but as long as you're breathing you can be hurt."

"Now you're just saying anything to say something," she said.

"Isn't that what we've both been doing?"

"Go," she said.

He raised the washcloth and kissed her wet forehead then put the washcloth back in place.

"I need to close up the bar anyway," he said. "But I have to tell you this one more thing and I hope you don't take it badly."

"What is it?" she asked.

"I didn't know you were such a weakling with the rum."

He laughed, this time loud and deep, and his laughter was not just keeping her from crashing but exuberantly filling the inside of her hollow-feeling head. She tried to laugh too, but wasn't sure she was doing it. Instead, she started unbuttoning her blouse.

"I'm not usually this weak," she said.

"Just tonight?" he asked.

"Just tonight."

She surrendered.

AMERICAN WORK

Richard Russo

BY THE TIME *Pickwick Papers*, Dickens's first novel, was published, he was already well known, thanks to the hugely popular *Sketches by Boz*. Still, the phenomenal success of *Pickwick* took both its author and its publisher by surprise. It's a brilliant piece of work, and it remained G. K. Chesterton's favorite among all of Dickens's novels. But novels don't exist in a vacuum, any more than success does, and *Pickwick*'s success is best understood in context, as the perfect book published at the perfect moment, a book *about* the emerging British working class that was being read and embraced *by* the same class, a novel that really took off—in terms of both art and commerce—with the introduction of Sam Weller, a working stiff who becomes both Mr. Pickwick's valet and his moral compass. Mr. Pickwick is a gentleman, both educated and prosperous, but also detached from the reality of the new world order that resulted from the industrial revolution. In other words, an elite. He and the other elites of his circle are not bad people, but they are buffoons who contribute little of real value to society. This turned out to be not just a winning satiric formula but a brilliant intuition about how, precisely, the world had changed. Many of Dickens's readers hadn't *been* readers before, and guess what? They liked seeing their lives reflected, and they particularly liked seeing the work they did acknowledged, even if, like Sam Weller, they shined boots. As they saw it, the work they did needn't be glamorous, just honest and necessary.

For many Americans the takeaway from the election that gave us President Donald Trump is that it was all about jobs. Sure, he promised to build a wall and restrict immigration, but the stated purpose of those initiatives was to create, return, and protect good American jobs. What were all those angry white men angry *about*? The loss of jobs, to Mexico and the rest of the world. But to see things in these terms may be to miss the larger point, because it wasn't just jobs these men believed they'd lost. They'd also lost their *work*, and the two are far from synonymous. When you lose your job, the impact is primarily financial. Overnight you have less money, which makes you anxious about your future. How will you pay your mortgage? Send your kids to college? Survive a major illness or injury? Nor are these small losses, small fears. But losing your work may be even more profound and soul destroying. If the loss is not only *your* job but a whole sector of jobs, then you're probably well on your way to losing both your dignity and your identity, your sense of your place in the overall scheme of things. If you don't know who you are or how you fit in, maybe you're nobody. Maybe you don't matter. Maybe your friends and your kids don't matter either. Losing your job makes you scared; losing your work makes you angry.

I, myself, don't have a job. My last full-time employment was more than a decade ago at Colby College in Maine, where I taught literature and creative writing. Since then I've been hired by film and TV producers to write scripts, gigs that typically last a couple of months. That's not a lot of employment, and there have been times when not having a job, or steady, reliable income, or consistent health care, has made me fearful about the future. But I never felt that my dignity or identity was imperiled, or that I didn't know where I fit in the overall scheme of things. That's because, even when I didn't have a job, I always had plenty of work, usually more than I could handle. I'm a novelist, and while not everybody understands what I do or why, the work itself is held in high esteem. Even more important, *I* hold that work in high esteem. Even if I'm not as good at it, I get to do what Dickens did, and I'm grateful for that opportunity. In other words, even when I'm unemployed, I *don't* feel what many Trump supporters report feeling: ignored, undervalued, denigrated.

Moreover, it's important to remember that many Trump supporters who feel this way *have jobs*. Some have lost high-paying jobs and had to take others that not only pay less but are not nearly as meaningful. Others may still have their original high-paying jobs, but many of them are angry too, often on behalf of friends and relatives who haven't been so fortunate. Suddenly these guys feel like they're on the wrong side of history, and maybe they are. Unlike the rising tide of the working class that Dickens recognized and tapped into, today's working class too often feel like they're circling the drain. Even those who have jobs that provide a decent living—electricians, plumbers, carpenters, mechanics—are all too aware that people who work with their hands are often looked down upon. Over time, probably since the GI Bill, the notion that in America you're nobody without a college education has taken deep root. It was certainly drilled into me, and I come from decent, honest people who did good, honest work. Nor was their insistence that I go to college rooted in self-loathing. They simply understood that in America education correlates with income. They wanted me to prosper.

Okay, but somehow we've taken that correlation between education and prosperity to mean that there's something demeaning about unclogging drains and pounding nails, somehow less essential to our national life than, say, writing computer code. Trump supporters don't just remember when guys like themselves had good jobs; they remember a time when the work they did was valued and respected. My own working class heroes, even when they're standing hip-deep in muck, take a certain stubborn pride in doing jobs that are necessary, no matter how disgusting or dangerous. And though I've educated myself out of the necessity for doing such work for a living, I still share the pride of those who are less fortunate. And nothing makes me angrier than that one-sentence Amazon review of a novel of mine (and you have no idea how many of them there are) that says, "Why should I care about these losers?" Really? Working people are losers? It seems unlikely to me that we're going to be one America again until such casual contempt is admitted and addressed.

Here's the bottom line, I think. Before anybody can be admired, they must first be seen. Dickens *saw* Sam Weller, saw in a shoeshine boy character traits—honesty, hard work, goodwill— that were worth something to the nation. Isn't it worth asking how often Trump supporters see themselves reflected on TV or in movies or novels? How many contemporary Mr. Pickwicks give them the time of day? Those of us with voices—writers and publishers, actors and producers, musicians and record companies, among others—bear some responsibility here. I've been surprised by just how often I've been called upon repeatedly for insight into "Trump's America" in the aftermath of the election. It didn't take much imagination to conjure up the conversations that were probably taking place in newsrooms all over America the morning after the election. "If the politicos got it all wrong, whom do we talk to? How about some novelists? Who out there writes about American working people with sympathy? Who's tackled the disappearance of high-paying jobs and the destructive impact of such losses on places where there are large concentrations of Trump voters?" In truth, there aren't that many of us. Since Steinbeck and the great proletarian novelists, have there ever been? And what about the geographical bias that's long been a feature of New York–based publishing? It's not that writers like Kent Haruf and Ivan Doig and Howard Frank Mosher are not widely admired and well reviewed; it's that they would have been even more widely read and admired had they been writing about more "important" people (read: urban, affluent, beautiful, educated) and places (read: coastal). *The New York Review of Books* was once parodied as *The New York Review of Us* for a reason. Be honest. Isn't much of the disdain that Trump voters feel for elites warranted? Haven't the elites of both political parties been blind to the travails of working people?

Okay, granted, there's a lot of willful blindness out there, more than enough to go around, and failures of imagination abound as well. One can be sympathetic to Trump voters without giving them a free pass. Feeling angry, undervalued, and ignored, they don't seem to grasp that these are not new feelings. They're just new to them. American blacks and Latinos and LGBT folks have been feeling the same way for a long time. And I want to be clear about the man himself. Donald Trump is a despicable human being—a full-blown narcissist, a pathological liar, a vulgarian, a groper of women and girls. He's completely unfit to be president of the United States. As regards the working class, however, he did what Dickens did. He held a mirror up to a whole class of people who were too often ignored. Because Dickens was both a good man and a great artist, what people saw in that mirror was their best selves. And because Trump is neither good nor great, his distorted mirror reflects little but his supporters' bigotry and anger. But give the man this much credit. To his supporters he was saying, *I see you. I see your value.* Which is more than can be said for the elites of either party.

FIELDWORK

Manuel Muñoz

MY MOTHER TOLD ME the story only once, when I was a teenager and didn't know any better about asking personal questions, about holding in pain, that, yes, it was true there had been a baby, the first one before the others came, but I had to understand that this was never something to ask a woman about, ever. It is none of a man's business.

I think I was fourteen when I asked her that question, just like she was when she had the baby, and I was thinking about why my oldest siblings had been born in Texas and the rest of us in the Valley. I was young enough to believe that something bigger—fate, destiny, God's will—was responsible for my being born in a place like Dinuba, one of the many dusty towns dotting the fields around Fresno. It could have been Yettem, my mother had told me. Or Seville, even smaller places on the map, but she was long done with towns that didn't have hospitals. This is how she told me the story about having her first baby at fourteen and how she was still fourteen when the baby developed a fever. They had driven to another town that had a hospital, the baby wrapped in a blanket. She didn't have the English to explain what was wrong with the baby and no one at the hospital spoke Spanish. This was in Texas and it was 1960. They took the baby from her and she tried to follow them into another room, but they wouldn't let her. She could see through the glass in the door, though, and she watched them lift the baby from the blanket, strip it of its diaper, and place it in a tub of water. She heard the baby wail from the shock of the water and then the crying softened, as if the fever had broken, and then the baby made no more noise.

The baby had pneumonia? I remember asking, because back then I thought there should always be an answer to everything.

My mother said only that she hadn't known English. It was her way of saying that she had always wondered, but that she had no way of asking, that it was something she had not been allowed to understand.

I had it in my mind back then that any place but our hometown—any place but the Valley—would have been a better place to be. I spoke of her Texas as if I knew it, as if it were a place that had been a mistake for her to leave and deprive me of, all because the Valley offered nothing. When I was younger, I dreamed aloud about leaving and my mother's question was always, To do what? She had come to the Valley in the 1960s because of the work; her older sister had gone ahead of her because of the work (though my mother later told me that my tía was all talk, that she never worked a day in her life). Her brothers—my tíos—hunched everywhere in the fields, no matter the season. The Valley was all about work if you wanted to do it, and Fresno was a city big enough for anyone. My best friend from the Valley told me that his family, like mine, had come to the Fresno area because of the fieldwork, too. His father and his mother drove a truck from town to town, looking for crops to pick, and they had lived like that for a while before the truck broke down on Highway 99 outside of Selma. They had had no money to fix the truck, so they had settled there.

My best friend doesn't know if this story is entirely true or not, but I can easily picture his father, cigarette in hand, standing at the side of the highway and wasting no time with a decision. His father, like mine, is pragmatic, with little patience for fruitless dreaming.

That's how it was for my family and their arrival in the Valley, as well as people like us: the poorest from Texas and from Mexico, looking for work hard enough to never disappear. My father had come to the Valley from Mexico, just as many other Mexican fathers had done before him; I asked him this question not as a teenager but as a much older adult, caring for him in the fluorescent dullness of a county rehab center while he recovered from a stroke, the words not coming to him. I wanted to get him talking, so I asked him what I thought was a simple question, so the simple words could arrive. To pick crops, he told me, in Spanish and with great hesitation, as if he had to think about it to be sure. Just like all the men who had gone up north to the Valley before him, and wired back money from picking oranges and grapes and peaches, mostly. But cotton and tomatoes, too, he recalled. And almonds, my father added, and figs and nectarines, there was so much work. Apricots, plums, corn, pistachios, the lemon groves over on the eastern slope of the Valley into the Sierras. Walnuts and cauliflower. Cherries and pears. He kept remembering things. Strawberries hiding in the dirt. Pecans. Persimmons. Avocado trees in the prettiest green rows you've ever seen. Olives and wheat. Hay bundled up for the horses and the cows. Apples, since the Americanos liked their pie.

You picked all of those things? I asked him.

He hesitated or he couldn't say, I don't know. But then he nodded his head yes.

The way people talked about the Valley, my father said, you could get rich.

Then, after a moment, he recalled, unbidden, the first place he had ever lived in the Valley, a trailer parked illegally near a highway overpass. The owner would move it every few nights, in case the county sheriff came by.

I didn't ask him if he was angry that he had lived this way, or why he was remembering this fact. I simply wanted to hear him say anything. In the first few nights of my father's rehab, I had a terrible feeling that he was not going to make it. We had been alternating overnights at the center, my mother and I, sleeping in my father's room and then switching off after the morning meal. None of it was completely necessary, I thought, but my mother had a fear that there would be no one to translate for him in the middle of the night if the nurse was English-only. I didn't tell my mother that he had been awakened in the middle of the night by a nurse for medications and a blood withdrawal, and his disorientation grew so strong that it translated into what could only be pain. He struggled to rise from the bed, as if he sensed that he was being kept in the room against his will, and the English-speaking nurse had no words to calm him. Tranquilo, tranquilo, I kept saying to him, but my voice was nothing he recognized. He seized against both of us for a good long while before the nurse tapped the call button and another nurse came in to assist, drawing the curtain around the bed, and leaving me to listen to him whimper quietly back into sleep.

After that came other episodes with the same pitch of uncertainty but I grew to realize that it was my father not knowing where he was, what day of the week, what year, his full name, his date of birth. His confusion and his stunted tongue would cause the moaning, as if he were trying to fill the room with some kind of noise to kill the confusing silence brought on by those simple questions.

We all die, he told me one night, as if he had known what I was thinking. A todos nos toca ese camino. We're all on that road.

The other hospital bed was mercifully empty of another patient and the night nurse had encouraged me to sleep there instead of in the uncomfortable armchair. I kept one foot on the ground and stared up at the ceiling, wondered if my father could discern where he was, that his road could end here, in a county rehab center in the Valley, thousands of miles from where he was born.

And so I decided to ask him about what I didn't know. I didn't care that it was nearly four in the morning and that he should be sleeping.

It's true, my father said, that he came to the Valley only because others had talked about it. If enough people had said go to Texas instead, he would've gone. Or if enough people had reported that good things could happen in Los Angeles, he would've gone. As long as word came back. As long as word reached him.

It was his bad luck that he had never known anyone who could have told him about Denver or Chicago. Or New York City. New York City, he marveled. Imagínate . . .

Look at your mother, he said. Look at your tía, with eleven

kids to feed and not enough work in Texas. Work that other people were too proud to do, even if their kids were hungry.

But you came here with no mouths to feed, I told him.

He had his mother in Mexico and plenty of cousins, he told me, young ones who couldn't do for themselves. Everyone is a hungry child in the end.

Did I know, he asked, the story of the man who had knocked on my mother's back door one Sunday morning because he had nowhere to go and he had wound up in our little town of Dinuba on a bright hot summer day while the whole neighborhood was at church and so no one answered his knocking? He was lost and he was hungry and he had nowhere to go and my mother (who wasn't a churchgoer) gave him two tacos wrapped in tinfoil and a drink from the garden hose, and she had to tell him to let it run a bit so the hot rubbery taste could pass and the colder water could come through.

My father was quiet after he finished telling that story, as if the effort of thinking and remembering had tired him. I thought he had drifted off to sleep. I could hear nothing in the hallways, nothing from the nurses' station, and thought about the story: I knew it and had heard it, but did not know why my father was telling it. I looked up at the ceiling, back to my thoughts of my father ending his days in the Valley, when he asked me what I was thinking.

I couldn't bring myself to say anything about him dying, so I asked my father why he had remembered that story.

Because that man was afraid and now he was afraid.

I had never known my father to be afraid, to be a fearful man, and I told him so.

Just one time, he said. Just once, many years ago, when he had been deported for the first time. He had been trucked somewhere in Arizona, or maybe it was El Paso, it was so long ago, but it was the desert and he knew the border was close by. He waited to be driven across and he was thinking of a river, because to cross over meant to cross a river. Instead, they were marched over to a wide expanse of cement that he realized was an airfield, and a transport plane, military green, waited with its engines running and a little ramp for them to climb aboard. All of them were young men and none of them had ever been on a plane before. They sat on thin benches that stretched along the sides and the two men in the cockpit told them that they should hang on if they knew what was good for them.

You've never been to jail, my father told me. You were too much of a good boy for that, but your brothers would know. Your brothers would know the inside of the walls, what people carved in there because they wanted someone to remember them. That was the inside of that plane, just the benches and the metal walls. I read those terrible things and I thought they were going to throw us out of that plane.

But they didn't, I said.

Pues claro, he said.

After a pause, he asked me if I was a fearful person and I told him that I didn't think so.

You're like your mother, he said. He was quiet again for a long time before I realized he had fallen asleep.

In the morning, I helped my father to the dining room and waited for my mother. A quiet man sat at the table, staring off at the door, disconsolate as his breakfast ran cold, his wife yet to appear. He didn't want any of the nurses to help him, his eyes fixed on the door. Another man ate unassisted, his hands spry with the plastic utensils. Both of these men were my father's age. The nurses liked my father because his improvement in speaking and understanding and responding was an encouragement to these two men in their recoveries. They talked like the old Mexican men who gathered at our town bakery at six in the morning.

My mother came in just as my father's tray was being served to him, but my father was busy beginning his conversation.

He wants to know, my father said—meaning me—why you—meaning the old man with the spry hands—came to the Valley.

I didn't have to say to my mother that I had never asked such a question. She knew how my father would take his hazy recall of the previous evening's conversation and use it to start some chatter at breakfast, no matter who was at the table or what the subject might be.

Don't worry, one nurse had assured my mother in Spanish, we know that half the things they say aren't true anyway.

The old man with the spry hands finished his breakfast and pushed his tray forward. He was thin, more on the gaunt side, and yet he cleaned his plate at every meal. He had come from Mexico as well, in the 1970s, and he had found work at a dairy farm, feeding and caring for the cows, the single job he had had for more than forty years. An older brother, who had gone up north before him, had told him to look for work in the dairies and he found the job easily, the first and only dairy he had ever approached.

In those days, my father said, you could find work everywhere. People these days don't want to work anymore. Turning to me, he said, You see?

My mother looked at me as if to ask what had gotten my father so interested in work, but then the quiet man's wife came in, rushed and panicked. Because there were no nurses around, she eyed my mother when she saw the full breakfast tray. My mother said buenos días to her anyway.

And you? my father asked, as the quiet man waited for his wife to cut up his pancakes.

Let him eat his breakfast in peace, my mother said.

Oranges, said the old man with the spry hands. Isn't that right, señora? Isn't that what your husband did for a living?

The quiet man's wife helped him spoon a bit of egg and looked at us, unsure about the question or why it was being asked. She had the look of someone who had been asked a lot of questions about work—if she had it, the kind she had, how long she had had it. If she had the necessary documents, if she understood how she would be paid. And she had the look of someone who knew better than to answer.

He picked oranges, said my father. ¿Te acuerdas? he urged the quiet man to remember.

You're from Ivanhoe, said the old man with the spry hands. You told us that you were from Ivanhoe. There's nothing but oranges over in Ivanhoe.

The whole east side, my father said. All those towns that are almost in the mountains. Orange Cove up north and Lemon Cove down south.

Citrus, said the old man with the spry hands.

Grapefruit, said my father. I picked those before. Some as big as your head.

Mentiroso, my mother interrupted. You never picked grapefruit in your life, she said. And then, to me, what have you been talking to him about?

Work, I said, but then I realized that wasn't what we had been talking about at all: my father, the man with the spry hands who struggled to recover any use in his legs, the quiet man who remained just as quiet through his pancakes. These men who worked all their lives in the fields of the Valley, making do with whatever the state could provide now that their bodies had given out.

You shouldn't believe everything he tells you, my mother said.

The quiet man's wife kept her attention on my mother as she fed her husband some cereal. She took occasional glances at me, too, surprised that a son was present to help in feeding. This was women's work.

Do you have other children besides him? she asked my mother. She gestured with her head in my direction, as if I were not in the room.

Yes, I do, my mother answered.

How many? asked the wife.

I thought my mother took too long to answer. But then she said, I had six.

It was the truth, though it was not something I expected my mother to say. I had always heard her say five. I thought of myself as the youngest of five. Maybe it had to do with the way the woman was cleaning her husband's chin, helping him hold a cup of coffee. Maybe it had to do with knowing my father, in his current state, would try to correct the smallest of facts, and it was better to keep him calm around the breakfast table, to let the quiet man eat in peace.

The wife fed her husband some more and he ate as if in great thought. She kept her attention on my mother and then my father asked her ¿Y usted? Where was she from and why had she come to the Valley?

I knew the answer would be Mexico and I knew the answer would be she came because of her husband. I knew the answer would be there was no other choice but to come north. I listened with the respect that my mother had taught me and I asked her no questions when she said that picking oranges was a good and steady job. It had been, she said, a good place to live. It had been hard work, but she didn't have any complaints.

We would have weeks of this, my mother and I, staying overnight even as my father slept quite peacefully through the late hours, his hands gaining in grip strength, his eyesight coming back from what he said were the silver clouds. We alternated our posts at the end of the daily breakfast, about eight in the morning, when my father was wheeled off to physical therapy. The quiet man never spoke a word in those weeks and the man with the spry hands continued his healing without a family member to help him.

Imagínate, I said to my mother one morning, near exhaustion, to be so broken after all that hard work, and to end up like this.

We all work, my mother said. All work is hard. Mira ésta, she said, so I could remember the therapist who told us she was originally from Canada, another person who had come from so far away.

I tied vines one year, my mother said, when the money was low. I was pregnant with you, about seven months, but there I was. It must have been seven months because you were born in March and tying is January work, in the cold and the rain. You know what tying is?

Yes, I told her. I had done it before, along with my sister.

She remembered, yes, because it's easy work for kids, for women, untangling the vines like it was unruly hair, pruning them back a little, and then wrapping them back tight around the wires, the rows tidy and ready for the hotter months. It was still hard work, my mother said, all that mud and cold, and you just two months away from being born.

We watched my father as he negotiated a walker across the room, careful step by careful step. The old man with spry hands practiced stretching his upper arms and the quiet man was tasked with buttoning a shirt.

They'll get out soon if they do their exercises, she said, as if to remind me that this place was not the end. No place is the end if you don't want it to be. If they work hard, they can leave and go home.

We watched my father quietly. Seven months, my mother said, as if lost in thought. And then a moment later, Men don't know how to suffer.

For the Ones Who Put
Their Names on the Wall

                       & no one knew them
For the ones taken in the rustle of thorns w/o stars
For the ones the color of water who slowly grew peaceful
Face down on the spikes of asphalt
For the ones I longed to give lettuce who turned fast away
When they noticed a truck-man hunched scribbling
Near the fence they could have been
Feathered round & desire-shaped w/
Black rubber-like feet & elegant noses
In search for a way out

This endless container
Lagoon of shadows

                                   —Juan Felipe Herrera

TRASH FOOD

Chris Offutt

OVER THE YEARS I've known many people with nicknames, including Lucky, Big O, Haywire, Turtle Eggs, Hercules, two guys named Hollywood, and three guys called Booger. I've had my own nicknames as well. In college people called me "Arf" because of a dog on a T-shirt. Back home a few of my best buddies call me "Shit-for-Brains," because I was alleged to be smart.

Three years ago, shortly after moving to Oxford, someone introduced me to John T. Edge. My understanding was that he also went by a nickname. The word "jaunty" means convivial, affable, someone always merry and bright. The name suited him perfectly. Each time I called him Jaunty he gave me a quick sharp look of suspicion. He wondered if I was making fun of his name—and of him. The matter was resolved when I suggested he call me "Chrissie O."

Last spring John T. asked me to join him at an Oxford restaurant. My wife dropped me off and drove to a nearby secondhand store. Our plan was for me to meet her later and find a couple of cheap lamps. During lunch John T. asked me to give a presentation at the Southern Foodways Alliance symposium over which he presided every fall. I reminded him of my inexperience—at the time I'd published only a few humorous essays that dealt with food. I lacked the necessary qualifications. Other writers were more knowledgeable and wrote with a historical and scholarly context. All I did was write personal essays inspired by old community cookbooks I found in secondhand stores. Strictly speaking, my food writing wasn't actually about food.

John T. said that didn't matter. He wanted me to explore "trash food," because, as he put it, "you write about class."

I sat without speaking, my food getting cold on my plate. First, I couldn't see the connection between social class and garbage.

Second, I didn't like having my thirty-year career reduced to a single subject matter. I write about my friends, family, and my experiences in the world, but never with a sociopolitical agenda. Writers who are motivated by politics often produce propaganda or agitprop. My goal was always art first, combined with self-examination.

Third, I'd never heard of anything called "trash food."

I found myself in a professional and social pickle, not unusual for a country boy who's clawed his way out of the hills, one of the steepest social climbs in America. As a native of eastern Kentucky, I've never mastered the highborn art of concealing my emotions. Unfortunately my feelings are always readily apparent. I should have been an actor and spent my life getting paid to expose my emotions. Instead, I'm nothing but a writer—about class, apparently.

Recognizing my turmoil, John T. asked if I was pissed off. I nodded and he apologized immediately. I told him I was oversensitive to matters of social class. I explained that people from the hills of Appalachia had to fight to prove they were smart, diligent, and trustworthy. It's the same for people who grew up in the Mississippi Delta, the barrios of Los Angeles and Texas, or the ghettos of New York. His request reminded me that due to social class I'd been refused jobs, bank loans, and dates. I've been called hillbilly, stumpjumper, cracker, weedsucker, redneck, and white trash—mean-spirited terms designed to hurt me and make me feel bad about myself.

As a young man, I used to laugh awkwardly at remarks about sex with my sister or the perceived novelty of my wearing shoes. As I got older I quit laughing. When strangers thought I was stupid because of where I was from or what I looked like—they were granting me the high ground. I learned to patiently wait in ambush for the chance to utterly demolish them intellectually. Later I resolved to stop wasting my energy. It was easier to simply stop talking to that person—forever. But I didn't want to do that with a guy whose name rhymes with Jaunty. A guy who'd inadvertently triggered an old emotional response. A guy who liked my work well enough to pay me for it.

By this time our lunch had a tension to it that draped over us both like a lead vest for an X-ray. We just looked at each other, neither of us knowing what to do. John T. suggested I think about it, then graciously offered me a lift to meet my wife. Our conversation had left me inexplicably ashamed of shopping at a thrift store. I wanted to walk in order to hide my destination, but refusing a ride could make John T. think I was angry with him. I wasn't. I was upset, but not with him.

My solution was a verbal compromise, a term politicians use to mean a blatant lie. I told him to drop me at a restaurant where I was meeting my wife for cocktails. He did so and I waited until his red Italian sports car sped away. Once it was out of sight I walked to the junk store. I sat out front like a man with not a care in the world, ensconced in a battered patio chair staring at clouds above the parking lot. When I was a kid my mother bought baked goods at the day-old bread store and hoped no one would see her car out front. Now I was embarrassed for shopping secondhand.

My behavior was class based twice over: buying used goods to save a buck and feeling ashamed of it. I'd behaved in strict accordance with my social station, then evaluated myself in a negative fashion. I sat on the patio chair and became mad, first at John T., then at myself. Even the anger was classic self-oppression, a learned behavior of lower-class people. I was transforming outward shame into inner fury. Without a clear target, I aimed it at myself.

My thoughts and feelings were completely irrational and I knew they made no sense. Most of what I owned had been used by someone else—cars, clothes, shoes, furniture, dishware, cookbooks. I liked old and battered things. They reminded me of myself, still capable and functioning despite the wear and tear. I enjoyed the idea that my belongings had a previous history before coming my way. It was satisfying to make the small repairs necessary to transform a broken lamp made of Popsicle sticks into a lovely source of illumination.

Twenty-five years ago I'd managed a nonprofit thrift shop in New York City. Since then I've lived in Boston, Florida, New Mexico, Montana, California, Tennessee, Georgia, Iowa, Arizona, and now Mississippi. Before each move I got rid of stuff. At each new place, I began gathering used possessions once more. A writer's livelihood is weak at best, and I'd become adept at operating in a secondhand economy. I was comfortable with it.

Still, I sat in that chair getting madder and madder. After careful examination I concluded that the core of my anger was fear—in this case fear that John T. would judge me for shopping secondhand. I knew it was absurd since he is not judgmental in the least. Anyone who knows him recognizes that he's an open-hearted guy willing to embrace anything and everyone—even me.

Nevertheless I'd felt compelled to mislead him based on class stigma. I was ashamed—of my fifteen-year-old Mazda, my income, and my rented home. I felt ashamed of the very clothes I was wearing, the shoes on my feet. Abruptly, with the force of being struck in the face, I understood it wasn't his judgment I feared, it was my own. I'd judged myself and found failure. I wanted a car like his. I wanted to dress like him and have a house like his. I wanted to be in a position to offer other people jobs.

The flip side of shame is pride and all I had was the pride of refusal. I could say no to his offer. I resolved not to write about trash food and class. Later, it occurred to me that my reluctance was evidence that maybe I should. I resolved to do some research before making a firm decision.

John T. had been a little shaky on the label of "trash food," mentioning mullet and possum as examples. At one time this list included crawfish because Cajun people ate it, and catfish because it was favored by African Americans and poor Southern whites. As these cuisines gained popularity, the food itself became culturally upgraded. Crawfish and catfish stopped being "trash food" when the people eating it in restaurants were the same ones who felt superior to the lower classes. The elite diners had to redefine the food. Otherwise they were voluntarily lowering their own social status— something nobody wants to do.

It should be noted that carp and gar still remain reputationally compromised. In other words—poor folks eat them and rich folks don't. I predict that one day people will pay thirty-five dollars for a tiny portion of carp with a rich sauce—and congratulate themselves for doing so. The situation is similar to a politician who wants to demonstrate he's a man of the people but doesn't know how to hold a mattock. Or a writer from the hills of Kentucky wearing a sports coat in a public forum. The only person fooled is oneself. The emperor's new clothes are not invisible, they're made of carp and gar.

At home I ran a multitude of various searches on library databases and the Internet in general, typing in permutations of the words "trash" and "food." Surprisingly, every single reference was to "white trash food." Within certain communities, it's become popular to host "white trash parties" where people are urged to bring Cheetos, pork rinds, Vienna sausages, Jell-O with marshmallows, fried bologna, corn dogs, RC cola, Slim Jims, Fritos, Twinkies, and cottage cheese with jelly. In short—the food I ate as a kid in the hills. Having such a feast is somehow considered evidence of being very cool and hip. Implicit in the menu is a vicious ridicule of the people who eat such food on a regular basis. People who attend these "white trash parties" are cuisinally slumming, temporarily visiting a place they never want to live. They are the worst sort of tourists—they want to see the Mississippi Delta and the hills of Appalachia but are afraid to get off the bus.

The term "white trash" is an epithet of bigotry that equates human worth with garbage. The connotation implies a dismissal of the group as stupid, violent, lazy, and untrustworthy—the same negative descriptors of racial minorities, anyone on the outside of the mainstream. A similar division between "us" and "them" appears in stories from the Old Testament that pit Jews against Romans, later co-opted to mean Christians versus Jews.

Long before that, the philosopher Socrates divided Europe's population into two groups when he said: "There are Greeks and there
are slaves." This deeply flawed way of thinking is popular because
of its simplicity, its reduction of humanity to either-or, to us and
them. It's a method of thinking preferred by politicians, preach-
ers, and bigots as a means of social control.

History has changed very little in this regard. What has
changed is the language itself. For example, here in Mississippi,
the term "Democrats" is code for "African Americans." Throughout the United States, "family values" really means "no homosex-
uals." The term "trash food" is not about food, it's about social
class. It's about poor people and what they can afford to eat.

In America, class lines run parallel to racial lines. At the very
bottom are people of color. The Caucasian equivalent is me—an
Appalachian. As a male Caucasian in America, I am supposed to
have an inherent advantage in every possible way. It's true—I can
pass more easily in polite society—I have better access to education, health care, and employment. But if I insist on behaving like
a poor white person—shopping at secondhand shops and eating
mullet—I not only earn the epithet "trash," I somehow deserve it.

I am trash because I'm white and poor.

I am trash because I'm from a specific region—the rural South.

Polite society regards me as stupid, lazy, ignorant, violent, and
untrustworthy. Use of the term "white trash" has gained promi-
nence as a term of class disparagement due to economics.

But human beings are not trash. We are the civilizing force on
the planet. We produce great art and great technology. It's not the
opposable thumb that separates us from the beasts, it's our facility
with language. We are able to communicate with great precision.
Nevertheless, history is fraught with the persistence of treating
fellow humans as garbage, which means collection and transport
for destruction. The most efficient management of humans as
trash occurred when the Third Reich systematically murdered
people by the millions. People they didn't like. People who had
little status and power—Jews, Romanis, Catholics, gays and les-
bians, Jehovah's Witnesses, and the disabled.

In World War II, my father-in-law was captured by the Nazis and placed on a train car so crammed with people that everyone had to stand. Arthur hadn't eaten in several days. He was close to starvation. A Romani gave him half a turnip, which saved his life. Arthur had been raised to look down on Romani people as stupid, lazy, violent, and untrustworthy—the ubiquitous language of discrimination. The man later died. Arthur survived the war and revised his view of Romanis.

Economic status dictates class and diet. We arrange food in a hierarchy based on who originally ate it until we reach mullet, gar, possum, and squirrel—the diet of the poor. The food is called trash, and then the people are.

When the white elite take an interest in the food poor people eat, the price goes up. The result is a cost that prohibits poor families from eating the very food they've been condemned for eating. It happened with tuna years ago. My family of six often ate tuna mixed with pasta and vegetables. Salmon and mackerel have endured a similar elevation in status. Gone are the days of subsisting on cheap fish patties at the end of the month. The status of food rose but the status of people didn't. They just had less to eat.

Without human intervention, all food is trash. Cattle, sheep, hogs, and chickens would die of disease unless slaughtered for the table. Lacking harvest, vegetables rot in the field. Food is a disposable commodity until we accumulate the raw material, blend ingredients, and apply heat, cold, and pressure. Then our bodies extract nutrients and convert it to waste, which must be disposed of. Like water and money, it's all secondhand one way or another.

In the hills of Kentucky we all looked alike—scruffy white people with squinty eyes and cowlicks. We shared the same economic class, the same religion, the same values and loyalties. Even our enemy was mutual: people who lived on the blacktop. Appalachians are suspicious of their neighbors, distrustful of strangers, and uncertain about third cousins. It's a culture that operates under a very simple principle: you leave me alone, and I'll leave you alone. After moving away from the hills I developed a different way of interacting with people. I still get cantankerous and defensive—ask John T.—but I'm better with human relations than I used to be. I've learned to observe and listen.

The circumstances of my life have often placed me in contact with African Americans throughout the country—as neighbors, colleagues, and members of the same work crew. The first interaction between a black man and a white man is one of mutual evaluation: does the other guy hate my guts? After generations of repression and mistreatment, will this black guy take it out on me because I'm white? And he wants to know if I'm one more racist asshole he can't turn his back on. This period of reconnaissance typically doesn't last long because both parties know the covert codes the other uses. Once each man is satisfied that the other guy is all right, connections begin to occur. Those connections are always based on class. And class translates to food.

Last year my mother and I were in the hardware store buying parts to fix a toilet. The first thing we learned was that the apparatus inside commodes has gotten pretty fancy over the years. Like breakfast cereal, there were dozens of types to choose from. Toilet parts were made of plastic, copper, and cheap metal. Some were silent and some saved water and some looked as if they came from an alien spacecraft.

A store clerk offered to help us, an African American man in his sixties. I told him I was overwhelmed, that plumbing had gotten too complicated. I tried to make a joke by saying it was a lot simpler when everyone used an outhouse. He gave me a quick sharp look of suspicion. I recognized his expression. It's the same one John T. gave me when I mispronounced his name, the same look I gave John T. when he used the term "trash food." The same one I unleashed on people who called me a hillbilly.

Due to my experience, I understood the store clerk's concern. He wondered if I was making a veiled comment about race, economics, and the lack of plumbing. I told him that back in Kentucky when the hole filled up, we dug a new one and moved the outhouse to it. Then we'd plant a fruit tree where the old outhouse was.

"Man," I said, "that tree would bear. Big old peaches."

He looked at me differently then, a serious expression, solemn, and said: "You know some things," he said. "Yes, you do."

"I know one thing," I said. "When I was a kid I wouldn't eat those peaches."

The two of us began laughing at the same time. We stood there and laughed until the mirth trailed away, reignited, and brought forth another bout of laughter. Eventually we wound down to a final chuckle and studied the toilet repair kits on the pegboard wall. They were like books in a foreign language.

"Well," I said to him. "What do you think?"

"What do I think?" he said.

I nodded.

"I think I won't eat those peaches," he said.

We started laughing again, this time longer, slapping each other's arms. Pretty soon one of us just had to mutter "peaches" to start all over again. Race was no more important to us than plumbing parts or shopping at a secondhand store. We were two Southern men laughing together in an easy way, linked by class and food.

On the surface, John T. and I should have been able to laugh in a similar way last spring. We have more in common than the store clerk and me. John T. and I share gender, race, and regional origin. We are close to the same age. We're both writers, married with sons. John T. and I have cooked for each other, gotten drunk together, and told each other stories. We live in the same town, have the same friends.

But none of that mattered in the face of social class, an invisible and permanent division. It's the boundary he had the courage to ask me to write about. The boundary that made me lie about the secondhand store last spring. The boundary that still fills me with shame and anger. A boundary that only food can cross.

SOME HOUSES
(VARIOUS STAGES
OF DISSOLVE)

Claire Vaye Watkins

Tecopa House

A miner's shack, expanded by our father before he was our father with whatever materials he could find. A Mojave valley, a wash, crumbly clay hills beyond. To the north a mound of ore with cacti and sage and horny toads all through it, so that it might be mistaken for a hill. Beyond the ore a plateau, a cemetery. At the pleat of plateau and ore, a spring: flaking iron water tank and a grove of bamboo. A garden, a parachute for shade, tented by a creosote-greased telephone pole. One planter box surrendered to any lizards or tortoises we caught, fed iceberg lettuce until they escaped. Horny toads we tagged with nail polish and cataloged in your diary that locked until our mom said they breathe through their skin and you're killing them. In fall Mom would open the front door and the back so randy tarantulas could migrate through. Green linoleum in the kitchen and once, a toddler, you practiced shaving with our dad's razor. I remember them holding you down, lots of red-black blood on the green floor. You remember me walking on a wall in front of the post office, playing Olympics. *Calif.* had just become *CA* but *–lif.* was still sun stamped on the block wall. I slipped and caught my chin. My blood red-orange in the noon sun. Later you watched them sew me up, nine black stitches ants along my jaw, makes my smile look sarcastic. A swamp cooler, Raggedy Ann and Andy bedding bought on lay-away. You and me, naked, leaders of a small pack of dogs—Barry, Spike, and Garfield. A larger pack of coyotes beyond the near ridge, yipping, cackling, waiting. They got Garfield, then Barry, but not Spike and not us, not yet. Rattlesnakes came out at dawn and dusk, a bobcat in the bamboo up by the spring.

The Trailer School

A single-wide, grades K through six in one room, seven through twelve in the other. In between: two bathrooms and a drinking fountain. The only girl in my grade, but can that be true? Four of us, me, two white boys, and a Shoshone. Something had happened to one of the white boys as a baby and it made him slow, made his front top teeth four silver ingots, made his voice always hoarse. I had a bad singing voice too. For this reason he and I were put in a closet whenever the class sang. There, a seam of light allowed us to hear the music and me to stare privately at his teeth. I wanted them.

Fifth Wheel

The first boy I ever loved lived in a fifth wheel his father had parked on a friend's property. An accordion door, cupboards that latched. K's bed was also the dinner table. He wore poverty like a fashion statement: ripped jeans, wallet chains, boots with soles flapping open like laughter. He worked at KFC, his Dickies velvety with vegetable oil, smell of sweet batter when I pulled them down.

Malibu

Somersaults in a busted hot tub filled with water from a hose at a guesthouse in Trancas Canyon. Half-drained swimming pool a pit of frogs. A neighbor's house a giant barrel, another's a geodesic dome, flowers called birds of paradise that looked just like them, snails—their shells crunching, salt shrinking—the beach. Where our father went to die and did, while I was in the busted hot tub doing underwater somersaults and you were counting them.

Shoshone

In the back office at our mother's rock shop and museum, making banners from dot matrix printer paper, making bird's-nest crowns with the shred bin, coloring with highlighters, picking pomegranates from the tree outside, walking back into the wash, alkali soil crunch, a river that was sometimes there and sometimes not. Parents scolding their kids and our mother nicer to them than she often was to us, gave them TV rock or pyrite, which she never called fool's gold. It seemed we were alone forever, the three of us. Then suddenly we were not, you and I not allowed in her bed anymore, not allowed to drink the Mountain Dew not ours in the fridge, a hulking Igloo lunch box on top.

Ann Arbor

Now I live in a movie about college written by a high schooler. There are actual letter jackets, actual cheerleaders, actual frats. There is an actual quad flung with Frisbees and an actual grove strung with hammocks. In the fall the leaves are blown into actual piles, though I never jump in. All the things we grew up thinking were real only on TV are real in the Midwest: rain pouring down windows and making the house a submarine; leaves turning gold, maroon, purple; raccoons; mailmen strolling the sidewalk with satchels; snow enough for igloos. When you come to visit you point and say, Look! A squirrel!

Mom

She wasn't cruel but she made her decisions quickly. She said we three had the same hands, artist hands. She taught me painting and you photography. Even though we looked exactly alike she said you got her Dutch parts, her Indian parts. I got Dad's fun Irish, the mean English. She said we both got the crazy because it came from both sides. Confirmed, years later, when I told a psychiatrist a severely abridged version of our family history and he said, "You're the reason they should do mental health screenings before marriage." Or years earlier, when you overheard your guidance counselor ask her colleague, "What kind of sixth-grader knows she is a lithium responder?"

Navajo House

Some rules: We could not call someone stupid. We could not say shut up. We could not answer the phone during dinner and never if the caller ID said UNKNOWN. If a person came to the door we were to sic the dogs on them.

Barney Road

In her trailer when they found her: dozens of try-me eyeglasses from Walmart, the antitheft sensors still on. A pack of six mail-order self-help cassettes called *Depression and You*, tape number two missing, found later in the boom box in the bathroom. Books I had read in college and passed along, thinking they would heal her (*The House on Mango Street*, *Love Medicine*). Every episode of *Star Trek: The Next Generation* on VHS. Every episode of *The X-Files*. A coin stamped PAUL LOVES MARTHA, DISNEYLAND, 1989. An answering machine with neither of our voices on it.

Watkins Ranch

Now, years after both our parents are gone, a boy who'd been in the grade above us at the trailer school messages me online. No one is living in your house anymore, he says. E moved out. E, once our babysitter, had been paying our mother one hundred dollars a month to live in the Tecopa house, money Mom spent on cigarettes and ice cream and methadone. After Mom died, we said E could live in the Tecopa house for free, since you were in San Francisco and I was in the Midwest, moving every year, always in August, to another apartment or another college in another city or to live with a different man. Neither of us had much of an address. E herself had no phone, no Internet, no e-mail, so after Mom died we told someone to tell her that she could live in the Tecopa house as long as she liked, on the condition that we could come and visit the garden, where our pet tortoises had once lived, where our mother had scattered our father's ashes, and where we had scattered hers. But this messenger person was not very reliable, we knew even then, and there is a good chance that E never got the message and kept sending checks. But to where? And who would they be made out to? I wanted E to live in the Tecopa house for years and years, rent-free, until she died a peaceful, painless death, and we'd be some kind of filial for once, bring some sort of serenity to someone, if only when it was too late. (E's husband had already swallowed a shotgun in the shed, which had been our father's workshop.) I realize I want all this only when I receive my former classmate's message online. I'd never seen a deed or a mortgage or any other paperwork for the miner's shack, which my classmate generously called "the Watkins Ranch." Family yarns had my father squatting there, hiding from his past lives. My mother joined him, had us, we four trespassing on BLM land. Last summer I visited a friend of my parents and he told me this was more or less true. I tell the boy from the trailer school that the house does not belong to us, has never belonged to us, is *public land*, and that in my opinion my parents would have been honored to have it preserved and protected. "I think my parents would have been happy to see the property restored as public land and thereby contribute to the preservation of that beautiful desert." I say this despite that fact that my mother considered the Desert Protection Act a land grab, Diane Feinstein a carpetbagger. I say this though my former classmate needs a place to live and I could easily say, Go for it. I said this because at the time some rednecks were hunkered down at yet another a nature reserve, stroking their guns, trying to steal something that belongs to no one, and I thought maybe my former classmate sympathized with them, though I had no reason to believe this except that he'd stayed. In fact I knew nothing about him, had long ago erased him from my feed because the yowls from his difficult life interfered slightly with my enjoying my comfortable one. I never did get skeptical of the authority bestowed on me by being born first.

Tecopa House

It's possible that one day we will go back and it will have been bulldozed. Sometimes I wish for this. The shack or house or ranch, the screened porch, the parachute, the telephone pole and courtyard, all mangled, splintered in a dusty scrap pile. The spring run dry, the bamboo dead, the garden scraped away. Inevitably someone would come and throw tires and other garbage on the heap, maybe they'd spray-paint it, shoot it up, burn it. People do these things to desert ruins, you'll notice. Still, they tug us.

Lola Lane

Where we had, for a time, two pet donkeys. Mine was called Buckwheat, yours was called Spark. We kept them in the dog run, fed them sheaths of alfalfa from the farm at the end of the road. We got them one day when we were driving through the desert and we passed a house that Mom knew to be foreclosed, which she mentioned as we drove by. Behind the house we saw a pen, and in it two donkeys: one iconic brown, black cross of Bethlehem on its back, bristly Mohawk mane, the other entirely white. An albino. I didn't even know the word *foreclosed*, didn't even notice their ribs or the empty trough turned over in the pen, but you started howling and didn't stop until we brought them home. Then the brown one—Buckwheat—we took out for a ride. (The white one, not yet named, was skittish and mistrustful, would not tolerate mounting.) We walked Buckwheat into the desert and back again, a strange sound echoing over the hills as we walked.

We returned and the sound had a source, the white donkey calling for her sister. When she saw Buckwheat, Spark leaped the fence. Atrophy and fear did not allow her grace—her hooves flinting the iron. And so she had her name. Everything of our childhood seems an allegory, you clamoring over an invisible fence after me, but it was also real. Real hooves, real sparks.

Navajo House

Each of us became immediately unhappy in that house and there were times when I considered it cursed. Everything seemed to change for the worse the moment we moved in. It was the first stick-built house we ever lived in, the first big house, a two-story, the style Mom described as Cape Cod. No insulation, instead a pigeon infestation. The sound of pigeons fucking day and night. Our stepfather an ex-felon, not permitted to have guns in the house, so Mom bought a pellet gun, sat in a lawn chair in the evenings, picked them off. You couldn't sleep there, had lava dreams, watched a lot of VH1. Our grandma bought you a porcelain doll and you were too gracious about it so she kept buying them, bought you more and more, one for every occasion, so your room filled with them—smooth glass heads, curls painted on, those drowsy eyelashes. I got into feng shui, broke the bad news: our front and back doors were perfectly aligned, inviting the worst kind of energy. The stairs were positioned in such a way that they shot all our blessings right out the front door. Open space upstairs but sound couldn't move through it. No one could hear anyone, ever, so by the time you got someone's attention you were already screaming.

Navajo House

Her hands began to shake there. One Christmas I waited for K to come pick me up (was it K?) and she said nonsense things to me, silly things she seemed to know were funny though not why, which amused me. I suppose she must have been in a great deal of pain—even now I cannot simply say: she was hurting. Cannot say: she was sick. She certainly was, but the question is with what? Addiction is one of those concepts I cannot recall learning. A notion I seem to have been born knowing. Others are depression, wife beating, molestation, the names for all the parts of my body. She taught us these because no one had taught them to her. She'd had to learn for herself, and told us when and where and how she'd learned, was learning. I knew addiction was a disease, cureless, though secretly I believed her cured, since she'd not had a drink— not even bananas flambéed in liqueur at the nice restaurant on Mother's Day—since I was maybe four years old. She was careful to never say she *used to be* an alcoholic. I always wanted her to—the present tense frightened me. I'd heard stories about when she drank, things she'd done to us when we were little, you protecting me, me protecting you, things neither of us remembered but which she confessed to anyway. For ten years she had cigarettes, coffee, work, gardening, petty fraud, making jewelry, making dinner. She was never still. She never played. I asked how come if people replaced one addiction with another like she said she couldn't just get addicted to playing with us? That's not how it works, she said. You can't get addicted to anything that's good for you.

Navajo House

Then suddenly she was very still. Hurting all over, she said, though no one could say why, meaning we waited too long. No one believed her, she said, and she was right. Lyme. Perhaps by then she was already her own doctor? (Most of it was out of pocket anyway.) She quit the museum or was fired, no one knew. The Navajo house filled with rocks, bared down on us, stick built with a brick-and-mortar mortgage. Our stepfather had been feeding his paychecks into slot machines, I learned when I asked him to fill out his portion of the FAFSA. The spring my classmates spent dropping out to have their babies and you spent raising our half sister I spent overexercising, baffled on the treadmill at how his tax returns said $100,000 per year and yet every day at lunch one of my girlfriends lent me two dollars so I could buy three Pizza Hut breadsticks or a seven-layer burrito. All the mail went into one massive drawer, unopened, envelopes white then yellow then pink. The phone rang and rang, we did not answer—the caller ID always said UNKNOWN. Soon there were morphine patches and a mortar and pestle so she could grind up her Oxy and snort it. Soon all the blankets and cushions had cigarette burns in them. She watched TV—*Star Trek: The Next Generation, The X-Files, Law & Order*—and we watched her fall asleep with a cigarette smoking between her fingers, caught the cigarette at the fabric's first singe but not before, for if she woke she'd accuse us of overreacting, of nagging, and we'd have no evidence to the contrary. Many mornings she did not wake up and on some of those she could not wake up. Often there were so many pills she still had some on her tongue in various stages of dissolve. We took turns waiting for the ambulance. We got to know the EMTs. One was a few years older than me, a friend of a friend, and did me the dignity of never acknowledging that we knew each other. I sometimes saw him at parties, sitting on old tires or tailgates, he and I the only ones not chugging Robitussin. He never let on that he'd carried my mother naked on a stretcher down our stairs on more than one occasion. And now I wonder and am often asked, how many occasions were there? So many that the emergency wore off. We called the ambulance and then argued who would wait for it, who had a test in first period, who had too many absences, whose teacher was more lenient and whose was a hardass. My first period was Drama 2. Yours was something hard, something you probably failed. Drama 2, Anatomy & Physiology, Civics, AP English. Volleyball and plays, answering the phones at Domino's pizza, lifeguarding and teaching swim lessons in the summer. She called her overdoses accidents. I believed her and you didn't, though you weren't unkind with your knowledge, allowed me some denial. So many years ago, when our father was dying, you'd been the one to tell me what dying meant. You'd explained permanence gently but exhaustively in the busted hot tub when I came up for air. So perhaps you thought you needn't explain it again. Still, it's a concept I struggle with.

Barney Road

One way to say all this is, Our mother was an addict and she overdosed.

Another way is, Our mother was suicidal and she killed herself.

Another way is, Our mother was poor and ignored and dismissed for years by doctors who put her on legal and extremely profitable heroin, which eventually killed her.

Another way is, Our mother needed help and no one, including us, gave it to her.

■ ■

And yet you and I have loved each other and her and been loved by each other and by her in all these houses, through all these memories which were once moments, real and felt even if forgotten. We have loved and been loved despite the fissures and losses, violence, cruelty, smallness, timing, deficits in money and attention, despite the betrayals and indifferences, the distance and weather. Despite developing different definitions of certain words. *Death, expensive, cold.* Why, I wonder, or how? Because the little one was kind, pliant with forgiveness, because you absorbed my failings and defects, made them your grace. *There was not enough to go around.* Such a handy phrase to describe such mean circumstances. Here is another:

■ ■

I was born at a good time.

MOBILITY

Julia Alvarez

WE WERE HURRYING through the Atlanta Airport, worried about missing our connection, as it would be the last direct flight to Vermont until evening the next day. Navigating our way in the world's busiest airport was like being in a large city, something my husband and I aren't used to, living as we do out in the country, on ten acres, next to a sheep farm. On the crowded train between terminals a canned voice warned us the train was about to move: to hold on; the doors were about to open: to step back; to watch our step stepping out. (Do travelers really lose all common sense?)

Up the escalator we entered a maze of branching corridors. Carts zipped by, mostly empty, as if the drivers were on leisure vehicles, cruising the sights, much like Vermont farm kids on their snowmobiles on a bright winter day. TVs, two or more to every waiting area, blared the same recycled news. Perhaps the intent was to numb us against the horrors or inanities being reported, the bombing in Brussels, an airstrike in Yemen, Syrian refugees in desperate exodus across Europe, Trump's latest trumpery. Those who couldn't bear one more round could follow George W.'s advice after 9/11 and go shopping. Stores were everywhere, selling books, magazines, luggage, eyeglasses, Montblanc pens, Swarovski crystals, MAC makeup, T-shirts—you name it. (When had airports turned into humongous, overpriced malls?)

Our flight wouldn't be boarding for another half hour—time enough to hunt down a bite to eat. A "market" offered a selection of pricey salads and wraps encased in plastic. My husband, a former farm boy from Nebraska who grows half a dozen varieties of greens, kept shaking his head at what people were willing to pay for a container of wilted leaves. There was nothing in the Atlanta Airport you could pay him to eat.

"Come on now," I coaxed him.

I was in a mood of surprising equanimity, rare for me in airports, where I'm usually the one on edge with the heightened anxiety of air travel these days, the long lines, the security checks, the magical three-point-four ounces under which all liquids are deemed harmless, the boarding by zones, ours always the last one to be called, by which time all the overhead bins are full, and we have to cede our carry-ons to baggage loaders who board the cabin and lug them out like bouncers at a bar.

But we had just come from Ohio where I'd met with a group of undocumented teenagers who had traveled unaccompanied all the way from Ecuador through deserts, flash-flood-prone rivers, rough towns—kids fourteen, fifteen, sixteen, one seventeen-year-old with her three-month-old baby. They were desperate to reunite with missing parents in el Norte or they had been sent away by desperate parents from hometowns afflicted by violence, poverty, gangs, drug cartels. Their stories were wrenching, disturbing.

Every once in a while, another reality breaks into the gated communities of what turn out to be our default entitlements as we complain vehemently when they are withheld. To use an old-fashioned word, I felt *chastened* by the encounter, a reminder of how most of the rest of the world lives.

An overpriced salad, a soggy tuna wrap—we could deal with that!

■ ■

We found a greasy, littered table in the noisy, crowded food court, more corral than court, a holding pen for travelers trying to grab a bite before boarding their flights.

"How is it?" I asked. Bill had just taken a bite of his wrap and most of its contents had oozed out the other end.

He leveled a bleary eye at me, shaking his head at the affront of what passed for food these days.

But looking around, we both cheered up. Inveterate people watchers, we feasted on the scene around us. It's the part I love about big airports (and cities) which we don't get in Vermont: the energizing diversity of people. A cross-section of America, if not the world, was gathered here: mothers and grandmothers in head scarves scolding a bunch of rambunctious kids chasing one another around their table; a raucous group of college-age guys besting one another's tales of spring-break misadventures; Indian women wearing saris so striking I stared; an orthodox Jewish family, the father with sidelocks, a hat, the mom with a velvet hair band over her wig, and four kids obediently eating from the containers she unpacked from a shopping bag while balancing a toddler on her knee. I recalled those lines in Whitman's *Song of Myself*: "I hear America singing, the varied carols I hear." And Walt didn't have a clue what was coming down, an America singing in such diversity and not always in English and not always harmoniously, in fact, judging from the vituperative presidential primary debates, America was coming apart at the seams. Along with the issue of immigration (whom to let in, mostly whom to keep out or throw out), the other most explosive issue was the growing economic inequality in this country. According to our own Bernie Sanders, the top one tenth of 1 percent own almost as much wealth as the bottom 90 percent.

The crowd assembled in this food court was definitely in the solid middle of that 90 percent, as the poor at the bottom would not have the money for air travel, or travel at all. The upper end would be dining in the enclosed bistros and eateries on white linen tablecloths, the cost of their meals the equivalent of the poor's food budget for a week, maybe two, depending on the number of drinks. Others would be ensconced behind the frosted doors of their airline clubs where they could rest, relax, get free drinks, e-mail, and nap, away from the hubbub of the hoi polloi, before boarding first on a special red carpet aisle cordoned off from the rest of us.

The airport was packed tonight, odd for a weekday—until we worked it out—we'd lost track of the upcoming holiday because of work travel: this was the beginning of Easter weekend. Which meant tonight was Maundy Thursday, my favorite holiday on the liturgical calendar. Something about the story still deeply stirs me: the table where all are welcome, the breaking of the bread, the foot-washing ceremony. Later that night, a hunted man awaits capture in an olive grove, a man so terrified he sweats drops of blood—or so he was depicted in my old holy cards—about to be apprehended by a migra who won't stop at deportation, while his sorry friends fall asleep, too exhausted to stay up and comfort him.

It was not lost on me that the young people I'd just met in Ohio, the Syrians splayed across the airport TV screens, or our own invisible Americans, secreted away in ninth wards and trailer parks until some "natural" disaster thrusts them into our awareness—all were in a similar fix.

■ ■

An announcement came over the intercom: our flight to Vermont was delayed, please check the monitors.

"Great!" my husband said. He began on the list of grievances we'd been adding to since the start of our travel six days ago: flight delays, lost luggage, found luggage delivered to the wrong state, rerouted flights, and now another delay.

"I know, I know," I kept commiserating. Like many long-term couples we tend to fall into good cop–bad cop routines, one person's nasty mood triggering the better angels of the other's nature.

My husband was giving me his detective look of trying to find a missing clue. "What's with the good mood tonight?"

"I'm making believe this is the Last Supper." I was quick to grin at what I'd just admitted. Given the bad rap fundamentalists have cast on Christians, it's embarrassing when my childhood faith shows up unbidden. Not that Bill would scoff at that. Lutherans are as prone as Catholics to be revisited by ghosts of their religious past.

If I could put a caption on the look he gave me, it'd be something like "Wake me up for the Resurrection."

■ ■

At our gate a small vocal group had gathered at the counter.

They were giving large, annoyed pieces of their minds to our airline representative—what they're called these days, perhaps to make us all feel we elected these poor, beleaguered, mostly-women underlings, the first line of defense for the CEOs in the aforementioned airline clubs who have packed too many people and too many flights into America's airways. The flight was delayed a half hour, though in another half hour, the screen showed another delay of a half hour, then again, as if that were the increment that the air traffic controllers had decided the public could tolerate at a time.

At each announced delay, the group gathered at the counter to complain. Our representative kept her cool, speaking to each increasingly agitated traveler in an even voice, not abusing whatever brief power she might have over us. I was impressed by her self-control and refrained from the impulse to add my own serving of annoyance to her already-full plate.

I wondered about her life. Middle-aged, with the pale skin of someone who doesn't see much sun or vacation, she wore the front part of her graying hair gathered up in a ponytail, loose in back, a kind of Alice-in-Wonderland look, belying her lined, tired face. A girl who'd gotten old before her time . . . working for this airline, probably taking whatever shifts were offered to her. She wore no ring, maybe single or divorced with teenage kids she called during her breaks to make sure they were safely home. It was already after ten p.m.

A woman in a flowing cotton outfit approached the counter. She had a freckled face, Quaker-kind eyes, wisps of hair fallen out of her barrette. That former-flower-child look of many Vermonters.

"Just be honest with me, okay? Before I move everybody." She indicated two young children lying on their coats on the floor. On the bucket seat beside them sat an older man with a head of tousled white hair and a vacuous look in his eye. "I've got two kids who haven't slept in the last forty-eight hours and a father with Alzheimer's, so, please, I just want to know the odds of us leaving tonight, because if not, I've got to get them to a hotel."

I could see our representative pause, considering whether to parrot the official line or give the woman the straight talk, one human(e) being to another. In a quiet voice so as not to alarm the rest of us, she advised, "If I had two kids and a dad in that condition, I'd find me a room for the night."

"Good luck!" a voice called out. It was the seasoned traveler among us, a consultant who went around the country giving advice on sustainable designs or renewable energy or green construction—I wasn't sure, though he had a lot to say about it. He had several watchdog apps on his phone and kept updating us on what was being reported about our missing flight. A cold front was blowing in. Flights were being rerouted, canceled. It was closing on midnight. Everyone was scrambling to reschedule and bed down. He'd been calling around, and there wasn't a hotel with vacancies within a twenty-mile radius. He was packing it up, going back to the city.

"We just got the last two at the Courtyard," a businesswoman on our flight announced to her two colleagues. Her male colleague had already rerouted their flights with the company's twenty-four-hour travel agent. Everyone else calling the airline's 800 number to reschedule their flights was being given a one-hour call-back delay. Off the group went, relieved their corporate big daddy had taken care of them.

Our representative was shutting down her computer for the night. The monitor had just flashed the news we'd all been expecting: our flight was canceled.

"Can't you let her use the club?" I asked on behalf of the mom with the afflicted father. They had couches in there. Carpets on the floor the kids could sleep on.

Our representative looked at me as if we'd been living in different universes until this night when our paths crossed in the

Atlanta Airport. Did I really believe she had the authority to grant that? "I don't have the authority to do that." She had read my mind reading her mind. "Try the HELP desk." I knew all about the HELP desk: its line was now so long, it reached as far down as our gate, and looped back up again.

It was my turn to vent to Bill. Damn airline won't let them use the club! And that business trio. Couldn't they have ceded at least one of their two rooms?

"Would you have?"

Bill gave me that chastening look I'd given him earlier this night.

■ ■

Chastened or not, I wasn't ready to admit that I, too, would have denied her. A woman I didn't even know. What I did know was that I was fed up with the airlines. Clubs left empty because policy trumps compassion. First-class passengers getting preferential treatment: an express security check-in line (don't we all pay taxes?), early red-carpet boarding, seats with more space, and a curtained-off section with a bathroom no one else can use even if she's peeing in her pants. I'd seen a recent CNN report on increased air rage among travelers. Turns out that passengers in economy seating were almost four times more likely to have an incident of air rage on a plane with a first-class section—especially when they had to walk through first class to board the plane.

But the system was more complicated than I'd even guessed. Figuring out the fine-tuning of who gets what is good preparation for understanding the caste system in India. Delta, the airline we were flying that night, offers five levels of what they call "service": Basic Economy, Main Cabin, Delta Comfort+, DeltaOne, and First Class. In the Basic Economy class (travel bloggers call it "Minus Economy Class" or "Last Class") you get the stripped-down service, no assigned seating, no free carry-on, additional charges for everything from a can of soda to the canned entertainment on your monitor (if you even have a monitor and it isn't pressed against your forehead, as the seats are so crammed). One day soon (and you heard it here first) Last Class folks will have to swipe their credit cards to get into the toilets at the back of the airbus.

The airline CEOs on the program kept defending their policies as just wanting to provide their customers with more choice. But the pundits dismissed the flimsy PR. Airlines are responding to Wall Street investors who want them to pack more of us into tighter seats so they can charge more and higher fees. As Bernie might have told you, airlines are increasingly mirroring some of the worst inequalities found elsewhere.

If you think there isn't a class system firmly in place in the most mobile of worlds, try getting stuck at a busy international airport on a dark and stormy night.

By now the Maundy Thursday influence had worn thin.

■ ■

A girl with a tiny red carry-on came running to our gate, breathless.

"Anyone here speak Spanish?" one of our reduced group of stranded travelers called out. Our airline rep had left for the night.

I popped right up to the counter. "Sí, sí, yo hablo español!" Maybe it just made me feel good to think I could fix anything at this point.

The girl turned out to be older than I'd guessed from a distance, mid- to late twenties, heavily made up with bright red lipstick that gave her a retro look. She was overdressed in spike heels, a short black velour skirt with a patent leather belt, and a blouse with a ruffled collar. Someone who hadn't traveled much and wears her very best to mark the occasion.

Her name was Estela and she was on her way from Mexico City to Oklahoma. Her ticket said her connecting flight would be at this gate. Had she checked the monitors to be sure? Except I couldn't remember the word for *monitor* so I used *television* instead. (Not many occasions to practice my Spanish in Vermont.) She looked confused. I walked her over to the monitor. Sure enough, her flight had also been canceled. I offered to go with her to the HELP desk and get her on the next flight. From then on, Estela was like the chick that imprints on the first moving/maternal object it sees.

We inched forward on the line. Time for a long chat. I'd guessed right. This was her first time ever on an airplane. She was en route to her boyfriend in Tulsa, and—she hesitated, as if afraid to be asking for more help than I was already giving—she needed to buy a phone card to call him as he'd be waiting at the airport, worried when she didn't arrive. She had pulled out a cell phone, an inexpensive brand in a rhinestone cover, the kind I recognized from my trips home to the Dominican Republic, sold by hawkers at street corners. Twenty bucks—five more for the cover—and you could talk to your gente in the Bronx or Boston.

"You can use mine," I offered. But my iPhone turned out to have too many bells and whistles for her to manipulate. I might as well have asked her to fly one of the 747s stranded on the runway. I dialed the number and a wary male voice answered. "Un momento." I put Estela on and her face filled with relief and happiness.

We'd been on the line at least a half hour when a call came through on my phone. It was Bill, exasperated. "Where are you?"

"The line is endless," I explained. "Just go to sleep, okay?"

"Fat chance of that!"

"I'll see if I can get us some blankets." I had seen reps wheeling carts with pillows and blankets and little bags with overnight supplies to the different gates. Ours at the end of the line seemed to have been overlooked. "Can I bring you back anything else? Another tuna wrap or something?"

For the first time that night, I thought I could hear him smiling. "Just you," he said endearingly.

Finally we reached one of a handful of representatives at the HELP counter, all African American, all women. In fact, as the night had worn on, and the shift changed to graveyard, the workforce had become increasingly darker, including the cleaning crew of dark-skinned immigrant women chattering in foreign languages I couldn't place as they wiped down counters, emptied trash, cleaned the floor with big industrial vacuums they turned off periodically to talk some more.

Our representative, a large woman with the I-suffer-no-fools attitude of a Sunday school teacher, listened as I translated Estela's story. And that was that. She was transformed into a lioness with her cub. I was just the imprint surrogate until she arrived on the scene.

She was determined to get this poor child into the hands of her boyfriend ASAP. Somehow she managed to reroute Estela on the very first flight to Tulsa the next morning—though we'd been told the flight was full by someone ahead of us on the line. Bill and I had less luck. We would have to wait a full twenty-four hours if we wanted a direct flight, or we could fly to Albany, rent a car, drive to the Burlington airport to pick up our own car, and, no, the airline could not pay for the rental car if we changed our destination. I decided then and there, I'd break the news to Bill in the morning or neither of us would get much sleep.

■ ■

Back at our gate, a cheerful man with the delicate bones of a bird and mahogany skin had arrived, pushing a cart of complimentary supplies: blankets and pillows, overnight packs with doll-size toothbrushes, sodas, power bars. We divvied them out, making sure everyone got what they needed. In the bathroom Estela and I joined a lineup of women at the mirrors, washing our faces, brushing our teeth, getting ready for whatever bit of sleep we were going to get. "What a pajama party!" one of the women quipped. We all burst out laughing, even Estela, who I'm pretty sure didn't get the joke. We all needed the release of a good laugh after the tensions of the night.

As we walked back to our gate area, we passed small encampments of stranded travelers, people who had not known one another before this night, now banded together, taking care of one another. Estela set up her bedding next to ours; another single woman asked if she could join us. She was afraid of burglars coming by as she slept and yanking her backpack away.

"I think we'll be all right," I assured her.

■ ■

For a while, I was unable to sleep. But I must have dozed off, because I woke up startled. A woman was pushing a broom around us. "I just clean. Sorry. Go sleep."

I thought I'd feel aggrieved, lying on that hard floor, rehearsing grievances about what those with the savvy, luck, and twenty-four-hour corporate travel agents outsourced to the subcontinents got that we had not.

But we got something better, a significant resource there for the tapping—a kindred care and kindness, apparent in a dozen encounters: the equanimity of our beleaguered representative, her humane response to the anxious mother; the cheerful service of the small, happy man wheeling in our rescue supplies; the determined African American woman at the HELP desk who got Estela on the overbooked flight and into her boyfriend's arms; the late-night shift turning off their vacuum cleaners, rolling them away in silence, so as not to wake the sleepers from our light, restless three-hour doze; the ways we made sure everyone got a blanket, power bars for breakfast, which actually tasted better when halved and shared (note to Bill: this might apply to tuna wraps); even our *The Waltons* moment when we called out to one another, "Good night," and, "Buenas noches."

Even though Easter was two days away, I felt a resurrection of hope.

Please don't tell the airlines, but I was glad for what had happened.

YOUTH FROM EVERY QUARTER

Kirstin Valdez Quade

WHEN I WAS TWENTY-FOUR, my then-boyfriend and I taught at a high school summer program at an elite New England boarding school, which I will call Elliot Academy. The summer school was a kind of cash cow, trading on the Elliot reputation, catering to a wealthy and not very diverse student body. Students were promised rigorous classes, stimulating friendships, field trips to area colleges and idyllic swimming ponds: a glorious New England summer.

One of the students in my boyfriend's English class was a rising sophomore, whom I'll call Ana. Ana was from rural Oregon. Her parents, farmworkers, were Mexican—and, though Ana did not say, I suspect undocumented—who traveled around the state following the crops: cherries, plums, pears. Ana was shy and serious, with frizzy black hair escaping her ponytail, off-brand sneakers, and modest, too-long khaki shorts. At home, she translated for her parents; she took care of her younger siblings; she excelled in school. When she and another girl from her town were granted one of the few scholarships to Elliot Academy's summer school, their conservative Christian church raised funds to cover the rest.

Ana had never been out of Oregon, had certainly never been exposed to the level of privilege on display at Elliot, with its columns and cupolas and manicured grounds. The other students were used to jetting off to this or that summer enrichment program, and arrived equipped with iPods and Tiffany necklaces, sleek new laptop computers and spending money for shopping trips to Boston.

"She's having a hard time," my boyfriend told me. "She feels isolated. Maybe you can talk to her." He meant because I was also Latina, because I'd also been a bookish kid, because I'd also moved around a lot as a child, and money had always been tight.

And I'd also found myself an outsider in this prep school world. A decade earlier, when I was thirteen, a recruiter from another elite boarding school, in an effort to seek "youth from every quarter," had visited my rough public middle school on Tucson's southwest side. I took a pamphlet, and, despite my parents' bafflement and skepticism (boarding schools *existed* outside of Victorian England?), submitted an application. I was awarded a nearly full ride. I bought six mock turtlenecks in jewel tones from the Fashion Bug, and set off across the continent to New Hampshire.

Those mock turtlenecks were only the beginning of what was wrong with me. I was one of a handful of Latino students, the only one, to my knowledge, not from either New York City or from wealthy families in Venezuela or Mexico City. I'd attended nine schools, mostly in the Southwest, but had never heard of field hockey or crew or many of the universities in the Ivy League. Social signifiers that were tossed around—North Face, Nantucket, Greenwich, Guerlain, Majorca—meant nothing to me, and I was sharply aware that I did not speak an essential language. Who knew that the category "middle class" was capacious enough to fit any number of summer homes?

My time in boarding school was, on the whole, pretty good. I made friends. I took classes and read books that changed my life. But I was desperately shy, skittish around teachers and peers alike, vaguely ashamed of my family and background: of sharing a bed with my sister, of having once lived in a trailer, of growing up without a television, of having a violent, alcoholic biological father. And I felt guilty, too, because even with the generous financial aid, the plane tickets were a burden on my parents. The distance between my experience and others' felt impossible to bridge, so I didn't even try to explain myself. For four years I revealed remarkably little about my life beyond the school grounds.

My time in boarding school was a tremendous, astonishing

gift, and it did, as the pamphlet promised, open doors—yet I always felt that my presence there was provisional. Certainly I never felt it was *my* school. I always had the sense of my inferiority, that my role was to be invisible and studious and grateful, to write tidy and effusive thank-you notes to the donors who'd funded my spot.

Which was all part of why I'd come to teach at Elliot Academy. That summer was my opportunity to return to boarding school, but to return as the person I wish I'd been in high school: poised, articulate, worldly, and with a clearer idea of how my jeans should fit.

■ ■

Ana's difficulties had started early in the session. Her roommate, a moneyed and well-traveled French girl, with a healthy sense of what summer school should be, was having a great time. This roommate and her new Elliot friends stayed up laughing late into the night, talking about parties and hookups and drinking. They compared notes on their SAT coaches and college application consultants. They whispered and rolled their eyes at Ana, who, on the other side of the room, tried to do homework or fake sleep.

In the second week, Ana and her friend from home had asked if they could switch rooms to live together. No, she was told. Roommate assignments were firm, and the girls needed to extend themselves, meet other people.

When my boyfriend introduced me to Ana, I realized I'd half-seen her on campus, standing apart from the happy clumps of students, either with her friend from home or, increasingly, alone. Her expression was strained and wary.

In addition to her English class, Ana had signed up for a pre-calculus class that she wasn't prepared for, and by the end of the second week it was apparent that she was failing it. She told me this as we sat on a curb in a campus parking lot, the wide, sweeping lawn behind us. Far above, the leaves of a massive, ancient tree tossed the sunlight.

Ana didn't seem particularly surprised at my interest in her situation, but she also didn't seem especially eager for my mentorship.

"I have to go home," she said, resigned. "I can't do Elliot."

"But surely the teacher can give you extra help?" I asked.

"He said I'm too far behind." She paused, then explained that she'd always gotten As at her Oregon public school and had registered for the class so she could graduate early. "I need to help my family."

"You're just in the wrong class," I said briskly, cheerfully. "You just need to be in a more appropriate level. We'll get you switched."

I was jollying her along, optimistic, but Ana's fatalism seemed impervious. "They won't let me switch," she said.

"Nonsense. We'll figure it out," I promised. "Another math class. Or maybe creative writing! I'll talk to the dean. This summer should be fun for you."

"Okay," she said, and though she didn't smile, I thought I detected a glimmer of hope.

That summer I'd seen plenty of rules bent; I'd been in the office making copies when parents called, demanding this or that for their kid. Some students had switched roommates or been given singles. When a student hadn't signed up in time for a college tour or field trip, a parent called, and a space was found on the bus.

So my hopes were high when I spoke with the dean about Ana. I understood, of course, that these other, wealthier kids belonged to a world where their needs were accommodated, and that Ana did not, but with my advocacy, surely, everything would be sorted out.

When I explained Ana's predicament, the dean shook her head regretfully. The other math classes were full, she said. I looked at her in disbelief. I liked the dean—or had. She had a kindly pink face and a soft white bob. In her shapeless linen dress, she resembled a liberal children's librarian. She was a grandmother. Surely it mattered to her that Ana succeed.

"Okay, then," I said. "What about my etymology class? Or the fiction workshop?" My boyfriend had already offered to let her join his fiction class, I told her. I spoke in the sweet, reasonable, good-girl voice I used around people in authority.

The dean told me that she would not allow Ana to switch classes. "The session is already under way and I can't set a precedent." She looked back at her computer, where, doubtless, many demands awaited her.

I shifted my weight uncertainly. "Well, then, what about getting her tutoring?"

There wasn't time for that, the dean told me; summer school was only six weeks long, and they didn't have the resources.

"But the class is just too advanced for her," I said. "That's not her fault. She feels like she's failing Elliot. She actually thinks she needs to *leave*."

The dean held my gaze and nodded. "It would be a shame if Ana left," she said, her voice even. "And you're nice to show concern. But not everyone belongs at Elliot."

I was stunned. But then again, not. I remembered my friend from high school, who, when she was deeply depressed, suicidal, and sleeping through her classes, was never offered mental health support, but was instead punished and put on academic probation. I thought of my own isolation and depression and the indifference of my dorm faculty.

I ought to have argued with the dean. I ought to have told her that Ana *did* belong; Elliot itself had made that call when she was accepted to the program. I ought to have said that if Elliot was, as it claimed, committed to diversity, then it had a moral obligation to support the students it accepted. I should have pointed out that the rules needed to be in service of students' learning; or that if rules were going to be bent right and left, then they should be bent for Ana, too. I should have made her see that Ana's leaving would be a loss for the whole Elliot community as well as for Ana.

"It's just summer school," the dean told me kindly. "It's not the end of the world."

But it wasn't just summer school; it was Elliot Academy. I understood what that scholarship represented to Ana, because a similar scholarship had represented the same thing to me: escape, welcome, possibility.

■ ■

Even a decade later, my anger at the dean and at Elliot Academy is raw and personal. I have to guard against overidentification with Ana, whom, let's face it, I knew only fleetingly. I had so many privileges that Ana didn't have: both my parents went to college, and I always believed I would, too; my dad, who is technically my stepfather, and who has always been extraordinarily loving and supportive of me, became a college professor when I was twelve; my family became middle class; I was never in the position of having to translate and navigate the adult world for my parents. Over and over I've benefited from institutional largesse, and have been the first in my family to have the option of pursuing an uncertain career as a writer.

But there was a time, when I was a kid in Albuquerque, when my life could have unspooled in a very different way. We were poor, and my single mother, who was without emotional or financial support, worked two and three jobs. We were constantly negotiating the role my violent and addicted biological father played in my life. I've always been aware of a shadow life running alongside my own, a life of curtailed possibility.

I was a smart, hardworking kid, but my acceptance to boarding school was a fluke. It was a fluke that the recruiter chose my middle school to visit; it was a fluke that I happened to be there the day the recruiter came (my parents frequently took us out of school when my geologist dad had fieldwork); it was a fluke that I managed to hang on to the pamphlet and request an application. And it was a fluke that I happened to fit the particular demographics that they were seeking to diversify the student body and that among all those other smart, hardworking kids, I was chosen.

And yet that first fluke was followed by others—scholarships to college, graduate school, fellowships, residencies—until it became clear that they were no longer flukes—that I'd been accepted into a rarefied world where such opportunities came more frequently. I'd learned how to navigate that rarefied world and to behave more or less as if I belonged there.

I didn't fully understand this when I was twenty-four. I don't flatter myself that in the end I could have made a difference to the dean's decision. But as I stood before her, I couldn't shake the sense that I was myself in that rarefied world only on sufferance, and not just because I was a new teacher at Elliot. My own sense of gratitude and indebtedness for having been allowed a seat at the feast kept me from fighting for Ana as hard as I should have.

■ ■

I dreaded reporting to Ana that I'd failed her. But I never had to, because the next afternoon, Ana approached me, walking stiffly across the grass. "I just wanted to tell you that I'm leaving tomorrow morning."

"Ana. Please don't leave." I was begging now. But for what? For her to stay and be told each day that she didn't belong at Elliot?

"I'm letting them all down," she said, meaning her parents and the people at church who'd donated to cover her flights and expenses.

"You're not," I told her. "They'll understand. It's just summer school."

Ana's head was bent. There was a long pause, and I knew she was crying only when the tears dropped onto her pink shorts. "I just really, really wanted to go to college."

I hadn't understood until then that Ana actually believed that her chances for college had been ruined by this summer school math class. I was furious that Ana was leaving this place feeling so diminished. Elliot Academy was supposed to broaden her horizons, to expose her to new ideas and friends. It was not supposed to crush her. "You'll go to college," I said when I caught my breath. "Of course you will. There are so many ways to get the things you want in life."

She nodded, unconvinced.

But we both knew that the one way, if you are born to a family without money, is to prove yourself smart enough and pleasant enough and eager enough to convince the gatekeepers to let you in, and then, once you're there, to try with all your might to convince them to keep you.

■ ■

It's a worthy, essential aim to seek "youth from every quarter." Institutions and individuals have a responsibility to work against centuries of structural inequality. And I've seen both as a student and as a professor the myriad ways diverse voices do indeed make for a richer learning environment. But it should go without saying that it's not enough for elite institutions to accept students from racially, ethnically, and economically diverse backgrounds if those students are then told in a thousand ways—ways tiny and large, oblique and direct—that they are there only at the whim of the powers that be, that they haven't paid for the privilege to err or falter, that, at root, they don't belong.

■ ■

I think about Ana frequently. I've imagined many futures for her. In my favorite, most self-indulgent fantasy, she's a leader in her field, a mathematician, say. She's invited to give an assembly at Elliot Academy, and when she stands on the stage before the dean and the rest of the Elliot community, she gives them hell.

What I really hope is that Ana is happy. I hope she went to college and found other mentors who did right by her, that she's doing a job she loves and that challenges her. The chances are good. The Ana I met that summer was smart and driven, and there are a lot of good teachers out there ready to encourage talented students to fulfill their promise. Someone, after all, told her about Elliot Academy. And Ana, who was, no doubt, already well aware that the deck was stacked against her, nevertheless found that application and filled it out.

OUTSIDE

Kiese Laymon

THE DAY I MET DAVE MELTON, he asked if I could help him get rehired at a job he lost for being black, poor, scared, and desperate. I was a twenty-six-year-old adjunct at Vassar College and Dave was the first person I met in Poughkeepsie, New York. On the ride home, Dave claimed we clicked not because of our bald heads or our love for midrange jump shots but because Dave "rocked gold teeth and Jordans, and people from the South love gold teeth and Jordans, ked."

I'm not sure anyone from my South loved Jordans as much as Dave, but I'm absolutely sure Dave never knew the correct pronunciation of my name. He never called me "Kiese." Sometimes he called me "Keece." Usually called me "ked," which was short—or long—for "kid."

While Dave Melton worked at Vassar, he sold drugs to sad people inside and outside Vassar's gates. Like nearly every black dealer I've known, Dave wasn't lucky. In the mid-nineties. Dave's initial sentence was six years. He did three. In 1999, while still on parole, Dave went to Maryland with his sixteen-year-old brother who had some weed in the car. Police stopped the car. For the parole violation Dave got sentenced to another seven months of boot camp. That's when he had to quit his job working Building and Grounds at Vassar.

For a few months, while on parole in Maryland, Dave worked two jobs and sent money back to his girlfriend, his mother, and his daughter in Poughkeepsie. Eventually Dave moved back to New York and traveled to Maryland once a week to meet with his PO. When money for bus rides got tight, Dave missed one week, then another week, and another. His PO told him he understood that Dave didn't want to leave his daughter and money was tight, but he'd have to arrest him when he reentered Maryland for unlawfully crossing state lines while on parole. A warrant was issued for Dave's arrest.

One winter night in 2004, I got a call from Dave's fiancée, Shauna. Earlier that day, Dave called my office and told me he wouldn't make our City League basketball game because he had to take his daughter, CheChe, to the carnival.

"Keece, they got Dave," she said. "Can you take me to see him? You're a professor. They'll listen to you. Can you talk to him?"

Shauna explained how two officers stopped Dave as he was paying a toll on the Mid-Hudson Bridge. The officer claimed Dave didn't signal when changing lanes. Shauna, who was in the car with Dave, says he didn't signal because at the last second, he saw that the tollbooth in his lane was closed.

"The last time he got arrested in Maryland," Shauna said, "they pulled him over 'cause they said he had too many air fresheners hanging from his front mirror."

After taking turns talking about how sick it was that Americans with the least access to healthy choice and second chances are given the harshest punishments, Shauna said she was calling the Kingston jail on three-way to see what they decided to do. "If Dave picks up, tell him some good words, Keece. Make my man feel better."

We were on hold for about five minutes when we heard a low-toned, gruff "Hello."

It was Dave.

Shauna told Dave how much she loved him and wanted to marry him as soon as he got home.

"I love you, too," Dave said. "Where CheChe?"

"She's in bed," Shauna said. "You think you can come home tonight?"

"Probably not," he said. "Maybe. I'm saying, you never know."

"Stop lying," Shauna said. "You know you ain't coming home. CheChe wouldn't stop crying."

"Yo, you act like I'm dead," Dave said. "I just wanna get this behind me, you know?"

"Keece on the line," she told him.

"You on the line, ked?"

"Yeah," I said. "I'm here. You maintaining?"

"You already know," he said." "I'm strong, ked. You know what? You about to see how I used to looked back in the day when I was in shape. I always lose weight when I go to jail, don't I, Shauna?"

Shauna ignored his question and told him that I had some words for him.

I sat there hanging in silence. I had three degrees and Dave hadn't graduated from high school. I paid my own rent and Dave stayed illegally in Shauna's Section 8 apartment. I earned nineteen hundred dollars a month after taxes for talking to young people about something called black literary imagination and Dave was legally unemployed because no one in the Hudson Valley wanted to hire a black man with several felonies on his record.

"I'll bring you some books next week," I told him. "And I'ma put some money on your commissary. When you get out, I got you."

"That's all you got to say?" Shauna asked me. "Ain't you a professor?"

Dave had neither the money nor the power to fight his arrest. I was the wealthiest, most powerful person Dave knew, and I had sixty-seven dollars in my banking account, a living room set filled with furniture students threw out, and plenty of family, friends, and students doing time in federal prison for murder, racketeering, counterfeiting, and drug trafficking.

"Just bring me some books, ked," Dave said. "I know this shit is awkward but can you write a little note on the front page of all the books? A nigga been locked up a lot and I never had no one write notes in my books."

Before and after Dave got out, white colleagues routinely put their hands on my back and called me lucky. They meant that

Southern black boys like me were more likely to end up incarcerated than working beside wonderful white faculty at so-called elite liberal arts colleges. I looked in the eyes of those colleagues and routinely shook my head. These colleagues were lucky, not simply because their students demanded less of them, nor because their identities were never threated by security or armed police officers; they were lucky that they got to share professional space with poor young black professors who materially never invested in notions of academic excellence being a stand-in for innocence.

Dave, the first person I met in Poughkeepsie, was a felon because he was black, scared, desperate, and guilty. My student Cole, a heroin user and dealer of everything from weed to cocaine, is a college graduate because he's white, wealthy, scared, desperate, and guilty.

I made good on my promise to bring Dave a new book with a new note every week before they shipped him out to boot camp. Every once in a while, Davie returned the books with notes he'd written on the second pages. Dave said he shared the books and notes with COs and other incarcerated men and they started a reading group. The books didn't take any time off his sentence. They didn't free Dave's imagination. The books gave us more to talk about and feel through when he got out. One of the last notes Dave wrote me before being released was "It's hard to get right when the free folks out there are more trapped than the criminal folks in jail. I just want to be free."

WHITE DEBT

Eula Biss

THE WORD FOR *debt* in German also means *guilt*. A friend who used to live in Munich mentioned this to me recently. I took note because I'm newly in debt, quite a lot of it, from buying a house. So far, my debt is surprisingly comfortable, and that's one of the qualities of debt that I've been pondering lately—how easy it can be.

I had very little furniture for the first few months in my new house, and no money left to buy any. But then I took out a loan against my down payment and now I have a dining room table, six chairs, and a piano. While I was in the bank signing the paper-work that would allow me to spend money I hadn't yet earned, I thought of Eddie Murphy's skit where he goes undercover as a white person and discovers that white people at banks give away money to other white people for free. "It's true," I thought to my-self in awe when I saw the ease with which I was granted another loan, though I understood—and, when my mortgage was sold to another lender, was further reminded—that the money was not being given to me for free. I was, and am, paying for it. But that detail, like my debt, is easily forgotten.

"Only something that continues *to hurt* stays in the memory," Nietzsche observes in *On the Genealogy of Morality*. My student loan debt doesn't hurt, though it hasn't seemed to have gotten any smaller over the past decade, and I have managed to forget it so thoroughly that I recently told someone that I'd never been in debt until I bought a house. Creditors of antiquity, Nietzsche writes, tried to encourage a debtor's memory by taking as collateral his freedom, wife, life, or even, as in Egypt, his afterlife. Legal documents outlined exactly how much of the body of the debtor the creditor could cut off for unpaid debts. Consider the odd logic, Nietzsche suggests, of a system in which a creditor is repaid not with money or goods, but with the pleasure of seeing the debtor's body punished. "The pleasure," he writes, "of having the right to exercise power over the powerless."

The power to punish, Nietzsche notes, can enhance your sense of social status, increasing the pleasure of cruelty. Reading this, I think of a white Texas trooper's encounter with the black woman he pulled over for failure to signal a lane change. As the traffic stop became a confrontation that ended with Sandra Bland facedown on the side of the road, she asked Brian Encinia, over and over, whether what he was doing made him feel good. "You feelin' good about yourself?" she asked. "Don't it make you feel good, Officer Encinia?" And then, when a female officer joined them, "Make you feel real good for a female. Y'all strong, y'all real strong." After asking the same question Nietzsche asked, the question of why justice would take this form, she came to the same conclusion.

When I was nineteen and in college, the head of campus police escorted me to an interview with the Amherst police. The previous night, a friend and I had pasted big posters of bombs that read "Bomb the Suburbs" all over Amherst, Massachusetts. *Bomb the Suburbs* is the title of a book by the graffiti artist William Upski Wimsatt, whom we had invited to speak on campus. The first question the Amherst police asked was whether I was aware that graffiti and "tagging," a category that included the posters, was punishable as a felony. I was not aware. Near the end of the interrogation, my campus officer stepped in and suggested that we would clean up the posters. I was not charged with a felony, and I spent the day working side by side with my officer, using a wire brush to scrub all the bombs off Amherst.

Twenty years later, I try to watch a video of a black man being shot in the head by a campus police officer. I don't want to see this, but then I think of Emmett Till's mother asking the whole country to see her son's body and mourn with her, so I search for the video. But I don't get past the first frame because the *Chicago Tribune* website runs an Acura commercial after I hit play, and the possibility that the shooting death of Samuel DuBose in his old Honda is serving as an opportunity to sell Acuras makes me close the window. With the long, slow pan across the immaculate interior of a new car on my mind, I reconsider the justice behind my own encounter with a campus police officer.

The word *privilege*, composed of the Latin words for *private* and *law*, describes a legal system in which not everyone is equally bound, a system in which the law that makes graffiti a felony does not apply to a white college student. Even as the police spread photos of my handiwork in front of me, I could tell by the way they pronounced "tagging" that it wasn't a crime invented for me. I was subject less to the law as it was written than I was to the private laws of whiteness. When the laws that bind a community apply differently to different members of the community, Bettina Bergo and Tracey Nicholls observe in their collection, *I Don't See Color*, then privilege "undermines the solidarity of the community." And that, in turn, undermines us all.

"The condition of black life," Claudia Rankine writes, "is one of mourning." Mourning this, I ask myself what the condition of white life might be. I write *complacence* on a blank page. Hearing the term *white supremacist* in the wake of the Charleston church massacre has given me another occasion to wonder whether white supremacists are any more dangerous than regular white people, who tend to enjoy supremacy without believing in it. After staring at *complacence* for quite a long time, I look it up and discover that it doesn't mean exactly what I thought it meant. "A feeling of smug or uncritical satisfaction with oneself or one's achievements" might be an apt description of the dominant white attitude, but that's more active than what I had in mind. I thought *complacence* meant sitting there in your house, neither smug nor satisfied, just lost in the illusion of ownership. This is an illusion that depends on forgetting the redlining, blockbusting, racial covenants, contract buying, loan discrimination, housing projects, mass incarceration, predatory lending, and deed thefts that have prevented so many black Americans from building wealth the way so many white Americans have, through home ownership. I erase *complacence* and write *complicity*. I erase it. *Debt*, I write. Then, *forgotten debt*.

■ ■

I read several hundred pages of *Little House on the Prairie* to my five-year-old son one day last winter when he was home sick from school. Near the end of the book, when the Ingalls family is reckoning with the fact that they built their little house illegally on Indian territory, and just after an alliance between tribes has been broken by a disagreement over whether to attack the settlers, Laura watches the Osage abandoning their annual buffalo hunt and leaving Kansas. Her family will leave, too. At this point, my son asked me to stop reading. "Is it too sad?" I asked. "No," he said, "I just don't need to know any more." After a few moments of silence, he added, "I wish I was French."

The Indians in *Little House* are French speaking, so I understood that my son was saying he wanted to be an Indian. "I wish all that didn't happen," he said. And then, "But I want to stay here—I love this place. I don't want to leave." He began to cry, and I realized that when I told him *Little House* was about the place where we live, meaning the Midwest, he thought I meant it was about the town where we live and the house we had just bought. Our house is not that little house, but we do live on the wrong side of what used to be an Indian boundary negotiated by a treaty that was undone after the 1830 Indian Removal Act. We live in Evanston, Illinois, named after John Evans, who founded the university where I teach and defended the Sand Creek massacre as necessary to the settling of the West. What my son was expressing—that he wants the comfort of what he has but that he is uncomfortable with how he came to have it—is one of the conundrums of whiteness.

"Tell me again about the liar who lied about a lie," my son said recently. It took me a moment to register that he meant Rachel Dolezal. He had heard me talking about her with Noel Ignatiev, author of *How the Irish Became White*. I had said, "She might be a liar, but she's a liar who lied about a lie. The original fraud was not hers." Because I was talking to Noel, who sent me to James Baldwin's essay "On Being White . . . And Other Lies" when I was in college, I didn't have to clarify that the lie I was referring to was the idea that there is any such thing as a Caucasian race. Dolezal's parents had insisted to reporters that she was "Caucasian" by birth, though she is not from the Caucasus region of Europe, meaning contemporary Armenia, Georgia, and Azerbaijan. Outside of that context, the term *Caucasian* is a flimsy and fairly meaningless product of the eighteenth-century pseudoscience that helped invent a white race.

Whiteness is not a kinship or a culture. White people are no more closely related to one another, genetically, than we are to black people. American definitions of *race* allow for a white woman to give birth to black children, which should serve as a reminder that white people are not a family. What binds us is that we share a system of social advantages that can be traced back to the advent of slavery in the colonies that became the United States. "There is, in fact, no white community," as Baldwin writes. Whiteness is not who you are. Which is why it is entirely possible to despise whiteness without disliking yourself.

When he was four, my son brought home a library book about the slaves who built the White House. I didn't tell him that slaves once accounted for more wealth than all the industry in this country combined, or that slaves were, as Ta-Nehisi Coates writes, "the down payment" on this country's independence, or that freed slaves became, after the Civil War, "this country's second mortgage." Nonetheless, my overview of slavery and Jim Crow left my son worried about what it meant to be white, what legacy he had inherited. "I don't want to be on this team," he said, with his head in his hands. "You might be stuck on this team," I told him, "but you don't have to play by its rules."

Even as I said this, I knew that he would be encouraged, at

every juncture in his life, to believe wholeheartedly in the power of his own hard work and deservedness, to ignore inequity, to accept that his sense of security mattered more than other people's freedom, and to agree, against all evidence, that a system that afforded him better housing, better education, better work, and better pay than other people was inherently fair.

My son's first week in kindergarten was devoted entirely to learning rules. At his school, obedience is rewarded with fake money that can be used, at the end of the week, to buy worthless toys that break immediately. "Welcome to capitalism," I thought when I learned of this system, which produced, that week, a yo-yo that remained stuck at the bottom of its string. The principal asked all the parents to submit a signed form acknowledging that they had discussed the Code of Conduct with their children, but I didn't sign the form. Instead, my son and I discussed the civil rights movement and I reminded him that not all rules are good rules and that unjust rules must be broken. This was, I now see, a somewhat unhinged response to the first week of kindergarten. I know that schools need rules, and I, myself, am a teacher who makes rules, but I still want my son to know the difference between compliance and complicity.

For me, whiteness is not an identity but a moral problem. Becoming black is not the answer to the problem of whiteness, though I sympathize with the impulse, as does Noel. "Imagine the loneliness of those who, born to a group they regard as unjust and oppressive and not wanting to be part of that group, are left on their own to figure their way out," Noel wrote recently in his own narrative of "Passing," the story of how he left a lower-middle-class family and a college education to work in factories for the next twenty-three years.

I met Noel after he left the factories for Harvard, when he was the editor, with John Garvey, of a journal called *Race Traitor*. In it, I read about groups of volunteers who worked in shifts using video cameras to record police misconduct in their cities. I read about the school board member who challenged the selection practices that had produced, in a district where only 22 percent of the students were white, a gifted program where 81 percent of the students were white. *Race Traitor* articulated for me the possibility that a person who looks white can refuse to act white, meaning refuse to collude with the injustices of the law enforcement system and the educational system, among other things. This is what Noel called "new abolitionism." John Brown was his model and the institution he was intent on abolishing was whiteness.

It was because I read *Race Traitor* in my twenties that I stopped, in my thirties, when I saw a black man being handcuffed by his car on an empty stretch of road next to a cemetery in Chicago. I was carrying my son, who was two, on the back of my bicycle. "What do you want?" the police officer yelled at me, already irritated, as soon as I stopped. "I'm just watching," I said. "Just being a witness." I didn't yet own a phone that could record video. He took a few threatening steps toward me, yelling about what the fuck I thought I would do differently in his situation if I was so fucking smart. My son was scared and began to cry. The officer kept barking at me. When my son broke into a loud wail, I memorized the number on the back of the police van and left. I now wonder what I was going to do with that number—report the police to the police? By the time I got back to my apartment my hands were still shaking, I had forgotten the number, and I was dismayed with myself.

Refusing to collude in injustice is, I've found, easier said than done. Collusion is written onto our way of life, and nearly every interaction between white people is an invitation to collusion. Being white is easy, in that nobody is expected to think about being white, but this is exactly what makes me uneasy about it. Without thinking, I would say that believing I am white doesn't cost me anything, that it's pure profit, but I suspect that isn't true. I suspect whiteness is costing me, as Baldwin would say, my moral life.

And whiteness is costing me my community. It is the wedge driven between me and my neighbors, between me and other mothers, between me and other workers. I know there's more, too—I have written and erased a hundred sentences here, trying and failing to articulate something that I can sense but not yet speak. Like a bad loan, the kind in which the payments increase over time, the price of whiteness remains hidden behind its promises.

"Her choice to give up whiteness was a privilege," Michael Jeffries wrote of Dolezal in the *Boston Globe*. "If giving up whiteness is a privilege," Noel quipped to me, "what do you call hanging on to it?" As Dolezal surrendered her position in the NAACP and lost her teaching job, I thought of the white police officers who had killed unarmed black men and kept their jobs. That the penalty for disowning whiteness appears to be more severe than the penalty for killing a black person says something about what our culture holds dear.

◼ ◼

The moral concept of Schuld ("guilt"), Nietzsche observes, "descends from the very material concept of Schulden ('debts')." Material debt predates moral debt. The point he is making is that guilt has its source not in some innate sense of justice, not in God, but in something as base as commerce. Nietzsche has the kind of disdain for guilt that many people now reserve for "white guilt" in particular.

Even before I started reading Nietzsche, I had the uncomfortable suspicion that my good life, my house and my garden and the "good" public school my son attends, might not be entirely good. Even as I painted my walls and planted my tomatoes and attended parent-teacher conferences last year, I was pestered by the possibility that all this was built on a bedrock of evil, and that evil was running through our groundwater. But I didn't think in exactly those terms because the word *evil* is not usually part of my vocabulary—I picked it up from Nietzsche.

Evil is how slaves describe their masters. In Nietzsche's telling, Roman nobles called their way of life *good*, while their Jewish slaves called the same way of life *evil*. The invention of the concept of evil was, according to Nietzsche, a kind of power grab. It was an attempt by the powerless to undermine the powerful. More power to them, I think. But Nietzsche and I disagree on this, among other things. Like many white people, he regards guilt as a means of manipulation, a killjoy. Those who resent the powerful, he writes, use guilt to undermine their power and rob them of their pleasure in life. And this, I believe, is what makes guilt potentially redemptive.

Guilt is what makes a good life built on evil no longer good. I have a memory of the writer Sherman Alexie cautioning me against this way of thinking. I remember him saying something like, "White people do crazy shit when they feel guilty." That I can't dispute. Guilty white people try to save other people who don't want or need to be saved, they make grandiose empty gestures, they sling blame, they police the speech of other white people, and they dedicate themselves to the fruitless project of their own exoneration. But I'm not sure any of that is worse than the crazy shit white people do in denial. Especially when that denial depends on a constant erasure of both the past and the present.

Once you've been living in a house for a while, you tend to begin to believe that it's yours even though you don't own it yet. When those of us who are convinced of our own whiteness deny our debt, this may be the inevitable result of having lived for so long in a house bought on credit but never paid off. We ourselves have never owned slaves, we insist, and we never say *nigger*. "It is as though we have run up a credit-card bill," Coates writes, "and, having pledged to charge no more, remain befuddled that the balance does not disappear."

A guilty white person is usually imagined as someone made impotent by guilt, someone rendered powerless. But why not imagine guilt as a prod, a goad, as an impetus to action? Isn't guilt an essential cog in the machinery of the conscience? When I search back through my correspondence with Sherman Alexie, I can't find him saying anything about white people doing crazy shit, but I do find him insisting that we can't afford to disempower white people because we need them to empower the rest of us. White people, he proposes, have the political power to make change exactly because they are white.

I once feared buying a house because I didn't want to be owned.

I had saved money with no purpose in mind other than the freedom to do whatever I wanted. Now I'm bound to this house, though I'm still free to lose it if I choose. But that isn't the version of freedom that interests me at the moment. I'm more compelled by a freedom that would allow me to deserve what I have. Call it liberation, maybe. If debt can be repaid incrementally, resulting eventually in ownership, perhaps so can guilt.

What is the condition of white life? We are moral debtors who act as material creditors. Our banks make bad loans. Our police, like Nietzsche's creditors, act out their power on black bodies. And, as I see in my own language, we confuse whiteness with ownership—for most of us, the police aren't "ours" any more than the banks are. When we buy into whiteness, we entertain the delusion that we're business partners with power, not its minions. And we forget our debt to ourselves.

LEANDER

Joyce Carol Oates

THAT EVENING A lone white woman appeared diffidently at the rear of the small redbrick Hope Baptist Church on Armory Street, Hammond, New York. She took a seat in the last pew, near the center aisle and the front door. No one was near: no one glanced in her direction, at first.

Already there were forty or more people at the front of the church talking together with much animation. Everyone seemed to know everyone else: of course. The lone white woman understood that she was (perhaps) a curiosity to them: not only a white woman in a company of (mostly? entirely?) black- and brown-skinned persons but a woman with a very white skin, a porcelain sort of pallor that suggested recent illness, and stark-white hair to her shoulders, of a length uncommon in women her age. And though this woman was dressed inconspicuously in dark clothing it was evident that her clothes were not inexpensive, and that her manner lacked the ease and camaraderie of whites accustomed to black activist occasions. This white-skinned woman smiled in greeting to anyone who acknowledged her but her smile was over-eager, uncertain.

She'd rehearsed the way in which she would identify herself should anyone ask. *I am Jessalyn, I am interested in SaveOurLives and would like to help any way that I can. I—*

It would be a relief to her, yet a disappointment, when no one approached to ask her name.

Alone in the last pew of the little church the woman listened to a sequence of impassioned speeches from the pulpit. She was shocked, appalled: she'd had no idea that so many unarmed and defenseless individuals in inner-city Hammond, ranging in age from an eight-year-old boy to an eighty-six-year-old woman, had been shot by Hammond police officers within the past decade. So many deaths, so many shootings and woundings, and not a single conviction of any Hammond police officer! In fact, not a single indictment.

Not a single apology from the Hammond Police Department.

The minister of Hope Church spoke, gravely and with dignity. The head of a New York State youth training program spoke, vehemently. A young black lawyer spoke, his voice quavering with emotion. Mothers spoke, holding pictures of their murdered children. Some were tearful and tremulous and some were angry and resolute. Some could barely speak above a whisper and others raised their voices as if keening. Young dark-skinned men and boys had been assaulted by Hammond police in the greatest numbers but no one was exempt from police violence—women, girls, the elderly, and even the disabled—a nineteen-year-old Iraqi war veteran in a wheelchair, shot dead by police officers for seeming to "brandish" a weapon; a twelve-year-old boy Tasered into unconsciousness by police officers for "suspicious behavior"—fleeing a police cruiser that braked to a stop in the street.

Jessalyn listened with mounting despair. She would have liked to add her voice to these voices but she could not bring herself to speak.

Such sorrow in this gathering, she dared not appropriate it as anything of her own. Driving into the *inner city*, as it's euphemistically called, exiting the expressway into a neighborhood of old, crumbling brownstones and row houses, driving cautiously along narrow potholed streets lined with derelict vehicles, she'd felt like one descending in a bathosphere, into a twilit world in no way contiguous with her own affluent, suburban world at the periphery of the city. (Yes, she'd locked the doors of her car before exiting the expressway. If another had been present she'd have made an embarrassing remark, an awkward excuse—but she would have locked the doors nonetheless.)

Eyes on her were curious, inquisitive; not hostile if not (evidently) friendly. The tall grave minister smiled in her direction but rather stiffly, guardedly. *White lady? Why's she here?*

As it turned out there were several white- or very light-skinned individuals at the meeting. One of these was lanky limbed with hair tied back in a slovenly ponytail—for a moment Jessalyn thought this might be someone she knew, a friend of her son's. (It wasn't.) Another was a tall gray-mustached man in a Stetson hat, wearing a dark-rose embroidered shirt and a black string tie—gentlemanly, Hispanic, of her approximate age.

But the tall mustached man was involved in an intense conversation with several others and took no notice of the (white) woman at the rear of the church.

A sharp-voiced white woman sporting a mane of ashy-blond hair, in gaudy quiltlike clothes, actually turned to stare at Jessalyn, and to glare at her; here was a middle-aged Caucasian hippie-activist, contemptuous of the diffident white woman of a very different, genteel background.

Her friend at the gathering was a massive black woman with a stern face, who also turned to stare at Jessalyn. This woman had spoken at the pulpit in a fierce voice denouncing the "tradition" of white racism and white indifference to black victims dating back to pre–Civil War times.

Jessalyn had never seen so large a woman, and she had never seen anyone stare at her with such hostility. The woman was in her midforties, perhaps, weighing as much as three hundred pounds; she was at least six feet tall, and wore a sacklike article of clothing that fell loosely over her bulk; her legs were columnar, and her arms were masses of slack, pocked flesh. Her face was massive as well, yet sharper boned, like a carved totem, and her eyes were accusing. "Yes? Ma'am? What you wantin' with us, ma'am?"—she called to Jessalyn in a mocking voice loud and assured as a bugle.

Jessalyn was stricken with embarrassment. Like a guilty child she all but shrank in the pew. Why had she come to the Hope

Baptist Church, to intrude upon these people who knew one another intimately, and had no need of her? Badly she wished she
could escape. In a hoarse voice she managed to stammer that she'd
wanted to contribute to SaveOurLives but her words were too
faint to register with anyone.

Fortunately the massive glaring woman and her ashy-blond-
haired friend had lost interest in Jessalyn almost immediately.
Nor did anyone else take notice of her except, out of politeness, it
seemed, the minister of Hope Church, who smiled in her direction, and seemed uncertain whether he should approach her, or
take pity on her embarrassment and ignore her.

How thoughtless and foolish she'd been, Jessalyn thought. An affluent white woman, a resident of Old Farm Road, hoping to align
herself with inner-city African Americans who'd suffered at the hands
of white police officers, and through white indifference, countless
times: what had she been thinking? Her son would charge her with
white-liberal condescension. Her daughter would charge her with lu-
natic recklessness. If he'd been alive her husband would be speechless,
as deeply shocked by Jessalyn's behavior as if she'd set out deliberately
to upset him.

*That's a dangerous neighborhood. Why are you there? Why alone?
What on earth are you thinking?*

Yet, the minister decided to come to speak with her. He had a
wan, worn face, kindly eyes, his impatience with the awkward
white visitor seemed to vie with his natural courtliness. Jessalyn
saw that he was older than he'd appeared at the pulpit, her de-
ceased husband's age at least. *Maybe he knew Jonny. Maybe they'd
worked together and had been friends. . . .*

It was the most tenuous, the most pathetic, of hopes. But Jessalyn dared not suggest it. There were no words she could offer to
anyone in the little redbrick church, no attitude that was not in
some way condescending, or inadequate; ridiculous, self-serving,
and (unavoidably) racist. The massive stern-faced woman had
peered into her white, shallow soul and annihilated her.

Vaguely Jessalyn had intended to donate money to SaveOur-
Lives. For that purpose she'd brought along her checkbook. She

had no idea how much money to give: one thousand dollars? But she was thinking now that such a sum was too much, that it might surprise and offend these people; the massive woman would sneer at her, and the ashy-blond-haired woman would sneer at her, as a rich white woman who hoped to absolve herself of racial guilt by giving money. But was five hundred dollars too little? Was five hundred dollars both *too much* and *too little*?

In his will her husband had left thousands of dollars to Hammond charitable organizations with ties to the black, inner-city community; he and Jessalyn had donated to these, as to the NAACP, for years. But the donations had been impersonal, mediated. The donations had, in a sense, substituted for actual encounters, investigations of the inner city, attempts to become acquainted with, still less befriend, individuals who lived in the Armory Street neighborhood; they had been oblique assertions of power, of the power to be *charitable*, a virtue of the Christian church to which, at least officially, Jessalyn and her husband had belonged. (And of course, the donations were tax-exempt.)

But here in the Hope Baptist Church, Jessalyn was personally exposed. Her generosity, or lack of generosity, could not be disguised.

The kindly minister stooped over her, introduced himself, and shook Jessalyn's hand. He did not ask her name (she would recall later) but thanked her gravely for coming. He did ask if her car was parked near the church. Rapidly Jessalyn's mind was working: should she make out a check for seven hundred dollars? (Not much, but nothing she could give would add up to much. The racial situation in the city seemed all but hopeless, during the very reign of the first black president of the United States.) Jessalyn wanted to apologize to the gentlemanly black man for having so little to give: her husband had left her money constrained by the stipulations of a trust fund, to prevent her giving extravagant amounts of money away to causes like SaveOurLives. . . . But of course Jessalyn couldn't give such an excuse: it would seem to be blaming her husband, the most generous of men.

In the end, as the minister looked on with some embarrassment, Jessalyn hurriedly made out a check for fifteen hundred dollars to SaveOurLives. It was more than she could afford this quarter but she could not explain that. Her face burned with shame, discomfort. "Ma'am, thank you!"—the minister smiled and blinked at her in genuine surprise, and shook her hand another time.

He had seemed to like her, at least. She felt a faint thrill at the touch of his hand, his long fingers closing upon hers, unusually long fingers, they seemed to her, with pale undersides; strong fingers, surely, but their grip of the (white) woman's hand was tentative, fleeting.

By this time the others, at the front of the church, speaking intensely together, had forgotten Jessalyn utterly.

The minister walked her to the door of the church, which he pushed open for her, as if to make sure that she left. In some magical way, a click of the long deft fingers, perhaps, he'd summoned a boy named Leander to "walk this lady to her car, please"—that happened to be in the parking lot of the Hammond Public Library just three blocks away.

Tall, spindly-limbed Leander was polite, taciturn with the (white) woman with long, shoulder-length strikingly white hair. He had not ever seen anyone quite like her close up—(was that possible?). He hadn't balked at the minister's request though clearly he was not thrilled with it. As he escorted Jessalyn to her car she tried to make conversation with him but he replied in mumbles— *Yes'm. N'm.* He was about the age of her eldest grandson, she gauged; though, in fact (she had to concede), she had no idea how old Leander might be, a teenager, or in his twenties, his skin was so dark and his features so—unusual—unfamiliar?—in her eyes.

To white police officers, black boys invariably looked older than their age, and larger than they actually were. Jessalyn had never quite understood this before.

■ ■

The thought came to her, both exciting and distressing—*Should I give Leander something? But—of course not. I should not.*

He would be embarrassed by the gesture. Possibly, insulted. (Would he?)

At her car Jessalyn thanked Leander for his kindness. Leander did not linger as if he expected anything more than thanks but muttered *Yes'm* and quickly edged away.

She could call after him—but she did not.

Of course, she *should not*.

In her car, at once she locked the doors. The parking area behind the library was lighted and there were a half dozen vehicles still in the lot since the library was open until nine p.m., but still her heart was beating rapidly as if she'd narrowly avoided a terrible danger.

How easily she might have given Leander a twenty-dollar bill—she would have liked to, badly; and the boy would have appreciated it.

Yet he might have been insulted by a tip. (He had acted out of kindness, not for a tip.) (She knew this: yet, knowing it, could she not in any case have given him a twenty-dollar bill as an acknowledgment of his kindness, and *not a tip*?)

"But when is a tip not a tip? Is a tip always a tip? Is there no escaping—*tip*? If you are *white*?"

There was something debasing in the very word *tip*. Flippant, insulting. No one wants a *tip*.

By the time Jessalyn arrived at the large, darkened house on Old Farm Road she was feeling very tired. Disgust and depression commingled in an ashy taste at the back of her mouth. The drive from Armory Street in downtown Hammond to Old Farm Road, North Hammond, that should have taken no more than twenty-five minutes at this hour of the day required nearly twice that long for her; in the haze of a steadily increasing headache pain she'd stared through the windshield at the highway as if she'd never seen it before. She was assailed by a dread of taking a wrong exit and becoming hopelessly lost in the very place in which she'd lived most of her adult life.

The fact was, she'd rarely driven into Hammond, and never at night; returning home from an event in the city, her husband had always driven.

And how dark Old Farm Road was, without streetlights! Set on large three- and four-acre lots, the houses here were spaced apart; the driveways were so long, like the graveled drive to Jessalyn's house, you could barely see the houses from the road. *Of course, it is a white enclave. Strangers are not welcome here after dark or before.*

■ ■

"Leander?"—in the morning and for many mornings in succession the name came to her, a mysterious name, it seemed, beautiful and strange and yet tinged with regret, reproach.

She had to think for a moment, before recalling why.

FAULT LINES

Ru Freeman

Mira

She crosses the street, comes up to me, bold as a rabbit in predator-purged territory, ferret-like herself, well-trained suburban calling card on a leash beside her, and asks me, right in front of all the other mothers, if I'm *looking for more work as a nanny.*

The other women have already recoiled, not from her, so much, as from the response they now know to expect from me, their one (fill in your chosen blank) friend. Perhaps at some primeval level they feel more sorry for her than horrified for me. It's too early, even for me. I choose clarity.

—Did you feel entitled to ask me that because I'm the only brown person standing here?

My daughters press against my body on either side, comprehending only its hardness, that chain mail that descends, the armor tossed as though from the hands of a benevolent deity all haste and consternation as he rushes through neighborhoods intuiting coming events casting shadows in each set of eyes that hood, each set of lips pursing its contents, that look that is turned inward asking: Is this it? Is this time for The Crazy Black Man/Woman or is there some mitigating element that must be considered? Time of day? Circumstance? A wrinkle or a smile? What other pressing duty calls that cannot now be derailed with a reaction or a rant? I feel their arms wrap, one higher, one lower, around my thighs, feel the pale strength of them, and do not move my own, crossed, waiting, face-off. Silence, and then the chug of the yellow bus coming up the road toward us, its sunshine color stippled by the old oaks that arch overhead and touch each other the way we neighbors will never do. She steps off the street and onto the pavement beside us, lingers there, lost in the shuffle of rituals in which she has no part, while we hustle our children inside and break into our directional cliques, leaving.

—I cannot believe

—What nerve

—Are you okay?

Ah, the vernacular of suburbia where we reserve our epithets for colleagues at workplaces where most of us are overpaid, for politicians we imagine give a damn about our vote, and for grouped people—the "those" of our stories—all the absent ones who need never feel nor fear our low-motility seeds of wrath. In the day-to-day, though, that's a different kettle of gefilte, that's a farce called civility, where the only people hurting are the ones who are hoping you might say fuck, just once, on their behalf. You're the one wearing whiteface after all. Fuck you, fuck off, fucking moron, any of those would do. I don't need the potluck or the block party, just give one flying fuck. Say it loud and clear.

I'm the last mother to reach her house, the farthest from the stop. The chatter of the Friedman toddlers catches up just as I reach my door, and I glance back for a moment to watch the double baby carriage making its vertiginous climb up the slope toward me. I make eye contact with the woman who shares no facial features with her four wards, but can only manage a commiserating grimace; I've got my own grievance to nurse today.

Iris

Iris Jones works down the street at the house with the sagging gutters and the haphazardly tended garden where the remains of the last tree felled are still being carted away, a few small logs at a time, by the neighbors who have begun to use their outdoor fire pits as they watch the first bulbs bloom along the edges of their own flower beds. There are six children there to fill up the three bedrooms of the house, the fifth still swaddled and kept beside his mother who is pregnant with the last. Iris manages the older four, all girls, aged six, five, three, and two. They are well behaved and expectant of an excess of attention in all aspects of their lives from baths to play to reading to naps, which they take religiously from one to three each afternoon.

Iris arrives by six in the morning. She passes Geraldo's Laundromat (where someone has pulled off various letters so it now read's Geraldo's Lat), two shops with wigs on display in colors that God never intended for human heads, and a salon with the "Nails" sign illuminated whether it is open or shut on her way to her transport. As she walks to the stop at Ridge and Susquehanna, she thinks about the fact that the prayers from four churches— Church of God of Prophesy, Jones Tabernacle AME Church, Bethel Presbyterian Church, and Faith Emanuel Baptist Church— always surround her as she stands within sight of her sons' high school, waiting for the 61. Each morning, just before the bus arrives, she turns toward the school and bends her head as she mentally gathers the prayers of all four churches to help keep her children safe until she returns. She boards the bus and nods to the same eleven people who are already sitting in their preferred places—only one, a teenage girl, chooses the aisle—changes to the 65 at the Wissahickon Transportation Center, and tries not to fall asleep before her stop at Bryn Mawr and City Line, where she gets off. It takes her 572 steps from there to reach the house on Upland Terrace. She lets herself in and hangs up her coat on the metal rack near the *ketubah*, which, according to the translation offered to her by Chana, tells the world that Yitzak Friedman and Chana Salzburg were married on the twenty-fourth of July, 2009. Every morning Iris does the same math and shakes her head, then changes the motion to a nod because Yitzak is always watching her from the dining table where he is already sitting down, drinking coffee and reading the Holy Book. In the kitchen that she is allowed to use, she makes herself a cup of tea and a slice of toast, and sets out breakfast for the children, each according to their taste; melon and yogurt for Acimah, banana and yogurt for Arashel, soft buttered white bread with the lightest touch of peach jam for Astera, and oatmeal for Aaliyah.

Upstairs, she wakes each one with soft words or stern, as required, and gets them washed, brushed, and dressed in time for them to kiss their father good-bye before he walks out of the house, still carrying the Holy Book, and, as far as Iris can tell, intending to do so all day long wherever he goes, as he does, each day, on foot. By the time their mother comes down, slowly, slowly, holding the banister with one hand, her baby clutched in her other arm, Iris has prepared breakfast for her and turns her back and does the dishes while Chana nurses her baby and feeds herself. Iris cleans and dresses the baby—and for the baby Iris has soft words and baby songs in unfamiliar yet melodious rhythms—while Chana gets dressed.

At around eight-thirty in the morning Iris pushes a double stroller down the middle of the street, the five- and the six-year-olds tagged on either side like long ribbons, and refuses to move for cars no matter how long and how hard they toot their horns, or how much their drivers yell out their windows. The ladies at the bus stop roll their eyes at her because Iris's stroller, arriving on its unpredictable schedule, delays the departure of the school bus, though the Jamaican bus driver with the wild hair who drives both the kindergartners and the high schoolers—and who insists that the boys in both groups wait until the girls have finished boarding, and also that they stop and greet him before they proceed to take their seats, quirks that generate smiles from the younger and half smiles from the older—never seems to mind waiting and watching Iris's progress down the road, which makes the mothers at the bus stop turn and gaze, like choreographed bit-part players in a drama where all of them tried and none of them made the leads, at Iris, and they cannot help but notice her stunning derriere, so they redo their ponytails and adjust their fitted baseball caps and blow extra-special kisses at their wee ones already distracted and otherwise engaged with the particular hierarchies arranged to terrify those consigned to riding public school buses. Only Mira smiles at Iris, though Iris remains oblivious to this virtual high-five as she wends her way toward the Bala Cynwyd Library, her thoughts on matters far more pertinent to her day-to-day than the shape of her arse or the politics of her audience.

By the time she is boarding the 65 for her return home, Iris has chalked up between twelve and sixteen thousand steps, which might have registered on her Fitbit or her iPhone if she possessed either one, but which register only on her veined calves, tight and raised like thin vagrant snakes. Iris also works until after dinner on Saturdays because on those days the Friedman family observes Shabbat and the laws of halacha, and would sit hungry in the darkness if not for her, and since she cannot leave until the ritual Havdalah is completed, Iris has come to associate the sour-sweet smell of wine and smoke and cinnamon with her long-awaited single day of freedom. On Saturdays the children are whiny and difficult because they are managed entirely by their parents in a routine neither side of the equation recognizes nor enjoys. (This does not make Iris feel special or loved.)

Before leaving her house in the Strawberry Mansions neighborhood of Philadelphia, she wakes up her son, Diem, sixteen.

—Baby, it's five I've got to go now. Wake your brothers at six. You be home right after school.

—Okay, Mom. Lock the door.

Then he goes back to sleep and doesn't wake until six-thirty and has to scream his brothers awake and through their corn-flakes and milk (if there is milk, dry if there isn't), and race out of the door to their school, which is just far enough that they are tired by the time they reach it, but too close for them to qualify for busing, and if there are blues out they have to slow to a stroll, which makes them late and gets them face time with teachers and the vice principal but never the principal, who has too many fires to put out to be bothered with these four smoldering pieces of coal. No matter how frantic their morning becomes, or how late they are—not even that time that he had to piggyback his youngest brother, Ozzie, all the way to school because he tripped right outside their door and bloodied both knees, or even the time that his second youngest brother, Jayjo, refused to go to school because he had not studied for his English test and swore that Mr. Bomze hated him and Diem had to drag Jayjo out and cuff his head and force-march him until he was within sight of the first teacher— Diem never forgets to stop and lock the door.

Gabriella

You never think that things will turn out as badly or as well. When you turn sixteen and you have no boyfriend and you are not pregnant and everyone says—yes, even Abuela, who has had you pegged as a *malparida* since you were seven years old and lifted your dress in front of the whole school while singing the national anthem—that you've beaten the odds and broken the family tradition of being knocked up before your *quinceañera*, you want to believe it. You stroke your flat belly and then you go and get one of those diamond-dust studs put in your navel, the type that has the thin dangling gold chain that points toward your not-available *cuca*, because you want to show it off. How off-limits you are, how you are not like the rest of the Roman sisters, or your mother, or your aunts, particularly not Titi Maria who was pregnant at four-teen, fourteen! or even your grandmother. The thing is that you put a sweet chain like that, which cost all your *quinceañera* money, in your belly button, your sweet diving-pool belly button, and the only thing you want to do is show it off. So you stop listening to the family chorus and you wear nothing but crop tops and low-rise shorts and jeans, and skirts with the waist rolled down, and you are just like all the stupid girls with tats that you scorned be-cause oh my god they carved the names of boyfriends and hearts between their breasts and on the skin over the angel-wing bones on their backs and could never after be seen in real clothes, only T-back tops and V-necked T-shirts that were not T-shirts, who were they kidding, they were whore-halters.

Ricardo said it was the jewelry in your middle that made him love you so much. That made him love you and bump into you in the hallways so he could see how the gold chain swung against your beautiful skin like a pendulum. So what if you had to spend junior year sitting sideways at your desk, and pretending you didn't notice Mr. Bomze staring at your ballooning chest all through English class, and you had to take the diamond-dust stud and its gold chain out, and you didn't get to graduate because whatever the hell that felt like, Luis is fifteen and Ricardo still treats you like you were already born a *princesa* before he made you his queen with all of that loving.

And now, after all these years, you might even get a nursing certificate or something in the medical field that you could use from the Philadelphia College of Osteopathic Medicine which is around the corner from your job, so close that you could go there after work. That's what Iris said when she handed you the brochure that she had brought home from the library near where she works. At first you had laughed because those brochures were not there at the library near where Ricardo works at the high school and where you have waited for him before on the evenings when he's taken you to watch Luis run at the track meets—and you love watching Luis run because his feet move as though god himself has taught him how to walk on air, but you don't mention this part to Iris because none of her boys can run—though both libraries belong to the same district and maybe, you joked, it was because that library was filled with *morenos* just like the community swimming pool near there, and maybe nobody wanted to encourage those people to go back to school. But Iris did not laugh. She just said, You got your GED, now give them a call. It's time.

And you felt sorry and made a tray of *asado de puerco* for her to take home because even though her boy, Diem, had also applied for the same program, only Luis was accepted and now Luis lives at the ABC house, not too far from where you both work, and is learning to tread water, he says, at the private pools of his friends' homes in the better neighborhoods because he goes to their school now, where he has a brand-new MacBook Pro computer for free like all the other students, and tutors and special attention because he is going to be A Success Story. That is what the program director had told you when you hugged him and cried when you had to leave him there and go home.

Of course Abuela scoffed. They want to take my boy (she calls Luis her boy even though you were the one who gave birth to him and she was so disappointed in you that she still only speaks indirectly to you), they want to take my boy and put him in the rich people's school so they can show off how rich schools can help poor kids? Why not give some of that money to *his* school so *all* the kids in the school can have what they have?

And you want to explain to her, the way the program director had explained to you, that it was not just money in poor schools but the *environment* that made the difference, that your community and your family and your general *trajectory* was what was holding kids like Luis back, but you couldn't get your tongue adjusted around all those words. So you don't say anything, because you know she'd just say *¡Vete a la mierda!* and make you feel stupid for having had the nerve to address her, but also because Ricardo is looking at you with that *I told you so* gleam and sucking his back teeth and so you just do the same and look away because you agree. You agree that there was nothing wrong with your community and your family and your *trajectory*. You got pregnant and you did the right thing and so did Ricardo and you got married and you had both always done the best you could for all your children. And if you were asked, you'd even say you were doing your best for theirs because how would Mira keep her job that takes her all over creation doing god knows what, and how would Ari (which is short for Aristides), keep his, that pays not only for his second family but also for his first, which comes with not one but two daughters in college on the other side of the country and a son and don't even get you started on the first wife who drives the car with the top rolled down every time she pulls out of her double driveway two doors from her ex-husband's house, the one she bought— so Mira says— just to spite him.

It makes you happy-sad-angry to hear about all the wonderful teachers, most of whom are male, in the school that Luis goes to over past City Line Avenue, when neither Rosita nor Ricky Junior have teachers like that because they still go to the school that Diem and his brothers do on this side, and the only male is the principal who is a *hijo de puta* who always stares at your chest and tells you how pretty Rosita is. You stay silent and you think that maybe they, too, will get to go to the other school and live in a house with tutors and all you can do is pray that they'll last, beautiful as they are—with Ricardo's eyes and your mouth and color—without babies to be looked after before they have finished being yours.

Mrs. Petralia, who prefers to be called Mira, is happy to hear that you are going to try to go back to school, though she insists she cannot manage without you because she and Ari are so busy all the time and her children need you.

—Ephie and Athena are so used to you being here when they come home from school, Gabby. How will we manage without you?

—The girls are old enough now, they will be all right.

You say that and it sounds heartless, and you know that it is probably not true—the only person those girls see reliably is you—but what else can you say? You are hoping that Ricardo will be able to find you work in the cafeteria at the middle school which would pay you more than you make now taking care of the Petralia children and then you could look at all the classes you might need to finish if you want to take this osteopathic medicine business seriously. You'd prefer the high school because then, like Ricardo, you'd get to see Luis every now and again as he walks through the halls or goes to the locker rooms after school to change for track, even if, like Ricardo, you would not wave, or meet his eyes, or in any way acknowledge any relationship even though that would be almost impossible for you, you'd do it, you're sure you would. Still, despite all that longing for what you really want, you know you will take what you can get because, as Iris says, *it is time*.

But it doesn't work out that way. That's the thing about things never being as bad or as good. Ephie breaks her foot so you have to keep working and now you have more hours, and enough money so you can call up the school and see what classes you might be able to take there, but too many late nights which means you obviously cannot enroll at the Philadelphia College of Osteopathic Medicine which does not sound like the kind of place that would make allowances for students like you. And you tell yourself it's all right. Because the middle school didn't have a vacancy anyway. And you should be paying more attention to Rosita, she is *that age*, as Abuela keeps saying, and *madre de dios* you do not want Rosita to have to drop out of school, even the same subpar school you went to, and isn't life like this anyway? And isn't family like this? What does it matter if only one of your children gets to go to the rich people's school, and if only one of you gets to watch your son in these last few years before he leaves home, and if only one of the females in your family finishes high school, when you put it all together aren't you A Success Story too?

Mira

The next time I see her I cross the road at the last minute and then I occupy the whole pavement with my stride so that she has to step off, hound and all, her eyes darting away from my stare. For the next few weeks, whenever she sees me on the road, she turns around and scurries back the way she came, her backside all flab and sway in her hurry. It isn't enough for me. Somehow she has crept under my skin and try as I might I cannot find the needlepoint tool with which to pry her out. The needlepoint tool with which to wound her in the precise measurement with which she wounded me.

Nanny. It's not that I haven't heard it before, or recognized it in the pass-over looks that I get from the mothers and fathers in this neighborhood. This neighborhood where every mother's son on a bike appears to be training for the Tour de France, every runner hooked up to the breast milk of ever-present bottles of water, suckling like pigs, every new mother doubling as a yogini. At the high school pool I was asked by a woman all diamond tennis bracelet and straw hat if I, too, was from Jamaica *like my friend's nanny*. I'd had afternoon sex, so I spoke upscale suburban and sailed on seemingly unscathed. But this one, this canine-led hussy and her words, just won't let me be. I lie awake at night counting the ways. I wake up ragged. I walk to the bus stop rearing for battle.

Things take time, but if you remain alert, the moment arrives.

Pescatore is still too new for a liquor license, and the fish is foul, but the desserts are worth the price of admission. I know the moment I walk in that this is it. There she sits, paramour or husband beside her, friends and their possessives surrounding. Here I sit, my own man, my friends and their partners surrounding. Each of us couples brought a bottle—Ari and I, two, since this had been our idea—and we carried it back out in our bodies. We all howled with laughter on our way home, drunk in ways that alcohol alone cannot arrange.

We paid our check and then waited until she had returned from the bathroom to send the note on the napkin over to her with the dregs of each of our bottles of wine contained in a glass with a lipstick stain on it. *Are you looking for more clients? My friend is also interested. Maybe after dessert?* Definitely not a paramour with her, definitely a husband; only a husband in good standing would assume betrayal, not insult. So it wasn't the fuck I so often want to hear from them, but it'll do; solidarity speaks many dialects.

Gabby has fallen asleep on the couch by the time we get back and I'm exultant so I laugh her awake, pay her double, and offer her Ari—still smiling, but also shaking his head, he's too drunk—to drive her home.

—No, it's all right, *gracias*, Ricardo will come and pick me up. He doesn't like me getting into another man's car. Even Mr. Petralia.

—It's a long way for him to drive. I can take you. Will he let me drive you home?

On the way back we talk about Ephie, and the injury. I ask her about the College of Osteopathic Medicine, whether she is still hoping to go. She says that she might think about it after her younger son and daughter are out of high school. For now, she'd like to stay close to home to make sure she can keep an eye on them. Her best friend's son was accused of dealing and thrown out of school.

—He didn't do anything. He's like gold, that boy. He takes care of his brothers all day while his mother works at the Friedman house as a nanny. Bad things happen even to the good kids.

—Friedmans? They live down the street? Five kids and the mother is pregnant? That's *your* friend who looks after those children?

—Iris, yes.

—Iris. I see her taking those children somewhere every morning.

—To the library. Iris likes the library.

—Maybe you should take Ephie and Athena there too?

—For what? Your house has books in every room! Maybe Iris should just bring the children there instead.

She doesn't join me when I laugh. Ricardo opens the door as soon as we pull into the driveway leading to the flat ranch-style house with its aluminum siding, the tiny square footage of its front yard fenced as though to protect something precious. Gabby calls out that it was only I who drove her back, and he nods and holds the door open for her. I get out of the car to prove my gender, shake his hand. He mentions the time and I feel reprimanded. I tell her to take the day off, that I will stay home with Ephie. The door shuts softly behind them. I wait until the thin porch goes dark and back out without turning on my lights.

Ari is asleep when I get back, the dank smell of alcohol rising from his body. In the cooled stale air of the bedroom, I feel nauseous. I go through the mail downstairs, pick up a few things, make lists, waiting for fatigue to find me. It is nearly dawn by the time I lie down on the couch next to the boxes I've filled with books for Gabby's family. I hope they are age appropriate. I fall asleep between figuring out how to ask the ages of her children and consternation that I do not know. Perhaps Ari does. If nothing else she could share them with her friend Lily, who must surely have a few children of her own.

Iris

He was late for all the same reasons he was late each day, he was running for all the same reasons he ran each day: he overslept, his brothers dallied, he had to make sure the door was locked.

When Iris got the call on her cell phone, it came from the principal. She dried her hands before she answered. She hung up the phone, finished getting the children dressed, set them at the dining table with coloring books and puzzles, changed the baby—though this morning she had no coos for her and her voice was low but not gentle—washed the dishes, and waited until Chana had finished breakfast to ask her for the rest of the day off.

—What's the matter? Are you sick?

—Yes.

—Is it the flu? Hold on just a minute. Chana got up and poured four glasses of orange juice, then added Emergen-C into each cup and handed them to her children before returning to the kitchen. Iris leaned against the fridge and waited.

—I feel dizzy and my chest hurts. I need to go home and lie down.

—You can lie down here. Chana gestured to the living room couch. She looked both concerned and distracted, her mind elsewhere.

—No, I need to go home.

Inconvenience was mentioned, and poor timing. How would Chana get to her mothers' meeting? There was a well-baby checkup later today too, and now she'd have to postpone it. Was she *sure*, Chana asked, was Iris *certain* it wasn't just fatigue? Perhaps a cup of tea, a little sitting down, might help. Hypochondria was suggested. A previous lapse in duty just like this was brought up. That was an illness associated with the personal interview that had been requested by the school guidance counselor after Diem had applied for the ABC program; school conferences and domestic emergencies were never mentioned by Iris; as far as Chana knew—nothing asked, even less volunteered—Iris lived alone and had no family to speak of. Still, when Iris began to wheeze, Chana hurried her out of the house and assured her that she wouldn't dock her a day's pay after all. Whether that registered as a saving grace on Iris, Chana could not tell. (It did not.)

The younger boys were called in to testify that, yes, indeed, they had made their brother late. Additionally, they said, they were often guilty of this because though he woke them up with due diligence at six each morning, they dawdled. It was not his fault. Why had he been running away from school rather than toward it, the blue asked, his belt, buckles, holster, and badge all gleaming and potent.

—I had to lock the door.

And Iris bowed her head, remembering. Once, just once, that door had been left unlocked. And as if he had been waiting all these years, watching the door for just that very day, Susa had come in, sat down, and waited for her to come home. Susa, whom she managed to forget each time she turned away from her boys and their milk-added coffee skin, but only then. Later, after he'd left, she had let her sons out of the room in which their father had locked them, and all night long Diem had tended her bruises. All night, without a single tear on either side, only the silence of alliance and resolve.

She asked, but only the science teacher—a new recruit already harried but clearly still hopeful of great undertakings—spoke on his behalf.

Gabby came with her some evenings to visit Diem. Some days she went alone, or Gabby sent Ricardo. Between the three of them, they did not miss a single day. At first, Iris's younger sons set an alarm and walked slowly and on time to school, but eventually only Ozzie kept trying. He wanted to be able to say that his brother did not have to worry about him anymore. One day, when Diem was allowed to come home. One day.

Gabriella

Your son walks into the house where you work and you say nothing. How could you not have known that somehow this whole thing couldn't work the way it was supposed to? You had done all the right things. You had not gone back after dropping him at the house, you never called him, you waited for him to call you, and when he visited you did not send him back with the kinds of gifts that you wanted to because you knew he had to cultivate different tastes now and you didn't want to remind him of the things he loved and missed with all his might. You had praised Ricardo each time he came home and said he'd seen Luis and had managed to turn away from your son, giving nothing away. Instead,

you had held him close, and pretended that it was not longing for
Luis but desire for you that was weighing his body down, and you
told him again and again that it was best, it was only four years
and then you would both have your son back for good.

But then you come back from picking up the girls at the bus
stop and you see him sitting at the dining table with Ari's son,
and you hear him talking in a way you don't recognize but can't
help but admire, and it is not your mouth but your hands that
betray you. You cannot help it. You reach out and you stroke his
head, and Theo laughs.

And you wouldn't have minded the laugh, you even smiled at
the sound of it, withdrawing your hand, folding the memory of
that silken hair into your palm as stealthy as a card shark, but then
Luis turns and sees you and he swears. He swears at you in language you will never repeat to Ricardo because you cannot break
Ricardo's fierce, strong heart that has loved you so well for so
long, right from the beginning, words that rise before your eyes
and blur as you see them written in letters as big as the sign outside the Faith Emanuel Baptist Church that you go to each Sunday, the one with the glassed-in sign that says in elegant font that
Jesus Loves You and that *It Is Not Too Late To Repent.* And how is it
that instead of lifting your hand and striking your son so he can
never speak to you again, his shame would be so great, his re-
morse so bottomless, how is it that you remember to cover Ephie's
ears? How is it that you can even think about the fact that Ephie
speaks Spanish almost as fluently as your own daughter, not because she has been born with your language ringing in her ears
but because she listens to language tapes that come in shrink-
wrapped yellow boxes, and spends her summers at camps where
they only speak to her in Spanish? How is it that you forget that
Theo, too, whose accomplishments were chosen and paid for by the
same father, must once have attended those same camps?

You take the girls into the kitchen and you only half listen
because what more is there to listen to?

—I can't believe she touched you! My father is fucking crazy to
have her around. C'mon man, let's go over to my mom's house.

And you think about that, about this business of having two houses and two sets of parents and two lives and you wonder if that is what makes people like Mira and Ari happy, the way they can separate what should be inseparable so easily and so neatly, like yolks from whites, and you wonder if Ephie and Athena ever think about that, about how their father once loved someone other than their mother, and whether that bothers them at all. You think about Theo and if he even thinks of Mira as a mother at all. You think about all kinds of things, but you don't think about what Luis has said, or the way the brush of his hair has stained your palm with a feeling you cannot rub out, a feeling you neither want to remember nor forget.

■ ■

At the library Iris picks up two sets of whatever brochures have been set out; for night classes, technical training, online colleges, language instruction, book groups, and summer programs for teenagers that combine sports, reading, and mathematics. She shares them with Gabby.

Iris keeps her set beside her bed and never opens them; they are a decoration.

Gabby flips through her brochures each night, and each night in rotation she pictures a new life that she might make, a life where nothing that should be together is ever pulled apart.

Across the line that divides the city, before turning out the lights for bed, Mira flips through catalogs for described clothing and other frivolities, dog-earing the pages that catch her eye.

Each woman dreams of purchases none of them will ever make. In their various beds, some hard, some soft, differently lonely, their children dream too.

WE SHARE THE RAIN,
AND NOT MUCH ELSE

Timothy Egan

FOR A TIME, I worked as a longshoreman in Seattle, during the twilight of an era when union workers could afford second homes on Puget Sound and no one ever asked you where you went to school. Pre–Microsoft boom, late Boeing bust. The hometown company—the Lazy B, it was called—had laid off more than sixty thousand workers in the early 1970s, almost two thirds of its peak payroll, prompting a billboard plea: "Will the last person leaving Seattle turn out the lights?" But here's the thing: not that many people left. The place was just too damn beautiful, surrounded by water and forests; on a clear day you could see three national parks from the top deck of the Space Needle. People "reinvented" themselves, though that term was not in vogue. It didn't take much to cover your nut, working part-time-this or helping-out-with-that, and the views, of course, were free. As always, being out on the far western edge, caressed by sea breezes born in some mid-Pacific tempest, was a recipe for possibility.

I wasn't a real blue-collar worker. I knew the gig was temporary. I had plans, vague and half shaped, but I knew I would not be using my back as a wrench or my hands as claws. I was studying Irish history at the University of Washington, and on select days my buddy and I would skip our classes and go down to the hiring hall at dawn, a block from the waterfront. We had used a connection to get on the union extra board, no small thing. If our names got called, we would work a shift offloading crap from

Asia, and a week later get a paycheck for that single day that was enough to cover a month's rent, and put a dent into quarterly tuition, which was even less. Hooboy—I always felt rich.

The scruff is gone from Elliott Bay, as is the union hall where we waited in folding chairs on a peeling linoleum floor. On a clear day, if you squint, you can still see a longshoreman or -woman, laboring in the shadow of a giant Ferris wheel, not far from the new offices of Expedia. When people talk about a city's soul, I think of those jobs, even though offloading container cargo is no more noble than steering people online to a chain hotel with free breakfast. Nor should we believe that a "working waterfront," to be authentic, must involve grease and sweat and people who didn't learn how to swear by watching movies about Wall Street. Whether we're in the market for cars from Japan or window seats on airplanes, somebody has to move the levers.

What was important about those jobs—what's lost in the new Seattle and all the other gilded brain capitals prospering in their lovely settings—is that they used to give longshore workers equal footing with citizens laboring in offices overlooking the sound. Today—forget about buying a getaway cabin with earnings from the dock, even at almost $80,000 a year in base pay. That kind of salary will not get you into one of the starter homes being bid up by people fleeing the $1 million tag for a leaky shack in the Bay Area.

Walk up the hill from the waterfront, past a place that used to have a six a.m. happy hour and another address that was a refuge for sailors called the Catholic Seamen's Club, and you find a town with barely a trace of its odiferous past. Looming among the other new buildings that snag the clouds is one that tourists take selfies in front of—the home for the fictional Master of the Universe in *Fifty Shades of Grey*. Our main pop cultural reference used to be *Sleepless in Seattle*, starring a houseboat community that was built, years earlier, by beats, banjo pluckers, and barroom socialists. Bohemians, I think they were called—another lost word.

For most of Seattle's history, when politicians came to town they held huge open rallies—Teddy Roosevelt on the waterfront, Bill Clinton at the Pike Place Market, a very young Barack

Obama at Garfield High School, whose former students included Quincy Jones and Jimi Hendrix. Now the politicians zoom through the city in a security cocoon to a rich person's home, Seattle as an ATM. The public, regular folks, are not engaged.

To lament the past is a perilous thing. Revisionism is only half right, at best. The easy mistake is to think it was always better *back then*, the past that brushes out racial segregation, closeted sexual lives, no cure for polio. Life was harder, surely, when women washed clothes on scruffy boards. And life is easier, surely, when most people have all the world's knowledge in the palm of their hand, at the swipe of a screen. But the past in Seattle—which is really nothing in the scheme of things, considering that the city is not even two centuries old—had a golden postwar period when people without college degrees, or GIs returning home after defeating Hitler, could live well, in the same neighborhoods as the swells. That past cannot be restored.

So when I walk the streets of the town where I was born, wading through the Amazon.com jungle that has replaced body shops and antique stores and affordable brick apartments, I try to restrain the nostalgic impulse. Those Amazon jobs pay well, though not enough to make a brogrammer feel as princely as the longshoreman once did. Better to have something new century than the ghosts that haunt Detroit. The way I try to make peace with the new era, knowing that the gulf between the rich and everybody else grows by the day, is to see some of Seattle's egalitarian essence in the new.

The city was one of the first to pass a law phasing in a fifteen-dollar minimum wage. Several years in, the sky did not fall, jobs did not flee, though you might pay an extra twenty-five cents for a fast-food burger. Not far from Amazon is the Bill and Melinda Gates Foundation, a hive of people working start-up hours to bring clean water to African villages and an end to diseases that no longer kill people in the developed world. We burned with envy—some of us, at least—when Microsoft was turning out millionaires by the boatload. But now, look! There are those same tech titans, late middle-aged and soft around the middle, trying to figure out how to give away more money than any private entity has ever attempted to do. A bit of the old socialist DNA, which manifested itself when Seattle became the only American city to stage a general strike in 1919, was alive among the billionaire class.

The things that give people a sense of belonging to their city, free for the asking, are still here. Those three national parks, visible as before from the Space Needle, are surrounded by public land that is the birthright of any citizen. You want to experience true wealth? Walk in a forest of five-hundred-year-old cedars, your land, a few miles from the city's edge. The public schools work, off and on, and there are ongoing crusades to make sure they remain at least a peripheral concern of the same people who attend those fund-raisers for liberal Democrats.

On the downside, the University of Washington is no longer cheap; no secondary school in America is. If college is still the best elevator to the middle class, crippling debt is the price of the ride upward. Once, well before my time, the UW was free. Why not go back to that future? Didn't somebody from Vermont run for president on that idea? I doubt if there are many people who dip their toes in the two worlds, the docks and the gothic towers of the university. Too bad. I learned as much from the people at one place as I did at the other. And they paid me for the education.

BLOOD BROTHER

Sarah Smarsh

YOUR BROTHER HAS A HOLE on the inside of each arm that never quite closes. A blood tap, really, like an oil well for drilling. He is a tall, strong man in his early thirties—an ideal source for plasma.

A woman calls his name. She takes his temperature and blood pressure. He gets to skip the full-blown health screening since he's been coming here twice a week for almost ten years. She pricks his finger to make sure his blood is okay today.

Some of the other regulars take iron pills for fear they'll get anemic and be turned away. There's a weight minimum of 110 pounds, so the smallest, frailest women, sometimes elderly or underfed or both, put on extra clothes or wear ankle weights to pass.

A technician wearing a white lab coat, a name tag, and a clear plastic shield over her face puts a needle in one of your brother's inner-arm holes. He's in a "donating bed," a high-tech recliner of sorts that elevates the legs and leans him way back.

Rows of these chairs on the donor floor hold people whose faces he sometimes recognizes. They look at cell phones, magazines, or televisions hanging from the ceiling while maroon fluid drains from their veins. Some of them are homeless. Some of them are like your brother: college graduates with beat-up cars, insurmountable credit-card debt, federal and private student loans. The state university where he worked and borrowed his way through undergraduate degrees is just four blocks away. Plasma centers like to set up shop near universities, where the blood is young and the wallets are light.

When your brother finally graduated, the economy was in the tank. As a first-generation college student he had no connections in the professional world, and no one to tell him that communications and history degrees were bad bets to begin with. A good job never turned up. For years he has worked at call centers, leasing agencies, shipping companies. Those paychecks don't cover basic living costs, though. Thus, his face has aged a decade going in and out of this place by necessity.

The plasma center, though, like hundreds like it across the country, always looks the same: The fluorescent lights. The rows of quiet people lying back with one arm hooked to a whirring machine. The white lab coats and the clear plastic face shields. The signs about what to eat the day before, the day of, and the day after giving plasma in order to keep your strength up.

Your brother's blood follows a tube to a centrifuge that separates out what they want: liquid plasma the color of Mountain Dew.

The materials around the place tout the life-saving service he's providing others; the plasma stripped from his blood will be turned into pharmaceuticals. Very expensive pharmaceuticals, ones he could never afford were he diagnosed with hemophilia or an immune disorder. He doesn't have health insurance and could use a trip to the doctor himself. The promotional pamphlets and websites call what he's doing a donation, but it's really a sale.

The buyers are corporations with names like BioLife, Biotest, Octapharma. Plasma brings thirty, fifty bucks a pop depending on how often you go and how much you weigh. Your brother is in the highest weight class, which means he gets twenty dollars for the first donation of the week, forty-five dollars for the second. Sometimes there are bonuses: prize drawings, scratch-off tickets. The place your brother frequents is running a recruitment special: *UP TO $400 THIS MONTH. Applicable for eligible, qualified new donors. Fees vary by location. Check with your preferred CSL Plasma donation center to see if they are participating in any other special promotions.*

Regulars like your brother are already on the donor loyalty program called Z Rewards. The more plasma given, the more points and the higher status they attain—bronze, silver, gold. If you're away too long, they want you back. "Lapsed donors," who haven't given plasma in six months or more, get fifty bucks each for their first five return visits.

Plasma is big business, a monopolized industry comprised mostly of five international corporations. After the 2008 economic crisis, when Americans lost their jobs and homes during the Great Recession, the plasma industry suddenly had a swelling source of eager plasma sellers. New centers popped up across the country, and total donations—transactions, really—nearly doubled in five years, rising from 12.5 million in 2006 to more than 23 million in 2011. In 2008, plasma was a $4 billion industry. In 2015: $20 billion.[3, 4]

The sort of drugs made with your brother's plasma came onto the market during the 1950s and have a grim history. During the sixties and seventies, private plasma companies siphoned their product from the veins of American prison inmates, paying them five or ten dollars a hit. From the late seventies to the mid-eighties, about half of all diagnosed hemophiliacs reportedly contracted HIV from infected drugs derived from the plasma of such a high-risk population.[5] The resulting class-action lawsuits revealed that one company knew it was flooding the market with dangerous supplies.

During the nineties, China turned poor, rural areas in Henan Province and elsewhere into springs of plasma. Chinese farmers' blood, it turned out, was worth more than their labor in the fields. In the process, dirty needles, other bad practices, and the resulting tainted plasma supply infected thousands, maybe hundreds of thousands, of Chinese people with HIV and hepatitis C. Every plasma station in the country would be shut down, but in the last few years

3 http://www.theatlantic.com/health/archive/2014/05/blood-money-the-twisted-business-of-donating-plasma/362012/

4 http://www.latimes.com/local/california/la-me-1025-lopez-plasma-20151025-column.html

5 https://www.hemophilia.org/Bleeding-Disorders/Blood-Safety/HIV/AIDS

they've blossomed again across the country. In 2012, a doctor who discovered the 1990s contamination published a letter warning of the dangers involved when "plasma collection once again becomes a profit-seeking route for some unscrupulous health officials and medical professionals on local levels, thus having devastating consequences for some of China's most vulnerable people."[6]

What if your brother came across this information in a magazine while hooked up to the plasma machine? Would he feel a kinship with the U.S. prisoners and the Chinese farmers? As it happens, your brother's grandpa went to prison a time or two; on the other side of his family he is the first man in generations not to be a farmer. He worked hard to go to college instead of to prison or the fields, but here he is, selling out his veins. If he knew the history of plasma as a product, would he feel afraid for his health, cheated by an economy?

Today in regulated markets like the United States, where collection methods are sterile and technology has gotten sophisticated in cleaning contaminated supplies, plasma donation and plasma-based drugs are considered exceedingly safe. On the receiving end, transfusion of whole blood, which enters recipients much the same way it left its donors, is more likely to spread disease. That's why blood is donated while plasma is purchased: The chance to make fast cash might incentivize disease carriers to lie about their health when showing up to give blood or plasma, but disease would be destroyed during industrial processing of the latter. The Food and Drug Administration thus requires paid-for blood, frowned upon by the medical industry, to be labeled as such. Paid-for plasma, most of which is transported to drug factories, doesn't have to be labeled.

Laws about what body parts can be sold as goods are complicated. The year your brother was born, 1984, the National Organ Transplant Act made it illegal to buy and sell organs. Since a 2011 federal court decision, you can sell some kinds of bone marrow.

6 https://chinachange.org/2012/11/30/in-china-hiv-hcv-transmission-through-blood -continues/

People in budgetary binds legally sell pieces of themselves for cash every day: sperm, eggs, hair. The poor have long been valued for how much work their bodies can do. Today, the body itself is a commodity.

The flow reverses and your brother's blood, its plasma gone like panned gold, is pumped back into him: red cells, white cells, platelets, sodium citrate mixed in as an anti-clotting agent. Promotional materials insist the process is harmless, but it isn't always. Some donors, including your brother, get fatigued and light-headed. Occasionally people black out. The anticoagulant bonds with calcium in the blood and, in rare cases, can lead to dangerous calcium depletion.

A healthy body rebuilds the plasma that's been sold, but that takes time. Plasma can't be given more than twice a week, per FDA regulations. The United States is the only Western country that allows even that frequency, though. Lenient regulations regarding donor wellness and financial desperation amid historic wealth inequality means American plasma accounts for about 70 percent of collections worldwide. The holes that don't heal in your brother's arms are in thousands, maybe millions of American arms.

He's your brother because you share a country, an economy, a land, a species. If you met him, you'd probably think he was witty. He'd reach out to show you pictures of his pit bull on his cell phone, and you'd pay little mind to the hole in his arm near his short sleeve.

If he were your *brother-brother*, though, you would know him so deeply that the thought of him laying his arm down to sell what's in his veins would make you wince. His blood and all its parts would represent to you something that cannot be assigned a monetary value.

You'd remember the first time you saw it run down his body. He was two, you were six. You were taking a bath together. Your parents had left the bathroom, so you were alone in the soapy water entertaining him with plastic toys. He tried to stand up and slipped, hitting his face so hard on the side of the tub that it split open the smooth, delicate skin under one of his gray eyes. The cut opened up in the shape of a third eye. The blood that welled out of it was the brightest red you'd ever seen. The damp flesh around it went white.

You'd remember the sound of his cry, primal and scared, and how bad you felt—like it was your fault. He had to get stitches. Your mom told the doctor they were sewn too tight in his soft baby skin, but the doctor didn't listen. She was right. He still has a scar under his eye that looks like the laces of a football.

After an hour in the recliner, though, while they take the needle out of his arm, your brother isn't fretting about what his blood means. He isn't regarding himself as a precious thing. He isn't thinking about the hemophiliacs who need medication, the drug corporations that will manufacture it, or the insurance companies that will pay for it after someone pays them. He is deciding what expenses to prioritize with forty-five dollars.

On his way to the check-out desk, he takes one of the cookies set out on a tray for staving off nausea. He gets the money he made applied to the prepaid debit card. His first purchase will have to be at the gas station, as the gauge in his beater is below E. When he gets behind the wheel he'll shake his head to lose the dizziness and pray he has enough fuel to make it to the pump.

HILLSIDES AND FLATLANDS

Héctor Tobar

MY SON WAS STILL sleeping in a crib. We set him down each night, my wife and I, in his cushioned cocoon, lined with bumpers festooned with dinosaurs in primary colors. When he woke up in the middle of the night, I'd pick him up and feed him, sway and coo, and sing him back to sleep, with "Hush little baby don't say a word . . ." followed by a series of improvised verses, "And if that wine don't make you dance, Papa's going to buy you a pair of pants . . ." Then I'd watch him sleep, brown skin and full lips, puffing infant breaths on a cottony rectangle, protected, my son.

I was a father for the first time. I'd given up on my dreams to be a novelist, and taken a job at a newspaper for the health insurance, because that's what fathers do. My home was filled with the baked-bread smell of regurgitated mother's milk, and I'd learned how to change diapers. In the mornings, I'd give my baby boy a kiss good-bye and leave for the newsroom, where my editors scanned their green-glowing computer screens for dispatches of overnight violence. They would then send me into the big, asphalted, graffitied, subdivided coastal plain of working Los Angeles, where the palm trees were as old as great-grandfathers. I believed it was my calling to bear witness, to speak for the voiceless, but an entry-level job those days required months and maybe years on the cop beat. So I traveled into the harried and sooty grid inhabited by people of African and Latin American descent. These were the early days of the Automatic Weapons Era, and there were bodies to be counted, witnesses and survivors and families to interview after the firefights of the night and the weekend before.

I was born and raised in a Los Angeles that did, and did not, resemble these battlefields. My Guatemalan parents and I were not well off, in our East Hollywood neighborhood; but the phrase "drive-by shooting" was unknown to me. Our neighborhood was gang-free and racially integrated. At least one murderer lived nearby, in an apartment that was less than a block from my family's—James Earl Ray, who went on to kill Martin Luther King Jr. But I remember no gunplay growing up. We lived on a humble grid of side streets squeezed between Sunset and Hollywood Boulevards, among assorted working people, artists, immigrants, and drifters. In our corner of East Hollywood, Jews and Armenians and white Southerners lived alongside Mexicans and Eastern European exiles. My best friends were from Arkansas, Lebanon, the Philippines, and Czechoslovakia. We played baseball on the tarry blacktop of our elementary school for hours on end, and walked home along streets lined with brick apartments built in the 1930s, and wide Craftsman homes, and birds of paradise and jade plants covered with dust.

My long Angeleno coming-of-age coincided with the city's long, steady postindustrial decline. Oil embargoes and plant closings, and a hippie apocalypse of bad drugs and cultish radicalism, from Free Love to the Symbionese Liberation Army to crack cocaine, and the tax revolt and the fiscal strangulation of the public schools. The 1970s, the 1980s, the 1990s. Unhappy decades for Los Angeles. When I started my own family, in 1996, we sought out a nook of urban peace away from the grid and the flatlands. We scanned elevated patches of real estate in search of a street with curved lines that hugged the topography of a mound or hillside, or the meandering routes of ancient watersheds. My wife and I bought our first home in a community called Mount Washington, at an elevation of approximately 725 feet above sea level, and about 300 feet above the Latino barrio below us. In Los Angeles, this small difference in altitude meant we lived in a mellower socioeconomic milieu, closer to nature and the looping flight patterns of red-tailed hawks and the scavenging routes of scrawny coyotes. Mount Washington was also one of the city's oldest bohemian getaways; at various moments in its history, our 800-square-foot two-bedroom home had belonged to a minor starlet of the silent-screen era, and to a sound engineer who'd won an Academy Award on a 1990s Hollywood blockbuster.

At night, while the coyotes feasted on our street's possums and feral cats, we'd hear the air-snapping reports of the occasional volley of gunshots coming from the barrio below us, the slinging of lead by the teenage armies of disorder and self-destruction; the sirens and helicopters of the Los Angeles Police Department usually followed. Nevertheless, I rarely felt any sense of danger driving through these adjacent barrios. Nor on my midday journeys southward into the districts where people were being killed in greater numbers. Lennox. Athens. South-Central. Nonlocals who first glimpse these districts are often puzzled. "This is a ghetto? But it looks sorta nice." There are avocado trees, and houses with lawns and cactus plants and rosebushes. Only the housing projects seem to fit the role. I wandered these neighborhoods at will and without fear—before sunset. Altogether, the poor southern districts of the metropolis spread out over close to one hundred square miles of flatlands and grids. A cruel, de facto segregation held sway. Only blacks and Latinos lived there.

One Thursday morning I was dispatched to the Florence district, an unincorporated community adjacent to South-Central Los Angeles, and specifically to East Sixty-First Street and Central Avenue. A nine-year-old boy had died the night before, three days after being shot in his family's 1976 Ford Granada. On Sunday night, a group of young men had taken an AK-47 and opened fire on the vehicle with brass-and-lead cartridge, penetrating the steel and glass skin of the Ford, where the boy had been sitting in the backseat with his brother and sister (ages three and six) and mother and father. According to the sheriff's department, the killers were members of a gang whose name I put into print then, but which I will now refuse to write out of respect for the dead. I turned off the freeway and entered the neighborhood, and noted the absence of bright colors, the earth-toned pallet of the southern districts of Los Angeles. A stucco, patched-over aesthetic reigned, one low-slung building after another wearing several layers of taupe and cement-gray paint. This was L.A.'s Rust Belt: the Goodyear Tire & Rubber factory, closed in the late 1970s, was located six blocks away from the scene of the shooting. In 1983, the actor playing the lead in the film *Bless Their Little Hearts* (an unheralded classic of African American cinema) drove a car through this neighborhood, and past the crumbling brick Acropolis of the half-demolished Goodyear plant.

This history was unknown to most of the locals. The neighborhood was by then 80 percent Latino, and Spanish and English were spoken in equal measures. In a series of sidewalk interviews in those two languages I was able to piece together the sequence of events of that violent Sunday night.

The Martinez family had moved out of their East Sixty-First Street apartment several years earlier. David Martinez was a mechanic, and he'd taken his family more than twenty miles away, to the Orange County suburb of Buena Park, home to another barrio and to the onetime boysenberry patch and now amusement park known as Knott's Berry Farm. Distance from the flat center of Los Angeles had brought the Martinezes a measure of safety and peace. But they still had friends in Florence and on a visit to see them their car had broken down in front of the apartment building on East Sixty-First Street where they used to live. Mr. Martinez returned with his family to Florence to see if he could fix and retrieve the car. When he parked and stepped onto the street, another car pulled up and several young men opened fire: they'd seen the Martinezes' car, and the silhouettes of the five people packed inside, and assumed they were rival gang members.

"They were blasting," one member of the local gang told me about the gunmen. "They were trying to get us," said another. They pantomimed their reactions and the actions of the gunmen with a lightheartedness that itself was deeply disturbing. Hector had been struck in the skull and back, and stumbled from the car holding his head in his hands. One of the gang members counted the votive candles at the sidewalk memorial to the dead boy: twenty-two. Another spray-painted the victim's name on the concrete: R.I.P. Hector. Other witnesses recounted how it had been a very warm, late summer night, with as many as thirty people gathered outside the apartment building, including families with children. As I scribbled into my notebook, I heard no statements of outrage. No one railed against the murderous demons who had perpetrated the crime, or against the neighborhood's poverty, and the grimness and hopelessness from which one murder, and hundreds of murders, had been born. (Years later, the apartment building was demolished. The Diego Rivera Learning Complex, a public high school, now rises from the site where Hector Martinez was killed.)

Next I drove to the Martinez home in Buena Park and found a carpeted living room, filled with mourning and suffering. Alejandra Murillo, Hector's mother, had herself been wounded. She still wore the bracelet from the hospital and the bandages on her wrist from an IV drip. There were two other journalists present, and as we sat and stood in the small space the dead boy looked at us from a studio portrait on a shelf near the television: Alejandra's mothering there to be seen in the straight part of his wet hair, the bright smile. A brown-skinned boy. His mother herself so young: twenty-five. Someone asked Alejandra about her own wounds, so she lifted up the corner of her blouse to show us the bruise and razorlike cut left by the bullet that had struck her on her side, just above her waist. Her six-year-old son, Christian, his knee still bandaged from a gunshot wound, sat on the floor, playing a video game. "They took my son from me," she said in Spanish, through the haze of a sedated numbness. *"Era mi adoración."* I whispered my question, the only question I could truly ask her: Tell me something about Hector. So that I can tell people who he really was.

"Tocaba el acordeón," she said, and she broke into tears and doubled over in pain at the memory of her beautiful son playing that big, boxy instrument, a symbol of his Mexican heritage, each mastered note and melody a testament to his intelligence and joy

and promise. She cried and cried, until one of the television reporters finally said one of the most narcissistic things I've ever heard: "*Señora, por favor*. Get ahold of yourself. Think of us. We have a job to do and this isn't easy for us either."

I offered Alejandra and the members of her family my deepest condolences and drove back to Los Angeles. The story I would tell was in my head and in my notebook. Now I just had to write it, which I would do, in green, watery letters on the pulsing screen of my computer terminal, in the three or four hours left before my deadline. I thought of Alejandra doubled over in pain, sitting on a big chair, and for a moment I thought of her loss and her sorrow as a kind of contagion that might take my own son from me. No, no, no. Please no. Please, God, protect my son. From bullets and car crashes and randomness. Protect him. I turned on the radio in search of a distraction, and thankfully the local public radio station offered stories from lands near and far that did not involve death. As I got closer to downtown, I listened to the story of a precocious, bright boy, a solver of impossible problems, recounting feats of mathematical prowess. His voice stayed with me as I reached the newspaper's garage, and when I pulled into a parking space the story ended, and I turned off the car, and stayed inside.

I thought of three boys: Hector Martinez and his accordion, alive in that portrait; this bright boy on the radio; and my own son, small and vulnerable in his crib. Three boys. Their beating hearts, their lungs, hungry for new breaths. Fragile and brilliant. One alive and balancing equations to show the world what smart boys can do; one soon to be buried at age nine, to be mourned by his mother for the rest of her life. And my son, my beautiful boy, the infant I held in my arms, asleep on a hillside. I am a father. I am powerless. And I am afraid. I began to sob, to weep uncontrollably. Cribs and sidewalk shooting grounds, mother's milk and flowers on a grave. After a few minutes, I wiped the tears from my cheeks, and walked into the newsroom.

INVISIBLE WOUNDS

Jess Ruliffson

Now A FREELANCE writer living in Southern California, former Sergeant Paul David Mansfield served with the Army National Guard from 1997 to 2009, deploying to Iraq twice as an infantry team and squad leader. The following is an excerpt from a forthcoming graphic novel, which collects interviews with veterans of the Iraq and Afghanistan wars.

I generally don't mind talking about it.

Particularly when I don't have to see the look on people's faces.

When a person finds out, I notice this change in them...

The tension building as they start to wonder if I'm dangerous and crazy.

If perhaps they say the wrong thing, will I freak out like a bad caricature of the crazy vet?

Screeee

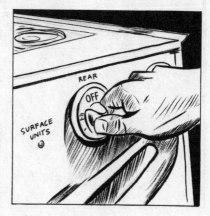

REAR
OFF
SURFACE UNITS

A neighbor whom I had known for awhile was visiting once, her daughter playing with mine.

The conversation turned to my being disabled, so I told her what the deal was. I mistakenly finished with:

I'm not dangerous or anything.

Should you ever find yourself in a situation where you need to reassure a person in regard to your stability, sanity, and general inoffensiveness, never, ever say those words.

I watched her gauge the distance to her daughter and to the door before she caught herself.

I gave her an out by excusing myself to the kitchen to make a cup of tea.

She took the opportunity to get her daughter home to start dinner.

HOW

Roxane Gay

How These Things Come to Pass

Hanna does her best thinking late at night when all the usurpers living in her house are asleep. If it isn't winter, which is not often, she climbs out onto her roof with a pack of cigarettes and a lighter. She smokes and stares up at the blue-black night sky. She lives in the North Country, where the stars make sense. Hanna shares her home with her unemployed husband, her twin sister, her sister's husband, their son, and her father. She is the only one who works—mornings, she waits tables at the Koivu Café, and nights, she tends bar at Karpela's Supper Club. She leaves most of her tips at her best friend Laura's house. Hanna is plotting her escape.

The most popular dish at the Koivu is the *pannukakku*, a Finnish pancake. If Old Larsen is too hungover, Hanna will heat the iron skillet in the oven and mix the batter—first eggs, beating them lightly, slowly adding the honey, salt, and milk, finally sifting the flour in. She enjoys the ratchet sound as she pulls the sift trigger. She sways from side to side and imagines she is a Flamenco dancer. She is in Spain, where it is warm, where there is sun and beauty. Hanna likes making *pannukakku* with extra butter so the edges of the pancakes are golden and crisp. Sometimes she'll carefully remove the edges from a pancake and eat them just like that. She's still in Spain, eating bread from a *panadería*, perhaps enjoying a little wine. Then she'll hear someone shout,

"Order up!" and she is no longer in Spain. She is in the middle of nowhere, standing over a hot, greasy stove.

Peter, Hanna's husband, comes in for breakfast every morning. Hanna saves him a spot at the counter and she takes his order. He stares down her uniform, ogling her cleavage and waggling his eyebrows. She feigns affection, smacks his head with her order pad, and hands his ticket to Old Larsen, who growls, "We don't do any damn substitutions," but then makes Peter three eggs over easy, hash browns with onions and cheese, four slices of bacon, white toast, and two *pannukakku*, slightly undercooked. When his food is ready, Hanna takes a break, sits next to Peter, watches him eat. His beard is growing long. A man without a job doesn't need a clean face, he tells her. She hates watching Peter eat. She hates that he follows her to work. She hates his face.

Her husband thinks they are trying to have a child. He wears boxers instead of briefs though he prefers the security of the latter. Peter once read in a magazine that wearing boxers increased sperm motility. He and Hanna have sex only when the home ovulation kit he bought at Walmart indicates she is fertile. Peter would prefer to have sex every day. Hanna would prefer to never have sex with Peter again, not because she's frigid but because she finds it difficult to become aroused by a perpetually unemployed man. Two years ago, Hanna said she was going on vacation with Laura downstate and instead drove to Marquette and had her tubes tied. She wasn't going to end up like her mother, with too many children in a too-small house with too little to eat. Despite her best efforts, however, she has found herself living in a too-small house with too many people and too little to eat. It is a bitter pill to swallow.

When she gets off work at three in the afternoon, Hanna goes home, washes the grease and salt from her skin, and changes into something cute but a little slutty. She heads to the university the next town over. She's twenty-seven but looks far younger, so she pretends she's a student. Sometimes she attends a class in one of the big lecture halls. She takes notes and plays with her hair and thinks about all the things she could have done. Other days she sits in the library and reads books and learns things so that when she finally escapes she can be more than a waitress with a great rack in a dead Upper Michigan town.

Hanna flirts with boys because at the Michigan Institute of Technology there are lots and lots of boys who want nothing more than to be noticed by a pretty girl. She never pretends she's anything but smart. She's too old for that. Sometimes the boys take her to the dining hall or the Campus Café for a snack. She tells them she's in mechanical engineering because Laura is a secretary in that department. Sometimes the boys invite her to their messy dorm rooms littered with dirty laundry and video game consoles and roommates or their squalid apartments off campus. She gives them blow jobs and lies with them on their narrow twin beds covered in thin sheets and tells them lies they like to hear. After the boys fall asleep, Hanna heads back across the bridge to Karpela's, where she tends bar until two in the morning.

Peter visits Hanna at the supper club, too, but he has to pay for his drinks so he doesn't visit often. Don Karpela, the owner, is always around, grabbing at things with his meaty fingers. He's a greedy man and a friend of her father's. Even though he's nearing sixty, Don is always breathing down Hanna's neck, bumping up against her in the cramped space behind the bar, telling her he'd make her damn happy if she'd leave her old man. When he does that, Hanna closes her eyes and breathes easy because she needs her job. If Peter is around when Don is making his moves, he'll laugh and raise his glass. "You can have her," he'll slur, as if he has a say in the matter.

After the bar closes Hanna wipes everything down and washes all the glasses and empties the ashtrays. She and Laura, who also works at the supper club, will sit on the hood of Hanna's car in the back alley and hold hands. Hanna will lean against Laura's shoulder and inhale deeply and marvel that her friend can still smell good after hours in that dark, smoky space where men don't hear the word *no*. If the night is empty enough, they will kiss for a very long time, until their cold lips become warm, until the world falls away, until their bodies feel like they will split at the heart. She and Laura never talk about these moments but when Hanna is plotting her escape, she is not going alone.

Hanna's twin sister, Anna, often waits up for Hanna. She worries. She always has. She's a nervous woman. As a child, she was a nervous girl. Their mother, before she left, liked to say that Hanna got all the *sisu*, the fierce strength that should have been shared by both girls. Hanna and Anna always knew their mother didn't know them at all. They were both strong and fierce. Anna's husband worked at the paper mill in Niagara until some foreign company bought it and closed it and then most everyone in town lost their homes because all the work that needed doing was already done. When Anna called, nervous as always, to ask if she and her family could stay with Hanna, she had not even posed the question before Hanna said, "Yes."

Hanna and Anna are not openly demonstrative but they love each other wildly. In high school, Anna dated a boy who didn't treat her well. When Hanna found out, she put a good hurting on him. Hanna pretended to be her sister and she took the bad boy up to the trails behind the county fairgrounds. She got down on her knees and started to give him head and she told him *if he ever laid a hand on her sister again*, and before she finished that sentence, she bit down on his cock and told herself she wouldn't stop biting down until her teeth met. She smiled when she tasted his blood. He screamed so softly it made the hairs on her arm stand on end. Hanna still sees that boy around town once in a while. He's not a boy anymore but he walks with a hitch and always crosses to the other side of the street when he sees her coming.

On the nights when Hanna and Laura sit on the hood of Laura's car and kiss until their cold lips warm, Anna stands outside on the front porch, shivering, waiting. Her cheeks flush. Her heart flutters around her chest awkwardly. Anna asks Hanna if she's seeing another man and Hanna tells her sister the truth. She says, "No," and Anna frowns. She knows Hanna is telling the truth. She knows Hanna is lying. She cannot quite figure out how she's doing both at the same time. The sisters smoke a cigarette together, and before they go in, Anna will place a gentle hand on

Hanna's arm. She'll say, "Be careful." Hanna will kiss her twin's forehead, and she'll think, *I will*, and Anna will hear her.

How Hanna Ikonen Knows It Is Time to Get the Girl and Get out of Town

Hanna and Anna's father, Red, lives in the basement. He's not allowed on the second floor, where everyone sleeps. When Peter asks why, Hanna just shakes her head and says, "It's personal." She doesn't share personal things with her husband. Her father used to work in the mines. When the last copper mine closed he didn't bother trying to learn a new trade. He started holding his back when he walked around, said he was injured. He collected disability, and when that ran out, he lived with a series of girl-friends who each kicked him out before long. Finally, when there was no woman in town who would give him the time of day, Red showed up on Hanna's doorstep, reeking of whiskey, his beard long and unkempt. He slurred an incoherent apology for being a lousy father. He begged his daughter to have mercy on an old man. Hanna wasn't moved by his plea but she knew he would be her problem one way or the other. She told him he could make himself comfortable in the basement, but if she ever saw him on the second floor, that would be that. It has been fifteen years since the mine closed but Red still calls himself a miner.

The whereabouts of Hanna and Anna's mother, Ilse, are un-known. She left when the girls were eleven. It was a Thursday morning. Ilse got the girls and their brothers ready for school, fed them breakfast—steel-cut oats topped with sliced bananas. She kissed them atop their pale blond heads and told them to be good. She was gone when they returned home from school. For a while, they heard a rumor that Ilse had taken up with a shoe salesman in Marquette. Later, there was news of her from Iron Mountain, a dentist's wife, with a new family. Then there was no news at all.

Hanna and Anna have five brothers scattered throughout the state. They are mostly bitter, lazy, indifferent, and unwilling to have a hand in the care and feeding of their father. When Hanna organized a conference call with her siblings to discuss the disposition of their father, the Boys, as they are collectively known, said it was women's work and if the Twins didn't want to do that work, they could let the old man rot. One of the brothers, Venn, offered to send Hanna or Anna, whoever shouldered the burden of caring for Red, twenty dollars a month. Simultaneously, the Twins told him to stick it up his ass and then they told the Boys to go fuck themselves. After they hung up, Hanna called Anna and Anna offered to take care of Red until he drank himself to death but Hanna worried that death by drink would take too long. Anna had a child to raise, after all.

It is an ordinary Tuesday when Hanna decides to go home after working at the café instead of heading across the bridge to the institute to play make-believe with college boys. She can feel grease oozing out of her pores and what she wants, more than anything, is to soak in a clean bathtub, in an empty house. When she pulls into her driveway and sees Anna pacing back and forth in front of the garage, Hanna knows there will be no bath or empty house today. She parks the car, takes a deep breath, and joins her sister, who informs Hanna that their mother is sitting on the Salvation Army couch in the living room drinking a cup of tea. Hanna thinks, *Of course she is.*

How Hanna Met and Married Peter Lahti

Anna fell in love when she was seventeen. His name was Logan, and he lived on the reservation in Baraga. She loved his long black hair and his smooth brown skin and the softness of his voice. They met at a football game, and the day after graduation, they married and moved. When Anna left, Hanna was happy for her sister, but she also hoped beyond all hopes that her sister and her new husband would take her with them. She could have said something. Years later Hanna realized she should have said something, but she became the one who stayed. She got an apartment of her own and started hanging out at the university sitting in on the classes she couldn't afford. Peter lived in the apartment next door and back then he worked as a truck driver hauling lumber downstate, so dating him was fine because he wasn't around much.

After a long trip where Peter was gone for three weeks, he showed up at Hanna's door, his hair slicked back, beard trimmed, wearing a button-down shirt and freshly pressed jeans. In one hand he held a cheap bouquet of carnations. He had forgotten that Hanna had told him, on their first date, that she hated carnations. He thrust the flowers into Hanna's hands, invited himself into her apartment, and said, "I missed you so much. Let's get married." Hanna, elbow deep into a bottle of wine at that point, shrugged. Peter, an optimist at heart, took the gesture as a response in the affirmative. They married not long after in a ceremony attended by Anna and her husband, Red, and three of the Boys. No one from Peter's family attended. His mother was scandalized that her boy would marry any child of Red Ikonen.

How Red Ikonen Got His Reputation

Red Ikonen had mining in his blood. His daddy and his daddy's daddy had been miners up in Calumet when mining was something that mattered up there and the town was rich and every Sunday the churches were full of good folks grateful for the bounties of the hard earth. As a boy, Red loved his father's stories about the world beneath the world. By the time it was Red's turn to head underground, there wasn't much mining left to do and that was a hell of a cross to bear. He was as a soldier without a war. Red started drinking to numb his disappointment. He married a pretty girl, had five handsome boys and two lovely girls, and continued drinking to celebrate his good fortune. The pretty girl left and he drank so he wouldn't feel so lonesome. Finally, drinking was the only thing he knew how to do so that's just what he did.

He was a tall man—six foot seven—and he had a loud voice and no sense of how to act right. That sort of thing just wasn't in him. There wasn't a bar in town where Red hadn't started a fight or done something untoward with his woman or someone else's woman. Things had gotten so bad he needed to drive over to South Range or Chassell to drink with the old guys at the VFW who really were soldiers without a war, because no one in town wanted to serve him a drink. When the Boys were still in town, bartenders would call and have one of them come get their father. By the time Red Ikonen was drinking so he wouldn't feel so lonesome he had become a mean drunk. He never had a kind word for his boys, who drove miles into the middle of the night to bring their drunk daddy back home.

One by one the Boys left home, tried to get as far away from their father as possible, until it was only the Twins left, and then he started doing untoward things with them and it was a small town so people talked and it wasn't long before no one at all wanted a thing to do with Red Ikonen.

How Laura and Hanna Became Best Friends

Laura Kappi grew up next door to the Ikonens. For a while in high school, she dated one of the Boys, but then he moved away, went to college, and didn't bother to take her with him. Laura was, in fact, a friend to both Hanna and Anna throughout high school. When Anna and Logan moved down to Niagara, Laura saw how lost Hanna was without her twin. She decided to do her best to take Anna's place. Hanna was more than happy to let her. They became best friends and then they became more than friends but they never talked about it because there wasn't much to be said on the subject.

How Hanna Reacts When She Sees Her Mother for the First Time in Sixteen Years

Before they go inside, Anna reaches for Hanna's waiting hand. They both squeeze, hard, their knuckles cracking, and then the Twins go inside. Ilse Ikonen is sitting on the edge of the couch. She is a small woman with sharp features. She has always been beautiful and neither time nor distance has changed that. Her hair is graying around the scalp, her features hang a bit lower, but she doesn't look a day over forty. Red is sitting where he always sits during the day, in the recliner next to the couch, staring at his estranged wife. He has tucked in his shirt, but his hands are shaking because he is trying not to drink. He wants to be clearheaded but his wife is so damned beautiful that with or without the drink he doesn't know up from down. Peter is sitting next to Ilse, also staring, because the resemblance between his wife and her mother is uncanny. They have never met. Anna's husband, Logan, is sitting next to Peter, holding their son, half-asleep, in his lap. He is deliberately avoiding any eye contact with his mother-in-law. He is helping his wife with the burden of her anger.

As soon as they enter the room, Hanna's and Anna's stomachs churn. Beads of sweat slowly spread across their foreheads. Ilse leans forward, setting her teacup on the coffee table. She smiles at her daughters. Hanna thinks, *Why did you offer her tea?* Anna thinks, *I was being polite.* Hanna bites her lip. "What are you doing here, Ilse?" she asks.

Ilse Ikonen uncrosses her legs and folds her hands in her lap. "It has been a long time," she says.

Hanna looks at all the broken people sitting in her living room on her broken furniture looking to her to fix their broken lives. She turns around and walks right back out the front door. Anna makes her excuses and rushes after her sister. She finds Hanna holding on to the still-warm hood of her car, hunched over, throwing up. Anna's stomach rolls uncomfortably. When Hanna stands up, she wipes her lips with the back of her hand and says, "I mean . . . really?"

How Laura Finally Convinces Hanna to Run Away with Her

Hanna sits in her car until Ilse Ikonen takes her leave and gets a room at the motel down the street. After her mother leaves, Hanna drives to campus and goes to the dank room of one of her college boys. She lies on his musty, narrow twin bed and stares at the constellation of glow-in-the-dark stars on the ceiling while the boy awkwardly fumbles at her breasts with his bony fingers. She sighs, closes her eyes, thinks of Laura. Afterward, when the boy is fast asleep, his fingers curled in a loose fist near his mouth, Hanna slips out of bed and heads back across the bridge to Laura's house.

Laura smiles when she opens her front door. Hanna shrugs and stands in the doorway, her cheeks numb, still nauseous. She shoves her small hands into her pockets, tries to ignore the cold. Laura wraps her arms around herself, shifts quickly from one foot to the other. "Why don't you come in?"

Hanna shakes her head. "I can't do this anymore."

Laura arches an eyebrow and even though she is barefoot, she steps onto her snowy front porch. She gasps, steps onto Hanna's boots, slides her arms beneath Hanna's coat and around her waist. Laura lightly brushes her lips against Hanna's. Hanna closes her eyes. She breathes deeply.

How Hanna Falls Even More in Love with Laura Than She Thought Possible

When Laura can no longer feel her toes, she says, "We better get inside before I get frostbite and I am forced to spend the rest of my life hobbling after you."

Hanna nods and follows Laura into her house. It is familiar, has looked mostly the same for the past twenty years, and in that there is comfort. Inside the foyer, amid coats and boots, a shovel, a knitted scarf, a bag of salt, Hanna sinks to the floor and sits cross-legged. Laura sits across from Hanna, extends her legs, resting her cold feet in Hanna's lap.

"Do you want to tell me about it?"

Hanna shakes her head angrily. "My mother's back."

"I mean . . . really?" she says.

Hanna doesn't go home. She calls Anna and assures her sister that she's fine. Anna doesn't ask where she is. She's starting to make sense of things. Hanna lets Laura lead her up the steep staircase lined with books. She lets Laura put her into a hot bath. She lets Laura wash her clean. She follows Laura to bed and for the first time in months, she falls asleep in a mostly empty house. She thinks, *This is everything I want*.

As Hanna sleeps, Laura calculates how much money she has saved, the tread on her tires, how far they will need to travel so that Hanna might begin to forget about the life she's leaving behind. It all makes Laura very tired but then she looks at Hanna's lower lip, how it trembles while she's sleeping.

How It Has Always Been

The next morning, Laura hears the knocking at her front door. She wraps herself in a thin robe and takes one last look at Hanna, still sleeping, lower lip still trembling. Laura has always loved Hanna, even before she understood why her entire body flushed when she saw Hanna at school or running around her backyard or sitting on the roof outside her bedroom window. Dating one of the Boys was a way to get closer to Hanna. Laura would kiss Hanna's brother and think of his sister, her smile, the way she walked around with her shoulder muscles bunched up. Being with the brother was not what Laura wanted but she told herself it was enough. For the first time Laura feels something unfamiliar in her throat. It makes her a little sick to her stomach. She thinks it might be hope. Downstairs, Anna is standing on the front porch shivering. She has a splitting headache. When Laura opens the door Anna quickly slips into the house. Anna squeezes Laura's hand and heads upstairs into Laura's bedroom. Anna crawls into bed behind her sister, wraps her arms around Hanna's waist. Hanna covers one of Anna's hands with hers. She is not quite awake yet.

"Don't make me go back there," Hanna says, hoarsely.

Anna tightens her arms around her sister, kisses Hanna's shoulder. Anna says, "You have to go back to say good-bye." There is a confidence in Anna's voice that reassures Hanna.

Hanna sighs, slowly opens her eyes. She sees Laura standing in the doorway. Hanna smiles. "You don't have to stand so far away," she says. Laura grins and crawls into bed with the Twins. Laura says, "Remember when we were kids and the three of us would lie on your roof at night during the summer to cool down?" Both Hanna and Anna nod. The three women roll onto their backs and stare at the ceiling—the cracks and water stains, how it sags. "We were miserable even then," Laura says.

How Hanna Finally Confronts Her Mother

Where Hanna has always been the protector, Anna has always been the voice of reason, able to make the right choices between impossible alternatives. When they were girls and Hanna would plot retribution against anyone who had wronged the Twins, it was Anna who would deter her sister from acting thoughtlessly. When Red Ikonen would stumble into their room drunk and Hanna would try to stab him with a kitchen knife or bite his ear off it was Anna who grabbed her sister's arm and said, "It's him or Superior Home." It was Anna who would sing to her father and stroke his beard and soothe all the meanness out of him. In these moments, Hanna would feel so much anger inside her she thought her heart would rip apart but then she would let the knife fall to the floor or she would unclench her teeth because anything was better than Superior Home, the state facility where motherless children were often discarded until they turned eighteen. They heard stories bad enough to make them believe there were worse things than the stink of Red Ikonen's breath against their cheeks as he forgot how to behave like a proper father.

Anna held Hanna's hand as they walked back to their house, a bracing wind pushing their bodies through the snow. Hanna tried to breathe but found the air thin and cold and it hurt her lungs. As they climbed the porch stairs Hanna stopped, leaned against the railing, her body heavy.

"I don't feel so good," she said.

Anna pressed the cool palm of her hand against Hanna's forehead. "You get to leave soon," she said. "Hold on to that."

Hanna stared at her sister. She said, "Come with us—you and Logan and the baby."

Anna shook her head. "It's my turn to stay."

"Bullshit. We've taken our turns long enough."

The front door opened. Peter glared at the Twins. "Where the hell were you last night?" He grabbed Hanna by the elbow, pulling her into the house, and she let him. She wanted to save what fight she had left.

In the living room the scene closely resembled the tableau Hanna stumbled into the previous day with Ilse Ikonen sitting on the couch, poised regally like she had never left and had no need to offer acts of contrition.

Hanna tried to squirm free from Peter's grasp and he finally relented when calmly, quietly, Anna said, "Let go of my sister." Peter held a natural distrust of twins. It wasn't normal, he thought, for there to be two people who were so identical. He also harbored no small amount of jealousy for the relationship twins shared. While he was not a bright man, Peter was smart enough to know he would never be as close to his wife as he wanted.

The Twins stood before their father, their mother, their husbands. They stood in the house where they had grown up filled with broken people and broken things. Anna thought, *This is the last time we will ever stand in this room*, and Hanna suddenly felt like she could breathe again. She tried to say something but she couldn't find her voice. Her throat was dry and hollow. The Twins looked at their parents and thought about everything they had ever wanted to say to two people so ill-suited for doing right by their children.

"I'm sorry to intrude," Ilse said, her voice tight, her words clipped. She crossed her legs and fidgeted with a big diamond ring on her left hand. "I wanted to see how you girls and the Boys were doing, perhaps explain myself."

Anna shook her head. "Explanations aren't necessary," she said. "Your leaving is a long time gone."

Hanna removed her wedding ring and dropped it on the coffee table. Peter sneered and said, "Whatever," and Hanna rolled her eyes.

The Twins stood before their father, their mother, their husbands. They sucked in a great mass of air, threw their shoulders back. They had rehearsed this moment more than once but then they realized that with all the time and wrongs gone by, there was nothing worth saying.

How Hanna, Laura, Anna, Logan, and the Baby Got Away

They piled into Laura's truck, their belongings packed tightly into a small trailer hitched to the back. They sat perfectly still, held their breaths, looked straight ahead.

ENOUGH TO LOSE

RS Deeren

THIS WASN'T LONG after Alice told me she was ready to start a family. She said we were ready this time but I think her definition of that word and mine don't exactly match up. I was riding shotgun in a no-bells, no-whistles F-150 that was more repairs and patches than actual truck. Rid drove, licking at the chew inside of his bottom lip as he barreled the Ford through the morning, the trailer swaying on the ball hitch. Fifteen minutes from the third house on the list. Half past seven in the morning and the humidity already bubbled up from the fields and the smell of dead grass and asphalt baked in the cab. The radio still worked but the first time I turned it on, Rid punched it off before half a note sang out. *Don't got time for that*, he said. I hadn't touched anything on the dash since, not that any of the knobs worked anymore. When the July heat caught up with the humidity June had left behind, I found out that the crank for my window was busted too. I brought it up to the boss but all he told me was that the tranny was new and the tires spun, and that was all I needed to get the jobs done.

Three months in with Secured Properties, mowing lawns for bank repossessions at ten bucks a pop, and I had inhaled more grass clippings, caked my eyes in more dust, and ridden more backroads than I had known were in Tip County. My ma told me about the job. I hadn't mowed a lawn since my dad let me lug his push mower around my neighborhood, ringing doorbells and offering my services, and even then, at fourteen, I was raking in at least twenty bucks per. Plus I could rely on one of the old folks in the area to come out with lemonade or sun tea. I didn't want to take this job but Pioneer Sugar hadn't returned my calls, not even for a seasonal job, and there was no way I was asking for my job back at Walmart. Alice sold Wrap-It—a plastic body wrap that was supposed to help people lose weight—from our home and at parties she organized. She had been able to get only her sister and my ma to work for her full time so the money only trickled in. I didn't want the job, but I needed it. So I called Secured, passed a piss test, signed a W-4, and drove out to the company garage when the new pay cycle started. That's where I met Ridley Bellows, leaning against the loaded trailer, sipping a gas station coffee.

"Morning," I said, "Name's Tim." I held out my hand. "You must be Ridley. The boss said you get out here early."

"Gives me more time for more jobs," he said. He shook my hand, not so much limp, as if he were a weak man, but as if he didn't want to bother. Like he didn't have anything to prove to me. "Got everything loaded this time but tomorrow you gotta get here early to help out. Let's go." We climbed in and pulled onto the dirt road, heading straight to the first yard.

'08 was bad for most people. Normal people. Bank people. People caught somewhere in between. Everybody. Normal people lost their homes, bank people lost their banks. Both lost faith in each other and all that was left behind were countless properties nobody could buy and nobody could sell. I was one of the in-between people. Alice and I got by, lost some things along the way but still had enough to feel more or less human. We married out of high school and rented the back half of a duplex on a dead end road that butted up to Scott's River. I had a few semesters' worth of college in me but the only thing I learned was that I could spend more than my share of time and money on something and still not feel like I'd learned anything. But I promised Alice, and she me, that we'd get enough put away and get ourselves a place.

The few people who came out of '08 ahead had more properties than they knew what to do with. That's where the in-betweeners like me and Rid came in. We kept those properties looking livable until they sold. Nobody wants to buy a shack sinking into a yard of chin-high weeds. We'd pull up to a double-wide or a split-level out in the country and before we unloaded, Rid walked around the whole place with a cheap digital camera, snapping shots of the house and yard. These were the before shots, he told me the first day. Then, once we finished with the job, he'd go back and snap the after shots. *So we can prove we did the job and didn't fuck it up or break in or anything,* he said.

Rid didn't say much that wasn't related to the job. On my first day out, he circled the house with a weed whacker while I wrangled with the mower. I'd never been on a zero-turn mower before, one of those speedy numbers that wasn't much more than a rubber seat cushion bolted above three sets of blades and a set of levers used for both acceleration and steering. Just a nudge would gun that sucker along and if you didn't give both those big levers the same amount of love, the whole thing would start spinning out of control like some redneck hovercraft.

"Lines gotta be straighter," Rid said when I passed. "Lines gotta be straighter." I swerved down the lawn, taking a wide turn at the road, and made my way back toward the house. "For the grace and love of naked baby Jesus, kid, you speak English? Boss don't pay if the job looks like shit. Straighten those lines out!" I squinted through the clippings kicked up in the wind and jerked side to side as I looped around the lawn. The job looked like hell, even after Rid tried a quick touch-up, and he still had to blur the after photos just enough to hide what looked like a drunk haircut. That first house, a boarded-up cottage on a half acre, took forty-five minutes. In the truck, pushing past seventy, Rid let me have it.

"Fifteen minutes per job, max. Got it?" he said. "Thirty-minute drive time between jobs. That paces out to twenty bucks an hour. You just cut that in half."

"Sorry, Ridley," I said. "It's my first time out."

"A job worth doing is worth doing right and quickly. The *first* time. Hear me? And call me Rid, only my ma called me Ridley."

And that was Rid. Twenty bucks an hour, speeding from one vacant house to the next with a twenty-seven-year-old nobody in tow and a work list that looped and spiraled wider and wider as more jobs came in. We would start the week mowing abandoned summer homes in Caseville and by the weekend wind up halfway to Flint spraying weed killer outside foreclosed apartment complexes. When the next pay cycle started, we'd be back up along Saginaw Bay, mowing those same summer homes. They stopped being homes by the time Rid and I got to them; they were only a crisp ten-dollar bill, calluses, and heat rash to us. It took only a couple more fuckups on the zero-turn and an earful from Rid before it all became routine to me. Pull in, unload, before shots, mow, weed, trim, after shots, load out, move on. Seventeen or so hours a day. At Rid's pace, it looked like something that resembled a sweet deal.

■ ■

A month in, I parked outside the duplex, beyond beat. I stayed out, listening to the grind of cicadas through the open windows of my truck, drinking a tall boy. The lights inside were off. Alice went to bed early so she could get to the gym at five to sell to the before-work crowd. The owner let her sell from a booth she set up behind the StairMasters and she pushed a sale or two most days. She passed her afternoons at home, posting to Facebook and fitness boards, trying to sign up enough people to earn a promotion from her higher-ups. Her sister managed to sign up some of her friends for a while. Those were a few good months. Alice had enough wraps and diet pills going out that we paid off one of the MasterCards. Then the school year kicked in and her sister's friends went back to class and stopped selling. Things got tight again and we maxed out the Visa. That's how things go. I was used to that up-and-down just so long as I could punch a clock and get another day behind me. Why bother looking back when you're never going to get closer to those days? That's just how time works, a straight line. But I have to admit, in those few moments alone in the dark car, maybe a little drunk, looking at the stained vinyl siding of my life, I'd pull the photo I kept behind the sun visor and think about the boy. The son Alice and I gave up when we were seventeen. I didn't have to look at the picture much by then, I already knew, no matter how long I stared at it, that I couldn't see him growing inside Alice. It was a wrinkled four-by-six snapshot that happened to find Alice and me standing next to each other outside our high school cafeteria. I had my arm around her waist and was trying to kiss her. Plant a sloppy one on her that only teenagers have the balls to get away with. But the wrinkled moment isn't the kiss, it's the half second where she pulled away and I missed. To anyone else it'd look like I was leaning to kiss her belly, our boy. But I know better.

He came a day after we turned our graduation tassels. Ten round pounds, twenty-one inches. A big, heathy boy with ten fingers and toes and adoptive parents sitting out in the lobby waiting to take him from us. All the papers signed and nothing left but the "thanks a lots" and the "have a nice lifes." When the nurse wrapped him and handed him to Alice, he didn't curl up to her. It was as if he knew, like he had heard from inside Alice as we interviewed couples who wanted him and could care for him. Maybe he felt it when Alice reached out to shake the hands of the couple we finally found and when their hands met, all the love and connection a boy can have for his mother pulsed from Alice's belly, down her arm, and into the bodies of his new mom and dad. When Alice brushed his cheek with her finger, he turned away and stared past her arms, past me, to the door of the delivery room. I can't forget his dark brown eyes. He had my father's eyes.

I finished my beer and took the empties inside, lining them on the kitchen counter with the other returnables, about three dollars' worth. There was a note on the fridge: *T., No sales today. Return bottles tomorrow. Buy bread. Love, A.* The mugginess in the living room escaped from a cracked window and in the quiet, the breeze sounded like music as it left the house and ran along the river. I didn't want to wake Alice with my smell; sweat and two-stroke gasoline doesn't make for good company in bed. I left my grass-stained clothes in a pile at the end of the couch and sat down in my underwear. If Alice had come out to see me, I wonder if she'd have said that I was what ready looked like.

It was noon a few weeks later when the boss texted me a new job: a ranch in a cul-de-sac outside Samson. We were supposed to get an updated list of jobs at the beginning of each pay period but if a "quickie" like this came across the wire, the boss would forward it to us. He never passed on one. The banks paid Secured Properties forty bucks per job so for every ten Rid and I made, the boss made twenty. We were also only one of three teams the boss had running across the region so I can only imagine how nice it was to be him. At least he paid for the gas and never bounced a paycheck.

"Got a quickie," I said. "Near Samson."

"Christ," Rid said, "that's twenty minutes the other way." By that time, Rid and I had worked into a kind of communication with each other, the kind of thing that's born from spending too much time together doing the same thing until it's a habit. Rid wasn't the kind of guy to double back. Our second week together, the weed whacker kicked up a faceful of poison ivy and he couldn't see straight for a few days. He had me drive and it took me missing only a couple of turns, no more than a few minutes burned, before he booted me back over to shotgun. Twenty minutes was a lifetime to Rid, either that or it was the line that separated life moving forward and life standing still.

"C'mon, Rid. It's ten bucks now instead of next payday. I know it's worth my time."

"You're the kind of guy who stops to pick up a dime, aren't you?" He rolled his fingers along the steering wheel.

"And you're not?" The job we were coming from had a small stable and a corral overgrown with Queen Anne's lace and dandelions that hid piles of sunbaked horseshit. The first hit with the zero-turn sent a cloud of it raining onto the two of us. When we loaded up from there, we smelled like the type of guys who would stop to pick up a penny.

"Only if it's right in front of me," Rid said. He kept the truck straight. "Plus it looks like it's gonna storm soon. Got two jobs almost right next to each other coming up soon.

"Yea, but we're driving into the storm. It could start any minute. Better ten bucks now than *maybe* twenty later." The truck moved on. "Rid, the boss wants it done. I need the sure cash. We're going. We can get back to Samson in fifteen minutes the way you drive."

"Shit, kid. What's with you?"

"Need the cash."

"We all need the cash," he said.

"The wife and I want a house. Want it sooner than later."

"Takes a lot of lawn mowing to buy a house."

"She used to babysit her cousins but they're old enough to be on their own now. She's been selling Wrap-It for about a year now."

"What's that?"

"You know, it's a body-wrap-type deal. You stretch it around your waist and thighs and it makes you thinner."

"So she sells girdles?"

"Not really; these make you lose weight. Like the ones sold on those late-night infomercials. Only Alice sells them in person. Hired a few people to sell for her."

"Like Tupperware and dildos?"

"What? Jesus, no," I said. "They're weight-loss apparel."

"How do you lose weight with them?" he asked.

"I don't know but my wife says it works. She sells diet pills too." He looked at me as if I had just thrown up in my lap. I remember the first time Alice came home with a neon-blue brochure filled with men and women with huge smiles, wearing nothing but underwear and their wraps. She said someone had an info desk set up at the Laundromat and had told her all about the benefits and earning potential while our linens were on the spin cycle. I love Alice, always have, and it's that love that kept me calm when the first shipment of wraps came and I opened a box of what looked more like flesh-colored cling wrap and caffeine pills than a good investment. She was thrilled, though, and kept saying that this wasn't just a second income, it was her ticket to getting back into the body she had "before." It never bothered me that I didn't know anybody who was in the same shape as they were when they were seventeen because I think Alice knew that to be in a seventeen-year-old body when you're pushing twenty-seven wasn't just unrealistic, it was unhealthy. What bothered me was the way she always said it: *before.* Period. As if the boy was an edit cut off the end of her sentences, off her memories from when we were kids.

"We do what we can," I said. The road hummed under the truck as Rid pushed toward the dark clouds in the west.

"All right, kid"—he pulled onto the shoulder of the highway—"we'll head back to Samson. Looks like we ain't beating the rain."

■ ■

Rid turned down the cul-de-sac and kept the truck slow as we passed a line of houses with actual people living in them. Two-car families one right after the other with wives and husbands and children. Lawns that people mowed themselves. Or lawns that people paid teenagers to mow. People who had made it. The job came up on the right just before the loop, a lawn so overgrown that it folded back onto itself in matted, brown clumps. Weeds cluttered along the sides of the house and the edges of the drive-way. The top of a Realtor sign poked through the mess like the face of a friend in a crowd of strangers. *Price Reduced* in red letters.

"Shit," Rid said. "Looks like nobody's had this job on their list. It's gonna take us over an hour to mow this place, not to mention the time to rake all this shit up." He glared at me and I saw him calculating all the money he wasn't making now that we had committed to this one job. He parked the truck in the street and we climbed out. From the house, I heard someone yell to us. In the shadow on the porch, propped back in a plastic lawn chair, a man in faded jeans and a torn flannel looked out to Rid and me.

"You people are late," the man said. He ran a hand down the stubble on his cheek.

"Excuse me?" I said. "This job just came to us."

"I don't pay you to *not* mow my lawn." Rid and I looked at each other and we both shrugged.

"You don't pay us, man," Rid said. "The banks do. They own this place."

"That's only till the loan papers go through." The man rocked in his lawn chair and began to laugh. "Been taking a little longer than I'd planned but don't you worry, loan's coming and I'll be moved back in quicker than it's taking you to mow this place." He didn't get up to talk to us, he was happy to just sit in his chair and yell across the yard at us. I looked around the neighborhood. I could hear the screams of children playing in one of the backyards and someone had fired up their grill with too much lighter fluid. I could smell the gassy smoke from the street.

"All right, buddy," Rid said. He turned to me. "C'mon, let's get this job done. We're gonna get rained on. I'd rather be less wet than more when we finish." He pulled on his leather gloves and dug into the bed of the truck while I lowered the trailer's tailgate.

I mowed along the side of the house slower than what Rid would've liked but I wanted to get a look at the man. A bedroll lay along the back of the porch and empty tin cans stood lined against the house. When Rid passed the front of the porch with the weed whacker, I saw the man point and mouth something to him. I couldn't hear over the mower but it looked like Rid was trying hard to ignore him and just get the job done.

Halfway done with the backyard and the rain came. Quicker than I had thought and harder than I had wanted. Damp grass didn't stop Rid and me but this was too much. I killed the zero-turn and ran to the truck just as Rid was chucking a pair of clippers into the bed.

"Goddammit," he said. He slammed his door, wiping water from his face. "You know we're not getting paid for this. And the day's shot, can't mow soaked grass and make it look good in the pictures." I wiped my face on my sleeve and leaned back. Fat drops pounded the truck and I wished I were back at home on the couch listening to the wind and Alice snoring in the bedroom.

"Well, we started early today," I said.

"We only got eight jobs in, so starting early don't mean much, does it?"

"Better than nothing," I said. I looked out toward the house and the man. He was standing now at the edge of the porch, positioning the empty tin cans under cracks in the eaves trough to catch the rain.

"This isn't much more than nothing," Rid said. He had his hand over his eyes as if the rain had been an inconvenience to him more than anybody else. Like it was an insult. "Get me my lip smoke out of the glove box," he said.

"Your what?"

"Chew, kid. Got a tin in there. Get it." I popped open the glove box and sitting on top of the truck's manual was a handful of tins all with their labels ripped off. I grabbed one on top. "Not that one," Rid said. "Can't you read?"

"Read what?" I looked down at the tin in my hands and saw a length of Scotch tape stuck across the top that said *Thursday*. The ink of the letters filled the tiny grooves of the tape, making the writing look old, like the tin had seen so many Thursdays that it knew nothing else.

"Move," Rid said. He leaned across the bench and grabbed another tin. He popped it open and wedged a healthy pinch under his lip. "We'll wait to see if this passes. If not, we'll load out." He tucked the tin under his thigh and looked up to the house. "Been doing this job for years now. Mowed a thousand lawns, three times over, and you know how many times I've run into shit like this?"

"A few?" I asked.

"Zero. Zilch. Goose egg. And do you know why?"

"No."

"Because most people know there aren't any do-overs." He cracked his door, spit, and came back dragging his teeth up his bottom lip. "People like our friend out there don't get that." He leaned back in his seat and closed his eyes.

We watched the rain for another half hour without many more words. Every couple of minutes, Rid cracked his door to spit. The man on the porch tended to his tins of rainwater. He didn't pay us any mind once the rain fell. It looked like even in his situation, he still had the ability to separate the necessary from the secondary. A mowed lawn means nothing to a thirsty man.

■ ■

I was home early that afternoon, soaked.

"Mowing at the bottom of a lake?" Alice asked. She smiled at me from over her laptop.

"I know, right?" I said.

"Don't think about leaving those clothes in a pile," she said. "Put them in a plastic bag. Tomorrow's laundry day." I grabbed a balled-up Walmart bag from under the sink and went into the bedroom to change.

"How was today?" I asked.

"Sold a wrap," she called. "Got a lady's e-mail. Said she'd be interested in selling too." I didn't know much about Wrap-It but Alice told me that if she could sign up three full-time sellers, her immediate boss would give her a larger percentage of what they sold. She had a hard time keeping her sister on board. Alice had me convince my ma to sign up and I remember the look on her face when I told her about it. It was the same look that Rid gave me.

"Do you think she'll sign up?" I asked. I came out in a pair of gym shorts and a stained Beatles T-shirt.

"She should." She didn't look up from the message board she was posting to. "What's for dinner?"

I opened the fridge and just stared. A few cans of tuna. Eggs. Half-gone gallon of milk. Loaf of bread. Mason jar of pickled asparagus my ma had made. Mustard bottle propped upside down so what was left didn't crust on the bottom. "Tuna sandwiches," I said.

"Wonderful!"

"Babe, it's only tuna," I said.

"What? No, no, I've been messaging this woman. She lives in Detroit. Says she is interested in selling." She tapped at the keyboard and didn't look up. "Just think, if I sign her up by the end of the week, I'll have a foothold in a whole new market. More people means more buyers." I turned on the stove and started mixing the tuna and eggs. "Then if she signs up a few more people, that automatically places me in the Sapphire Salesman category."

"And that's a good thing, right?" I dug in the cupboard for some salt and pepper.

"Of course it's a good thing." She turned to me, propped up on an arm of the couch. "That means I can start selling the Pro-Fit–style wraps and vitamins!"

"And those are better than what you're selling now?"

"I would guess so." She got up and pulled down her pants. "See?" She had wraps around her butt and her thighs, stretched past the elastic of her panties. With her pants around her ankles, she shimmied around to show me her backside. "This Basic-Fit style just comes in a rectangle shape. The Pro-Fit forms to curves and targets trouble areas."

"And what does that mean?" I really didn't know and it looked like my wife was wearing a sweaty diaper so I think I was allowed to be a little confused. She pulled her pants up and fell back to her laptop.

"It means more money, Timothy."

There was a silence while I mixed the ingredients into a passable meal.

"And who can beat that?" I said.

I scooped up a handful of eggy tuna and molded it into patties before sliding them into the pan. I watched the oil pop and hiss from under them and thought about the man and his cans of water. I mean, I can live on canned tuna just fine and I'm sure even the pickiest of eaters would eventually get used to it. But when I saw that row of cans, placed just so under the steady streams of gutter runoff, I think a part of me planted itself into that lawn like a patch of crab grass, unable to remove, unable to forget.

■ ■

Every ten days or so, that ranch rotated to the top of the list and before we could unload the equipment, the man would holler from his lawn chair.

"You guys should be out here once a week. Grass grows too quickly to have you slacking off." Beyond the grunt he gave when we parked outside the house, it was easy for Rid to ignore the guy. He just put his ear protectors on, cranked the edger or the weed whacker or the clippers on, and went to work.

But it wasn't that easy for me. Every time I swung the mower close to the house, I'd stare at the man. He wasn't old, around forty, forty-five. The age where you have enough to lose that you'll lose yourself in the process. The third time we hit that place, I put half of a sandwich I'd bought on the front step before I hopped on the mower. I nodded at the man before walking back to the truck but all he did was suck on his lip and shout to Rid that he'd better make sure to not crack the siding with the edger. The next time we stopped out, I found that bag wedged under the propane tank out back. Looked like a raccoon had gotten to it.

■ ■

Five months into the job, Alice told me that she stopped taking her birth control. I came out of the shower and she was sitting, tapping away at the laptop, scrolling past pictures of people in underwear and cellophane. Her telling me that was something that ages a guy a couple of years when he hears it. I asked her why and she pointed at the computer screen and read: "Too many toxins, like alcohol, drugs, and even contraceptives, can hinder the effectiveness of Wrap-It products." *Besides*, she said, *we're ready.*

■ ■

It was past six, the sun had just come up, and Rid and I were pulling out of the day's first job. On the highway, heading toward the ranch outside Samson, I couldn't stop replaying the nonconversation Alice and I had the night before. Rid had been hollering at me while I was on the mower but I didn't hear him. To hell with the straight line.

"You go stupid overnight, kid?" he asked. "Or do you just not care?"

"Sorry, Rid. I got lost in my head. That's all."

"Lost? This job doesn't need a map." He slowed as we came close to Samson.

"It's my wife," I started. "We got into it last night."

"Fighting with the woman, eh. First time I ever heard of such a thing."

"Well, you see we don't fight. She just kinda, you know, *tells*. And that's that."

"What? You go out with the buds too much? She find a girlie mag on the back of the toilet?"

"She wants to start a family."

Rid looked over to me and just stared. Lines of dust folded into the creases of his mouth and dry grass stuck to the hair at his temples. "So what's the fucking problem?"

"We don't own a home yet," I said.

"So what?"

"So how you suppose to raise a kid without a house?" I knew I was talking at a guy who I had no business talking at. And maybe he was thinking, *Who the fuck does this kid think he is?* but I didn't feel the need to justify myself. Sometimes you just want to talk and damn whoever is stuck listening to you. "There's a way of things, Rid," I said. "A plan of action."

"It's all broad strokes, kid," he said.

"Excuse me?"

"You heard me. All this"—he waved his hand over the steering wheel, across the windshield. "Chaos." He turned down a dirt road. The way he said it, so convinced, maybe not of what he was saying but of himself saying it, sounded like a man familiar with stupidity. He'd seen a world of zero-turn know-nothings and empty houses. He heard too many people say too many things about everything from bank loans to weight-loss Reynolds Wrap. And he didn't buy any of it. He just wanted his jobs, one at a time, looping forever. Part of me hated him at that moment, hated the dismissal of how the world was according to eyes that weren't his, but also knowing that he'd probably been some kind of stupid at some point in his life.

"Yea, but—"

"But what?" he asked. "But nothing. So your old lady wants you to throw one in her? That's her right and who are you to keep that from her?" He pulled into the cul-de-sac. "Not what you had planned? Tough, man up and do it." He stopped the car before we got to the house. "Now, what in Jesus' pecs is this righteous mess?" Out the windshield we saw two police cruisers parked in the yard, cherry tops blaring.

"Might as well pull up and see what's what," I said. A cop met us outside the house.

"What do you two want?"

"We're the guys who take care of this place," Rid said. "We're with Secured Properties."

"Not today, you're not," the cop said. He looked into the back of the truck and then at me.

"What happened?" I asked.

"Neighbors heard a crash and saw someone moving around inside. You happen to know the squatter here?"

"No," I said. Rid shook his head and looked at his watch.

"But you knew he was living on the front porch?"

"Not my job to report the homeless," Rid said. The officer looked over his sunglasses at him and clicked his teeth.

"We only cut the grass, sir," I said. "The guy sat on the porch and watched us, nothing else. Been here every time we've come around." I heard someone yell from the house.

"I told you I'm waiting on the loan. Call the bank. Call them!" The man came from the front door, handcuffed and pushed by two officers. They led him to the back of one of the cruisers. I watched as they tucked his head past the doorframe and could feel the officer's hand on my own head. Feel the fingers as they matted my hair and locked me away.

"He busted in the front window," the officer said. "We found him asleep on the living room floor, using a landscape brick as a pillow. Listen, you guys aren't working here today."

"We don't work, we don't get paid," Rid said.

The cop didn't listen. He tapped on the hood of the truck and walked toward the cruisers, pointing and directing the other cops. The car with the man backed out of the lawn, tire tracks rutted into the soft earth, and I wondered how Rid would hide them in the after pictures. As the cruiser passed us, I looked for the man. Here was someone who was being kicked out of his house for the second time. The first time for failing to keep it, the second time for succeeding to get back in it. What else was left for him? I didn't know but I thought that maybe, if I could see the man, see his eyes, have them tell me across the space of two passing cars that this was all right, that I'd get my answer. I needed that. But I didn't see the man. He must've laid himself down in the back-seat because it was like he disappeared as soon as the car left the property, as if, without the house, the man was nothing.

■ ■

"Here." I handed Alice the picture I'd kept in the truck and walked to the kitchen to start dinner.

"What's this?"

"It's us," I said.

"Where did you get it? Did your mother find it?"

"It's just been around."

She smiled and pulled her laptop from her knees, folding it on the couch next to her. She came next to me at the sink, wrapped an arm around my waist, and held the picture in front of us.

"That was back when people liked you," she said. She squeezed me.

"And when I didn't talk back," I answered.

"You've always talked back," she said. She unwrapped herself from me and set the picture on the sill above the sink. We'd been saying the same thing to each other for forever. My grandfather used to say it to my mother and then to me when I got older. He passed before Alice came around but she picked up on it anyway.

"You could trade me in for a model that doesn't," I said. She was back on the couch now, laptop opened. I peeled some carrots.

"No," she said, "I think you're worth keeping." She leaned toward her laptop and scrolled through more pictures.

■ ■

Rid and I parked in front of the house the next day. Plywood replaced where the front window had been. Police tape crisscrossed the porch. We got out of the truck and the smell of lighter fluid blew across the neighborhood. I heard the kids scream again and though I wanted to keep my thoughts of the boy tucked behind my sun visor, my mind focused on him. He'd be just about ten years old. On the ride home the night before, I thought real hard about walking into the bedroom and waking Alice up. Tell her no. Tell her that ready isn't a vinyl-sided duplex and plastic wrap. Ready wasn't ready just because you said it was. I wanted to tell her she was wrong.

But I didn't. After dinner, Alice joined me in the shower and we stayed in there until the hot water ran out.

"So," Rid started, "I'll get the weeds, you tackle the yard. Fifteen minutes. Easy as that."

"Sure thing," I answered. I climbed up on the zero-turn and started her up. I wheeled it up and down the front yard, past the porch where the man watched us all those weeks. His bedroll and returnables were gone; his chair tipped over the edge of the porch.

I spun the mower around at the street and let it idle. The yard stretched below me, the straight line of new-mown grass wedged in between an expanse of shag, and for a moment, I swore I could see the grass I had just cut begin to grow again.

TO THE MAN ASLEEP IN OUR DRIVEWAY WHO MIGHT BE NAMED PHIL

Anthony Doerr

WELL, YOU'RE NOT sleeping anymore, thank goodness, though was that even sleep? It seemed a deeper, scarier condition; the kind of state people don't always wake from.

At least the cops are treating you well. They're surprisingly patient, aren't they? Gentle, even, standing with their hands behind their backs, waiting for you to walk the line the male officer has scratched with chalk on the pavement of our cul-de-sac. You shuffle your boots, hang your head. It's Friday night, ten-thirty p.m., plenty of places for a police officer to be, but no one's rushing you.

I feel a need to explain myself, Phil, to beg a measure of forgiveness, though I understand you may not want to grant it. It's just that we don't often find strangers asleep in our driveway. And, look, we were heading home from one of our kids' flag football games, a long drive after a long week, and my feet were cold from standing on the sidelines, and my bladder was overcapacity, and when we pulled into our street and saw your '88 Taurus parked crosswise across the bottom of our driveway, I didn't know what to think.

Your headlights were off, but your dome light was on, and all I could see inside was the shape of a man sitting very upright in the driver's seat. Which was weird, I guess, but what was weirder was that your head did not turn to watch our headlights as we pulled up. Nor did it turn when I tapped the horn.

I squeezed my truck around your rear bumper and pulled into our garage, and you did not turn to watch as I did this. My son said, "Who's here, Dad?" and I said, "Don't know, buddy," and sent him into the house in his cleats. Then I approached your car.

To be clear: we live in a dead-end subdivision of late-eighties homes high in the foothills above Boise, Idaho. Our garages are large, our roofs deteriorating. It's full of kids and dogs and it's hopelessly Caucasian. On a busy night, maybe one car turns into our street every hour. Our cul-de-sac, in particular, is not easy to find: we have friends with PhDs who can't find our house even after they've had two or three dinners here. In the eleven years we've lived in this house, we've found bull snakes, mule deer, baby robins, three-inch-long Mormon crickets, and a peregrine falcon in our driveway, but never a rusty '88 Taurus.

Were you a hearing-impaired traveler with car trouble? One of those meat salesmen who drive door-to-door hawking frozen rib eyes? Why didn't you get out and say hi, or head to the front door and ring the doorbell? And if what you were doing was sleeping, how in the world were you holding your head so upright?

The rear half of your car looked as if it had been painted with black house paint. Your backseat was stuffed to the roof with bulging trash bags. In the dim glow of the dome light I could see that your hair was stubbly, you were pale skinned, and you were dressed in camouflage. I called "Hello?" but you didn't move your head one millimeter.

Louder: "Hello?"

Not a twitch.

Which, I admit, spooked me.

So I backed away, closed the garage, telephoned my wife, who was returning from a lacrosse game with our other son, and said, "There's a guy asleep in our driveway, so when you come home, pull around him and I'll close the garage behind you," and she said, "Huh?" and I peed in the downstairs bathroom, feeling both guilty and grateful that our house has three mostly operational toilets, and sent my son upstairs with some postgame Oreos, and tiptoed to the bay window.

Could a man really sleep with his neck plumb straight? Or were you actually awake, enthralled by something I couldn't see: an owl, a comet, a vision?

When my wife's car arrived and raked your Taurus with light, your head still did not move, and she squeezed her car past yours and I closed the garage and we asked our other son, still in his lacrosse uniform, to go upstairs and join his brother, and he looked at us like, *I'm missing something cool down here, aren't I?*

Then my wife and I stood together in the dark.

I said, "I'm going back out there."

She said, "No, you're not."

But in the *Odyssey*, I wanted to tell her, pretty much every time Odysseus rolls up to a stranger's house, his hosts feed him and offer him wine. In Shakespeare's play, Macbeth's biggest crime in murdering the visiting King Duncan might not be murdering him but violating the sacred trust of a guest. In New Zealand in my early twenties, all I'd have to do is show up at a sheep farm and offer to work and they'd give me dinner, a place to put my sleeping bag, and as much beer as I could drink.

That, I wanted to say, is the kind of hospitality we should practice.

But there was a reason my wife didn't want me to go back into the driveway. I knew because I was worrying over it, too.

Guns.

In Idaho we have the sixth most firearms per capita of any state; you can buy a Baby Glock at Ridley's supermarket and drop it in the cart next to your cream cheese. You can carry your firearm in your car, you can buy a big, scary semiautomatic without a permit, and the governor just signed a law allowing you to carry a concealed weapon inside city limits anytime you want, permit-free, no questions asked. So even in our driveway, two miles from the state capitol, it's probably safer to assume unresponsive trespassers in camo have weaponry than to assume they don't.

My wife suggested you might have been a guest of our neighbors who was sleeping off some wine before driving home, so we called them and Sue picked up on the second ring, Sue who is always up for anything, and said, "Nope, no guests tonight!" I agreed to meet her in her driveway, and together we approached your Taurus, Phil, so that Sue could take a photo of your license plate, but she had trouble with her phone, and you were so still that I started wondering if maybe you were dead, if you might have chosen our driveway as a place to end your life, but as I drew within arm's reach of your window, I swear, a cloud closed over the moon, dimming what little light there was, and some trick of the shadows made it seem as if your eyes swiveled in their sockets, that you were staring *right at me*, and what felt like a gallon of antifreeze poured down my vertebrae and some atavistic part of my brain imagined your trash bags full of body parts, your trunk full of blood, and I hotfooted it for my front door.

Fear. Mistrust. Why was it so close to the surface? Sue followed me in and we stood in the bay window with the lights off and called the nonemergency number for the police, and waited on hold, but the call dropped because reception at our house isn't good, so Sue called a second time and a dispatcher asked some questions, and the three of us drank tap water in the dark.

Ten or fifteen minutes later, a police cruiser rolled into the cul-de-sac. No sirens, no flashers. It pulled up behind your Taurus and sat for a long time with its spotlight on your rear window. It sat so long I wondered if the police, too, had fallen asleep, if some sleeping enchantment had befallen our cul-de-sac, but then a bunch of lights on the cop car came on, and two policewomen got out of the cruiser and walked to either side of your car, one with a flashlight and the other with a hand on her weapon, and the first one shone her light in your face, and the policewoman on the other side of the car stepped back a little, and all this time you didn't move. The first policewoman rapped on your window and you didn't move. She rapped a second time, a third, loud louder loudest, seemingly enough to shatter your window, and still you didn't move.

Then, just as the officer stepped away, finally thank God you turned your head.

They got you up out of the car, and you were tall and thin and though I couldn't see clearly through the branches in front of our window, your pants didn't look like they were in good shape, the hems ragged around what might have been laceless boots, and you sat down in our driveway, right where our sons wrote *Welcome Santa!* in huge chalk letters one Christmas Eve, and this was when I began to dislike myself.

I thought of all the human beings I'd seen asleep in parks in San Francisco, on benches in Cleveland, on curbs in Nairobi; I thought of Ryszard Kapuściński, who upon arriving in New Delhi for the first time came across a river of people sleeping in the middle of the airport road, and was amazed at how the bus honked its horn to rouse them, and then by how everybody climbed back into the road and fell asleep again as soon as the bus had passed.

Why is it okay to sleep in some places and not okay to sleep in others?

Even with the window cracked I couldn't hear what the officers were asking you. Soon a second police cruiser arrived, and a male officer got out, and he stood you up, and I heard him say, "Minnesota, huh?" and he seemed to be calling you Phil.

Phil? I'm failing here, failing in some big way I don't understand. I pay my taxes, read Krugman, read Chomsky, donate to the homeless shelter, drop coats off at the Youth Ranch, regurgitate party lines about the need for more social services, but then a stranger shows up in the driveway and like some Bronze Age villager I close the stockade and bar the gates. Wouldn't a better version of me have offered you something? A bed, a cup of tea, a pair of wool socks?

Or maybe you didn't need anything from me, let alone some self-congratulatory attempt at decency; maybe you just needed some quiet, some darkness, and I came along and wrecked that.

The policeman gestures for you to walk his chalk line. You walk the line more slowly than any man has ever walked ten feet. I press my ear to the window screen.

The policeman says: "Done this before?"

You say, "A few times."

It would take most folks ten seconds to walk that line and walk it back; it takes you three minutes. But you manage it. The officers shine lights in your eyes; Sue and my wife whisper; I can't hear any of it. Finally the cops hand you something, maybe your ID, and you balance it on both palms as though you've received Communion, and carry it to your car very, very slowly.

You turn the ignition several times, and your engine coughs to life, and your Taurus pulls away.

I walk out to the driveway.

"Something's off there," says one policewoman.

"Something not right," says the other.

Down the street you take a wrong turn into the other cul-de-sac, make a U-turn, and vanish up the road.

"Thank you for treating him so respectfully," I say. "We weren't sure what to do."

The policeman says, "You did the right thing."

The last snow of winter gleams on the ridges above the neighborhood. Our breath shows as we exhale. The officers say goodbye; Sue walks home; my wife puts our boys to sleep. I stand in the darkness and wonder.

If you were in a brand-new Prius, if you were wearing a suit and tie, if your car wasn't stuffed full of trash bags, would we have called the cops? If we lived in a poorer neighborhood, would the police have come so quickly? If your skin was a different color, Phil, would they have let you drive off into the night?

Something's off there.

Something not right.

Once, at my wife's office, they did a team-building exercise where facilitators stood everybody hip to hip along a line. If you were read to as a child, they said, take a step forward. If you had health insurance as a child, take a step forward. If your parents took you to art galleries or plays as a child, take a step forward. If you studied the culture of your ancestors in elementary school, take a step forward. If your family owned the house where you grew up, take a step forward. If English was your first language, take a step forward. If you never had to skip a meal, take a step forward. If you were able to complete college, take a step forward.

You know who gets to decide who's right and who's wrong? The people who take the most steps forward.

Out here in the driveway, I'm remembering Saint Augustine. "Since you cannot do good to all," he wrote, "you are to pay special attention to those who, by accidents of time, or place, or circumstance, are brought into closer connection with you."

You did the right thing.

Did I?

SOUP KITCHEN

Annie Dillard

ON SOME DAYS a writer can't write. Some days a painter can't paint, and a composer can't compose. These wretched men and women know they are eating the food, burning the fuel, and adding nothing. How can they get through the days? How can they relieve their despair?

They can work in a soup kitchen. They can give blood. No one can hate herself, no one can despise himself, who has fed a hungry stranger or saved a life. That's a good day's work.

Howlin' Wolf

In Parchman   Prison
in stripes   standing
guitar gripped   like a neck
strangled   strummed
high strung   & hard.
Mostly   you moan
see how   heavy
your hands   hang with-
out women   or words
we cannot
quite know.   How is this
not hell   being made
to make music   here where
music only   makes time
go slow   cloudy
like blue
Depression glass?   Under
the hard sun   of your smile
we see   stripes like those
that once   lined the slave's
unbent back
blood   & gunk
spit   it out
like a song   low down
gutbucket
built   for comfort
not built   for speed.
Gimme   the brack
of the body   the blue

the bile   all
you sing   or howl.
If a wolf   then lone
then orphan   then *hangry*
enough to enter   into town
to take food   from the mouths
of low houses   a hen
a stray   it is never
enough.   You don't need
tell me   why
we here   you know
better   black
as an exclamation   point
the men   all around
you   in stripes
how long   their sentences
their dark   faces ellipses
everywhere accidental.
The white   man
in front   proud
or is it   prideful
he wears   no number
& now   exiled under
the earth   no one
recalls   his name.
Yours   a dark wick
waiting   we burn
wanting you
to step   into song
to again   howl
till you sweat   through
your shirt   & two
white   handkerchiefs
as if   a revival
preacher   waving
praise   no flag

of surrender—
the guitar   a blunt
instrument   your hair
your shoes   even your
voice   shines.

—Kevin Young

LOOKING FOR A HOME

Karen Russell

In May 2014, I moved to Portland, Oregon. It was my seventh move in five years. My boyfriend and I found an apartment with a month-to-month lease, a coup at a moment when Oregon's apartment vacancy rate had been hovering around 2 percent—the lowest in America. Central Eastside, Portland, is rapidly gentrifying, but our neighborhood retained a gritty heterogeneity. We lived half a mile from the warehouses and the train tracks near the Willamette River, and catty-corner to an H. P. Lovecraft–themed bar where goth fairies drink highballs under a mural of purple tentacles (herbal tea is also available).

Our new apartment building was built in 1890; the landlord told us that it was on the National Register of Historic Places. It had beautiful Italianate window bays and Victorian trim, and looked to me like the architectural offspring of a castle and a cupcake, somewhat incongruously fronting a Shell station. Barber Block, as it is known, had housed a mortuary firm, a nickelodeon theater, a restaurant, a women's dormitory, and a bank. We would pay $940 a month to live in a spacious one-bedroom, well below the market rate for Portland. How was this possible? A friend speculated that we were the hapless couple stepping into a B horror movie—storing our bikes in the old crematorium, turning a deaf ear to the wailing ghosts. My boyfriend countered that any ghosts had likely long ago traded up to a riverfront condo.

As it turns out, Barber Block *is* haunted, haunted by the living.

Our apartment was above a homeless shelter. This was the reason why the rent had remained so low.

My first night in the apartment, I was awoken many times by a shrill minor-key chord. This was the train horn. Wide awake, I became alert to another chorus, much closer to our open window. Invisibly, anonymously, our neighbors introduced themselves to us. Voices flowed under the window, leaving a residue of muddy sound without clear meaning; out of the general eddying came the occasional metallic flash, a scream or a distinct curse. A man started howling threats around three a.m.; it was impossible to know if his interlocutor was real or imaginary. City dwellers everywhere have likely played a version of this grim midnight game, Does That Screaming Require My Intervention?

At a softer, pinker hour on that first night, just below our window, a woman began to wail. I went to the window but I saw only the lagoon of streetlight—nobody was visible. If I had gone outside and really looked, I'm sure it would have been quite easy to find hers and many other sleepless faces.

■ ■

The voices that we heard at night emanated from living bodies. You could not forget this. These voices had homes, walls of flesh and bone. The bodies they belonged to did not. This was confirmed for me the following morning, when I opened the door to the street and found a man curled in the alcove that separated our building from the street. To exit, I'd either have to wake this person up or take an awkward, lunging step over his unconscious body. I opted for the latter, telling myself that I did not want to disturb him.

This became a daily exercise in empathy suspension. The stranger in the doorframe was rarely the same man—people often turned up for a few days and disappeared just as suddenly. Sometimes I'd leave bottled water or food, but I don't think I ever knelt to introduce myself or ask what else I could do. I was ashamed of this routine—the literal sidestepping of a suffering person. I kept telling myself that I did not want to wake these men; wasn't that the reason I tiptoed around them? But it was my own equilibrium, I fear, that I did not want to disturb.

More than once, when the stunned broken-neck angle of a person's body suggested something worse than sleep, I called 911. The first time the paramedics responded to one of my calls, they asked me to dial 211 for future nonemergencies. Then they gave me some tips for determining whether a person was overdosing or simply unconscious. The paramedics were on a first-name basis with some of the homeless residents of Barber Block. As one of the guys living at the shelter told me, as we watched EMTs tend to an unconscious man, "Turns out when you're calling the paramedics night after night, it's the same three guys that come out."

■ ■

Daylight had revealed the members of the nightly choir to us. So many people were asleep under the bright sun or curtained inside the rain, depending on Portland's moody weather. They were laid out in the open caskets of the medians, and camping under the loony-looking cherry tree near the Burger King. Dozens of sleeping bags were lumped in the dewy scrub grass near the river, forming a surreal tableaux. Nylon cocoons, large and shimmering, pupating under the lightly falling rain of Oregon. But this was a reverse metamorphosis. Very quickly, I lost access to that vision of the campers' sleeping bags as a rainbow of cocoons. Under the gray skies of Oregon, I started thinking of the blue morgue, body bags.

■ ■

By June, I was feeling less like an intruder in the apartment, and more like its tenant. Walking through the rolling heat at dusk, I loved coming back to Barber Block. I loved the sound of the toothy key turning in the lock. Sometimes I'd call my boyfriend on the apartment intercom, just for the pleasure of being buzzed up. I couldn't start up the stairs without pausing to look at the mailbox, where our surnames shared the white slot under an apartment number. My mind often felt like an overexposed photograph; it took me a few weeks to understand that I was experiencing simple happiness.

Temperatures were unusually high that spring, and then in July there was a terrible heat wave. Whenever I ran into someone on the stairs of our apartment building, we'd smile through a mask of sweat and commiserate about our lack of air-conditioning. I was getting to know my indoor neighbors, too. There was the young woman who looked like Velma from *Scooby-Doo*, the always-hoarse middle-aged musician, the Indian woman with the beautiful baby, the neurotic blond guy who patrolled the laundry machines. Certain voices bled through our bedroom wall at night, and now I could picture the faces of our indoor neighbors to which they belonged.

Outside was a different story. I'd gotten used to the train horns at night; the human screaming still woke me. How often did I get up and go to the window, to see if there was something I could do? After the first few nights, not very often at all.

Some of our homeless neighbors who we saw on a routine basis:

The young Mexican guy with tuba-player cheeks who slept on the cement steps near the apartment Dumpsters.

The white woman who flashed a pink, childlike smile at all passersby, revealing a single tooth. Who was watching out for her? She seemed to have no friends, no protectors. She was mentally ill and well over sixty years old. Anybody could do anything to her body, I often thought. Crimes against her body would go unrecorded and unprosecuted, and likely had. When I say that she seemed defenseless, I mean that the very air around her felt unshelled—yolky and violable. If auras existed, hers would have been spigoting rosy light. Yet she'd smile at anyone, everyone.

The horseshoe-bald man with ginger sideburns who was not quite five feet two, pacing the intersection with the harried aimlessness of a pigeon.

The white guy with a chronic sunburn and Ripley's Believe It or Not! yellowed toenails who sat outside the Jackson's gas station, holding loud, abusive conversations with himself.

"D'Nuts," who was briefly my friend and then not, who once

asked to take a photograph with me. Weeks later, he reappeared with a red Walgreens photo album, sweeping his hand over our photograph like a magician, as if the proximity of our two faces inside the plastic sleeve was as stupendous a violation of natural law as a levitating building.

■ ■

I wish I'd done a better job of getting to know these people, so that I could give you a fuller portrait of them. But the truth is that during my year and six months living on Barber Block, I did not make a single real friend. At best, you could say that I became friendly with my homeless neighbors. We exchanged smiles, or a few words of conversation. The urgency of their needs could generate a kind of atmospheric pressure on the smallest of small talk, charging our brief interactions with something that felt like intimacy. But at the end of the day, I disappeared into my apartment, and we were still largely strangers to one another.

Most of these faces were white; most of those experiencing homelessness here are Oregon natives, and the population of Oregon is overwhelmingly white (the original state constitution had a "whites only" clause). Oregon has a history of racial exclusion and discriminatory housing practices that are very much a part of its present; as of this writing, thousands of Portland's African American homeowners have been pushed out of their historic neighborhoods (which were created by redlining) to the city's edges. But if you're looking for diversity in Portland, the shelter is a good place to visit. Between 2013 and 2015, the number of unsheltered African Americans jumped by 48 percent. African Americans make up 7 percent of the general population in Portland, and 25 percent of those without housing. Homelessness is also on the rise among other minority groups, women, and families.

Why is this happening? Homelessness, as everyone to whom I spoke kept reminding me, is a multidimensional problem. An incomplete list of reasons might include housing costs that have risen twice as fast as incomes; sharp declines in public assistance;

deindustrialization, the automation of many jobs, and declining wages for low- and middle-income workers; discriminatory housing policies and practices and a housing system that perpetuates racial inequality; concentrated poverty that leaves generations of people moated without access to the opportunities available in wealthier neighborhoods; inadequate or unavailable psychiatric and health care; systemic racism in our criminal justice system, our schools, our job market, our public services; breakdowns in the foster-care system; and decades of erosion of the federal budget for housing assistance, which, adjusting for inflation, is about half of what it was in 1979.

Our poorest citizens—disproportionately people of color—continue to function as America's fleshy insulation system, the shock absorbers who bear the brunt of the impact when rents skyrocket or jobs dry up. For many chronically homeless people, today's "housing crisis" has been ongoing for decades. But it's only recently—now that the blast radius has spread to white middle-class families—that we have begun to define Portland's lack of affordable housing as a "state of emergency." Upsettingly and unsurprisingly, the greater the incomes of those impacted, the more attention we pay to escalating rents and no-cause evictions. A 2016 report from Metro's Equitable Housing Initiative noted: "Even households with moderate incomes are finding themselves priced out of neighborhoods where they work or go to school."

■ ■

In September 2015, Mayor Charlie Hales declared a "state of emergency" to address homelessness, as did Los Angeles, Seattle, and the state of Hawaii. Practically, this permitted West Coast mayors to fast-track new emergency shelters and to jump certain bureaucratic hurdles, with the goal of improving the lives of the thousands of men, women, and children sleeping outside each night. Hales's decision came at a moment when Portland's unsheltered population outnumbered the available beds three to one. Josh Alpert, Hales's chief of staff and point person for the new strategy, said that Portland should be able to do much more for those living on its streets, much faster. The city opened a stopgap shelter for men in a former business school. It opened a temporary shelter for women and couples in the Army Reserve Center. City and county leaders pledged $30 million toward shelter beds, affordable apartment units, and rental protections.

Not everyone embraced the new initiatives. Some Portlanders complained about feeling unsafe in their neighborhoods; many business owners and homeowners alike were upset about what one commenter referred to in an online post as "the recreational homeless who are camping, fucking, and doing drugs in our doorways." And I'll admit to feeling alarmed by the marked increase of tarps lashed to trees and pup tents pitched on the sidewalks.

"We are making it far too easy for people to be homeless," I heard several people complain. Was this true?

On a rainy October morning, I put the question to Dan, one of the men who staffed the shelter next door, a funny middle-aged guy and a benign flirt who could drink his body weight in Mountain Dew. He shook his head.

"Portland is a liberal city, it's tolerant, it's got a temperate climate." But he told me he doubted that people were getting on buses in Philly and Dallas and "coming to Portland to be homeless," as if it were the Disney World of homelessness. "Most of the people who you see on the street here were born in Oregon."

I've heard this referred to as the "perverse incentive problem," the idea that offering more services will draw even more homeless men and women to Portland. A version of "If you build it, they will come." Those involved in homeless advocacy work call it "the magnet myth"—the notion that Portland, because of its progressive politics and relatively mild weather, holds a special attraction for homeless people, particularly young ones. In 2015, the *Oregonian* ran a special section on homelessness, which called this view an "oversimplification." Portland does seem to attract more people without shelter than other parts of the country; but that appears to be true of cities generally. Urban areas usually have more services for the homeless than rural places, and if you are carless, or disabled, or sick, or penniless, the density of a city makes these services easier to access.

The Portland Housing Bureau issued a reminder that part of what presumably has made Portland so attractive to many liberal-minded people is its "culture of caring."

"The wider community also has a stake in ending homelessness. As members of a community," writes the Portland Housing Bureau to Multnomah County, "we want to take care of our citizens, including those with illnesses or disabilities who cannot care for themselves. In addition, all of us want safe, clean and livable streets and neighborhoods."

Who would disagree? But some Portlanders felt that the campsites under bridges and on public property had made their neighborhoods less clean, less safe, less livable.

Biking down the Springwater Corridor during this period, a gorgeous twenty-one-mile trail along the Willamette River, you would have found a blue heron sanctuary and scenic buttes covered in firs and also hundreds of tent campers. Local residents who lived near Eighty-Second Street, where most of these tents were concentrated, complained of crime, drug use, pollution, and noise. Some bike commuters reported that they no longer felt safe along the trail, and asked the city to clean up a strip they'd nicknamed the "Avenue of Terror."

"I mean, we're calling it the 'Avenue of Terror'? That's not a nature trail anymore," a comedian joked at an open mic near our apartment, where my boyfriend and I went not long after we'd moved to Barber Block.

The room was mostly silent (it was also mostly white, a bald, inescapable fact of life in Portland that nearly all of the comedians worked into their sets, finding dozens of scaldingly funny ways to tell us how discomfiting it felt to play to a nearly all-white house). I remember thinking that maybe everybody's conflicted attitudes about the homeless camps had created some kind of impenetrable fog in the bar, an earnest anxiety so thick that no joke could cut through it.

Despair can function as an analgesic, numbing us to our shared responsibility for this crisis in progress. It can be almost comforting to yield to despair, in the face of vocabulary like "growing wealth disparity," and "climbing housing costs," which evoke a sense of inertial forces, ungovernable and unstoppable as the shifting of tectonic plates, continental drift. Or, for an even uglier metaphor, the runaway growth of subdividing cancer cells. In Portland, for example, journalists have been writing about the homeless camps "mushrooming" throughout the urban woods and public plazas of downtown Portland—a word I've used myself to describe the scene, as if the proliferation of human beings sleeping under tarps and cardboard were the result of unusually heavy rains.

But just like "natural" disasters in the Anthropocene, housing bubbles and market crashes have human authors:

"'Millions die' was ultimately a policy choice . . ." writes Mike Davis in *Late Victorian Holocausts.* "The victims had to be comprehensively defeated well in advance of their slow withering into dust."

Davis was talking about famines in the "golden age" of liberal capitalism, but the same statement applies to the overlapping crises of our present moment.

A Room Becomes Home

One day at the end of my first Oregonian summer, I surprised myself by calling the bank and requesting that they change the address on my checkbooks. I started buying my insurance through Oregon's Health Co-Op. My boyfriend's sister gave me a Ducks T-shirt, so that I could camouflage myself as a local sports fan. My agent shipped all the mail she'd collected for me over the past half decade to the Barber Block apartment. My boyfriend gave me a waterproof jacket for the winter rains, the knee-length shroud of resignation that Oregonians wear from October to March. I watched the salmon become suicidally amorous in late red September, muscling up Eagle Creek with the last of their strength to spawn and die. I learned that Couch Street in downtown Portland is actually pronounced "Cooch," as in 2 Live Crew's "Pop That Coochie." I watched leaves curl and fall off the trees in our neighborhood, snow ghosting over them. I ceased to feel shock when I looked up from lacing my sneaker on the Burnside Bridge and rediscovered the flickery outline of Mount Hood. The cashiers knew my name at the Jackson's minimart. One of them, Janice, gave me a Christmas card with a candy cane taped on it; I felt elated, even after I watched her hand one to the guy buying Max Caf coffee behind me. Once or twice, a new acquaintance greeted me by name on the street, a dizzying collision in the middle of an otherwise anonymous weekday. I started feeling a little less like a silhouette. We bought a table with feet like lion's paws, or perhaps a lion pretending good-naturedly to be a table, and a chest of drawers. I unpacked the rest of my seventy-pound suitcase.

Feeling less like a silhouette did not always feel good. Despite the entropic costs of moving every few months, there is also something liberating about traveling light. I'd felt unmoored for a long time, but my rootlessness was always my choice. I crossed state lines and hopped continents, knowing that I had a sturdy net.

Some of the older men I met in the shelter below our apartment also described themselves as inveterate wanderers. Even if they'd had the option, they said, they would not have wanted to settle down. Many of the younger campers I saw by the river that summer also seemed to be camping volitionally, smoking dope and sharing food and booze in the sunset. Some told me that they'd chosen to live outdoors, for a season or for a lifetime.

But most of the people to whom I spoke on Barber Block did not strike me as people with choices.

At night, in the starkly lit theater of the bank parking lot, the residents of Barber Block with south-facing windows often saw a stencil of a man, his age impossible to determine, dancing spastically while grunting and clapping his hands. It was like looking into hell. His moves were sugary, insane. He was still visible to the rest of us, but he was on the wrong side of the mirror now.

And who did I mean by "us," exactly? The domiciled? The lucid? The sober? The solvent? The lucky? The loved?

■ ■

On my side of the window, I'd now been living in Portland for eight months. It was my longest stint in one place in many years. I felt so happy that my mail kept coming to the same address. I loved knowing that we owned the silverware in the drawers. I'd stand under the showerhead while my boyfriend cooked dinner, knowing that in a few hours we'd go to bed together, and wake up in the same place. Warm water hit my neck, my naked back, and a knowledge softly drilled its way into my body: I wanted to stay here. This was what it felt like to choose to live somewhere.

"Ours" had become my favorite word. My boyfriend had become my fiancé. I had truly never known this kind of intimacy; I had never before been capable of sustaining it. To exist in an overlapping sphere, where everything was shared—I felt a joy I hadn't known since early childhood. "Ours" thrilled me applied to anything. "Our" kitchen. "Our" shower liner. "Our" dubious Robo Taco leftovers.

One day, I called the apartment "our home."

But pronouns can become exclusionary, gated communities. "We," for example. "Us."

Grammar can erect a false wall. Look at how I keep falling into this trap, writing this piece. To refer to the thousands of diverse individuals with unique histories who are sleeping on the street tonight as "the homeless" certainly expedites a sentence. But it inadvertently reinforces an ugly and false idea, perhaps secretly consoling: that "the homeless" are a monolithic population, a different species of person from those of "us" lucky enough to have jobs and homes.

How do we begin to bring down these walls—to create a more elastic "we"? For starters, I'd need to exhume and revise a largely unconscious assumption: that the audience of this piece will be primarily people "like me," people reading by electric light indoors, people with the resources to buy a literary anthology and the *space*—literal and figurative—to read it at their leisure. That may well prove to be the case, but if I slip into writing for "us" about "them," I'm certainly part of the problem, reinforcing the false wall. We all want a safe place to live in the future, wherever we presently bed down. We are all vulnerable. In fact, for an increasing number of people in America, the difference between living indoors and living on the street is an injury, an accident, a family emergency, a bad season, a month's salary.

"Us" versus "them," that binary view, fails to recognize that sickness and health and solvency and bankruptcy are of course porous states; that sanity and insanity exist on a continuum; and that every house standing is a house of cards, be it a brick-and-mortar duplex or a human body. Some people have far more resources than others to rebuild with when disaster strikes. But nobody is indestructible.

"Two missed paychecks," one of the men outside the shelter told me. The condensed history of how he went from living indoors in Washington to sleeping in his van.

Mike

"I'd like to live in a tiny house."

Mike had a nose like a red pepper and extraordinarily luminous eyes, lake-water blue. He was a fixture on the corner, sitting in the shade for hours with his motorized wheelchair parked next to the shelter. Even in repose, his face had the angular integrity of origami, the creases sharpened by decades of smiling. He often volunteered at a senior center—Mike was a magician—where he bragged that he could make anyone laugh. A botched operation when he was an infant had severed a nerve and left him legally blind. He preempted all pity: "People feel sorry for me, but I tell them not to. For me, this is what is normal."

"I grew up living on a boat," he said, "so I really don't need much space at all." He liked the idea of a little house, because he was tired of the shelter's noise, the lack of privacy.

"They want you to want what *they* want for you," he explained. "But I want my own place."

I'd seen the tiny houses going up on Division. I asked Mike if he was working with the city, or perhaps a nonprofit.

He shook his head. Then his voice dropped to a whisper, as if he did not want the other men to overhear the plan he'd hit on.

"I got the Yellow Pages, and I called an architect."

I must have been silent a beat too long, because Mike's voice lifted an octave:

"He said he would try to help me. I need to call him again. I wanted to find a quiet place to call him today, but it's too late now. He is expecting my call."

His hand swept his head, and his eyes followed the line of men moving into the shelter; now there was a hitch of anxiety when he spoke.

"I just need to find a quiet place to call him."

■ ■

At the shelter next door to our apartment, dinner was served at five-thirty p.m., but somewhere between fifteen and forty people were always milling around outside the blue door. Across the Willamette River, on the other side of the bridge, people coagulated in slow, colorful clots around different entryways and arches: the Portland Rescue Mission, the Union Gospel Mission. It rained all January, and people were always smoking in the rain, sheltering small flames with their hands. Smoking kills, as the label warns, but I found myself admiring these smokers' commitment to its ritualistic aspects, even in the bone-chilling damp. Their lit cigarettes looked like miniature scrolls to me, leaking blue prayers.

I often found myself walking home at dusk with a bag of groceries, carrots leafing cartoonishly over the paper bag. "Excuse me, excuse me," I murmured, wending through the men queued up for dinner service outside the shelter. Passersby could travel through this crowd like ghosts through walls. In their midst but also, somehow, by mutual agreement, invisible. I sometimes tried to make eye contact, but I often felt hot faced and flummoxed. I was very aware of my bags loaded down with fresh food, and of the safe, warm home waiting for me half a block away.

Occasionally a phrase rattled in my ear, *and there's plenty more where that came from.* A very American phrase, abundance leveraged like a threat. This experience of "plenty" should be available to everyone, as a basic right; who would disagree? But doesn't *that* ambition sound Utopian—a word synonymous, by today's definition, with "impossible," "naïve"?

Indicting our impoverished vision of paradise, Toni Morrison warned against our tendency to envision Eden as a private garden. A place where the abundance is inversely proportional to the number of inhabitants:

"Plenty, in a world of excess and attending greed, which tilts resources to the rich and forces others to envy, is an almost obscene feature of a contemporary paradise. In this world of outrageous, shameless wealth squatting, hulking, preening before the dispossessed, the very idea of 'plenty' as Utopian ought to make us tremble. Plenty should not be understood as a paradise-only state but as normal, everyday, humane life."

In half a minute, I would be stepping over a disabled man zippered into a gray nylon bag to enter my home. On a cellular level, this felt entirely wrong. A fizzing pressure filled my chest, one like suppressed laughter but far more terrible. On more than one occasion, it turned out, the stranger in the doorway was awake, and we both apologized at the same moment; he moved to make a space for me, and I crossed the threshold with my overflowing bags of groceries. *How did we let it come to this?*

■ ■

Hermit crabs were a popular pet when I was growing up in South Florida. At the pet store kiosk in the Dadeland Mall, some sadist had given the naked crabs no option but to choose from decidedly inappropriate housing: One crab was struggling around inside a

Magic 8 Ball. Others had been forced to move into artificial shells painted like football helmets.

In Portland, men and women without a roof or a room to call their own must improvise shelters out of salvage, the garbage of people living inside four walls. People who lack what the city has euphemistically named "indoor alternatives" build homes out of whatever raw materials are available to them. It is heartbreaking to see a medically or mentally frail person sleeping outside, on asphalt, under a tarp thinned to the violet transparency of a nail bed. But there are also cases where, whatever your perception of its inadequacy and shoddiness, the campsite you are looking at is very clearly somebody's *home*. Filled with kitchenware and clothing and floral duvets and musical instruments. I have seen pup tents and plywood shacks and ancient dust-orange RVs that shelter whole families.

I have been truly shocked by how many people can emerge from a single tent: one, two, three, four adults, the tent heaving like an overcrowded womb. Dogs, too, clicking around the bricks of rubble and foam. On numberless occasions in Portland, I've been humbled by the sight of an older camper stooping to feed her animals.

I've also seen kids doing their homework on a dirty bean bag chair propped outside their camper, a toddler wandering unchaperoned around the clustered tents.

Portland is also home to several self-organizing outdoor camps, like Dignity Village, Right 2 Dream Too, and Hazelnut Grove, where campers live by a code that includes no stealing, no weapons, and no drug use. These are laudable places and a sanctuary for many people. But most people without permanent homes, let's assume, would really prefer an "indoor alternative."

According to the *Oregonian*, "A higher percentage of long-term homeless men and women sleep outside here than almost anywhere in the United States."

The sheer volume of campers means that we are becoming accustomed to the sight of men and women huddled under bright blue tarps, hidden in plain sight on the city steps. Hales's "state of emergency" was intended in part to shine a light on the urgent and recurring needs of those experiencing homelessness; to remind those of us with homes that thousands of our neighbors are in crisis, even if, to passersby, these campers' suffering is often dismissed as stasis. As their numbers climb, will the homeless camps become easier for everyone with a home to ignore? The danger, it seems to me, is that our "state of emergency" will again come to seem like a regular Wednesday; that many of us will exempt ourselves from working for change, lulled by a hopelessness, a false sense that the growth of the camps is both inevitable and irreversible.

How do we continuously refresh our sense that Portland's homeless city within the city *is* an emergency state, an inhumane state—that we cannot risk becoming inured to the suffering of our neighbors? How do you keep homeless camps in cities from becoming an ordinary sight, the status quo, while also welcoming people with nowhere else to go?

American Mobility/Who Gets to Go Home?

I'm going home, I'd sometimes think in the car. Just that one thought, looping like a song. Accelerating over the steel bridge, I felt the knowledge travel from my heels to my scalp. I felt it along the gumline, which was vibrating like a plucked string; I felt happy everywhere, even in my teeth. After a few months of this, the thought slid out of my consciousness. One day, I caught myself driving home on autopilot.

By this time I'd come to the awestruck realization that this feeling of home was portable, transferrable to another space; somehow it had happened, a home had extended its awning over me and another human. We'd carry that invisible awning with us, I now believed, even if we moved. But I also knew that we owed a great debt to this first home in Southeast Portland, the room on Barber Block that physically housed us for those first fourteen months together, held us in space and time as we turned a fantasy blueprint of home into something shared and real.

In April 2015, we began looking at houses. I loved the authorized trespassing that was the "open house." Houses seemed like sentences to me—some had straightforward layouts, some kept subdividing and ramifying, spinning off stairways and corridors like a complex German syntax. You could move from clause to clause, imagining your own nouns and verbs animating the empty spaces. In the beginning, we loved touring homes; this was before we started placing offers, anteing with all the savings we had, and discovering that this was still not enough to purchase a home in the neighborhood we'd chosen, inner Southeast Portland.

That spring, we learned that list prices meant nothing. We placed offers on seven houses; every one of them went to all-cash buyers who offered between $30,000 to $90,000 *over* the list price. We were competing with developers, new hires relocating to Portland, equity refugees from the Bay Area. We expanded our search. We toured a house where the selling feature was a building that looked like a torture shed in the backyard ("Accessory Dwelling Unit Potential!"). We placed an offer on a house in a nice neighborhood that sounded like the title of a seventies-era porno, Sullivan's Gulch. The house fronted the I-84, which we'd convinced ourselves sounded almost like a rushing river. This house was sold to someone else, for nearly $100,000 over the asking price.

We felt torn about how much to offer. We felt torn about what school district to choose, how much debt we could afford to take on. We felt torn about what compromises we were willing to make on things like bedrooms and street noise and commute time.

Something occurred to me then, something so embarrassingly obvious that I'm reluctant to include it here:

People with options feel torn. People with options feel pulled, tugged—people who *can* move in multiple directions. Whereas those without homes are often immobilized by illness and poverty and addiction. They lack stable shelter, a bed in which to dream.

Without this most basic infrastructure, how does a person so much as imagine alternatives, let alone move toward them, inhabit them? Feeling "torn" is yet another luxury of the highly mobile. Feeling "torn" is a symptom of freedom.

Homes and Sleep

One of the greatest milestones of my adult life occurred on an arbitrary weekday, maybe fourteen months after moving to Portland: I slept straight through the night. I blinked awake into pale, natural light. I was astonished that its source was the sun and not the moon. I honestly could not remember when I'd last shut my eyes at midnight and woken with the sun.

I felt so safe! It was a miracle. My body had slyly reset its default assumptions. Now, for the first time in my adult life, I regularly slept in darkness. Whenever I'd lived by myself, in various sublets, the place looked like a ship ablaze. I couldn't fall asleep without the lights on. I'd wake at 2:00 a.m., at 3:30 a.m., at 4:00 a.m. I kept a journal of gibberish that I'd named "Night Thoughts." It was an indescribable relief to turn that thinking off, and sleep until dawn.

Of course, this also meant that I was now sleeping soundly through the cries of my neighbors outside the window.

Mount Hood no longer surprised me, looming with its ghostly grandeur over the city; but neither did a catatonic teenager sitting on a horsehair blanket on the Burnside Bridge, holding up a sign sun-faded to illegibility. Neither did the growls and sobs I heard inside of tents pitched near the elementary school on Stark; this was background music now, and I walked right past it.

Geometries of Echoes

When I moved to Portland, I wasn't certain that I'd succeed at "putting down roots" or "making a home." The only true home I'd ever known was in Florida, and it now existed only in my memory; it had been twice destroyed, once by Hurricane Andrew and, more finally, by its new owners' bulldozers. Could I stay some-where for two years, longer? And could that simple, static act make a city my home?

It is hard to answer this question looking forward. Homes, after all, are places where the past collects in pockets, where a memory might ambush you at any tiled or carpeted coordinate. Until my family's Miami home was destroyed, I'd walk into a closet, and 1985 would flash into view: my young father on a lad-der, gushing sweat in December, getting down the artificial tree. Or I'd catch the septic whiff of low tide and remember, for some reason, my siblings and I burying our toothbrushes in the jungle-like backyard. Time rippled into form, a menagerie of moments, antlered and feathered and scaly episodes, some welcome and do-mestic, some feral and terrifying, all arced inside that house.

Home to me has also meant "family," a metaphysical spandrel created by the close proximity of five consciousnesses (seven if you counted our fat, narcoleptic dogs). Home meant sleeping in the bedroom that I shared with my siblings, snugly centered in the familiar shadows, wishing to be nowhere else. The sight of orange blossoms in the driveway, blowing like Florida snow. The ocular ticklishness of staring into the red hibiscus flowers, with their furry orange pistils. Home was a hundred black ants crawling around inside our mailbox, as if the font of the catalogs had mag-ically come to life. Home meant knowing which drawer to open. It meant not jumping at the sight of tiny lizards glued to the shower door. The ubiquitous smell of water—salt water, Miami weather. That smell of rain, recent and imminent. Home meant everyone in your family asleep under one roof. A terrific collective vulnerability, grouped within the same four walls. Family still means this to me.

Even after Hurricane Andrew came marauding across South Florida, flooding buildings and hanging boats in the trees, it did not diminish our house's power to locate me in time and space. I'd internalized its layout, which was the grid that supported my mental life. When our house was bulldozed, it continued to stand indestructibly in my imagination. My siblings and my parents are still living ghostly lives in that house; sometimes we bump into one another there, reminiscing.

Not everybody gets a sturdy brick-and-mortar binding for this compendium of sense experience. So many people do not have that real estate in their past. It's a luxury property, I've come to realize—a childhood home in the imagination. A stable referent, a sanctuary from which you can never be truly exiled. If you never had a home in the past, to what do you anchor your present?

"I ran away when I was very young," one of the men at the shelter told me. "I became a night boy."

■ ■

In November 2015, our eighth offer was accepted, our mortgage loan was approved, and to our astonishment and joy, we owned a home in Southeast Portland. After the apartment, it felt cavernous to me. It was a three-bedroom Victorian house, one of the oldest on the block, built in 1888, a "historic charmer," as the Realtor kept referring to it, while sliding a pocket door into and out of the living room wall like the tongue of a cartoon frog. A wavy green light filtered through the many windows. Shadows flowed over the walls in the late afternoon, fluctuating ultra-sounds of the weather moving all around us. We had a real yard, with a no-shit cherry tree and vividly hued mosses that really looked a lot like grass to me, a sort of psychedelic grass. I thought it was the most beautiful place I'd ever woken up in. Our new house was just south of Powell, a busy street, and within sight of a Jack in the Box. "Check your privilege at that Jack in the Box," joked a New York friend when she visited. But to me, this street felt residential, in a very unfamiliar way. It was tree lined, and blushing with rosebushes. The house did not feel like it belonged to us, not at all, but I was grateful to live in such an old place, one that felt happily haunted by many other families' stories.

After we signed the papers, we drove over and stood on the lawn under a full moon. All the windows were dark, and I had a disorienting moment looking up at them and imagining our view from

Barber Block. Here, the streets were so quiet. We were two miles from our old apartment. Easily, I could imagine how quickly a sort of amnesia might kick in; how tempting it would be to let this new silence swaddle us. "Happiness" does not have to be synonymous with "complacency," of course. But now I better understood how a person might unconsciously begin to draw the curtains, turning a home into a walled garden. Would we forget about our homeless neighbors if we were no longer living within earshot of one another? If we weren't literally rubbing shoulders? On our first night in the new house, this seemed like something dangerous to guard against.

Not long after we moved in, between February and March 2016, rents rose by 14 percent—again, the fastest escalation in the country. My fiancé and I felt like we'd run into a fortress just before the drawbridge closed; we were relieved to be in our new home, and for me it was a guilty relief, a queasy relief. Tell me, how do you celebrate a homecoming when you know that so many people are being left on the other side of the moat? How do you keep your relief, your happiness, from moating you further? I was afraid to come home, to relax into the new happiness. Personal happiness seemed like a limp response to a problem that required, as the friend of mine in politics put it, "an Iron Giant." The more intensely I came to know the pleasure of coming home, the more outrageous it seemed to me that so many thousands of Americans living on the streets had been abandoned to "their" fate, while "we" fell safely asleep. Home prices soared. Inventory was at a historic low. No-cause evictions were on the rise, with some people reporting five-hundred-dollar jumps in their rent overnight.

Almost everybody in Portland was now feeling insecure about housing. At precisely this moment, the city took bold action on behalf of its homeless citizens. In February 2016, Mayor Hales legalized overnight camping on sidewalks and public rights of way, the "Safe Sleep Policy." Between the hours of 9:00 p.m. and 7:00 a.m., homeless people could now sleep in their cars in certain authorized parking lots; they could pitch tents in well-lit areas without fear of being moved along by police. The city released a statement explaining the rationale behind the policy:

"Most of our homeless population are simply looking for a safe night's sleep, and have suffered needless trauma that comes with uncertainty about where that safe night's sleep can be."

Hales's chief of staff, Josh Alpert, described this as a temporary measure—a way to make life safer and easier for people living without housing until the city could get the funding together for more shelter beds.

In late April 2016, half a dozen business and neighborhood groups, including the Portland Business Alliance, filed a lawsuit against the city. As I write, they are currently seeking an injunction to bar the mayor from enforcing the policy. The plaintiffs say they are not antihomeless; some are activists who fear that Hales's measure is "inhumane." Hales's response? "We are going to tolerate some level of street homelessness until we have enough shelter beds." Wasn't it inhumane, he countered, to sweep people who had nowhere else to go, when the city is running such a deficit of shelter space?

A friend of mine who works in city politics expressed his frustration with people blaming the mayor's office for the growing ranks of Portland's homeless: "They don't understand how the city is hamstrung. We need an extra hundred billion a year at a national level. No local entity or state has that fund-raising power. If it's not a federal solution, I think we are in trouble."

And I thought of the faceless bodies sleeping in bags on the streets, which I continued to see in our new neighborhood, as I crossed the train tracks at Division on my way home. Zip up. Good luck.

Homelessness in Portland: Worse or More Visible?

In Kevin Brockmeier's novel *The Illumination*, human pain begins to glow. Auras appear around people's fractured bones and migraines, their pain now fanning out of them, a global light show. A disk of fire hovers above an athlete's ruptured disk. Ulcerating sores shine as bright as lightbulbs through a woman's closed mouth. Skin becomes a lampshade for radiant pain.

What is the dark genius of this premise? It indicts all of us. It exposes the willfulness of our daily blindness. And the myth that it's our ignorance of the suffering of others that prevents us from acting on their behalf. It's a book about the open secret of suffering.

According to the most recent Point-in-Time count performed by the city, the number of unsheltered people in Portland on any given night did not increase between 2013 and 2015. At that time, there were more than thirty-eight hundred people sleeping on the street or in shelters. Nearly everyone here will tell you that the crisis is getting worse. But perhaps the city's lenient camping policy has simply made the suffering of homeless people more visible.

I was worried that if I moved off Barber Block, I'd lose touch with our homeless neighbors' need; in fact, the challenge has not been losing sight of it but staying sensitized to it. An ambulatory example, from my ordinary commute down Milwaukie Avenue toward our new house:

On my walk home, I do not give a dollar to a tall, furious white man who stumbles down the street cursing at me, choking on the bone of some undislodgeable pain.

On my walk home, I pause over the sleeping body of an obese African American man, his unconscious body flung over a tree root, a Big Gulp alive with ants next to his walker. He is sleeping on the bare ground, exhaling a sticky stillness. If he were a character in Brockmeier's novel, I would be blinded by the radiant light pouring out of him. A nova would have fanned out of his skull, perhaps, or exploded from his heaving chest, slicing through the Douglas firs and X-raying the baseball diamond, dilating the pupils of the three young blond children on the Go Wheelie. But in this universe, I barely break pace. This is not an unusual sight in my neighborhood, a man sleeping with his head on a tree root.

St. Francis Dining Hall/Staying on the Pommel

"Socks! Oh, *please* ask people to donate socks."

Sue Unger, the director of Social Ministries for St. Francis

Church, stared hopefully up at me, her soft eyes' powerful appeal focused and magnified by her glasses. It was April, and I'd asked Sue if I could interview her, to learn more about her work as the director; I had served food and scraped plates alongside Sue, but this was our first in-depth conversation. Her tone gave me the definite sense that if our hour together produced even a dozen more clean, balled socks for her guests, she would deem this interview time well spent.

I had started volunteering at the St. Francis Dining Hall after we'd moved to the new house. It's located a few blocks south from our old apartment. For a while, I'd been resistant to the idea of working at a shelter. My fear was that I'd drown there. The need seemed overwhelming. I grew up in America. Horrifyingly, I have internalized a warping, heart-deforming attitude toward basically all verbs—a market logic when it comes to evaluating the risk: reward/cost: value of every human activity. Unregulated, the drive to "maximize" profit from every investment of time would, I'm certain, destroy my life. If I'm not vigilant, these kinds of calculations, of which I'm often barely aware, can tilt me toward failures of compassion. For example: I saw the work being done at the St. Francis Dining Hall, and I thought, *Fuck, this is Sisyphean.*

Volunteers were wiping tables in circles. They were setting out rounds of bread, vases of fresh lilacs, salt and pepper shakers. Two hours from now, they would clear the dining hall and begin to prepare the next meal. I saw this, and I must have done some quick, unconscious math, because I had this thought: *Your time would be worth more elsewhere.* The ugliest voices in me, invoking the "big picture" and the "grand scheme," protested: *Keeping a few dozen people fed, what good does that really do?* Surely this was simply "treating the symptom," handing out a piece of buttered bread. I'm really not sure what my grandiose advisers thought I should do instead. But according to this chorus, serving bread and salad and chicken to fifty or so homeless men and women was a bad investment. Energy unwisely spent, when I *could* be helping by . . . and here, the voices fell silent. Revealed for what they are:

voices that cover for fear, laziness, selfishness, hopelessness, a cowardly egotism.

The first thing I learned at St. Francis is that many different kinds of sustenance are exchanged between servers and guests at a dining hall, and that the nourishment is very mutual. I also learned from veteran servers that this is a skill: giving of yourself without going numb, staying open, avoiding burnout. The people who work at the shelter have learned how to swim through the need without drowning in it. They are shrinking the ocean of need, drop by drop. Many of the volunteers I've met at the St. Francis Dining Hall are parishioners, and many are simply committed to helping this population; at least half of the volunteers on my first night were homeless themselves.

"If we had funding for a few steady employees, it would make a big difference." Sue sighed. "When Eric gets sick, we have no cook. If I'm sick, there's nobody to back me up."

The St. Francis Dining Hall is plagued by the same week-to-week instability as the population it serves. Nevertheless, they keep their doors open; this past winter, they hosted an emergency cold-weather shelter, sometimes single-handedly staffed by Sue for hours at a time.

"Hospitality," Sue told me. "That's our mission, to extend hospitality to our guests."

It is hard to be hospitable. The need is bottomless; how much should we give? At the shelter, I saw an outflow of energy that cannot be quantized.

The people who work here, day after day, have developed a remarkable equipoise. It's not callousness—Sue has highly sensitive antennae out, attuned to the fluctuating emotions of everyone under this roof, staff and guests. But somehow she isn't knocked off the pommel. I watched her go from table to table with the affect of a no-nonsense den mother, checking in on people. She brought people clean socks and Q-tips, Advil for a headache or a fever. She seemed to know everybody's name, and I thought about my first months in Portland, what a joy it had been to exist for someone as

"Karen," a word floated out to me, buoylike; it was my birth name, and it was always a homecoming to be greeted and known.

After ladling out salad greens and cheddary macaroni, I was asked to help with cleanup. In the kitchen, I found a bearded, middle-aged man staring down with rapt concentration at a flat object on his palm. He had a walking cane painted purple and gold, decorated with swirling peacocks. His eyes loomed over me, clouded with agitation. Now I recognized what he was holding: the mixing blades. And I, too, was hypnotized by the way the steel tapered to a point.

"You know you're not supposed to be back here, Michael."

Sue materialized behind me; before I could ask what to do, she calmly plucked the mixing blades from him and guided him toward the door.

On his way out, Michael accidentally kicked the doorjamb loose. Now the door refused to stay open. Twelve times, twenty times, he tried to kick it back under the door. A three-inch triangle of wood had plunged Michael into hell. His face was balloon-taut and agonized. He kicked with such urgency that I was afraid to approach him. He would be tethered to this spot forever, it occurred to me, unless somebody could help him to stake that door back into place.

A teenage volunteer from the high school, a sweet kid who scooped ice cream like he was digging toward Jules Verne's center of the Earth, his small bicep bulging, paused to see what was causing Michael such distress. He knelt and made a gentle adjustment, and then Michael exhaled in relief, free to go.

■ ■

On another shift at St. Francis, several weeks later, I went after the tall stock pots with steel wool. Very old stains webbed the bottoms and sides of many of them; scrub as you might, certain stains would not lift; I found this a tough reconciliation. Things were cleaner than they'd been, but they did not look clean. The part of me that wanted everything sparkling had a hard time volunteering in this kitchen.

The next time, I volunteered to wash the trays with the aid of a heavy-duty industrial dishwasher. All I had to do was rinse and load them. Immediately, I blinded myself with the spray from a high-pressure nozzle. Was there no way to modulate this fire hose? Too embarrassed to ask for help, I got everything wet. By the time the pots were clean, I looked like someone who had just returned from a day pass at the water park. My hoodie was thoroughly soaked, my hair matted to my skull.

John, a man who looked so much like my father, who had been living on the streets for most of his life, came in to see how I was doing. Watching me from the splash zone, he did not disguise his alarm.

"Try stacking them like this," he said, and then completed a load in approximately a quarter of the time that it had taken me.

"Okay," I agreed. "I'll try."

The trays were coming so much faster than I could wash them.

Dozens of ketchup-colored trays piled up beside me. I shot water at the brainlike spatter of calcified spaghetti, aware that I was close to tears.

"You will learn your own system," John kept repeating kindly by my side, as if trying to convince himself of this. "We all have to start somewhere."

■ ■

I am writing this having recently cast my first ballot as an Oregonian for Portland's mayoral election. Our mayor-elect, Ted Wheeler, put affordable housing and homelessness at the center of his campaign. He has proposed a Tenant Bill of Rights to protect people from spiking rents and no-cause evictions. Citing Salt Lake City and San Antonio as models, Wheeler has promised to help people transition from the street to safe, stable homes. In a statement issued by Wheeler in December 2015 while running for election, our future mayor committed to ensuring that everyone on Portland's streets would have "the option to sleep inside" by the second year of his administration. He also made this bold pledge: "For every investment made to place someone in a shelter bed, parallel dollars need to be spent on permanent housing." And a collection of Multnomah County advocacy groups, politicians, and service providers plan to put a $350 million bond campaign on the November ballot to build more affordable housing.

Of course, these positive changes alone cannot counter the global economic trends that drive income inequality, or the slow violence, decades in the making, of federal budget cuts.

I spoke by telephone to Rich Rodgers, a former adviser to the Portland City commissioner in charge of housing, and the volunteer chair of Wheeler's housing committee, to ask for his veteran perspective on the affordable housing crisis and homelessness in Portland.

"For the first time ever, housing is the *number one* issue here in Portland," he told me.

We discussed Mayor Hales's permissive camping policy. Rodgers commended his chief of staff, Josh Alpert, for changing the policies around police sweeps of homeless camps. He described past raids that had ended in the destruction or confiscation of men's and women's few possessions—"It literally does kill people." Camp sweeps are no longer indiscriminate; if they occur, they are meant to target criminal activity that endangers the public. Police officers are now trying to build relationships with the campers in their neighborhoods. The city is coordinating with campers to get them access to clean water, footlockers, and regular garbage pickup.

"People visit Portland and they are shocked by what they see," said Rodgers. "They tell me, 'No decent society should let people sleep on the street.' This is true."

But for now, with such a scarcity of affordable housing units and shelter beds, you could make the argument, as Hales has done, that helping to make campers' lives easier is the most humane option in our present "state of emergency." The goal, of course, is to secure permanent housing for everyone living on our streets. What would it take to make that goal a reality?

Rodgers endorsed our mayor-elect, Ted Wheeler, and called Wheeler's initiatives "a huge step forward," but warned that they will not be enough to make up for lack of involvement by the federal government.

"The difficulty is, how much can any mayor do? The entire landscape needs to be remade."

Here are some more numbers, just for context. Portland has 4,000 people on the streets. Seattle? 10,000. Across Los Angeles County? 46,000.

Rodgers also complained that no presidential candidate has pledged to do enough for housing and homelessness, in part because the issues that plague Portland have yet to affect many other regions of the country; housing is still affordable in Buffalo and Cincinnati.

"What's a crisis here is not in Oklahoma yet. . . ."

I mentioned to Rodgers that we'd purchased a home in November, after nine months of looking with a Realtor and seven offers. "You were lucky," he said, and I agreed. We started discussing the influx of tech money that has contributed to the 14 percent annual increase in Portland's housing market—again, the fastest in the nation.

"If you're wealthy and plugged into the economy, you're doing as well as you've ever done. . . ."

And if you're not?

Wages have stagnated or declined since 2000, at a time when one in three Oregonians are spending half their paycheck on rent. It's getting more expensive to be poor everywhere. According to a recent Pew report, the poorest third of Americans now spend about 50 percent more on all their housing costs than they did in 1996. If you are spending half your income on housing, the scepter of eviction is always near. It's a nightmare that many people camping outside tonight have lived through—their worst fear becoming a foregone conclusion.

In a recent article, "Let Them Drown," Naomi Klein discussed the poor who bear what she makes literal reference to as the "toxic burden" of our policies: "This is happening because the wealthiest people in the wealthiest countries in the world think they are going to be OK, that someone else is going to eat the biggest risks, that even when climate change turns up on their doorstep, they will be taken care of."

Klein is talking about climate change, but when I read this my mind leaped to the tents *mushrooming* across downtown Portland. I saw the hundreds of campers living by the river, their tents extended infinitely in the glassy facades of the new luxury apartments. When I'd mentioned Klein's piece to Rodgers, he immediately said, "We don't treat the housing crisis like a natural disaster and we should." Rodgers contrasted the outpouring of emotion and aid that follows a natural disaster to people's often benumbed, resigned, apathetic response to our homeless.

"If I told you a tornado swept through here and left thousands of people hungry and without shelter tonight, how would you respond?"

Rodgers is on the board of directors of *Street Roots*, a newspaper that covers issues related to homelessness and poverty; the vendors of *Street Roots* are often people who have been homeless. He described his joy at watching vendors "rewired" back into the community. He mentioned a man named Raymond who lived in chronic orthodontic pain—that kind of shooting red tooth pain that keeps you riveted to your gumline. The trick candle of chronic pain, a fire that never goes out. Night and day, for all his waking time on the planet, his mouth had been pulsing.

Standing on the same corner, selling the *Street Roots* paper, he began to form friendships and connections to the neighborhood. Rodgers told me, "Thirteen people got together to buy Raymond a new set of teeth. It really changed his whole life."

We'd been talking about the danger of letting the global statistics depress and overwhelm you to such a degree that you opt out of caring entirely. Stalling out in the cul-de-sac of guilt. You'd be justified, Rodgers said, in feeling extremely pessimistic about the likelihood that we are going to "solve" America's homelessness crisis. You'd be correct to note that an extra hundred-billion-dollar commitment per year from the federal government to America's poorest citizens is nowhere in sight. You'd be in good company if you found yourself daunted by the massive structural changes that would be necessary to prevent more Americans from becoming homeless. At the same time, none of the above negates the value of our individual, eye-level efforts to reach one another: the homespun web of neighbors helping neighbors.

"Because you might also think of it as, 'Raymond's doing a lot better.'"

Visible City

Washed in a green, webby light, festival, playing
A chord, playing the near-most exotique
For a sterner nation, a brass mirror, a song where the word

Sin stands out, is thought to, anti-puritan but not
Anti-god, playing a flirt, saying you could land a landed kiss
Here, *quick*, *lick*; and,

Later, this city washed more literally and more blue
With waters as close as cousin Cuba, as far as the far-walked
    shores
Of my playful Brazil,

So that it was its image, not just its people, not just our bodies
    puffy
As a hemorrhoid against the water's
Advancing image, that was flooded; and

If sense is true, sight like a deeper speech,
An art, if *that* is true, then it is between these many poles
The city is seen:

The city, not just the given
Notion of the city, that screen we call myth, call the dark,
But the brick and spit of it, iron, horseshit, the river,

A mosquito vetting it for blood, mud, August,
The cathedral in August—it is in these, first, the eyes build
    their purpose,
Build a line: New Orleans

As that modern text, witnessed and revised by the light as
   radically
As by the water, which is history, which
Slips through your hands. This city is a ghost I wear.

—Rickey Laurentiis

PORTION

Joy Williams

ARTHUR HAD BEEN going to the asylum to visit a friend he had betrayed who foolishly had become quite undone. The young man had once been mesmerizingly attractive and desperate but was now slack, slothful, and weepy. He had also fallen into the habit of repeating the vatic phrase *When you think of chocolate think of Sparrow,* which Arthur felt to be a particularly annoying British affectation. They had never favored chocolate as a couple. Chocolate had never been a feature of their relationship.

It was during one of these utterly unsatisfying visits that he caught the Governor's eye, or his presence did not escape the notice of the Governor, Arthur was no longer sure.

When you think of chocolate think of Sparrow, the addled and former lover was intoning desperately when the Governor with smooth assurance escorted him to a corner of the hobby room where jigsaw puzzles in much mended cardboard boxes were stacked, their lists of missing pieces printed neatly on the lids to forestall distress, disappointment, or rage as the case might be.

PART(S) OF:
Cloud   4
Paw 2
Big Wave   7
Little Wave 9

The Governor then returned to Arthur and held his hand.

"Let me ask you something, let me ask you something," the Governor whispered, "that phrase 'I'm going to send a letter to the Governor . . .' how did that start? Someone going to the crapper says, 'I'm going to send a message to the Governor.'"

"I don't know," Arthur whispered. "I've never heard it."

"Why are you whispering? People say it all the time. Vulgar. Folks are vulgar. The problem with people who say they love nature is that they're crazy. You know the last leader of this nation's largest environmental organization—the one who holds an alligator over his head and screams *From My Cold Dead Hands*—he's got Alzheimer's. Doesn't know his dick from a fountain pen. . . ."

He looked at Arthur merrily, then shrugged. "That was the head of the National Rifle Association, holding a flintlock rifle over his head. I'm speaking phatically here. Just establishing tolerance for our mutual presence. Chitchat. I'm trying to get a feeling for you. Friend or foe? Phatic talk serves to prolong the moment before the possibility of communication. No other purpose to it. Now, you might be curious about my term as Governor. This is a sore subject with me. I didn't complete my term. Wolf took out a state trooper stationed outside the kitchen where I was having breakfast. It was the morning of the shortest day of the year and I was being served breakfast, at my request, by a young woman in a white nightie with candles in her hair. The wolf, Darling Bea, jumped the trooper. What was the fellow to do, shoot the Governor's wolf? He went down like the man he imagined himself to be, without a cry. It was unfortunately the public's first glimpse into the style of my administration. Had to whisk her off in protective custody. She's with monks now. God knows what they're trying to teach her. They promised me they wouldn't punish her until she understood. They assured me of that. I asked them pointedly. Still, I know men dissemble and deceive other men. I know men. I had brothers. I was the youngest. They hung me on the doorknob by the back of my underwear. They went out, they came back in. I laughed with them, this is how you survive.

All dead now, those boys. But enough gloom. Tell me, what's the state of the state? Has my legacy of infrastructure endured? Subsidence continuing to be a problem? How is the road?

"The road . . ." Arthur began. What a peculiar word . . .

"Agriculture's in decline too, I suppose. I've heard that farmers are turning their fields into mazes to make a buck. Disaster fields all the vogue too. Farmers are sly ones, they press any advantage. Lives freely taken, people dropping out of the sky on their worthless fields. Plane crashed, everyone amazed, disbelieving, horrified. How could this happen! Then someone figures out that a human disaster of a certain magnitude makes the area sacrosanct and eligible for public funding and tax deferral. Or a lesser magnitude will do if the circumstances have an innovative resonance. Once the fields are cleaned up farmers can start charging. Enforced donations to keep order, keep it nice, maintain it as contemplative space. This is what I would tell my environmental friends who have never considered me their ally, I'm afraid. Take a page from the farmer's book: Only way left for them to preserve land. Presence of a rare moth won't do it. Those little flower-faced owls no bigger than your fist, forget it. Not a rumor of one of the last of the big cats. Certainly not a rumor of one of the last of the big cats. Has to have a human angle. And they can't be choosy. Land may not be ecologically ideal but they should claim it early on, swoop in soonest before teddy bears and bouquets start piling up, stake it out as a pioneer space with all due respect, of course, but quick on the heels of death's untimely unfair undiscriminating mass transit operation. Then if beast or bird does manage to make its way there they will be seen as acceptable symbols of hope and healing and will be tolerated by those seeking comfort."

The Governor paused.

"But I can get by without the environmentalists. Does the environmental vote even exist anymore? I'm now recollecting that those people took a hit when they protested the draining of the Everglades when that airbus went down and all those passengers plus crew vanished into the muck. Their 'Let them be a part of the great Everglades which has no counterpart anywhere on earth' didn't sit well with the next of kin. Just made them mad. Environmentalists flat-footed around most people. First part of the statement was okay, should have left it at that. Second part was where they went astray. The next of kin felt it as their lost loved ones that had no counterpart on earth and not some nasty melancholy swamp. So they sucked each rag and bone out, divvied it up for proper burial and drained the place right down to the pandemonium rock. Now there's a Legoland in the works there. Going to be a Taj Mahal totally made out of Legos. The actual Taj is a mausoleum, that's how they got the concept approved."

When the Governor laughed he hissed a little.

"Ever made it to India?" he inquired. "Had an opportunity to converse with a Hindu?"

Arthur looked at him sleepily.

"Too late now," the Governor went on. "Cultures everywhere being suppressed by mass civilization, by agnostic humanism. There's a hatred of what's considered the picturesque. The annihilation of the picturesque is quite acceptable. Assimilation is no longer the vogue. You might ask why I am addressing you. Your sweet inquiry breaks my heart. Whole goddamned state breaks my heart. It should be put on a ventilator. I made mistakes before, I admit. Built too many roads. Liked clever argument, was fond of peculiar grammars, but I was no one's creature. I made my way sucking no one's toes. Now I have amends to make, wrongs to right, wealth to spend, and I can't do it because I'm here you see."

"Yes," Arthur ventured. "You are."

"I have a proposition for you," the Governor said.

But a black-smocked orderly appeared and announced lunch, another odd word . . . *lunch, road*. Who came up with these things . . . and the Governor was led away.

■ ■

He had been christened Arthur Barrow and had been a clever imaginative lazy youth. Before the arrangement with the Governor in the activities room of the asylum, before he had signed the contract, he had made a harmless and modest living by bilking everyone he met but now, little more than a year later, he felt himself the bilkee, and by a dead man, cornered rather like a noble cougar, treed by petty dogs. The arrangement was that he, Arthur, would take on the Governor's life when the Governor felt no longer qualified to do so which, the man had the remaining marble to realize, was a shade past imminent. For a considerable amount of money and the interesting contents of several footlockers, Arthur would assume the Governor's guilts and strive to make amends for his unfortunate decisions when in office. Those roads. He had directed ten miles of new asphalt to be laid down for every woman and child in the state, not including parking lots and private driveways.

They even discussed the Governor's—rather Arthur's—final gesture in this fallen world. Arthur suggested that when the time came, after the money was gone and, of course, all reparations had been made, he would go into one of those thousand-acre car and bulldozer dealerships and immolate himself in the showroom. Strip to a snowy white diaper—the Governor liked that detail as he was both fond of ceremony and vain about his sinewy limbs— and combust, but the Governor argued that the days were past when an event like that would give anyone pause, to say nothing of bestirring further consciousness.

"You ever see one of those gummy bears on fire?" he said. "One of those candies? You'd go up like that. Mean no more to people than that."

"Death as protest might have lost her bump," Arthur agreed.

"Such an exit opens no doors," the Governor said. "But it might be the best we can do. The important thing is not to wait too long. You don't want to die of pneumonia. That's what they call the old person's friend. Some friend. Like having a three-hundred-pound officer of the law sitting on your chest advising you that it's not in your best interest to draw that next breath." "The leaving will be in as magisterial a way as possible," Arthur promised.

The scam seemed innocent enough. What was the harm?

The Governor imagined all the other inmates in the dreary facility to be the dim-bulbed legislators he had known though with larger heads, but Arthur, he believed, had the potential to be himself, that is, the Governor. Arthur began visiting him regularly and the details of their accordance were hammered out. After this was done to the Governor's satisfaction, the Governor seemed to lose all interest in him, devoting his days to protecting the piano, which existed, marginally, in the hobby room along with the tower of puzzles. The Governor had taken it upon himself to not let anyone near the beat-up out-of-tune old thing, believing like the innocent young Nietzsche thrust into a brothel that of all the beings there it was only the piano that still possessed a soul.

A burlish inmate finally had enough of the Governor's behavior and attacked him, banging his head with the piano's scarred lid, crushing his skull actually beneath the lid. The smirking spineless attendants were affording themselves sundaes in the adjacent ice cream parlor and were slow to react. By all accounts—Arthur had not been present—the murderer then sat down to play, and quite brilliantly, before he was wrestled away from the trembling instrument.

So the Governor died. By piano.

He had once confided to Arthur that he did not wish to play the piano, he believed himself to be the piano. Glenn Gould said that players want to be either the music or the piano, they hate being middlemen. As a child the unparalleled performer had begun an opera about nuclear destruction. In act I everything dies. In act II a superior breed of frog emerges.

Another nut, Arthur thought. Not that he didn't think frogs were underrated in this life.

Arthur wished he were an unparalleled performer but he was not and the opportunities afforded by the Governor's faith in him were, he had to admit, unrealized. He had not taken on the other man's guilts nor had he reflected much on expiation. But after pretty much racing through the Governor's assets and down to the surprises of the last trunk, he had been thinking more and more about the clause imposing substantial penalties for early withdrawal—or had it been serious penalties? But the contract couldn't be valid, the man was insane: He hadn't even been a governor.

He had no idea what he'd been. He'd certainly accumulated a great deal of money. Which was gone. Arthur was subsisting on the generosity of some do-gooder encampment in a beetle-compromised wood. His benefactors were a faintly perceived lot, last of a breed really, at odds with the more generally accepted belief that compassion was nothing more than self-cannibalization. The more an individual doesn't care the freer he becomes. This was the current thinking.

When he'd first arrived he'd had the companionship of rats, like Paul in prison, but the rats, never a playful lot, had long abandoned him. For a while there were the occasional mice, white ones trying to clamber out of the toilet, but they too vanished after the nearby research facility tightened up their disposal practices.

His small cabin was comfortable enough though it seemed to be shrinking, the walls creaking closer, the glass of the single window moaning in its frame, which was riddled by the tireless efforts of those beetles. And the rain, pounding upon the roof, was relentless. He remembered when rain fell so prettily and the smell without exaggeration was divine. But that was a while ago—fourteen months ago—goodness, the Governor was still in the bin. Fourteen months ago rain had changed its nature.

He mused on the number fourteen. Some philosopher—the name failed to present itself—maintained that it was impossible for fourteen minutes to pass. Something about it corresponding to infinity. This philosopher was greatly influenced by an earlier philosopher whom he had misunderstood completely, which is how all great discoveries are made, through misunderstanding.

A bovid plastic duck with a nasty expression floated in the bathtub. It was one of the Governor's effects that Arthur sometimes fancied. He tended to avoid taking baths in the daytime, not only because he considered it bad form but because it was then that the grout between the tiles looked unequivocally filthy. Still, he was spending long hours in the tub lately, thinking about this and that, sipping from a bottle of Hirsch Selection rye, reflecting on the fabled concept of a continually stocked honor bar, the rows of shining bottles that trusted you would do the right thing. He'd come across only two of these marvels in his life and he had advantaged himself of them shamelessly both times.

He placed a fetid washcloth over his head.

Arthur used to think that we all feel so strange and nothing is right because there are more people alive today than all the people who ever lived but then he learned that those who are alive today comprise less than 6 percent of all the people who ever lived. Or something like that. Which is an even better explanation as to why we all feel so strange and nothing is right.

When he had arrived trolleying the last of the Governor's footlockers it had harbored a full case of rye and though he thought he'd been provident, only one bottle remained. He promised himself that he would put off its retrieval as long as possible. For one reason it was the last and for another it was wedged between a bag of filthy pink candy imprinted with an unflattering image of George Ivanovitch Gurdjieff (worth something to someone, he was sure) and Darling Bea's immense hand-tooled leather collar with the coral inlays. Arthur felt fortunate that he'd never made the acquaintance of old Bea. He was sure he would have been judged unfavorably as her master's ancillary, maybe even devoured. He could visualize with unsettling vividity Bea in some freezing Franciscan kennel, mangy and enraged, eyes green as peridot, plotting night and day her return. He saw ice in her water bowl, on her muzzle, between the pads of her gigantic paws, ICE, the very subject of a massive book which was the only other occupant of that wretched trunk, Hans Horbiger's 1913 *Glazial-Kosmogonie*. Another total nutcase, Horbiger had written a pseudoscience classic—lengthy, ponderous in style, and utterly without value—in which he argued that the most important material in the universe was ice. It was the cosmic answer. Arthur could understand the Governor's interest in this theory for it suggested the irrelevance of Florida. Thus all the disastrous decisions the Governor thought he'd made on that unfortunate state's behalf had been irrelevant as well.

The rye was gone, the bottle empty. He had deceived himself in believing there was another, for holding his breath, closing his eyes, he had reached into the depths of that trunk several days ago, braving the touch of Bea's frightfully disorienting and cold collar, and removed it. This had been that. Nothing more to take there was.

In the asylum one of the Governor's fellow travelers had remarked that all he wanted from life was a competent portion.

A competent portion.

Marvelous! I'm going to remember that! Arthur had exclaimed.

Sweet old guy in a shiny soiled seersucker suit, always talking about eating companions. Arthur thought he'd meant an eating club, recalling the black tie dinners and dances at glorious Harvard where he claimed to have matriculated, until he was informed by the Governor that "eating companions" were well-known etheric world entities that invisibly attach themselves to one's body and suck from it all vital force, and the pitiable wasting fellow in seersucker had them in spades.

Arthur became aware that the plastic duck was listing near his groin. There was something wrong with it, it wasn't balanced properly. Just kept circling his groin as though it were a drain. He swatted it away.

He felt old. He was old. The last fourteen months had aged everything excessively. It had something to do with the rain, the rabid rain. Or was it the birdless dawns? He no longer had communion with the Governor. His dreams weren't even the Governor's anymore. Truck-sized butterflies, radiant women, sustained applause—repetitive but pleasant. He missed them.

The Governor didn't want to be in here, of that he was certain. But he didn't want to be out there either. There was where people who couldn't imagine the earth without them plundered on, unconcerned as to the probationary nature of their exertions. And even with the apocalyptically hammering rain that would drive anyone off the rails, there were billions and billions of them.

Gee, he was tired.

He thought sentimentally of his grandmother and sniffled a little. She used to say that a robin singing close to a window meant sorrow was on the way. She was Welsh and gloomy as they come. But his mother had been part of the Blessed Assurance crowd, the visualizing the world without you crowd. *I left and the birds stayed singing.* Down in the lovely valley, down by the glittering brook. It was supposed to put a joyful steel in your spine. *I left and the birds stayed singing*, his mother would say, her mouth trembling. And now it was his turn. But the birds no longer sang, there were no birds.

Arthur gripped the slippery curved sides of the tub and began the process of hauling himself out. The image of a pale, struggling, and determined mouse came easily to mind.

He carefully patted himself dry and put on a silk bathrobe of excellent quality from the Governor's extravagant years.

The rain screeched. He had seen one of the do-gooders try to catch it in a bucket and it had thickened like an eel and snaked away.

He shivered.

He was ready, but he was a little hungry. Just one more thing. One little bit of something. He went into the tiny kitchen and opened the refrigerator. There should be one more serving of integrity-raised beef in there. There were many who didn't care about the integrity of their food overmuch but he was not one of them. He thought the Governor would approve even though the man had limited himself to rice balls and water in the weeks before the piano incident. But there was no last portion of integrity-raised beef in the refrigerator, no calf raised to prime by loving kindergartners, petted a hundred times a day by tiny hands, fed flowers and clover, surrendered in the final moments by the most loyal and trusted and affectionate of caregivers, the ones who had named it and taught it to know that name as its own. No Tunnel of Death, no blood-slick and reeking duckboards. No inept stickers or angry leggers, no prodders or stunners. No knocking gun going *kachunk kachunk kachunk.* Just a last embrace in a lush and sunny field, the little children's piping voices. Not a whiff or inkling in the air for it.

The last of Geryon, raised by Mrs. Ricky Hormel's advanced kindergarten class of Hopewell, New Jersey, was not in the freezer. He must have finished it off sometime back and just forgotten.

APARTMENT 1G

Nami Mun

THE OLD NURSE hovered above him, sniffing at the fresh wound at the top of his head, picking at it with her fingernails until he could feel the wet lesion writhing like an oyster. The nurse's two front teeth were black and smelled of infection. *Confirm your name for me*, she said. *First name? Last name? And what part of your body are we working on today?* When he twitched with pain, she giggled, every note sounding like tiny, dry brakes. Hanju Lee wanted sleep. The kind that turned the world into a dark, muddy slime. But the old nurse's lips, peppered with prickly hair, scratched against his earlobe as she whispered a list of his failures into him—the Laundromat that had kept his wife washing other people's underwear twelve hours a day; the motel that lost money the second they took it over; past due rents, past due gas bills, past due water bills, electric bills, supply bills, medical bills, and Songmi's college tuition, so on and so on, and of course the little girl—the one with the birthmark shaped like a whale—found only blocks away from their motel, her tiny body bloated by the morning dew. And then the Russian. The supposed answer to all of their problems. The answer that took a square piece of his scalp as collateral.

The old nurse was now shoving something cold and metallic down his throat, making him scream. A furious white light screamed back, straight into his eyes. Lee squinted and hand-blocked the glare as the nurse chanted *Count backward from a hundred* as if on a loop, her head ballooning to the size of the sun and then shriveling back down, just as quickly, to a hard dried lemon. *Count backward from a hundred, because honor can't be bought and yet one pays highly,* she said, wiggling her finger in admonishment. Soon, Lee fell headfirst into that slime, into a warm molasses where nothing lived, except maybe a burp of dialogue overheard in the orphanage where he grew up—*No one will take him with that scar on his face*—and then a sliver of thought about one of the monks who smelled of burned sugar, the sweet bitterness spiraling him down to a cup of coffee, his wife stirring it slowly, hypnotically, the spoon clinking against porcelain sounding robotic and medical, like the cold gray room where Songmi was born—how breakable she seemed, how his hands felt so dirty holding her.

Then came the thread of a long silky dream: bells ringing, a flash of bright orange. The air rippling with the smell of diesel. People bustling by, their heads whipping toward a monk who has lit himself on fire.

The monk is wearing an orange robe and sitting like Buddha in the middle of a busy street. High winds. High heat. Other monks encircle, ringing their bells. The hems of their orange robes flap like flags. *Che yong, che yong, che yong,* they chant. The flame waves wildly and black smoke rises. Everything is chaos. People are sobbing. Some scream. Some cover their ears, while others run for help.

The only one not moving is the monk in flames.

He is stone still. A gust of wind blows the flame to the right, and for a moment Lee can see the man's unflinching face. The brows quickly vanish. The lids disintegrate and melt down his cheeks. Then he is simply *eyes*. Nose and lips meld into a lump on the chin, and the skin on his neck bubbles, then pops, the sound loud enough to make people wince. His shaved head blackens, then drips like grease. The skull is revealed. His bones fuse, and soon everything smells like hot sand.

In the end his entire cross-legged frame tips over like cheap furniture. Only then do fellow monks put out the fire. The casket arrives but the monks cannot fit his scorched body into it. His bones do not bend. So, upon their shoulders the casket flows down the street, a charred knee sticking out from under the lid. Black flakes of flesh sprinkle the air.

Lee couldn't breathe. The scent of bones bit his nose. *Che yong, che yong, che yong,* for the roots and the branches make up the tree. *Che yong,* the nurse said, hovered over his face again, and as she spoke, her rotting teeth, all of them covered in fuzzy mold, fell from her mouth and plopped into his.

He clamped his lips shut and jerked side to side but one nurse morphed into three, and their six hands and arms whipped like tails and conspired to pin him down, pinch his nose, vise-grip his jaws open. Each nurse took turns looming over his mouth and let their teeth pebble down his throat, one by one, choking him, until his eyes foamed, until his hands fisted. And all he could do was moan for his daughter, over and over, like a long, foggy siren.

Songmi.

Lee's eyes snapped open. *You ready to tell us what happened?* The ceiling fan above him wobbled and whined. *Who did this to you?* The light flickered. The room still smelled of gasoline, and maybe fish. *Who scalped you like this?* Bedsheets stuck to his back. The mattress was a pond. Just above his forehead the bandage sat heavy. A cold wet sock. In three blinks he saw he was no longer at the hospital but in his own apartment. Two more blinks and his wife slept soundly to his left, snoring, even. Only the guilty can sleep so well, he thought.

He lit up a cigarette so as to breathe and tracked the smoke up to the flickering bulb. At the age of fifty-one, Lee still slept with the light on, something his wife had found charming at first. *What do you think you're afraid of?* she had asked once, as if it were that simple.

When the phone rang, it startled him. He was about to answer but his wife placed a cold hand on his shoulder.

"What if it's Songmi?"

"Then we really mustn't answer," she said, and rolled to her side.

After six rings the answering machine clicked. "Yeah, this is Joe McGill from the *New York . . .*" He didn't finish his sentence, seemed distracted. "Anyway, I'm sure you're getting a lot of calls but if you have anything you wanna get off your chest, anything about the little girl, I'd make sure to do right by you."

The reporter went on but Lee stopped listening.

"How long have you been awake?" his wife asked, still with her back to him.

"Does it matter?"

The ceiling fan took up the silence. "You're not the only one suffering," she said evenly, and then: "Go back to sleep."

Lee got out of bed. He wanted to show he wasn't that easy. But then he stood at the desk in his underwear and socks, not knowing what to do. And wasn't *this* the problem. He never knew what to do. For him, the time between inaction and action could be measured only in oceans. Oceans of doubt. Wasn't this why he was now staring at his suit, cleaned and pressed, hanging over the back of his chair? The pants dragged along the carpet, as if someone had hammered the knees and snapped the legs into a backward *L*. And next to the legs, the two cans of gasoline.

From his desk he picked up the picture of Songmi. A moment from her high school graduation. Her face a perfect diamond. Her smile soft, as if apologetic. The girl who grew up eating ramen and doing homework in the utility closet of their Laundromat was valedictorian. He was proud of her, not because of grades but because she'd remained humble. And kind. He tried to feel proud of himself—tried telling himself that he had made her, that he'd had a part in creating this goodness, but then he looked around and saw where he was—a one-room ground-floor studio apartment that contained one desk, one chair, one bed, two burners, and a coffee table where he and his wife ate rice porridge and kimchi nearly every night, and salted fish when lucky. There was no sofa, no dining table, no TV, no life, unless one counted the small family of mice squeaking under the kitchen sink.

No, it was impossible for the proud to live here.

"Don't be frightened." His wife had pulled back the covers, and through the sheer nightgown he could trace her long slender back as it dipped at the waist and rose at the hips to meet her red

underwear. Even at rest, she was in control, which only made him
want to revolt. He picked up the phone and dialed.

"Calling her will only make things worse."

His hands trembled.

"She'll think she had a chance to stop us but couldn't."

When the line rang on her end, his mouth dried. He could picture the pay phone just outside her dorm room, a triangle of light
painting the hallway as Songmi opened her door and squinted at
the ringing made conspicuous by the early hour. She'd be in her
pajamas, the panda slippers he'd bought her, and she'd walk slowly
to the phone because she was smart enough to know that at five in
the morning it could only be bad news. Only bad news ever had
the right.

On the twelfth ring she answered. "Hello?"

Lee opened his mouth. Nothing.

"Hello?" she whispered this time, sounding frightened.

Lee couldn't believe how much he wanted to cry.

"Who is this?" she asked, and he wanted to answer her—to say
the things a father was supposed to say to a daughter. Advice on
boys and love and how to change a tire or how not to trust people
who say "Trust me." Most of all he wanted to apologize. He was a
failure—not because of losses financial, but because he had viewed
life through glass so stained and dense, not one ray of truth could
shine in or out. He failed, in the end, in seeing truth—the truth
in others but mostly the truth about himself. And now it was too
late. Even if he were to break the glass, all that lived on either side
were molds of neglect. He wanted to say all of these things but
something like cold gravel clogged his throat. "Dad, is that you?"
she asked, and, as if his hand had been struck, he hung up.

He stared at the phone.

"All you ever think about is yourself," his wife said. Her eyes
turned tight as bullets.

She understood nothing. All he had ever done was think of
others. That was the problem. He thought too much about how
others saw him. Including his daughter, who, after today, would

see him as a liar or, worse, a coward. And especially his wife, whom he'd wanted to impress the moment he met her. All those years ago. So many miles ago. Just outside their window a bus shrieked to a stop and sighed, and a woman wearing a head scarf got on. It was early and the woman's features got lost in the dirty light of morning, but Lee could tell by the crook of her back that she was a hard worker—someone who'd never be rewarded while she was alive.

"Instead of feeling sorry for ourselves, why don't we just get dressed." His wife was sitting up now, reaching for his pack of cigarettes.

Her dress lay on the coffee table. On top of that, a necklace. The previous night she announced that appropriate attire was important, adding, *For many are called but few are chosen.* Christian nonsense. For most of their twenty-five-year marriage she went to church and recited verses as though she had written them herself, but Lee knew all along that to her, church was just a vessel for networking. Every Sunday she sat in the front pews, her face shining with piety, and every Sunday afternoon she tried to shake hands with the right people, hoping that someone would introduce her to a smart investment, a quick moneymaker, anything that could catapult her into one of those immigrant success stories she'd read in *Korea Daily.* That was how they'd gotten involved with the motel. And now Lee understood why the money, at first, came so easily.

He picked up the necklace and held the tiny cross in the center of his palm.

"We're doing the right thing," she said and took a long drag.

"I wasn't disagreeing."

"But I can feel you turning weak. I always can."

"I'm not as weak as you think I am," he said, feeling bold.

"Well, I'm not as strong as you think I am so perhaps today, just this once, you can be a man."

Without much thought he flung the necklace at her. "I am your husband and you will not talk to me that way."

The necklace had missed her. She laughed, her mouth slacking wide enough to show the gaps in her upper row of teeth. "We're not in Korea anymore, my dear. It's much too late for you to have the upper hand."

He wanted to hit her. He wanted to stomp her face and break that smile.

"And if you think beating me will finally turn you into a man, you have my blessing." She slid out of bed, picked the necklace up off the floor, and coiled it around her wrist as she walked up to him, stood close enough for him to smell her breath. She was tall for a Korean woman. Slender and taut. A human knife. "But there are other ways to prove your manhood." Her hands swirled against his chest and then coaxed the sides of his arms, chilling the nerves along his spine. "You have to trust me and know that we are doing right."

"How can you be certain?"

"Because . . ." Pulling him in gently she spoke into his ear. "It's easy to be certain when you don't have options." She tilted his chin and kissed him lightly on the lips, twice, before walking him back to the bed and sitting him down so she could examine the top of his head. She fingered the outer edges of the bandage and peeled up a corner, gently, and blew into the wound.

"Does it hurt?"

He lied and said no.

Her hands smoothed the stubble on his face. "Soon, nothing will ever hurt you," she whispered, her eyes closed in prayer. "The path has already been built, not by God but by us. Now we must simply walk down it."

"We can tell the police how little we were involved." He squeezed her hands, wanting her to open her eyes, but she kept them closed.

"Our duty in life is to die with a little more honor than we were born with."

"We didn't know what they were doing. With the girls," he said.

Her face opened and looked at his, searching for something, a flicker of understanding. But he didn't understand, never could. On the coffee table her dress waited. She touched the fabric, the bright white a contrast to the room's sickly gray. "No one will believe us. We're immigrants. We're nobodies."

"Maybe the journalist can help. Jimmy Park can translate for us. He wants to help. I don't know why but he keeps offering."

"Jimmy's a useless man. And he keeps offering help precisely because he knows he's useless."

For months Lee had wondered if she and Jimmy had been having an affair. Now he was certain. And certain it had not gone well. Her affairs never surprised him. The fact that she found time to have one was what confounded him most.

"He's a good man," he added, wanting to see her reaction.

"I'd rather have a useful one than a good one. Why do you think his wife tried to kill herself?"

Lee slid off the bed and sank to the floor. "When did you get this cruel?"

"When?" Using the window as a mirror, she put on her necklace. "The real question should be how, my dear husband."

"You weren't always this way."

"Whereas you have always been *this* way," she said too quickly.

"And what way is that?"

"Someone who makes *me* this way." She went to the desk and began straightening it, pushing the mound of bills into the trash can with dramatic indifference, repositioning the phone, putting away a roll of stamps inside a drawer. "You would've kept us washing dirty underwear for the rest of our lives. You would've let Songmi grow up to also be a nobody. What have you done to get us out of this apartment? Nothing. And what have you done to accept that you knew *exactly* what the girls were for?"

"I knew nothing."

His wife got on her knees and took his face in her hands. "Listen to me, Hanju. I'm begging you. We must admit to what we did. We must know we did wrong. One has many good reasons in lying to others but there is no use in lying to oneself. Not at this point. Do you understand?"

He looked up, at her eyes, that efficient mouth of hers. "But *you* were the one who shook hands with the Russian. And *you* were the one who wanted the motel."

She let go of him.

"Oh God," he heard himself say. He stood up and backed away from her. "You knew."

The silver cross winked from the base of her neck. "It must feel good to blame others."

"You knew it all along."

"We were in debt."

He walked to the desk, grabbed the chair for support.

"Somebody had to do something," she said.

"But nobody asked you to."

"You're absolutely right. You never *have* to ask for anything. I just take care of things, don't I? I do all of the dirty work so you can go on believing you're a good man. Well, being good in America is a luxury. A luxury I never got to have."

She took off her nightgown and began getting dressed. She hadn't changed much since they'd first met. Skin as white as paper. Jet-black hair tapering at the middle of her back, pointing to the rest of her. Her beauty only confused him. She was far more beautiful, even at this age, than any of the girls the Russian had brought over—from Vietnam, Laos, Korea, from wherever, to be hostesses. That's what they were supposed to be. In retrospect, the idea of hiring girls from other countries to be restaurant hostesses sounded absurd. And now the truth reverberated through him, endlessly, like the bells that kept on ringing long after the monks at the orphanage had left the courtyard. Only then did he remember his dream. Then the little girl, the one they found in the empty lot, just down the road from the motel. Why did she have to be Korean? Why did she have to be so young? Just barely twelve years old. Legs bent unnaturally. Blood smeared across her face, as though someone had tried to wipe it. He wanted to vomit. He shut the image out because none of it mattered now. None of them mattered. He finally understood. He had to sit down.

"Put on your suit," his wife said. She was dressed now. White dress, tight at the waist, with a pair of white stockings, white shoes. Funeral colors.

"You're the one," he said, barely able to get the words out.

She put on earrings.

"You took the girl's body out to the lot, didn't you?"

His wife walked up to him and turned. "Help me with the zipper."

He couldn't move.

"Help me," she said again, this time taking his hands and putting them to work.

When he finished, all she said was, "I'm not a monster," in a voice he had never heard before. Now look who is lying to oneself, he wanted to say but didn't because she was crying. He couldn't see her face but her shoulders shook. She cried often but this time felt different. This time, he could tell, she actually believed she was a monster—and her denial had simply been a wish for the truth to be untrue.

"How could you do it?" he asked, knowing that even this didn't matter. Today wasn't about truth or lies or blame or monsters or money. Today was about the end, and the beginning—that day in Seoul when she walked through the doors at the watch repair shop where he worked as a clerk. Today was about the silk blouse she had on. Her cream-colored shoes. Her eyes as bright as apples.

When she came into the shop all Lee had wanted was to wake up every morning to that face. To be graced by those hands. He straightened his posture so as to seem taller, counted money at the register as though his family owned the place, as though he had family, and tried not to think of himself as the thug that he was, the high school dropout that he was, the part-time employee that he was, getting paid under the table, mostly in cash but sometimes in unclaimed watches, which he sold in the black market. *In two years I'll have my own business*, he remembered saying as she was leaving.

She paused at the door. *Hope the watch will be ready before then.*

Friday, he told her.

She nodded and made to leave again.

At five, he said, stepping out from behind the counter. *Then we'll go out to dinner afterward.*

She turned and smiled that smile of hers. Tiny fishhooks in his heart. *What else will I be doing? You seem to know my schedule.*

On Saturday you'll be at the beach. I'm done at noon.

I can't swim, she said.

Neither can I, he said.

Two years after that he didn't have his own business but he proposed anyway, only to have her family object. Her father threatened to disown, and then disowned. And as if her parents' actions had lit a fuse in her, she left everything behind—her name, her inheritance, her country, her seat at Seoul University where she would have studied medicine, her silk blouses, her chauffeur, her cook, her maid—to accompany Lee to the States. First to Oklahoma; then to Daly City, California; then to the Bronx, to end up working at a Laundromat, washing clothes at fifteen cents per pound. All those years, Lee wondered why she never left him. Only now, as he held her in his arms, did he understand that maybe her loyalty was nothing more than unwavering spite.

He watched her now, her hands covering her face, and he imagined those very hands dragging the girl's body into the empty lot in the middle of the night. He imagined his wife trying not to look at the girl's face, a face that, even in the dark, would've reminded her of a younger Songmi. How could she do it, he asked himself, but then the answer hit him almost immediately. She had done it, as she had done everything, because she knew he couldn't.

She held out his shirt. Lee took it, got dressed, each layer of clothing helping him stand straight. A kind of armor that arrives only after one accepts all of one's actions in life. And in Lee's case, his inactions. Today, this moment, was not about truth or lies. It was only about whether one wanted to die with or without love. "You're not a monster," he finally said.

She wiped her tears and then fixed his tie, the knot hitting his Adam's apple.

"There," she said and stepped back for a look.

Minutes from now, Lee will focus on his wife, his beautiful monster wife. "You be the strong one," she'll say, and he'll guide her to the bed, straighten the folds of her dress as she lies on her side. First he'll pour the gasoline on his half of the mattress, then around her, outlining her shape, before letting the clear solvent splash her legs, her trembling chest. The bright white dress will sag to a brown, and his wife will whimper like a child lost in the woods. The fumes will bend the air. Everything will turn to a sheet of glassine. He'll sit on the bed and pour the entirety of the second can onto his head and shoulders, the gasoline showering the back of his neck at once cold and burning.

He'll grab the lighter. His wife will tug on his elbow and try to pull him down beside her. She'll cry *Please* between tears and Lee will hold the lighter inches from his chest and understand that he has never loved his wife more than in this moment.

Minutes after that, their studio apartment will be the brightest it has ever been. The mattress Lee and his wife have slept on for nearly a quarter of a century will go up in flames, the fire tickling the ceiling fan before melting the blades into taffy. People in the apartment above and adjacent will wake up to the smell of smoke. They'll grab their photo frames, their immigration papers, their soda cans of cash, their cigarettes, their check-cashing cards, social security cards, bus cards, green cards, parole cards, their plastic rosaries, their food stamps, their eye-rubbing children. Sirens will wail. Firemen will sweat. The sun will rise but the sky will darken just above their building, and coughing tenants will be ushered across the street and they'll stand there, in their bathrobes and socks, trying to figure out who the hell lived in apartment 1G.

HAPPY

Brad Watson

WHEN I WAS a boy in Meridian, Mississippi, my mother, who'd thought she had a happy life of mid-twentieth-century home-maker ahead of her, had to go to work. I was five and not happy about it, but she went anyway. And though my father wasn't mak-ing much money (sometimes none), and she wasn't going to make much on her new job, she needed a caretaker for my little brother (then one and a half or two) and me, so she hired a maid.

In the South then, if you were a middle-class or even lower-middle-class white family like us, you could hire a maid. The maid would be a black woman, maybe young, maybe not so young. Ex-perience was good, so not too young was best. In any case, the reason a woman like my mother, a mother of very modest means, could hire a woman to look after her children—and cook, clean house, do laundry, handle discipline—five days a week, eight hours a day, was because these women came from a segment of our soci-ety in which women pretty much had two "honorable" livelihoods they could pursue: schoolteacher, or what everyone called a maid. (I know maid has long been a common term for a general house-keeper and child-care person. But when you apply it to a fully grown, usually married woman with children of her own, the word takes on a particularly onerous quality.) If the woman had a college education, she likely worked as a schoolteacher. There were jobs in the offices of black male professionals—businessman, dentist, doc-tor, merchant, etc. But there weren't many of those jobs.

If the woman did not have a college or even high school education, chances were she worked as a maid in a white household. And because the competition was pretty tough, and because black people had no economic or political power in those days, a white mother/head of household affairs could get away with paying her maid a phenomenally low sum.

There came the day I was old enough to be standing next to my mother when she wrote out the check for our maid's weekly pay.

Even at that age—I must have been twelve or thirteen—I was flabbergasted. I won't say how little it was, but I will say that even by then I knew that I could make that much money mowing three yards, and I could make it in one day. I could make, mowing yards, in one day what our maid was paid for a forty-plus-hour week.

And I said something about it. About how I couldn't believe she paid the maid that little. My mother got angry. She got defensive. "That's all I can afford to pay her!" she said, upset. And this may very well have been true. If I'd been able to mow four lawns a day five days a week for a month, I would have been able to make more than half of what my mother was making at the clinic where she worked. And she was, in the worst times, supporting a family of five on it.

Still. I'd seen the run-down house where our maid lived with her family. It was pretty much a wooden shack on brick foundation posts. It had no running water. It may have had electricity, but I'm not sure. There was no grass in the yard (until sometime into the twentieth century, of course, no one in the South had grass in their yards except a few town people, so this had very recently been common among country folk, but still).

I brooded over it. But of course I let it go. It wasn't me paying the maid, who was still needed to look after my younger brother, and whom my mother still needed to help keep the house clean and the laundry washed. It wasn't my call, finally.

There came the day, though, when my mother accused our maid of stealing our (my and my brothers') underwear. She'd noticed some underwear missing, more than once, and she came to the conclusion that the maid had to be stealing it. So she fired her.

I remember the morning she fired her. We were backing out of the driveway in my mom's economical three-on-the-tree small sedan when the maid came charging out of the house toward the car. Before we could pull away, she was on us, shouting into the window past my older brother sitting up front, saying to my mother, "Ms. Watson, I did not steal that underwear, you can't accuse me of stealing, I'm not a thief, and you can't call me a thief, you can fire me for whatever you want, but I'm not a thief!" My mother put the car into first gear and drove off. The maid stormed back into the house.

She accepted the firing. Or maybe she quit after being accused. I don't remember. But I do remember how ashamed I felt at being, even inadvertently, the cause of yet one more humiliation, an outrage, really, toward this woman, who I must say I felt great affection for, even if it was pretty much impossible for me to get to know her, to really get to know her. We lived in different worlds, in those days. Especially the very poor black and the middle- (even lower-middle-) class white. Any black and white, really.

I remember thinking, If her children don't have underwear, she can have my underwear. I don't care if she steals my underwear. It's not right to fire a woman because she can't afford to buy her children underwear, and that she can't afford to do that because she has to work for wages about five times less than what an adolescent white boy could make for less skilled labor than she was doing.

There was nothing I could do to rectify the situation. My mother hired a new maid, not nearly so nice or efficient as the one who quit or got fired.

Years later, I saw the first maid, the good maid, at a bus stop. She was wearing a hospital worker uniform. She had a pretty good job. But I can practically guarantee it was one of the lowest-paying, if not the lowest-paying, job in that place.

She was happy to see me. She sure seemed so, anyway. And there was no real reason anymore for her to pretend that she was.

A GOOD NEIGHBOR IS HARD
TO FIND

Whitney Terrell

I USED TO worry about a boy. He lived next door to me in a small
airplane bungalow on the east side of Kansas City. My writing
room was at the back of my house and in the afternoons, when I
was working late, I would hear him playing trumpet in his own
room, which was at the back of his house. It was a mournful and, to
be honest, very imperfect sound—a teenager fumbling through
scales on snow-bitten afternoons when the light was flat, in a depressed African American neighborhood, where playing the trumpet no longer seemed like a realistic method of escape. No Miles
Davis over there. Just a kid who was about to get beat.

■ ■

My neighbor, Jackie Eason, rented the house. She was black; I was
white. The boy with the trumpet had suddenly appeared at her place,
a sweet, quiet, almost furtively gentle kid who one day hopped down
off a school bus and loped up her cracked concrete steps, instrument
case in hand. It was 1998. No announcement, no explanation.

Our houses were maybe twenty yards apart, separated by a
waist-high fence, along which the prior owner had planted orange
day lilies.

"What's up?" I said one day. "My name is Whitney. I live
next door."

The kid nodded politely. He was bright eyed and long limbed, wearing a collared shirt and khakis, and he tucked his chin and bit his lower lip as if he'd just witnessed something amusing—for instance, my announcement that I lived next door, made while standing in the yard next door—and he was debating whether or not he should share this with anybody. "What's your name?" I continued, circling the fence.

"Terry."

"So you're staying with Jackie for a bit?"

I was fishing for information, of course. Terry who? Terry Eason? Were he and Jackie related? Not related? Where were his folks?

Then Jackie's wry, smoky voice issued out through her darkened screen door. "Watch out, Terry. You talk to him too much, he'll put you to work."

She pushed out the door in her slippers and a pair of jeans. Jackie was in her fifties, on disability, and rarely left the house—and yet, despite these difficulties, she always seemed formidably collected, hair done in a perm, nails painted, clothes pressed. I myself tended toward cotton work shirts with holes in the elbows and filthy khakis.

"Is he busy?" I asked.

This got a shy laugh from Terry, which pleased me.

"No, he ain't," Jackie said, observing Terry with her arms folded across her chest. "But he should be because he's got a pile of homework he needs to do in here."

"Come on, Granny," Terry said, tilting back his head.

"It's better than anything *he's* got to offer," Jackie replied.

This was said in a friendly tone, like a joke, so I took it that way. But it was also a warning, which I spent a lot of time trying to figure out whether I should ignore or heed.

■ ■

I found out that Terry Hemmitt (that was his full name) *had* no father. That's what people said. That's what *he* said. Of course this wasn't true. He had a father out there somewhere. He just wasn't around. Ever. And his name was never mentioned in my hearing, either by Jackie or by Terry. There was a zone around that name, a force field, that he and Jackie had deliberately erected, which told you: *Do not ask about this man.*

That was what I felt when Jackie said: "It's better than anything *he's* got to offer."

She didn't just mean that I didn't have anything better to offer than homework. She meant that I should not under any circumstances present myself as a substitute, a mentor, a big brother, a "male presence." The warning also involved the admission that Terry would be vulnerable to wanting that.

■ ■

A journal entry dated Thursday, February 15, 2001. I'd just finished teaching Flannery O'Connor's *A Good Man Is Hard to Find* to the white kids at the nearby Catholic college, where I taught comp for ninety-two hundred dollars a year. I heard a high-pitched squabbling outside my house and found about twenty African American schoolchildren in a pushing, screaming mass across the street. Their bus was inching forward, as if the driver wanted to leave. When I walked down the steps from my house, he did, and I was alone with the fighting kids. "Hey, nigger, why don't you stay out of this?" said a boy in a Packers parka, whose head came up to my elbow. "Just let them fight. Let them be."

Two girls circled each other on the sidewalk. It was cold. The aggressor wore a white cotton T-shirt and was bare armed. The other girl wore a red coat with a floral pattern stitched onto it. My lecture on O'Connor's story had focused on the white family's lack of curiosity and empathy. I had no real curiosity or empathy for these kids; I just wanted them to go away. But during my lecture, I'd angrily recalled Jackie's claim that I had nothing to offer. As I approached, the girl in the white shirt pushed me away and then looked me up and down in a slow, deliberate manner as if she didn't understand *what* species of being could be stupid enough to be standing in her path.

"All right, let's go," I said. "Get out of here. Break it up. No fighting on this street." Even to my own ears, I sounded unconvincing.

"Hey," the Packers kid said, plucking my sleeve. "Would you *please* step out of the way? Would you *please* step out of the way? Now I asked you three times nicely, would you please step out of the way." There was the grave suggestion in his eyes that something horrible would happen to me if this incantation were disobeyed.

The aggressor in the white shirt taunted; the girl in red stood her ground with a blank stare. The mob egged them on: "What you waitin' on? Hit that bitch!"

A fusillade of "motherfucker!" and "shit!"

Jackie Eason came out on her porch and said she was going to call the cops.

"Fuck the cops!" one kid said.

The cops came. Both girls were cuffed and arrested. I stepped away.

■ ■

Terry Hemmitt hadn't been on that particular bus. But the fight—unreasoning, brutal, pointless—reminded me of the world he lived in when he wasn't at Jackie's place. Like those kids, he was in the Kansas City, Missouri, public school system. The KCMO public schools were a horrific wasteland because the white residents of our city had fled across the state line to Kansas during the battles over school desegregration in the 1960s and 1970s. In Kansas, which housed our newest suburbs, built expressly for these fleeing whites, there were no black residents. Thus nobody to bus. Thus higher property values.

Thus lower property values in the neighborhoods they'd left behind, like the one where Terry and I lived. Lower tax revenues. Worse teachers. Failing schools.

■ ■

After that incident on the street, I started spending a bit more time with Terry. Part of this was vanity. A silent assertion that I wasn't a total misfit. We went out to dinner occasionally. Royals games. I watched him play football. In his presence, I often felt like a much younger and smaller version of Terry was very cautiously protecting himself inside a fortress of good manners that he wasn't sure was going to hold up. The kid who played those mournful scales on the trumpet was inside the fortress. He was appreciative that I'd come up to the ramparts for a visit, but he wasn't coming out.

Fair enough. I still wasn't going to play his friend or father. But I also wasn't sure what I *could* offer, other than a lot of unsolicited advice. For instance, about girls.

"You dating anybody?" I asked one day.

"Not seriously. There's one girl I'm kinda seeing. Doing stuff," Terry said. He had a very pleased look in his eye when he said the words "doing stuff."

"No," I said.

"Whaddya mean, 'no'?"

"I mean, I don't care. You want to have sex with her, have sex with her. But you have to be very, very careful not to get stuck in anything."

This was one of the times when Terry deployed his shy laugh, as if to remind me that he was now old enough to make a joke out of that last phrase.

"I know what I'm doing."

"I do *not* doubt that," I said. "Just so long as you are doing it with a condom. Right?"

Silence. The ramparts of the fortress whistled in the wind.

"You don't think this matters? What about your future? And hers?" I was sputtering here, offering an incompetent version of a talk that my father had once incompetently given to me. "What about college? You ever think about that? Your grades are good. Football. Music. Extracurriculars—"

Terry also found this phrase, "extracurriculars," to be funny. But I could also see that he was curious about college. A bright brown eye peeked at me through the ramparts.

"I am serious about this, man," I insisted.

"Maybe you are."

"This college thing is no joke. You could totally go if you wanted to. The only thing that would prevent you would be getting in some kind of trouble between now and when you graduate. Some kind of responsibility that you might not be ready for yet.—"

"You mean like getting my girlfriend pregnant?"

Terry's chipper, innocent expression was slightly exaggerated, as if to remind me that he had experience with the consequences of somebody getting pregnant when they weren't prepared to take care of a child.

Like his mom, for instance. I always felt better when I saw this glint in his eyes.

"Okay," I said. "So we're on the same page?"

"Yeah. I heard about that page."

■ ■

College. That was it. I wasn't fit to be a father—I didn't *want* to be a father—but I could be a college counselor. That was something I knew about. I gave Jackie my entire spiel. Terry was an A student. He'd recently gotten into Lincoln Academy, the best high school in the otherwise disastrous KCMO school system. He played football. He played *trumpet*. And he was a young African American male from the urban core. Sure, he'd been marked for a different destiny by his neighborhood, school district, and city. But the people who'd done the marking felt a very vague and distant sense of guilt about this. They were willing to do certain things to assuage this guilt, and one of those things was to allow pointy-headed academics at their universities to favor students like Terry.

"So he gets in, what then?" Jackie asked me. "I can't pay for this."

Which was true. "He can get a scholarship."

I almost lost her here. Jackie's face broke into a scowl. She handed back my sheaf of application requests. "He is *not* good enough at football for that."

"An academic scholarship," I said.

"For what?"

"For grades. For being a good student. And for being a good student while he was living here." We were sitting on her porch and I nodded out at our neighborhood.

Jackie took a deep sigh and pulled the paperwork back, pursed her lips, and gave it another look. "You better be right," she said.

■ ■

I'm not going to portray myself as being omnipresent in Terry's life during these last few years of high school. I wasn't. I had my own life. I published a book in the summer of 2001. I got fired from my adjunct teaching job. I got married in 2003. I was working hard to finish my second book. The book was late and I was terrified it wouldn't be any good. But somehow during this time, his college application to the University of Kansas got turned in. Financial aid forms were filed. Personal essays written—that part I remember helping with, editing, though I have no actual memory of what they said.

And then, as I'd hoped, he got in. The University of Kansas offered him an academic scholarship and financial aid.

■ ■

I drove him up to Lawrence for a campus visit in late May.

"It'll be great," I said. "It's really beautiful. The whole university is set up on a hill. Big limestone buildings. There's a river. Allen Fieldhouse. You're going to be a Jayhawk, man. You're going to love it. It's like nothing you've ever seen."

Terry was nervous. The bright, shy smile didn't show up during these conversations. I chucked him on the shoulder. Maybe he felt bad about leaving Jackie.

"It's okay," I said. "You do *not* have to feel guilty about success."

■ ■

The term "white privilege" wasn't common yet in those days. Neither were the terms "institutional racism" or "structural racism." I'm happy that these terms are in current use now. But as shorthand, they fail to convey the human feelings that Terry and I experienced when we drove forty minutes west of Kansas City to Lawrence, Kansas, for his campus visit to KU. As the son of a KU graduate, I'd always felt very comfortable in Lawrence. My father told stories about being in a fraternity there. We'd gone to basketball games together. My mother had a college friend who lived in Lawrence and I'd grown up visiting and playing at her house. As an adult, I'd taught at KU for a semester, and as a writer, I'd read at The Raven, the local bookshop.

That was what I brought with me as Terry and I exited I-70 and pulled into Lawrence. He'd been quiet on the ride out, so I thought I'd take him on a cruise down the main drag, Massachusetts Avenue. That street is like a postcard for the "college experience." Filled with the kinds of things you'd imagine that college kids would like: hip record stores, coffee shops, pizza restaurants, artsy movie theaters, and bars, bars, and more bars. Crowded, too, with kids. I'd driven down it a hundred times and always loved it, always felt at home, but then, for the first time in my life, cruising down that block with Terry, it made me queasy and frightened. Nervous. Anxious. A sheen of sweat glossed my forehead, and I began to curse myself for my vast stupidity and blindness because, for the first time, with Terry riding beside me, I was looking at that street through his eyes. I was searching the sidewalks, and the bars, and the packs of laughing coeds, for somebody, anybody, who looked like him.

Maybe there were a few African American faces there. Surely there must have been. But my memory of driving down that street, and then up the hill onto campus, was of a vast, impenetrable sea of whiteness. Happy. Self-assured. But to me, right then, wanting to reassure Terry, terrifying and inane.

■ ■

Terry bravely went in for the campus interview that I'd set up for him, dressed in a pair of khakis and a collared shirt that he'd carefully picked out. I waited in the car, rehearsing things that I could say. It was a big school. Lots of students. There were African American student groups. African American frats. You didn't have to get involved in, or even pay attention to, the white fraternities and sororities whose mansions we'd cruised past on our way in. Once he got assigned a dorm, he'd meet people on his hallway. He'd find his way into making friends. It would be scary, I understood it would be scary, but it was scary for everybody when they first went away to school.

He could always come back home and visit. It was a short drive away.

All of these things were true, in the narrow sense of the word. But none of them, on that particular day, felt true because they were in the shadow of a greater truth. There are a *ton* of KU graduates in Kansas City. They live in Johnson County, Kansas. This is a huge swath of Kansas City, just across the state line. A vast white republic that extends south from 55th Street clear to 160th Street and beyond. They are people who *left* the neighborhood where Terry and I lived. Their descendants are the kids whom we drove past that day as we silently left Lawrence and headed back to our part of the city.

■ ■

The process of reinscribing oneself, of covering over the destiny that our economic system has written on all of us, isn't easy. Thomas Wolfe is credited with coining the phrase "You can't go home again." My version of that line would be "You can't leave home if you try." During the years I lived next to Terry, I always expected to be the one who left Kansas City. My writing was useful only if it served to get me out.

I've tried several times to leave, believe me. But I'm still here. Sometimes, I think, it's because, no matter how openly I rebel against my past, the fact is that there are still benefits to being tattooed with the marks of a white son of privilege in Kansas City. These are diminishing and dying out. They aren't the future. But they exist and are applied indiscriminately, even to the rebels, no matter how loudly they complain.

Terry, however, got out. It was painful, merciless, and hard, as all such operations have to be. But most important, it was *his* plan, *his* decision, *his* escape route—which is, of course, the only true path anyone can take. After his first semester at the University of Kansas, he gave me a call.

"I don't think I'm going to stay at KU," he said.

"Okay," I said. I was sitting in my back writing room and I glanced up, out my window, at Terry's bedroom in the back. It had been a long time since I'd heard him practicing that trumpet.

"I appreciate what you did. What you were trying," he said. "And I also—you know, I just . . . I don't want you to be upset with me."

"I'm not, Terry," I said. "I'm not."

"It's not that I don't think it's important. School. I like it. I can do it, I know I can do it, it's just that . . . even with the scholarship, I can't afford it. I'm working full time and I'm still five thousand dollars in debt."

"That's fine, Terry. That's fine. It's my fault. I didn't see that. I should've been able to anticipate that. I mean, there's other places we can look. You can take a year off. We can reapply—"

This was the opposite of the advice that I'd previously given him, because it was the opposite of the advice that my college counselor had given me. Taking a year off was suspect. I'd argued that it was crucial he apply to college right away.

"No," he said.

"No?" I understood then, by the quality of his silence, that he wasn't just informing me of his decision about KU. There was something else, some kind of help he wanted from me. "Well, that's fine. But you've got to have some kind of backup plan. You can't just stay around here and do nothing. You've done too much work for that."

"I've got a plan," Terry said. "I'm going to join the air force."

"What?"

"I know you've been all worried about the war. I know you've been writing about it. And Granny, she's a little worried about me doing this, so she asked me to call you. Before I signed up. So I promised I would."

I'd had no idea. Terry was right, though. I had been writing about the war in Iraq. My desk at that moment was covered with notes, transcripts, and news articles about some infantry soldiers who'd executed Iraqi detainees and were now in jail.

"Holy fuck," I said.

Terry's soft, shushing laugh whispered to me over the line. "Yeah," he said. "That's what she thought you'd say."

"What branch is it again?" I asked.

"Air force."

"Not the army?"

"Not the army. So if I go—"

"No, when you go."

"*When* I go," Terry said, agreeably. "I'll be up in the air. In a plane."

When I got off the phone with Terry half an hour later, my eyes were wet. I'd given him the third degree, talked over every option, listened to the details of his contract. He'd thought things through pretty damn well. Worried over details. And he was right—the air force was a lot less dangerous than the army, especially if he wasn't going to train to be a fighter pilot, which he wasn't going to do. He'd have a staff position. He'd learn a language. And the air force *was* harder to get into than the army. More exclusive. More elite. The grades he'd worked so hard on had come into play.

I couldn't have described then the emotion that I was feeling. Loss? Concern? Failure? No, not exactly. It was much fuller, much more painful, than that. I made calls to my military contacts. I asked questions. And then, a few days later, I knocked on Jackie's door when I knew Terry wasn't home, sat with her on her porch, overlooking our street, and told her that I thought Terry should accept the offer from the air force.

Jackie cried. She was a tough person. I'd never seen her cry over anything. I sat across from her and held her hand. "I know he's got to do it. I know he's gotta be happy. I just don't want to see him get hurt. I'm afraid," she said. "I'm afraid."

At that moment, I understood why I was there. This was the one true, useful thing I could do for Terry. The one thing he had asked: lie to his grandmother. Guarantee his safety, even if I couldn't really do that. Even if I was afraid.

"I checked it out," I said. "There's nothing to worry about. I promise. He's gonna do great."

■ ■

I've stayed in touch with Terry during the many years that have passed since that summer. As it turned out, he did go to war, flying missions in Afghanistan as well as Iraq. He was a crew member, not the pilot, but still he was there. He won't tell me what those missions were about, either. What he did, why he was there. As it turned out, I went to the war, too, as an embedded reporter in Iraq during 2006 and 2010. There were times when I wondered if Terry was up there in the sky above me, invisible, reading his instruments, and, in an inversion of our fortunes, somehow watching out for me.

I still own the house next door to Jackie's place. My first son was born when my wife and I still lived there, right around the time that Terry went away. I wrote two novels there. I loved it. I loved my neighbors, the day lilies, the tall, calming, majestic white pine that shaded both Jackie's house and mine. I live in a different house that's only seven blocks away, so I still visit the old place, tend the yard, clean the gutters, light the pilot light for the renters when winter comes. I go over and talk to Helen Palmer, who still lives across the street. When I look up at Jackie Eason's porch, I sometimes wonder if maybe the two of us weren't afraid for Terry. We were afraid for ourselves, for getting left behind. Which was why that fear felt so different, fuller, like happiness, in a way.

In that sense, Jackie was right to be afraid. When she got sick, in 2011, I was on a fellowship in another state. Terry was overseas, though he made it back before she died. And now? Terry's a grown man. He's still in the air force and lives in Washington, D.C.

He's not coming back, I don't think. Which makes him a stronger man than me.

Here in a State of Tectonic Tension

Its geography similar to Istanbul's—
read for Lake Huron, the Black Sea,
for the St. Clair River, the Bosporus,
for Lake St. Clair, the Sea of Marmara,
for the Detroit River, the Dardanelles,
and for Lake Erie, the Mediterranean—
a natural place for Ford and Olds to open factories,
strategically near the Pittsburgh steel mills, Akron
rubber plants, Mesabi iron ore range.
Here, in ultimate concentration, is industrial
America—Chrysler, Continental, Budd, Hudson,
in an area not much larger than two square miles,
ninety to one hundred thousand employed on two
or three shifts—the capital of a new planet, the one
on wheels. Whacked-out, stamped-out connecting rods,
the steady blown-out flare of furnaces, hammer-die
brought down on anvil-die, oil-holes drilled and oil-
grooves cut—Fordism was Gramsci's word to describe
mass assembly based on systems of specialized
machines operating within organizational domains
of vertically integrated conglomerates fed by small
and medium-sized units coordinated by methods
of marketing exchange—an epical, systemic violence.
Anonymous's eyes pop as he laughs and says
"dragged the old coon from his car, kicked him till
he shit himself, and then we set the auto on fire—God
Jesus was it a show!" How many summers after that
the Motor City burned to the ground? Soon several new
regimes of redistributed wealth would alter the way

capitalism proceeded, a squad of police breaks down
the union hall door, swinging crowbars and tossing canisters
of Mace—around the time the long depression started.
There are stalks of weeds in sunlit snow, an abandoned
house surrounded by acres of snow. The decay apparently
has frightened the smart money away. Metaphorically
underwater—more is owed on properties in Detroit than
they're worth. His hands and feet were bound, found
beaten in a field near Post and Fort, he's in intensive
care at Receiving Hospital, says Sergeant Ollie L. Atkins,
investigators yet to ask him who he is or what happened.
Notice that on the high school baseball diamond is a herd
of goats—attended by whom? Notice, a few doors down,
the stucco plastered house painted baby blue, walking in front
in a red stocking cap, green specks on his shoes—what
do you think he is thinking? Drive Woodward to Seven Mile,
west on Seven Mile to Hamilton, Hamilton south to the Lodge
Freeway, then the Lodge downtown, and measure the chaos,
drive Mack Avenue east to Seminole, south on Seminole
to Charlevoix, then west on Charlevoix to Van Dyke, south
on Van Dyke to East Jefferson, and remember what isn't.
Ionic pillars carved with grapes and vine leaves no longer
there, deserted houses of gigantic bulk, in which it seems
incredible anyone could ever have lived, no longer there,
Dodge Main's nocturnal gold vapors no longer there,
the constellated bright lights reflected on the Rouge River's
surface no longer there. Narco-capital techno-compressed,
gone viral, spread into a state of tectonic tension and freaky
abstractions—it'll scare the fuck out of you, is what it'll do,
anthropomorphically scaled down by the ferocity of its own
obsolescence. Which of an infinity of reasons explain it?
Which of an infinity of conflagrations implode its destruction?

—Lawrence Joseph

ONCE THERE WAS A SPOT

Larry Watson

I'M NOT so idealistic or naïve as to suggest that the Bismarck, North Dakota, that I lived in from the age of five to the age of twenty (1952 to 1967) was a classless society. Not at all. It was a largely middle-class community, and it certainly had people living in poverty, just as it had people of wealth. But here's the thing: While the poor aspired to a middle-class life, so did the wealthy.

Let's say you were a lawyer or you owned a lumber company or you ran a construction company or you owned the city's taxi service or you were a successful real estate developer. (These were the occupations of homeowners on my parents' block; my father was one of the lawyers.) You could afford a nicer house than a school-teacher or a cigarette salesman, yet the homes of all these families looked the same. When my wife moved to Bismarck with her family in 1958 they lived on the same block as the governor of the state, and I'd defy anyone who didn't already know which house was the governor's to pick it out from its neighbors. Later her family lived across the street from the mayor, and his house was as ordinary and unpretentious as any on the block.

The city had its grander houses, to be sure, but for the most part those had been built in an earlier era; they were older houses clustered near the center of town. The dwellings of newer construction were invariably modest, and almost all single-story ranches or split-levels.

In the company of friends, I entered more than a few of those houses, and once I was inside I could see that some had features that made them nicer than others—a plusher carpet, a paneled basement rec room, an extra bathroom, a console color television, a sectional sofa. But these touches were for the comfort, convenience, or taste of the residents; they didn't affect the impression of the house—or of its inhabitants—from the street.

How to account for the middling effect in that place and time? Perhaps it was a collective memory of the Depression, which so many of our parents lived through. Since they'd witnessed what it was to lose everything, they might have believed it was better not to accumulate too much. Maybe it was ethnic influence. The ancestors of many North Dakotans came from Norway and Sweden, and to Scandinavians ostentation was a sin only slightly less grievous than murder. It was all right to keep up with the Joneses; it wasn't all right to show them up. Many of the men had served in the military during World War II, and in the military almost everyone lands in the middle ranks. Maybe it was some strange influence of setting, of place and time, that made people believe the middle was where they belonged; they lived, after all, in the middle of the continent in the middle of the century. Or perhaps this was an era when the citizenry still took to heart their Christian religion's lessons on humility. Whatever the cause, the city could have had a credo: Don't try to show you're better than your neighbor.

When did it change? I'm not sure. My wife and I moved away, but on one of our annual trips back to Bismarck, probably in the mid-1970s, we noticed that on the once-bare hills that surrounded and looked down on the town, houses were being built, grand houses, many of them, and over the years there were more and more of them, and they became bigger and more imposing ("big-roofed houses," my architect brother-in-law calls them). At some point the houses that our parents had bought with the idea that they would live out their lives in them (true for my mother; she died in the house she'd lived in for more than fifty years) weren't large enough for school principals or doctors or oil company executives or heads of state agencies. Families believed they needed *more*. One bathroom certainly wasn't enough. Three bedrooms wouldn't do. A triple garage was a necessity. Soon Bismarck became a city with houses that grandly declared that their occupants belonged to the higher socioeconomic classes. Anyone driving down this block had to know that the people here had more money than the people on that block.

Of course matters of social class are always complicated by culture, region, ancestry, history, politics, race—to say nothing of the eyes of those making observations and coming to conclusions. It's entirely possible that when I recall a city that tried to show itself to the world as a community of equality of class I'm completely full of shit. But maybe, just maybe, on the wind-swept, heat-blasted, blizzard-besieged northern Plains, once there was a spot . . .

HURRAY FOR LOSERS

Dagoberto Gilb

AT THE BEGINNING I took auto shop because it didn't make me yawny or sarcastic to be there, and Uncle Willie—what kids called the teacher—might yell now and then, but mostly he left us alone, talking, doing. I liked cars, especially driving them instead of walking or the bus. And better when they were bad looking. Also for work, yes, but of course there was after work, cruising the starry boulevards, eyeing girls, the summer wind blowing through open windows all year round. These were the best times, the very best, all the older, mature veterans of life would say. I remember, I listened. None talked college years or the kind of jobs that were for them. All my friends, ones who weren't into glue, or likely headed to county a few times, or fantasizing too much about music careers (because they listened, not out of talent), talked about jobs and income as soon as they got out. Loading docks and trucker training, fireman, bartender, carpenter, plumber, jet mechanic, butcher. I had one high school friend who came from New Zealand. Poor, his mom and younger sister (his dad, an abusive drunk biker, didn't live with them) were set up by the Mormon church. He planned to go to BYU but in my mind that was because it was a Mormon thing, nothing to do with normal. Like me. Another friend, a girlfriend, she had a cousin who started college, but when her mom went to Mexico for her sick mother, she had to take care of the family instead. Another friend I made had come from Colorado. The Rocky Mountains. That was impressive to me in itself. He lived with his mom, a secretary at a parts factory.

One day his dad came to town. He'd never mentioned him before. His dad, unemployed, was once an engineer. Of course, yes, I thought railroad. I knew older people who worked at the yards. Not that, though. And more, he had a master's degree. I didn't know what that was, where it ranked in the educated order. It was out there and up high special, like from another land. One day my new friend got horrible news. His dad had shot himself. I don't remember if I even asked what kind of weapon, if I only imagined a shotgun. And my friend had to go to his apartment and clean it up. Brains and blood on the wall and floor is all I heard of it that one day he told me, and never again. Educated people were unusual.

Then, tenth grade (though it didn't change in eleventh or twelfth), the only colleges I knew of had headlining football teams. In L.A. it was USC and UCLA in the sports pages. I didn't know where either of their campuses were, had never seen a campus even, only that they both played at the Coliseum. Nobody I knew of went to a college like that. Actually, any college at all. Excluding the few off-the-books types, people I knew of, older, had jobs in construction, shops, factories, or delivering things in trucks. I had a friend whose mom was an *executive* secretary. A "rich" girl in high school's dad delivered the U.S. mail. Before she married the one after my dad, my own mom had a job at a dentist's office because she was pretty, not because she knew anything about offices or teeth. She dated lots of *culos* whose employment I didn't care to learn until she married one that became a temporary stepdad. My dad had worked full time at an industrial laundry since he was thirteen. I got to start working there the summer I turned fourteen. And during school I worked four hours every day and eight on Saturdays. Most adults I knew and spoke to worked there. Around 30 to 40 men and women where at least 150 were employed, all minimum-wage level. About a fourth of them whose origins were the Deep South, who knew about sports in town, the other three-fourths, who didn't follow any college sports local or national, from Mexico and Central America. They of course didn't talk a lot about any high school days, let alone the prep for what came after.

Nobody ever told me to go to college. That I should. Not one adult, in an office or on the street or in my home—or my father, who I only saw at work. Nobody expected me to go to college. Nobody discussed what it took to go to college. I remember—not even sure of the language then—that when asked on a form, like that, I picked college prep as my plan. Maybe it was the other options that were so bad. But the reason, for me, that I picked it was that it was the best choice. The top. Because I was aspiring to be, if not already, an elitist. I wanted more, better, the best possible at whatever it was. I didn't know what that was exactly, or at all, or how you made it happen, but I had confidence in my abilities, whatever they were supposed to be once they were in front of me. I liked cars, but no way I wanted to be a mechanic.

I'd say I wasn't as less than average as my grades. I got Bs in a couple of subjects. Like Spanish. Not an A because a grade wasn't about what you knew only. The teacher wasn't particularly fond of me, and I don't blame him, though he was a bloated fart and deserved me and other pains in the class. I might have gotten As in PE and auto shop and even math once or twice. Maybe Bs. Probably, maybe. Grades weren't about skills. Cs in the rest. Except English, where I got at least three or four or even five Ds. Not just that I never did homework—I never carried a book home—unless it was in-class, and I kept having specific trouble with those teachers. The only time I asked for a meeting with a counselor and vice principal (instead of one being called about me) was because I figured out the teacher planned to flunk me. I wanted a transfer to any other class so I wouldn't be held back or have to take it again. She agreed to pass me at the meeting.

My senior year my mom married again and I found a full-time graveyard-shift job as a janitor at McDonnell Douglas—had to get military-grade government clearance for that, and it came even though I just turned seventeen, in high school, and lied. I was allowed to go half day to a better neighborhood school, because clearly I was so advanced. I wanted the diploma. I always missed my first morning class to have breakfast and slept in the next. The next two classes weren't ones really. They gave a group of the special students like me a special "class" that was like two.

And so I graduated. Like most of my friends did too. I was the only one who pushed on and stuck to it at the community college level. And I was pure lucky. When I first got, for example, an F in a freshman English class (I had no belief that could happen, especially when I was trying—I got Ds on papers, and gave up), I soon after received my please come to the induction center letter in those Vietnam draft days, and I went (not a cheerful place). I visited my draft board office right after and asked if I could have a second chance for a student deferment. And they let me. Working full time, I took a night class at a "lesser" junior college, where I suddenly became smarter, and got a B in that freshman comp course. Well intentioned, I wasn't close to a high-level student then, but, given information, I was someone who could take what I knew I could do and figure out what came next.

Like me, my friends, all of them, did what they did, what they'd learned, harmlessly almost always. We were the mess-ups. We were the ones who didn't sit in the front of the classroom and join school clubs and organizations and government. Some guys played sports, some girls were on drill team and cheerleaders and a homecoming princess, but none of us got the best grades or worried about them, knew one thing about the best schools or even good ones. There were the ones who bought a car that was too expensive and worked to pay it off, to make it cooler, faster, lower, or were losing it to thieves or collection agencies. Ones that took too many drugs, though mostly only mota, weed. A couple moved on to juvie or prison. They got pregnant. They got married too early and had babies too young. They were in love or they were trying to do right. They stayed together and they didn't, either full-time occupations. Some jobs were awful, really shitty bosses, or so boring that nobody human, young anyway, could bear it. They tried studying fire science or health care at a junior college and then, oh well. Or business, and no thanks. They worked construction and in department stores or welding and wanted oil pipeline jobs or mining or to go to the wilderness or desert or Mexico and some went kind of hippie or semihippie until it was just a job job. Most stayed within a few miles of high school and worked at the familiar there, or there, and they had rent, lived with someone new and maybe a nice, modest wedding. Or they were drafted or joined. Or just had work that came out of the family, lived near all of them. They just did what they'd been doing, what they learned to do.

Little did they or I realize that by graduation it was all set. By *all* I mean 99.9 percent so. I mean the big shit. The grand, good whole front and backyard, and briefcase dad, and beautifully painted bedrooms life visualized on TV or movies. I mean, does one exception—which in many ways is me, I'm aware, because, miracle, I became a writer—out of ten thousand (and that's not generous, because isn't it more like a state lottery number)—make a braggable trend? You know, how a certain America rah rah likes to have it. Actually it could have been settled even sooner than that. A bet-able wager. Clearly we were traveling on a different American highway than those better behaved than us. And I'm saying there are a lot more of us than those who had a wise father mother grandfather grandmother neighborhood history inheritance and who genetically did everything just right. Better grades, better schools, better family, better manners, better breakfasts, better homework, better birth, better land. Never screwing up. Always hitting it right, with winks and wows coming back at them.

It's not like at first I didn't believe myself that anything was possible. I didn't consider probability, the odds, favorites. I was an elitist to my mind, or at least someone who believed in the better being better, that some can and will do better than others and should. Of course that meant that I could. Maybe I'm too short for an NBA squad, but I could make a major league baseball team! If I'd gone for it. If I'd have thought about it instead of an hourly job I wanted. What I didn't know and couldn't were what I didn't know that I didn't know. In the wide space of anything is possible, I could name like five side trails and maybe heard of five more. I thought that was a lot—I was doing better than any expectation—and I was off. New York, Paris, Rome, Yale, Harvard? Of course and sure I heard about all of them! What I knew about was, e.g., South Gate and Watts and Imperial Highway and say the campuses of ELA and Harbor and Compton colleges. Sure I was aware of the biggie deals, of the White House and president and cabinet and their offices, and attorneys and doctors and architects—like I knew of India, the Amazon, like I knew of astronomy, like I knew so many movie stars who lived in L.A. where I too lived and grew up.

You know these stories well: At twenty-two he or she accomplished this or that and what a job to land on! Admirable greatness, we are left to believe. And we do accept. But . . . by twenty-seven he runs this, controls that, invented, achieved, defended, wrote, and and and. At twenty-two I was still learning to read better, struggling with vocabulary, which is to say my thinking ability, and at twenty-seven I couldn't get a job (by then I had a master's degree in philosophy and religion) but somehow so-and-so didn't have any of that kind of problem ever of any kind. Ever! Not that I don't and didn't believe it, but here's what really underneath I was being told to take away from this: They are just smarter. More talented. More ambitious. More skilled. More accomplished and able. Work harder. Super trained. Perfect personality, mesh with the world, with the biz. More fluent, articulate, focused. In sum, the best, they earned it. And I say okay. And I do not believe it isn't true. I am sure it is. Such are the breaks. *Así es.* Life. Whereas . . .

Here's where the bad kid in me will be sent to the vice principal's office yet again, where my attitude has gotten my butt fired from let's say a number of jobs over the years. Because here comes another list that starts with a Whereas . . .

A step sideways first: I was a construction worker into two decades after I received my master's degree. Union high-rises generally. A one-crane job would be like thirty to seventy-five men there, depending on what stage of what. There were usually a couple of Chicano carpenters on downtown jobs, a few *mexicanos*. A few more percentage of black carpenters, especially at the bigger projects, of two or even three cranes. One job I remember, in West L.A., they'd had this one apprentice, black, who didn't work directly with me but was around and who seemed in every way normal and capable from my distance. Who at break would sit with me and another two Chicanos and one drawling Tejano and a few laborers—except for the dude from outside Houston, we were all Dodger and Laker fans and the apprentice was too. Then one day he was gone. Let go. The foreman said he was tired of him coming in late and being lazy, that he had too many screwups, and that he didn't like his mouth. Like I said, I barely knew the guy, and what the foreman said was all possible, and I didn't give it much more thought. In the trades, jobs came, jobs went. Then there was a layoff. The two Mexicano carpenters and the two big, older black carpenters were given checks. Job slimming down as we got closer to the top seemed like a plausible explanation. Keeping the younger, faster dudes who also could speak English to the boss. Soon enough two new carpenters appeared, both friendly and easy around the foreman. And in a blink a new apprentice too, who seemed connected to the new boys. I had to be around him more, and he wasn't too pleased about that, and I for one didn't enjoy him much either. He was a fucken jerk. If I asked him to do something, he'd frown, like it was beneath him. He was a hothead, got outraged at laborers for not doing what in fact should have been his job, wronged if anyone of us (not his buddies) suggested that maybe he forgot this, didn't do that well enough—normal advice for apprentices—and maybe he should buy his own tools so he didn't borrow and lose ours. And he missed days and was late often enough and hungover bad on Mondays. What the boss said? He's young, feeling his oats. His mouth? Fiery, full of spunk. Shitty work? He's learning, how it goes at first.

And so it is for all the very special people treated most specially from the especially special lands. Yet even that can seem sort of like nature's way—power picking what suits it. More money, for instance, goes to those who are living around more money places, and people in the wealthier places have more money to have and choose more. Up to a point anyway, and up to the point when, in a bit of less equanimity, when yet again it's one of them and not one of us, one of me mine, when it's the layoff check here and not there, when it's didn't even get an interview unless it's like Princeton—you know, I could go on and on—and that's when I'm *fuck you. That is what your only "best" is? Duhhh, gee, every and all the time, huh? You think I don't know better? Do you think I think it's okay? That I'm good with it? Do you really?* And that's when the Whereas pops out. Not uttered through the lips, not one word like the following (unless maybe you push, freaking hard, except then you're at a construction site, you're not talking about high, sophisticated power that doesn't have a stupid Trump-like face even thinking it): Whereas you, sir, you are just not our winner kind. Proof? This outburst. We go with winners and winners start as winners. You, sir, are no winner.

Oh god is that true. I grew up in L.A. and when I got out, I went not to New York or San Francisco, but straight to El Paso of all places. I didn't even know Princeton was in New Jersey until a few years ago. But you do know I'm not really talking about me, right? I'm not. I'm okay. A lot better than I and anyone who knew me when would have ever imagined. What I am talking about is what I love. America? Sure, lots I am grateful for, my birth here instead of there. And of course what I mean by America includes its history of what is below its southern border, and what I mean is what I have imagined was the best of America, the openness, the range and grandness of space real and dreamed. And the honest prospect of opportunity, not just for the privileged clutter at the top, way over there and all about there. I'm an elitist. That is, I believe in the best and that it should be admired and learned from and supported. It's just that my own view of best isn't what goes for best in this country of my birth.

A few years ago I was living in Oaxaca, one of the most beautiful cities in Mexico. Every morning I walked down a hill to get a cafecito. At a corner a block up from the café, a lady in a typical Mexican housedress would have set up a table, selling morning chilled *frutas* all cut into cubes and in plastic containers. They were *mango, piña, melón, sandía,* and sometimes even coconut. My second visit to her I bought two and she suggested that my girlfriend might prefer some *limón* and *chile* on the *coco.* When I told her I was solito but especially liked mine that way, she laughed—at sorry me or lucky me, I couldn't tell—and gave me one for free. I went every day and began to sit next to her for an hour to talk and listen and eat a little fruit and hear stories (and learn words and phrases in her native language) and watch people buy her fruit. She always saved me a *coco* when she brought them. She was Zapotec, from a village not far, but now lived nearby. Every morning she got up by four-thirty and went to the market and picked out the fruit and hurried back to her home where she cut and boxed them so she could be on the street early.

Almost eighty, she'd told me this was what she learned to do, and she had been doing it for decades, though not always in the same spot. That she lived on these pesos, from twenty-five, thirty-five fruit boxes. Of course it occurred to me to ask her how it was that she was this. But I couldn't. Couldn't treat her as a subject. She was more friend, a respected elder, and after a month she treated me, for that hour, as part of her life, sharing. I was already as lucky as I could be, able to be there, the large of it, the small of it. And what else but my luck? The big metaphor of that, the small connotation. She was so good, so lively and happy to be living her fate. So quick to talk and to laugh. There could be no better than her, no harder working, ambitious, accomplished. Like pure water. The best. She was just, normally, unseen. A few pesos, a *gracias*.

In these days, these last decades especially, it's as if privilege is taken for granted by those who live inside it, who don't know a world that is not it—that exotic, other world where there are other, poorer, lesser people who . . . just don't and probably, certainly, didn't have what it takes, weren't born better. Lately, these days, in these years, privilege isn't simply accepted, it's entrenched and it is assumed it is true, right. Privilege has made the special more so. It's advancing the special and calling only those therein "the best." And though it could be so, I'm not buying that fruit.

LA CIUDAD MÁGICA

Patricia Engel

You see them walking along the shaded perimeters of parks, dressed like nurses in pressed white uniforms, pushing strollers, talking to the babies in their care. You see them sitting together on benches near the playground, watching the children on the swings, occasionally calling to them not to climb so high on the jungle gym.

You see them walking along the road, carrying the child's backpack on the way home from school, while the child walks a few steps ahead, laughing with a friend. You see these women waiting outside of karate and ballet class, sitting in church pews beside the children on Sundays.

You see these women at the supermarket, pushing the cart down the aisle, the child perched atop the seat, legs dangling between the metal rails, while she pulls food from the shelves to buy and prepare for the family. You see these women sitting at the ends of tables in restaurants, keeping the children entertained with coloring books and video games, cutting their food into small pieces, whisper-begging the child to take another bite, so as not to interrupt the parents' dinner conversation.

You see these women in the morning, as early as sunrise, stepping off the bus from the downtown terminal, walking quickly along the avenue to arrive at the place of their employment in time to wake the children, feed them breakfast, and get them ready for school.

You see these women in the evening, sitting five to a bench

beneath the bus stop shelter, shielding themselves from the summer sun or from the winter rain, waiting for the bus to come to take them home.

■ ■

A group of mothers dressed in exercise clothes, adorned with jewelry and painted with makeup, gather for lunch at a café in Coral Gables—where streets lined with ficus and poinciana trees have Spanish names like Valencia, Minorca, and Ponce de León.

You overhear their lunch conversation, comparing nannies by country of origin.

"I prefer the Panamanians and Nicaraguans," says one woman, picking at her salad, "because they know their place. They don't try to get too friendly with me. I *hate* that."

Another woman jumps in. "Oh, you mean when they address you directly? My God, it's like, 'Who gave you permission to open your mouth?'"

"Brazilians are just crazy, and you can't trust Colombians or Ecuadorians. They steal and they'll flirt with your husband," offers another woman. "Don't even bother trying them out. And Guatemalans come with too many problems. They're always crying about something. Like, *hello?* I hired a nanny, not a charity!"

The women laugh, then brag to one another how their children are fluent in Spanish, and though it annoys them that now the nannies and their offspring can have private conversations, at least it's still cheaper than hiring an American babysitter or paying an agency commission for a European au pair.

■ ■

Tuesday morning at a bakery in The Roads.

Two men ahead of you on the counter line catch up after not having seen each other in a while.

One man tells the other he and his family plan on moving away soon.

"We're tired of feeling like foreigners around here. You can't go anywhere in this city without hearing Spanish spoken. I don't want my children growing up around that."

He says they're thinking about moving north to Broward or Collier County. "Somewhere *spic-free*."

"But they're everywhere," his friend says, laughing. "You can't escape them."

"We want to get away from the Miami kind. They're the ones taking over."

Then each man takes his turn at the counter, ordering a dozen empanadas to go.

■ ■

After eight days at sea, twenty-four Cuban migrants making their way to Florida shores on a shabby vessel spot the coast guard in their wake. They throw themselves into the water and climb the American Shoal Lighthouse six miles off the coast of Sugarloaf Key, hoping it will amount to having touched dry land. It takes an entire day for officials to coax the Cubans off the red iron lighthouse rails. They are detained for a month until a judge rules that the lighthouse, despite its name, does not count as U.S. soil. The Cubans will be repatriated and will likely serve prison sentences for having fled their island.

The Magic City.

La Puerta de las Américas.

The Capital of Latin America.

■ ■

The rainbowed Brickell Avenue high-rises, made as famous as the flamingos in the opening credits of *Miami Vice*, are now tiny folds in a much taller and more congested panorama of mirrored towers that glisten like machetes; the Miami that cocaine and money laundering built.

Brickell Avenue snakes into Biscayne Boulevard, cutting through downtown, a place everyone but the diamond and drug dealers used to avoid, now lined with new condos and chic restaurants, with a view of the restored waterfront parks, unfolding along the bay into urban pockets where longtime residents have been edged out by developers and hiked rents, christened with catchy names and written about in travel magazines as the trendy new neighborhoods to explore.

■ ■

Far down Biscayne, in a sleepy subdivision built along the Intracoastal, your friends Joe and Nicole live in a small stucco house with a red-shingle Spanish roof. Their next-door neighbors recently moved out so their baby could pursue a career in toddler modeling in Atlanta. A single guy in his forties moved in a few weeks later.

You all assume he's a bachelor because of the different girls coming to the house. Young, beautiful. Some in fancy cars. Others dropped off. There is a girl who arrives on a skateboard. Another, on her own Ducati.

One day while barbecuing in the backyard, Joe decides the neighborly thing is to invite the bachelor over.

The guy arrives and drinks tequilas around the patio table till long after dark.

At one point he leans over to you and says, "I hear you're Colombian. I've got a couple of Colombian girls working for me. They're the best. Second only to the Russians."

You ask what sort of business he's in.

"Film production."

"What kind of films?"

"Well, not really films, per se. More like video production. For the Internet."

Another tequila and the guy admits he's running a porn studio out of his house. Each bedroom outfitted with lights and cameras operated from a central control room. The girls perform for subscription

Internet channels. Most have loyal followings and do private shows, sometimes alone, sometimes with each other.

"Where do you find these girls?" is all you think to ask.

"It's easy. One girl tells another. I've got a waitlist thirty girls deep."

He pats your hand as if to assure you.

"Believe me, it's all perfectly legal. I don't hire minors. I leave that to the guys up in Fort Lauderdale."

■ ■

In the mailroom of your apartment building, you say hello to another resident checking her box near yours. She's the type who complains about anything. The weather. The color of the paint on the walls. A speck of lint on the lobby floor. "This country is screwed," she always says, "especially Florida." She kicks herself every day for moving down from Delaware twenty years ago and constantly threatens to go back.

"How's work?" you say.

She's a masseuse and tells you her least favorite clients are the "Latins" because they make her use the service entrance when entering their homes—the same door meant for the maids, cooks, and plumbers.

"Can you imagine?" she says, horror streaked across her face. "They treat me like a servant. They don't even want me to walk in the front door. They act like they own this city. They're so entitled. They've ruined Miami, turning it into their own colony."

"Now you know how it feels," you say, dropping your junk mail in the garbage.

Your neighbor stares at you, her pale cheeks flushed with anger, but says nothing in response and walks away.

■ ■

There's a saying locals throw around:

The best thing about Miami is how close it is to the United States.

■ ■

They come from other cities and from other countries, looking for paradise by the sea; looking to be South Beach models, to marry rich and become queens of Star Island, but instead find themselves in the republic of pills and powders and paid sex.

You see them standing outside of hotel lobbies on Collins Avenue, dressed in designer clothes, balanced on sharp high heels. Legs tanned and shiny. Breasts large and fake. You see tourist men come out of the building to look for a girl to take in to the hotel bar, or up to a room. You see red rented Ferraris pull up to the curb and the women step over to them casually, as if the man were just asking for directions, and then climb into the passenger seat. He doesn't even open the door for her.

You see them walking along Biscayne Boulevard, even in parts the city has worked so hard to clean up. You see them outside of the Wonderland strip club on Seventy-Ninth, ignored by cops patrolling the area, and among the homeless and stray dogs in the concrete yards beneath I-95 that used to hold the Mariel refugee tent city.

You see them standing outside the motels among teenagers smoking cigarettes and working as lookouts for drug dealers. You see them wandering the few vacant lots still left along the bay that haven't yet been bulldozed and flattened to make room for more skyscrapers; the ones where body parts often wash up—a hand, a foot, even a whole leg, that will remain forever unidentified.

■ ■

You knew one of these girls once. A white Texan named Toni who worked a five-block stretch on lower Biscayne where your boyfriend at the time lived with his bandmates. She was always high and would get in the car of any guy who whistled her way, but always said hello and watched after you when you walked alone to your car late at night.

"This city's not safe for nice girls like you and me," she used to say.

One day her father came from Dallas to collect her. Everyone in the neighborhood heard her shouting that she didn't want to leave. You and your boyfriend watched from the second-floor window as she fell to her knees on the sidewalk and cried. But then her father scooped her up, embraced her long, and she let him take her home.

■ ■

A dozen Cuban migrants land on the beach near your apartment building. They arrive in a motorless wooden boat loaded with broken paddles, empty water jugs, and a torn plastic sheet they used as a sail during their two weeks at sea. They are sunburned and filthy, thin, their faces crusted with sea salt. A mob of beachgoers gather on the sand around them, welcoming them to Miami, offering the migrants their sunglasses, hats, towels, and shirts with which to cover their charred shoulders; water and beers from their coolers, until the police arrive to process them for amnesty, and release them to their relatives.

La Ciudad Mágica.

La Ciudad del Sol.

Cuba con Coca-Cola.

■ ■

Down U.S.-1, past the waterfront mansions of Coco Plum and Gables by the Sea, the sprawling estates and ranches of Pinecrest, a few turns off the highway onto a narrow dusty road, you find people selling fruit out of tin shacks; papayas the size of footballs, guanabana, carambola, and unbruised mangos, perfectly ripe, erupting with nectar.

Here you will drink straight from the coconut while, a few yards down, another vendor offers barbecued iguana—the same ones they sell in pet stores that owners grow bored of and release to the wild, and people in the suburbs pay to have removed from their property—or wild hog, alligator, and diced python, served with hot sauce and rice, freshly hunted down in the Everglades.

Out here, you can pick out a pig from a corral and they'll slaughter it right in front of you, ready to take home, head and all, to roast for all your friends in your caja china; or you can whisper your request to a guy who knows another guy, and in a few minutes find someone to sell you horsemeat.

Out here you can watch a live dogfight, buy a peacock to take home and keep in your backyard to protect you from the evil eye of your enemies, have your illnesses cured by the polvos of a curandero, and a spell cast by a brujo so you'll be lucky in money and in love.

Nobody will ever know you were here.

■ ■

The shrine to La Virgen de la Caridad del Cobre sits on Biscayne Bay, with its own replica of the Havana malecón. Elderly people are bussed in daily from retirement communities and senior centers; families come together in pilgrimage from all over the state. Here, people gather to pray to Cuba's patron saint, and to leave sunflowers for her other face, the orisha Ochún.

A year ago, on a day like any other, as the viejitos sat before the altar praying for freedom from Fidel, as they often do, President Obama entered the church unannounced, walked down the aisle, and knelt beside the faithful in the pews.

Your friend Alejandro's grandmother was there.

She said it was like seeing Jesucristo himself.

Alejo was born in Cuba and spent three months in a Guantanamo refugee camp before his family received permission to enter the United States. His father worked as a dishwasher in Sweetwater. His mother sold watermelons at the intersection of Eighty-Seventh Avenue and Coral Way. He's a lawyer now and plans on running for a public office.

"Why do you think Obama came that day?" he says. "It's because every politician knows that without the abuelos of Miami in your pocket, you won't make it to the corner."

He says there are other major Latino cities. Los Angeles. Houston, San Diego. Even Chicago and New York. But none like Miami, where a national minority is the ruling majority, with 67 percent of the population, where the money and the political power sit firmly in Latino hands.

"Miami is the city of the future," Alejo says, "and in a few years, the rest of the country will finally catch up."

■ ■

Your Miami begins in New Jersey where you were raised far from the ocean in an Anglo suburb near woods and mountains, speaking Spanish among family and close friends, while outside your home, classmates and townspeople mocked the color of your skin and your parents' accents, asking with suspicion how they managed to come to this country, and they'd answer that they came on a jet plane.

Your only community was your family. From the world beyond your tíos and primos, you were made to understand, before you could spell your own name, that even if you were born in this country, even if you speak the language, you will always be an outsider; this country will never belong to you.

Your Miami begins in New York, where you moved to at eighteen, lived in different downtown apartments and tried on different lives for more than a decade before finally deciding to leave.

Your Miami begins in the Andean highlands, across the mountainous cordillera, low in the valleys of the Río Cauca, and deep in the wetlands of the Orinoco; before Bolívar, before the conquest, before Colombia was Colombia, when you were Muisca and spoke Chibcha; and before that, it begins across the Atlantic, on the northern coast of Africa.

Your Miami begins in Puerto Rico, where your older brother was born, and before that, it begins in the other América, where your father worked since age fourteen to support his family of eleven in Medellín; where your parents married in a chilly church in Bogotá; your Miami begins in Colombia, the country your parents loved but left, like so many others, so you, the child they did not yet know they would have, might have a chance at something more.

■ ■

After they settled in the United States, as soon as they could afford it, your father took your mother on vacation to Miami. There is a photograph of her leaning on a crooked palm tree in the last pink hour before sunset. She stares at your father, who holds the camera. She is barely twenty-two. Her long hair colored a rusty red, still pearl-skinned from the lifelong overcast of Bogotá despite her indigenous blood.

There is a picture of you holding your father's hand a decade later; you, a child of two or three years old. Your mother took the photograph from the beach while your father led you into the shallow and flat edge of the ocean. He stands above you like a tower; you, in your red gingham baby bikini. They tell you that you hated the ocean when you first felt it on your skin. You tried to stomp and slap it away. You cried and reached for firm land. But then something changed and you began to swim on your own before you could speak full sentences. And then they couldn't pull you out of the water.

As you grew older, despite the years you spent in other cities, feeling their claim on you, you knew Miami would one day be your home, at least for a little while.

You are not a refugee, but here in Miami you believe you have found a sort of refuge.

■ ■

You walk along a nature trail in one of the city's spectacular ecological reserves, canopied with thick banyans and mangroves lining a lagoon. As you pass him standing on the edge of the trail, an old man with a thick belly and a T-shirt crescented with pit stains calls you over to him and points out a fat, furry golden weaver, what locals call "lighting spiders," centered on a web shining like glass in the fractured sunlight.

"That is one big spider," you say.

"I used to practice shooting on them when I was a kid. Till I got bitten by one and my hand swelled so much the skin split like a banana peel."

He misses the old Miami, he says, when it was vast and empty, and you could walk for miles from what's now the Palmetto Expressway to Dinner Key and not run into a soul.

"Now it's crazy and crowded and full of foreigners. It's like watching your first love turn into a junkie and finding her begging for pennies under the highway."

You tell him you still think there's a lot of beauty to Miami. Just look around.

"You didn't grow up around here. I can tell."

"That's right. I didn't. But I've lived here for twelve years so far."

"You're real brown. How'd you learn to speak English so good?"

You look back at the spider and then at the man, tell him to have a nice day, continue on your way down the trail, leaving him alone by the trees.

The man calls after you.

"You watch out for those big spiders, girl. Miami is dangerous territory. Remember, there are people like *me* out there."

American Arithmetic

Native Americans make up less than
one percent of the population of America.
0.8 percent of 100 percent.

O, mine efficient country.

I do not remember the days before America—
I do not remember the days when we were all here.

Police kill Native Americans more
than any other race. *Race* is a funny word.
Race implies someone will win,
implies *I have as good a chance of winning as*—

We all know who wins a race that isn't a race.

Native Americans make up 1.9 percent of all
police killings, higher than any race,
and we exist as .8 percent of all Americans.

Sometimes race means run.

I'm not good at math—can you blame me?
I've had an American education.

We are Americans, and we are less than 1 percent
of Americans. We do a better job of dying
by police than we do existing.

When we are dying, who should we call?
The police? Or our senator?

At the National Museum of the American Indian,
68 percent of the collection is from the U.S.
I am doing my best to not become a museum
of myself. I am doing my best to breathe in and out.
I am begging: *Let me be lonely but not invisible.*

In an American city of one hundred people,
I am Native American—less than one, less than
whole—I am less than myself. Only a fraction
of a body, let's say *I am only a hand*—

and when I slip it beneath the shirt of my lover,
I disappear completely.

—Natalie Diaz

THE WORTHLESS SERVANT

Ann Patchett

IN THE MIDDLE of June in Nashville, a few days before the summer became unendurably hot, I was in the car with Charlie Strobel, driving out toward the river. To grow up Catholic in Nashville is to know at least some of the members of the Strobel family, and long before Charlie and I became friends, I knew the stories of what he had accomplished, and what he had lost. We were on our way to the Stadium Inn to visit some homeless men who were about to get their own apartment, and while he drove, Charlie told me a story about Father Dan Richardson. Father Dan was the priest at Assumption, the North Nashville parish in the poor neighborhood where Charlie grew up. It was not too far from where we were headed now.

"Father Dan was a father figure to me," Charlie said, his own father having died when he was four. "We lived down the street from the church, and by the time I was in the third or fourth grade, I was an acolyte."

Assumption was a parish with an older congregation, and Charlie remembered the funerals coming one after the other. For every funeral, Father Dan gave the exact same homily. "We knew it word for word. We could mouth it along behind him," Charlie said, and though he is sixty-nine now, a good distance from his altar boy self, he begins the recitation: "Father Dan would say, 'We're on this earth to get ready to die. And when we die, God's not going to say, "Charlie (Ann, Sally, John, fill-in-the-blank), what did you do for a living? How much money did you make? How many houses did you have?" God is only going to ask us two questions: "Did you love me?" and "Did you love your neighbor?" And we can imagine that Charlie (Ann, Sally, John, fill-in-the-blank) will answer truthfully, saying, "Yes, Lord, You know I loved you. You know I loved my neighbor." And then God will say, "Well done, good and faithful servant. Now enter into the kingdom of heaven."'" Charlie smiled at the thought of it. "He nailed it *every single time*. He had this soft voice, and his cadence was perfect. Even though I knew exactly what was coming, it never failed to grab me. It was sad, especially if I knew the person who had died, but I never heard it as anything but a positive and hopeful message. We come from God, we return to God, so death was never frightening."

Charlie realized then that he had missed his exit. Neither one of us had been paying attention to the interstate, and neither of us was sorry. It gave him time to finish the story.

"Even after I grew up and became a priest, I could never call him Dan. It was always Father Dan. I'd always say to him, 'What are you going to get me for Christmas this year?' And he'd say, 'A bridge,' because the homeless lived under bridges." Father Dan, who was Irish, was always one for a joke. "When I went to see him for the last time before he died, we had a personal talk, a father-son talk, and I told him how much I loved him. Then I said, 'Now I'm going to be your priest,' and I did his whole routine— We are on this earth to get ready to die, and when we die, God's not going to ask, 'Dan, how much money did you make?' He's going to ask two questions: 'Did you love me?' and 'Did you love your neighbor?' And I know you'll say, 'Yes, Lord, you know I loved you. You know I loved my neighbor.' And God will say, 'Enter, good and faithful servant.'"

I was struck by how often the lessons we learn when we're young, the things we could never imagine needing, make it possible to meet what life will ask of us later. "I've grown to be who I am," Charlie said, "because of those life experiences each of us has."

In its finest hour, the Stadium Inn must have been a cheap motel where fans of the opposing teams could spend the night after a football game. But any football fan who booked a room there now would be able to realize the error of his ways without ever getting out of the car. When we pulled up to the front, Charlie stopped and looked at the men sitting on the steps, then he looked at me. "I'll leave the car running," he said, trying to calculate how long he might be inside. "You lock the doors and wait."

When I told him I was happy to go with him, he gave me an enormous smile. "Oh, that's wonderful," he said. He reached in the backseat and pulled out a two-burner hot plate. The Stadium Inn was what my policeman father would call a flophouse, a pay-by-the-week motel of the lowest possible order. Charlie greeted every man and woman who leaned by the door or sprawled in the lobby. He announced our plans to visit Ron and Sid to the woman at the front desk, who claimed to have no idea who they were. Then he told her he was Charlie Strobel, and that he was expected. "Oh," she said, smiling and nodding. She gave us the room number and directed us to the elevator. Ron and Sid would soon be moving into their own apartment, an apartment that had no stove. They would be needing a hot plate. We took the one we had upstairs.

Every human catastrophe the carpet in the hallway had endured over the years had been solved with a splash of bleach, which rendered it a long, abstract painting. Beneath the low yellow light, the row of closed doors each thumped out a distinct musical beat, including the door we were standing in front of. I saw an eye study us at the peephole and then pull away. I stepped to the side, certain that I must look like a parole officer. "Sid," Charlie called out in the tone of a cheerful and persistent relative who had dropped in for a visit. "It's Charlie. Open up the door." He waited, and then he knocked again.

It was a long wait, but finally the door cracked open and a

single dark eye peered out of a cloud of cigarette smoke, then the door opened wider. "Father!" the man said, and gave Charlie a hug. (Charlie can do without the title, as he thinks it creates a distance between people. Still, if the word "father" makes anyone feel better, he accepts it.)

Sid and Ron are salt and pepper shakers, Sid with dark brown hair and a heavy brown beard, Ron with faded red hair and a graying beard going halfway down his chest. Both men wore loose jeans, tank tops, baseball caps. Neither could have weighed more than one hundred pounds, their upper arms no bigger than their wrists. Introductions were made and they shook my hand. For all their reticence about opening the door, they were clearly pleased we had come. There were two unmade beds in the room with a heaping ashtray between them, a console television playing the country music station. A shopping cart was parked against the wall, neatly packed, its contents tarped over and tied. "We're ready to go," Ron said, giving the cart a pat. "We've got somebody coming tomorrow to help us move."

"Are you staying sober?" Charlie asked, his voice making it clear that he will be proud of them if they are, and love them still if they are not.

"We are, Father," Sid said.

"Four days, Father," Ron said.

Charlie tried to lead them in a conversation about how much better it was to be clean, and though they clearly wished to please him, their hearts weren't in it. They planned to find jobs once they settled, maybe dishwashing. Ron took off his baseball cap and pushed back his hair to reveal a long scar running across his forehead. "I don't know, though," he said. "I don't think so clear since I got hit."

Charlie gave them the hot plate and they marveled at the newness of the thing, still in the box. They talked about the move, and Charlie promised to get them bus passes. When we were finally ready to leave, both men hugged him again and promised good behavior for the future. They told us about a man five doors down the hall, someone who wasn't doing as well at staying out of trouble, and so we went and knocked on that door for a long time, but despite the music blaring from the other side, no amount of calling could draw anyone out.

"That's the best I've seen them look in a long time," Charlie said cheerfully as the shuddering elevator dropped to the first floor. "Their eyes looked good, didn't you think?"

I hadn't seen their eyes before, but I was struck by the sweetness of both men, and how more than anything they looked tired. Homelessness is an exhausting and dangerous state of being.

■ ■

Charlie has a good story that he likes to bring out for fundraisers—that his career with the homeless can all be traced back to a single peanut butter and jelly sandwich he made for a man who knocked on the rectory door when he was a young priest at Holy Name. The next step came soon after that, as he explained in a lecture he gave at the local Unitarian church, "They were in the church parking lot, sleeping under my window, and the temperature that evening was dropping below freezing. I didn't think too long about it, probably because I knew I would talk myself out of it. As a pastor, I knew the consequences of such a decision were far greater than simply giving a dozen men one night's lodging. What do you do tomorrow night when they return? And the next night and the next night and on and on? One simple decision could be parlayed into a lifetime commitment. What would the parishioners say? Or the bishop? Or the neighbors? For the moment, I decided that it was the thing to do. Like Scarlett O'Hara, I found myself saying, 'I'll worry about that tomorrow.' So I invited them to spend the night, and they've been with me ever since."

It was while he was trying to meet those immediate needs that Doy Abbott arrived.

"He was my terrorist," Charlie said. "Every morning he woke me up to demand breakfast. He was a regular back at Holy Name. He kicked in the screen door. We had to have that door replaced three times. He cussed out everyone in the parish. He expected everything to be done for him. My mother used to say to me, 'Doy is your ticket to heaven.' And I'd tell her, 'If he's my ticket to heaven I don't want to go.' Everyone in the parish was afraid of him."

Everyone except Mary Hopwood. She was the housekeeper and the secretary and the bookkeeper for the parish. She'd come to work at the age of fifty-five, after raising twelve children of her own. With Doy her tone was always quiet and respectful, and he was respectful in return. They listened to each other.

"About that time I read something Dorothy Day had said. She said what she wanted to do was love the poor, not analyze them, not rehabilitate them. When I read that it was like a light clicking on. I thought about Mrs. Hopwood. I realized that Doy was not my problem to solve but my brother to love. I decided on the spot that I was going to love him and not expect anything from him, and overnight he changed. He stopped the cussing, stopped the violence. I feel we became brothers. I was his servant and he was my master. I was there with him when he died."

■ ■

Charles Strobel founded The Room in the Inn and its Campus for Human Development in 1986 as a center of learning, respite, shelter, and relief for the homeless. Like the homeless, he can pretty much be found there seven days a week. Originally, it was formed as an organization of local parishes of all denominations that welcomed the homeless in for a meal and to spend the night once the cold set in. The first building they had was traditionally dismal, with some classrooms for AA meetings and art projects, showers, clothing, and a place to pray. Charlie's primary gift may be his ability to serve the poor, but he possesses the equally necessary gifts of being able to work with a board, the local government, the police, religious organizations of every stripe, and the people who have the money to underwrite his vision. His radical idea was that the homeless need not be served in low, dark places, and that people with nothing should be able to stand beside people with everything and hold up their heads. The building that now comprises the campus is new and looks it, as stylishly modern in its glass and steel construction as the expensive condominiums that sprawl through Nashville a few short blocks away. The dignity with which Charlie had always treated the homeless was finally reflected in their surroundings. The mission statement of the campus reads: *Emphasizing the Scriptural ideals of love and community through service to the homeless, the Campus provides faithful people of Nashville an opportunity to respond directly to the broken and disenfranchised among us. This fellowship with the poor is at the heart of our purpose.*

Which basically means that *I* am the person the campus is serving. This center is there to give me the chance to experience what has been the enormous joy of Charlie's life—the opportunity to respond directly to the broken and disenfranchised among us.

"All you have to do," he tells me, "is give a little bit of understanding to the possibility that life might not have been fair."

The trouble with good fortune is that people tend to equate it with personal goodness, so that if things are going well for us and less well for others, we think they must have done something to have brought it on themselves. We speak of ourselves as being blessed, but what can that mean except that others are not blessed, and that God has picked out a few of us to love more? It is our responsibility to care for one another, to create fairness in the face of unfairness, and find equality where none may have existed in the past. Despite his own dealings with unfairness, this is what Charlie has accomplished.

When Charlie's father died of a heart attack at the age of forty-six, he left behind four children between the ages of eight years and four months. Afterward, Charlie's mother, Mary Catherine Strobel, who had lost her own mother in a house fire when she was an infant and her much-loved father when she was sixteen, took a job working as a clerk for the fire department for $185 a month. There were also two great-aunts whom she took care of, Mollie, who was eighty-one at the time, and Kate, who was seventy-eight. The way Mary Catherine interpreted her husband's death and their subsequent hardships was that none of it was

God's fault. God, along with their father, would be right there watching over them.

And while God, in the newfound company of Martin Strobel, watched the children from heaven, Aunt Kate and Aunt Mollie watched them during the day while Mary Catherine worked. "They were the reason it was so easy for me to believe Jesus' words 'I am among you as one who serves,'" he said of his aunts. "And that led me to the next step in logic, to believe that God loves us and provides for all our needs—just as any devoted servant would—because I had experienced it so lovingly from Aunt Mollie and Aunt Kate."

He told me a story from Luke 17, in which the servant who does everything that is asked of him and then, joyfully, does more is called a "worthless servant" (or an "unprofitable servant," or "a servant who deserves no credit," depending on the translation). It is a state of loving service so deep, so all-encompassing, that the servant loses himself, so that the worthlessness becomes a kind of transcendence. "They were worthless servants," Charlie said, remembering his aunts, his mother. "They wanted nothing more than to serve us, which means that we were their masters. They did everything they could for us. They never disciplined us. I never remember their asking me to help them around the house." Charlie asked if I was following him, because the concept of the achievement to be found in worthlessness can be a murky one. It is not the stuff of Sunday sermons. Certainly, I could think of many instances in which people who had been served were not then inspired to go and serve others, but if being profoundly loved enabled us to love profoundly then, yes, I understood.

"Wouldn't that be a wonderful thing to have on your tombstone?" he said to me. "Worthless Servant?"

I told him I wasn't there yet, but that I could see it as something to aspire to.

"I hesitate to say this," he said, and then he gave such a long pause that I wondered if he did in fact plan to proceed, "so many people have struggles with their faith, but God has never been a struggle for me. *I've* been a struggle for me, but I could never honestly believe in the nonexistence of God."

It was the only thing he hesitated to tell me for the entire day. He felt it might be cavalier to admit that something that was so difficult for so many had come to him, and stayed with him, without effort.

In the main lobby of The Room in the Inn there is a sculpture of a tree on the wall with more than 650 leaves. Every leaf bears the name of a homeless man or woman who has died in Nashville, and the presence of God did not waver any time a new leaf was added. It did not waver in December 1986, when Charlie's mother, Mary Catherine Strobel, then seventy-four, was kidnapped from the parking lot of Sears in Nashville and murdered by an escaped convict from Michigan, the first victim in a spree that ultimately took six lives.

But the way the story was remembered over the years was that she had been working at the Room in the Inn at the time, and that she was killed by a homeless man. People said that Mary Catherine had started the Room in the Inn, and that Charlie took up her work as a penance. By making her murder a consequence of her own associations, people could safely distance themselves from such a random act of violence. Charlie was often asked if he would continue his work after his mother's death. "If it was worth doing before," he said, "why wouldn't it be worth doing now?"

"Many have said that she did not deserve to die the way that she did," her son said at the funeral Mass. "Yet for years, we have heard it said that 'God did not spare his only Son but delivered him up, and the Son emptied himself and humbled himself, obediently accepting even death, death on a cross.' In Mama's death, our family believes that the viciousness inflicted on such gentleness and kindness, as was her way, brings about a great *communion* with Jesus. So how can we question its course? It seems to run true to the form of Jesus' own death. And why speak of anger and revenge? Those words are not compatible with the very thought of our mother."

"Of course her death changed all of us," he told me that afternoon after we had left Ron and Sid, while we were on our way to visit a formerly homeless woman in the hospital who was struggling to care for her grandchildren as her health declined sharply.

"But maybe not the way people thought it did. Our mother's death helped me focus on what was important. After that I became more single-minded about what I should be doing with my life."

There is throughout the course of life a long line of fathers and sons, parents and children, servants and masters, forgiven and forgivers, and at different moments we are called on to take up one role and then the other. When we do it right, we are bearing the example of Christ in mind. When we finally made it back to the Room in the Inn, it was past eight o'clock in the evening and still light out, the longest day of the year. The achievement of Charlie's life surrounded us, not the dazzling building or the flowers stretching out in front of the property, but the crowd of people spreading out in every direction. This was the place they had come to feel safe, to feel loved. These are the people he serves.

CONTRIBUTORS

Julia Alvarez has written novels (*How the García Girls Lost Their Accents, In the Time of the Butterflies, ¡Yo!, In the Name of Salomé, Saving the World*), collections of poems (*Homecoming, The Other Side/El Otro Lado, The Woman I Kept to Myself*), nonfiction (*Something to Declare, Once Upon a Quinceañera, A Wedding in Haiti*), and numerous books for young readers (including the Tía Lola series, *Before We Were Free, Finding Miracles, Return to Sender*, and *Where Do They Go?*). A recipient of a 2013 National Medal of Arts, Alvarez is one of the founders of Border of Lights, a movement to promote peace and collaboration between Haiti and the Dominican Republic. She lives in Vermont.

Eula Biss is the author of *Notes from No Man's Land*, winner of the Graywolf Nonfiction Prize and the National Book Critics Circle Award for criticism, as well as *On Immunity* and *The Balloonists*. Her essays have appeared in *The New York Times Magazine, Harper's*, and *The Believer*, and in *The Best American Nonrequired Reading* and *The Best Creative Nonfiction*. She has received fellowships from the Guggenheim Foundation, the Howard Foundation, and the National Endowment for the Arts, and she has won the 21st Century Award from the Chicago Public Library Foundation. Biss teaches at Northwestern University and lives in Chicago.

Sandra Cisneros is the author of two highly celebrated novels, a story collection, two books of poetry, a memoir, and *Have You Seen Marie?*

She is the recipient of numerous awards, including National Endowment for the Arts fellowships, the Lannan Literary Award, the American Book Award, the Thomas Wolfe Prize, and a MacArthur fellowship. Her work has been translated into more than twenty languages. Cisneros is the founder of the Alfredo Cisneros Del Moral and Macondo foundations, which serve creative writers.

Edwidge Danticat is the author of several books, including *Breath, Eyes, Memory*, an Oprah's Book Club selection; *Krik? Krak!*, a National Book Award finalist; *The Farming of Bones*, an American Book Award winner; and the novel in stories *The Dew Breaker*. She is the editor of *The Butterfly's Way: Voices from the Haitian Dyaspora in the United States*, *The Beacon Best of 2000: Great Writing by Women and Men of All Colors and Cultures*, *Haiti Noir* and *Haiti Noir 2*, and *The Best American Essays 2011*. She has written six books for young adults and children, *Anacaona: Golden Flower, Haiti, 1490*; *Behind the Mountains*; *Eight Days*; *The Last Mapou*; *Mama's Nightingale*; and *Untwine*; as well as a travel narrative, *After the Dance: A Walk Through Carnival in Jacmel, Haiti*. Her memoir, *Brother, I'm Dying*, was a 2007 finalist for the National Book Award and the 2008 winner of the National Book Critics Circle Award for autobiography. She is a 2009 MacArthur Fellow.

RS Deeren was the 2016 Union League Club of Chicago Library's Writer in Residence. His fiction, nonfiction, and poetry appear in the *Great Lakes Review*, *Midwestern Gothic*, *The Legendary*, the *Corvus Review*, and elsewhere. Before moving to Chicago to earn his MFA in fiction from Columbia College Chicago, he lived in the rural Thumb Region of Michigan working as a line cook, bank teller, teacher, and lumberjack.

Natalie Diaz was born and raised in the Fort Mojave Indian Village in Needles, California, on the banks of the Colorado River. She is Mojave and an enrolled member of the Gila River Indian Tribe. Her first poetry collection, *When My Brother Was an Aztec*, was published by Copper Canyon Press. She is a Lannan Literary Fellow and a Native Arts and Cultures Foundation Artist Fellow. She was awarded a Bread Loaf fellowship, the Holmes National Poetry Prize, a Hodder fellowship, and a PEN/Civitella Ranieri Foundation residency, as well as being awarded a U.S. Artists Ford fellowship. Diaz teaches in the Arizona State University MFA program. She splits her time between the East Coast and Mohave Valley, Arizona, where she works to revitalize the Mojave language.

Annie Dillard has written twelve books, including the nonfiction titles *For the Time Being, Teaching a Stone to Talk, Holy the Firm*, and *Pilgrim at Tinker Creek*. She is a member of the American Academy of Arts and Letters and the American Academy of Arts and Sciences.

Anthony Doerr was born and raised in Cleveland, Ohio. He is the author of the story collections *The Shell Collector* and *Memory Wall*, the memoir *Four Seasons in Rome*, and the novels *About Grace* and *All the Light We Cannot See*, which was awarded the 2015 Pulitzer Prize for fiction and the 2015 Andrew Carnegie Medal for Excellence in Fiction.

Timothy Egan is a Pulitzer Prize–winning reporter, a *New York Times* columnist, a winner of the Andrew Carnegie Medal for Excellence in Nonfiction, and the author of eight books, most recently *The Immortal Irishman*. His previous books include *The Worst Hard Time*, which won a National Book Award, and the national best seller *The Big Burn*. A third-generation westerner, he lives in Seattle.

Patricia Engel's most recent book, *The Veins of the Ocean*, was a *New York Times* Editors' Choice. She is also the author of *Vida*, a *New York Times* Notable Book of 2010 and a finalist for the PEN/Hemingway Fiction Award and the Young Lions Fiction Award; and *It's Not Love, It's Just Paris*, winner of the International Latino Book Award. Her books have been translated into several languages and her stories have appeared in *The Atlantic, A Public Space, Boston Review*, and *The Best American Mystery Stories 2014*, among other publications, and honors she has received include a fellowship in literature from the National Endowment for the Arts. She lives in Miami.

Ru Freeman's creative and political writing has appeared internation-ally. She is the author of the novels *A Disobedient Girl* (Atria/Simon & Schuster, 2009) and *On Sal Mal Lane* (Graywolf, 2013), a *New York Times* Editors' Choice book. Both novels have been translated into sev-eral languages including Italian, French, Hebrew, and Chinese. She is the editor of the groundbreaking anthology *Extraordinary Rendition: American Writers on Palestine* (2015). She blogs for the *Huffington Post* on literature and politics, is a contributing editorial board member of the *Asian American Literary Review*, and has received fellowships from the Bread Loaf Writers' Conference, Yaddo, Hedgebrook, the Virginia Center for the Creative Arts, and the Lannan Foundation. She is the 2014 winner of the Sister Mariella Gable Award and the Janet Heidinger Kafka Prize for fiction by an American woman.

Roxane Gay is the author of the novel *An Untamed State*, which was a finalist for the Dayton Peace Prize for fiction; the essay collection *Bad Feminist*; the short story volume *Difficult Women*; *Ayiti, a* multigenre collection; and *Hunger*, a memoir. She is at work on a comic book in Marvel's Black Panther series. Her writing has appeared in *The Best American Short Stories 2012*, *The York Times*, *The Guardian*, and many others. She is a recipient of the PEN Center USA Freedom to Write Award, among many other honors. She splits her time between Indiana and Los Angeles.

Dagoberto Gilb is the author of *Before the End, After the Beginning*; *Woodcuts of Women*; *The Magic of Blood*; and others. He has been pub-lished in *Harper's*, *The New Yorker*, *The Threepenny Review*, *Zyzzyva*, and many more. He founded the magazine *Huizache* to promote Latino lit-erature centered in America's West.

In 2015 **Juan Felipe Herrera** was appointed the twenty-first United States Poet Laureate, the first Mexican American to hold the position. Herrera grew up in California as the son of migrant farmers, which, he has commented, strongly shaped much of his work. He is the author of thirty books, including collections of poetry, prose, short stories, young adult novels, and picture books for children. His collections of poetry include *Notes on the Assemblage* (City Lights, 2015); *Senegal Taxi* (University of Arizona, 2013); *Half of the World in Light: New and Selected Poems* (University of Arizona, 2008), a recipient of the PEN Beyond Margins Award and the National Book Critics Circle Award; *187 Reasons Mexicanos Can't Cross the Border: Undocuments 1971–2007* (City Lights, 2007); and *CrashBoomLove: A Novel in Verse* (University of New Mexico, 1999), which received the Américas Award. In 2014, he released the nonfiction work *Portraits of Hispanic American Heroes* (Dial), which showcases twenty Hispanic and Latino American men and women who have made outstanding contributions to the arts, politics, science, humanitarianism, and athletics in the United States.

Lawrence Joseph's sixth book of poems, *So Where Are We?*, will be published by Farrar, Straus and Giroux in 2017. He is also the author of two books of prose, *Lawyerland* (FSG, 1997) and *The Game Changed: Essays and Other Prose* (University of Michigan, 2011). He is Tinnelly Professor of Law at St. John's University School of Law and lives in New York City.

Rickey Laurentiis was raised in New Orleans, Louisiana. He is the recipient of numerous honors, among them a Ruth Lilly Poetry Fellowship and fellowships from the National Endowment for the Arts, the Atlantic Center for the Arts, and the Civitella Ranieri Foundation in Italy. In 2016, he traveled to Palestine as a part of the Palestine Festival of Literature. His first book, *Boy with Thorn* (2015), won the 2014 Cave Canem Poetry Prize and the 2016 Levis Reading Prize, and was a finalist for a 2016 Lambda Literary Award and the Thom Gunn Award from the Publishing Triangle. He teaches at Columbia University and Sarah Lawrence College.

Kiese Laymon is a black Southern writer born and raised in Jackson, Mississippi. He is the author of the novel *Long Division*, the essay collection *How to Slowly Kill Yourself and Others in America*, and the forthcoming memoir *Heavy*.

Nami Mun grew up in Seoul, South Korea, and Bronx, New York. For her first book, *Miles from Nowhere*, she received a Whiting Award, a Pushcart

Prize, the Chicago Public Library's 21st Century Award, The Hopwood Award, and was shortlisted for the Orange Prize for New Writers and the Asian American Literary Award. *Miles from Nowhere* was selected as Editors' Choice and Top 10 First Novels by *Booklist*; Best Fiction of 2009 So Far by Amazon; and as an Indie Next pick. Previously, Nami has worked as an Avon lady, a street vendor, a photojournalist, a waitress, an activities coordinator for a nursing home, and a criminal defense investigator. After earning a GED, she went on to receive degrees from the University of California, Berkeley, and the University of Michigan, and has garnered fellowships from organizations such as Yaddo, MacDowell, the Bread Loaf Writers' Conference, and Tin House. Her writing can be found in *The New York Times*, *Granta*, *Tin House*, *The Iowa Review*, *The Pushcart Prize* Anthology, *Evergreen Review*, and elsewhere. She lives in Chicago with her husband, the novelist Augustus Rose, and their son.

Manuel Muñoz is the author of two collections of short stories, *Zig-zagger* and *The Faith Healer of Olive Avenue*. His first novel, *What You See in the Dark*, was published in 2011. The recipient of fellowships from the National Endowment for the Arts and the New York Foundation for the Arts, a Whiting Award, and two PEN/O. Henry prizes, his work has appeared in numerous publications, including *The New York Times*, *Glimmer Train*, *Epoch*, *American Short Fiction*, and *Boston Review*, and has aired on National Public Radio's *Selected Shorts*. Muñoz has been on the faculty of the University of Arizona's creative writing program since 2008.

Joyce Carol Oates is a recipient of the National Humanities Medal, the National Book Critics Circle Ivan Sandrof Lifetime Achievement Award, the National Book Award, and the PEN/Malamud Award for Excellence in Short Fiction. She is Roger S. Berlind Distinguished Professor of the Humanities at Princeton University and has been a member of the American Academy of Arts and Letters since 1978. In 2016, she was inducted into the American Philosophical Society.

Chris Offutt is the author of the short story collections *Kentucky Straight* and *Out of the Woods*; the novel *The Good Brother*; and three memoirs, *The*

Same River Twice, *No Heroes*, and *My Father, the Pornographer*. His work is included in many anthologies and textbooks, including *The Best American Short Stories* and *The Best American Essays*. He has written screenplays for *Weeds*, *True Blood*, and *Treme*, and has received fellowships from the Lannan and Guggenheim foundations. He lives near Oxford, Mississippi.

Ann Patchett is the author of seven novels, *The Patron Saint of Liars*, *Taft*, *The Magician's Assistant*, *Bel Canto*, *Run*, *State of Wonder*, and *Commonwealth*. She was the editor of *The Best American Short Stories 2006*, and has written three books of nonfiction, *Truth & Beauty*, about her friendship with the writer Lucy Grealy; *What Now?*, an expansion of her graduation address at Sarah Lawrence College; and *This Is the Story of a Happy Marriage*, a collection of essays examining the theme of commitment. In November 2011, she opened Parnassus Books in Nashville, Tennessee, with her business partner, Karen Hayes.

Kirstin Valdez Quade is the author of *Night at the Fiestas*, a *New York Times* Notable Book, which received a 5 Under 35 award from the National Book Foundation, the John Leonard Prize from the National Book Critics Circle, and the Sue Kaufman Prize from the American Academy of Arts and Letters. She teaches at Princeton University.

Jess Ruliffson is a nonfiction cartoonist hailing from Biloxi, Mississippi. In 2017, her comic *I Trained to Fight the Enemy* was shortlisted for Slate's Cartoonist Studio Prize. Her work has been published by Pantheon Books, *BuzzFeed*, *The Boston Globe*, *The Gainesville Sun*, *The Oxford American*, and *Wilson Quarterly*. Her forthcoming graphic novel, *Where Eden Once Stood* (Fantagraphics), collects interviews with veterans of the Iraq and Afghanistan wars. She teaches comics at The School of Visual Arts in New York City and The Sequential Artists Workshop in Gainesville, Florida. For more, visit www.jessruliffson.com.

Karen Russell is the author of the story collections *St. Lucy's Home for Girls Raised by Wolves* and *Vampires in the Lemon Grove*, the novella *Sleep Donation*, and the novel *Swamplandia!*. She lives in Portland, Oregon.

Richard Russo is the author of nine novels, most recently the best-selling *Everybody's Fool* and *That Old Cape Magic*, two short story collections, and the memoir *Elsewhere*. In 2002 he received the Pulitzer Prize for *Empire Falls*. He lives in Portland, Maine.

Sarah Smarsh is a journalist who has reported on public policy and socioeconomic class for *The New Yorker* and *Harper's Online*, *The Guardian*, *Guernica*, and others. Her essays on cultural boundaries have been published by *Aeon*, McSweeney's, the *Morning News*, *Creative Nonfiction*, *Vela*, and the *Texas Observer*. Smarsh's book on the American working poor and her upbringing in rural Kansas is forthcoming from Scribner. She lives in Kansas.

Danez Smith is the author of *[insert] boy*, winner of the Kate Tufts Discovery Award and the Lambda Literary Award. He was awarded a Ruth Lilly and Dorothy Sargent Rosenberg Poetry Fellowship from the Poetry Foundation. His second poetry collection, *Don't Call Us Dead*, is forthcoming from Graywolf Press in September 2017.

Writer, historian, and activist **Rebecca Solnit** is the author of eighteen books on environment, landscape, representation, disaster, politics, hope, and feminism, including a trilogy of atlases and the books *Hope in the Dark*, *Men Explain Things to Me*, *The Faraway Nearby*, *A Paradise Built in Hell: The Extraordinary Communities That Arise in Disaster*, *A Field Guide to Getting Lost*, *Wanderlust: A History of Walking*, and *River of Shadows: Eadweard Muybridge and the Technological Wild West* (for which she received a Guggenheim, the National Book Critics Circle Award for criticism, and the Lannan Literary Award). A product of the California public education system from kindergarten to graduate school, she is a columnist at *Harper's*.

Whitney Terrell is the author of three novels, *The Huntsman*, *The King of King's County*, and *The Good Lieutenant*. He was an embedded reporter in Iraq during 2006 and 2010 and covered the war for *The Washington Post Magazine*, *Slate*, and NPR. He teaches creative writing at the University of Missouri–Kansas City and lives nearby with his family.

Héctor Tobar is the author of four books, including the critically acclaimed *New York Times* best seller *Deep Down Dark: The Untold Stories of 33 Men Buried in a Chilean Mine and the Miracle That Set Them Free*, a finalist for the National Book Critics Circle Award.

Claire Vaye Watkins is the author of the story collection *Battleborn* and the novel *Gold Fame Citrus*. She was named a National Book Foundation 5 Under 35 fiction writer, and has been awarded the Story Prize, the American Academy of Arts and Letters Rosenthal Family Foundation Award, and a Guggenheim fellowship. Her stories and essays have appeared in *Granta*, *One Story*, *The Paris Review*, *Ploughshares*, *Glimmer Train*, *Best of the West 2011*, *Best of the West 2013*, and elsewhere. Watkins teaches at the University of Michigan in Ann Arbor with her husband, the writer Derek Palacio, with whom she cofounded the Mojave School, a creative writing workshop for teenagers in rural Nevada.

Brad Watson was born in Meridian, Mississippi, and has lived there, as well as in Alabama, Boston, California, and, most recently, Wyoming, where he teaches in the University of Wyoming creative writing program. He previously taught at the University of Alabama; Harvard; the University of West Florida; Ole Miss; and the University of California, Irvine. His books are *Last Days of the Dog-Men*, *The Heaven of Mercury*, *Aliens in the Prime of Their Lives*, and *Miss Jane*, all from W. W. Norton & Co. His work has received two awards from the American Academy of Arts and Letters, an NEA grant, and a fellowship from the Guggenheim Foundation. *Aliens* was a finalist for the 2011 PEN/Faulkner Award for Fiction. *Mercury* received the Southern Book Critics Circle Award and the Mississippi Institute of Arts and Letters Award in Fiction (as did *Aliens*), and was a finalist for the 2002 National Book Award. He lives with his wife, Nell Hanley, and their dogs and horses on the prairie south of Laramie, Wyoming.

Larry Watson is the author of the novels *Montana 1948*, *American Boy*, *Let Him Go*, and others, including the most recent, *As Good as Gone*. He teaches writing and literature at Marquette University in Milwaukee.

Joy Williams is the author of four novels, five story collections, and the book of essays *Ill Nature*. She's been nominated for the National Book Award, Pulitzer Prize, and National Book Critics Circle Award. Her most recent book is *Ninety-nine Stories of God*. She lives in Tuscon, Arizona, and Laramie, Wyoming.

Kevin Young is the author of eleven books of poetry and prose, most recently *Blue Laws: Selected & Uncollected Poems 1995–2015*, longlisted for the National Book Award, and *Book of Hours*, which won the Lenore Marshall Poetry Prize from the Academy of American Poets. He is director of the Schomburg Center for Research in Black Culture, and incoming Poetry Editor of *The New Yorker*.

ACKNOWLEDGMENTS

"Death by Gentrification" by Rebecca Solnit first appeared in *The Guardian*. Reprinted by permission of the author.

"i'm sick of pretending to give a shit about what whypeepo think" by Danez Smith, copyright © 2017 by Danez Smith.

"Notes of a Native Daughter" by Sandra Cisneros, copyright © 2016 by Sandra Cisneros, first delivered for the Hispanic Housing Development Corporation, Chicago, March 2016, and first appeared in print in Chicago magazine, August 2016.

"Dosas" by Edwidge Danticat first appeared in *Sable* in spring 2007. Reprinted by permission of the author.

"American Work" by Richard Russo, copyright © 2017 by Richard Russo.

"Fieldwork" by Manuel Muñoz, copyright © 2017 by Manuel Muñoz. By permission of Stuart Bernstein Representation for Artists, New York, N.Y. All rights reserved.

"For the Ones Who Put Their Names on the Wall" by Juan Felipe Herrera, copyright © 2017 by Juan Felipe Herrera.

"Trash Food" by Chris Offutt first appeared in the *Oxford American*. Reprinted by permission of the author.

Tales of Two Cities

The Best and Worst of Times in Today's New York

In a city where the top one per-cent earns more than a half-million dollars per year while twenty-five thousand children are homeless, public discourse about our worsening wealth gap has never been more sorely needed. This remarkable an-thology is the literary world's response, with leading lights in-cluding Zadie Smith, Junot Díaz, and Lydia Davis bearing witness to the experience of ordinary New Yorkers in extraordinarily unequal circumstances.

"A bristling portrayal of New York in the tradition of Jacob Riis." —*Guernica*

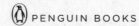 PENGUIN BOOKS